"A mandrake," Iz said, chalk from her khaki breeches.

"I've never seen one so large. But don't worry. They're quite docile. He probably just got lost during his migration. Let's try to herd him back down."

With hands raised, Warren advanced upon the mandrake, nattering pleasantly as he inched toward the heaving golem that resembled an ambling yam. "There's a sport. Thank you for keeping off my rug. It's an antique, you know. I have to be honest—it's impossible to match and hard to clean. I haven't got one of those newfangled carpet renovators. The salesman, wonderful chap, wanted three hundred and twenty gallets for it. Can you imagine? And those suck-boxes are as big as a bureau. I have no idea where I'd park such a—"

The moment War inched into range, the mandrake swatted him with a slow, unyielding stroke of its limb, catching him on the shoulder and throwing him back across the room and violently through his tea cart. Macarons and petits fours leapt into the air and rained down upon the smashed porcelain that surrounded the splayed host.

The mandrake raised the fingerless knob of one hand, identifying his quarry, then charged at the royal secretary, who sat bleating like a calf.

Praise for
Josiah Bancroft and the Books of Babel

"It's rare to find a modern book that feels like a timeless classic. I'm wildly in love with this book." —Pierce Brown, author of *Red Rising*

"*The Hod King* is a compelling and original novel; the Books of Babel are something you hope to see perhaps once a decade—future classics, which may be remembered long after the series concludes." —*Los Angeles Times*

"Josiah Bancroft is a magician. His books are that rare alchemy: gracefully written, deliriously imaginative, action-packed, warm, witty, and thought-provoking. I can't wait for more."
—Madeline Miller, *New York Times* bestselling author of *Circe*

"*Senlin Ascends* is one of the best reads I've had in ages. I was dragged in and didn't escape until I'd finished two or three days later."
—Mark Lawrence, author of *Prince of Thorns*

"Deeply compelling. . . . A classic in the making."
—*B&N Sci-Fi & Fantasy Blog*

"Wonderfully unique and superbly well written. I loved every page."
—Nicholas Eames, author of *Kings of the Wyld*

"Senlin is a man worth rooting for, and his strengthening resolve and character is as marvelous and sprawling as the tower he climbs."
—*Washington Post*

"*Senlin Ascends* crosses the everyday strangeness and lyrical prose of Borges and Gogol with all the action and adventure of high fantasy. I loved it, and grabbed the next one as soon as I turned the last page."
—Django Wexler, author of *The Thousand Names*

"What is remarkable about this novel, quite apart from its rich, allusive prose, is Bancroft's portrayal of Senlin, a good man in a desperate situation, and the way he changes in response to his experiences in his ascent."

—*Guardian*

"Brilliant debut fantasy. . . . This novel goes off like a firework and suggests even greater things in the author's future."

—*Publishers Weekly* (starred review)

By Josiah Bancroft

THE HEXOLOGISTS NOVELS
The Hexologists

THE BOOKS OF BABEL
Senlin Ascends
Arm of the Sphinx
The Hod King
The Fall of Babel

THE HEXOLOGISTS

A Hexologists Novel

JOSIAH BANCROFT

orbit

orbitbooks.net

This book is a work of fiction. Names, characters, places, and incidents are the product of the author's imagination or are used fictitiously. Any resemblance to actual events, locales, or persons, living or dead, is coincidental.

Copyright © 2023 by Josiah Bancroft

Cover art and design by Ian Leino
Map by Ian Leino and Josiah Bancroft
Font of Magic illustration by Josiah Bancroft
Interior ornaments by Ian Leino
Author photograph by Kim Bricker

Hachette Book Group supports the right to free expression and the value of copyright. The purpose of copyright is to encourage writers and artists to produce the creative works that enrich our culture.

The scanning, uploading, and distribution of this book without permission is a theft of the author's intellectual property. If you would like permission to use material from the book (other than for review purposes), please contact permissions@hbgusa.com. Thank you for your support of the author's rights.

Orbit
Hachette Book Group
1290 Avenue of the Americas
New York, NY 10104
orbitbooks.net

First Edition: September 2023
Simultaneously published in Great Britain by Orbit

Orbit is an imprint of Hachette Book Group.
The Orbit name and logo are trademarks of Little, Brown Book Group Limited.

The publisher is not responsible for websites (or their content) that are not owned by the publisher.

The Hachette Speakers Bureau provides a wide range of authors for speaking events. To find out more, go to hachettespeakersbureau.com or email HachetteSpeakers@hbgusa.com.

Orbit books may be purchased in bulk for business, educational, or promotional use. For information, please contact your local bookseller or the Hachette Book Group Special Markets Department at special.markets@hbgusa.com.

Library of Congress Cataloging-in-Publication Data
Names: Bancroft, Josiah, author.
Title: The hexologists / Josiah Bancroft.
Description: First edition. | New York, NY : Orbit, 2023. | Series: The Hexologists
Identifiers: LCCN 2023000605 | ISBN 9780316443302 (trade paperback) |
    ISBN 9780316443401 (ebook)
Subjects: LCGFT: Fantasy fiction. | Novels.
Classification: LCC PS3602.A63518 H48 2023 | DDC 813/.6—dc23/eng/20230106
LC record available at https://lccn.loc.gov/2023000605

ISBNs: 9780316443302 (trade paperback), 9780316443401 (ebook)

Printed in the United States of America

LSC-C

Printing 1, 2023

For Sharon, my is-and-always-will-be.

the FONT of MAGIC

WIZARDRY · HYPNOSIS · ILLUSIONS · HALOISTS · ALCHEMY · FLAILS · BRAID MAGIC · WITCHERY · JINXES · HEXEGY · WARDS · CURSES · SUMMONING · NECROMANCY

CONJURING · BINDING · FORGING · DIVINATION · PROPHECY · SALUTARIAN · BOTANICAL · EMPATHIC · DEFECTIVE · POSSESSION · ANIMATION · POISONS

THE YOKED GOD
AND THE TRANSMUTATION
OF SPLEEN

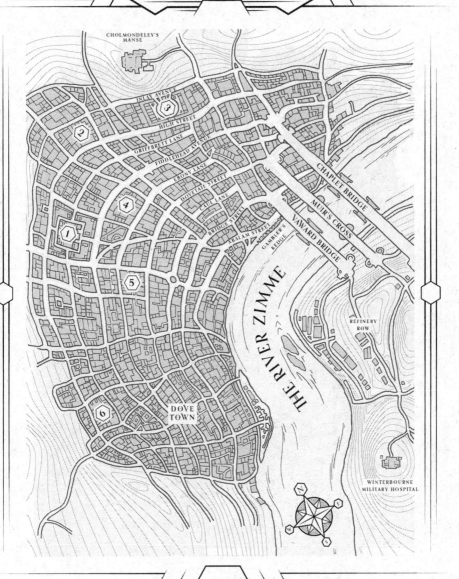

BERBITON

CHOLMONDELEV'S MANSE

INLAY AVENUE

HIGH STREET

GRIFFBRETT LANE

FIDDLEHEAD AVENUE

EBONY LANE

DOVETAIL STREET

CAUL LANE

BRIDGE STREET

ABALAM STREET

GAMBLER'S KEDGE

CHAPLET BRIDGE

MUIR'S CROSS

VAWARD BRIDGE

THE RIVER ZIMME

REFINERY ROW

DOVE TOWN

WINTERBOURNE MILITARY HOSPITAL

MAP KEY

1 · THE ROYAL CHATEAU
2 · THE SAFFOI TOWERS
3 · HONEWORT CEMETERY

4 · THE CARDINAL LIBRARY
5 · THE WILBIES' HOME
6 · DE LEE & GWATKIN

OUR CAST OF CHARACTERS

Alman, Horace, Royal Secretary — One of King Elbert's advisors who has taken it upon himself to investigate the king's malady.

Atterton, Florian, Duke — Rudolph Atterton's older brother.

Atterton, Lily, Lady — Rudolph Atterton's older sister.

Atterton, Rudolph "Rudy" Elias — Lance corporal in the Luthlandian Armed Forces and batman to the future king, Captain Yeardley.

Blessed, Henry — Jessamine Bysshe's son and ultimate participant in Victor Cholmondeley's orphan experiment.

Bysshe, Jessamine Rutha — A nurse at Winterbourne who was given the appellation "Jess Blessed" by her peers as a result of Prince Sebastian's connection to her.

Cholmondeley, Victor — An industrial alchemist and famed social experimentalist who adopted ten children. Formerly impoverished under the name Victor Gill.

Constance, Princess of Yeardley — The king's younger sister, a noted socialite and proponent of the study and practical applications of hexegy. Mother of five children.

Darlington — Nurse Percy Slorrance's hotheaded henchman.

De Lee, Charlotte — A midwife and monthly nurse who witnesses a terrible crime.

Dursun, Emin, Captain — Captain of the *Sangfroid Hand of Heaven*, husband of Nimet, father of Sema.

Dursun, Nimet — Wife of Emin, mother of Sema.

Dursun, Sema — Nimet and Emin Dursun's daughter who was abducted by chimney wraiths and rescued by the Hexologists.

Elbert III, King of Luthland — Formerly Sebastian, Prince of Yeardley, Captain Yeardley in the Luthlandian Armed Forces.

Eynon, Ms. — Victor Cholmondeley's housekeeper.

Gwatkin, Beatrice — A midwife and monthly nurse.

Hollins, Arnold — The groundskeeper of Honewort Cemetery.

Joyns, Lenard "Len" — A gravedigger at Honewort Cemetery.

Katsaros, Sherman — Warren's tailor who is leery of buttons.

Larkland, Valerie, Lady — Jessamine Bysshe's cousin and adoptive mother.

Larkland, George, Sir — Jessamine Bysshe's cousin and adoptive father.

Magnussen, Lorcan — A journalist for the *Berbiton Times* and vocal critic of Isolde Wilby's methods. Author of *The Hexed Court: A Rationalist's Critique of the Gray Arts*.

Mary, Queen of Luthland — Formerly Lady Mary Soames of Keene. Married to Elbert before her death.

Morris, Emma — One of Victor Cholmondeley's adopted daughters and current seamstress.

Mayer — One of Victor Cholmondeley's protective alchemists.

Neesland, Louis — The new royal secretary to King Elbert.

Obelos — Formerly known as Alexander Larkland, student of Wynn University of the Thaumatic Arts. A wizard.

Offalman, Annie — Warren's adopted sister.

Offalman, Irmmie — A butcher and Warren's mother.

Offalman, Morris — A butcher and Warren's father.

Our Cast of Characters

Old Geb — An incubus that haunts the drunk regulars of the Spillway Public House. The imp shares a special attunement with the dead, specifically those who've been buried.

Pyle, Eric — The publican of the Spillway Public House.

Reames, Jonathan — A prolific art forger exposed by Isolde Wilby.

Silva — A devoted guard and alchemist to the industrialist Victor Cholmondeley.

Slorrance, Percy, RN — A nurse, formerly employed by Winterbourne Military Hospital and the current leader of an antiroyalist faction that presently squats within the abandoned grounds of Winterbourne Military Hospital.

Snag, Mr. — Professor Wilby's mysterious benefactor who is only identified by a simple glyph of a dead tree.

Tamm, Margaret, Dr. — Doctor of Phantasmagoria, faculty member of Wynn University of the Thaumatic Arts.

Timmons-Wilby, Luella, Dr. — Librarian at the Cardinal Library, Doctor of Letters, Isolde's mother.

Wilby, Isolde "Iz" Ann Always — One half of the Hexologists, private investigators of the paranormal, and former head of the Office of Ensorcelled Investigations. Married to Warren.

Wilby, Silas Roner, Prof. — Isolde's long-absent father, once the nation's foremost explorer and collector of antiquities.

Wilby, Warren "War" — The second half of the Hexologists. Married to Isolde. Formerly known as Warren Offalman.

THE
HEXOLOGISTS

BY THE LIGHT OF
THE LOST

THE KING IN THE CAKE

T he king wishes to be cooked alive," the royal secretary said, accepting the proffered saucer and cup and immediately setting both aside. At his back, the freshly stoked fire added a touch of theater to his announcement, though neither seemed to suit what, until recently, had been a pleasant Sunday morning.

"Does he?" Isolde Wilby gazed at the royal secretary with all the warmth of a hypnotist.

"Um, yes. He's quite insistent." The questionable impression of the royal secretary's negligible chin and cumbersome nose was considerably improved by his well-tailored suit, fastidiously combed hair, and blond mustache, waxed into upturned barbs. Those modest whiskers struck Isolde as a dubious effort to impart gravity to a youthful face. Though Mr. Horace Alman seemed a man of perfect manners, he sat with his hat capping his knee. "More precisely, the king wishes to be baked into a cake."

Looming at the tea cart like a bear over a blackberry bush, Mr. Warren Wilby quietly swapped the plate of cakes with a dish of watercress sandwiches. "Care for a nibble, sir?"

"No. No, thank you," Mr. Alman murmured, flummoxed by the offer. The secretary watched as Mr. Wilby positioned a triangle of white bread under his copious mustache, then vanished it like a letter into a mail slot.

The Wilbies' parlor was unabashedly old-fashioned. While their neighbors pursued the bare walls, voluptuous lines, and skeletal furniture that defined contemporary tastes, the Wilbies' townhouse decor fell somewhere between a gallery of oddities and a country bed-and-breakfast. Every rug was ancient, ever doily yellow, every table surface adorned by some curio or relic. The picture frames that crowded the walls were full of adventuresome scenes of tall ships, dogsleds, and eroded pyramids. The style of their furniture was as motley as a rummage sale and similarly haggard. But as antiquated as the room's contents were, the environment was remarkably clean. Warren Wilby could abide clutter, but never filth.

Isolde recrossed her legs and bounced the topmost with a metronome's precision. She hadn't had time to comb her hair since rising, or rather, she had had the time but not the will during her morning reading hours, which the king's secretary had so brazenly interrupted, necessitating the swapping of her silk robe for breeches and a blouse. Wearing a belt and shoes seemed an absolute waste of a Sunday morning.

Isolde Wilby was often described as *imposing*, not because she possessed a looming stature or a ringing voice, but because she had a way of imposing her will upon others. Physically, she was a slight woman in the plateau of her thirties with striking, almost vulpine features. She parted her short hair on the side, though her dark curls resisted any further intervention. Her long-suffering stylist had once described her hair as resembling a porcupine with a perm, a characterization Isolde had not minded in the slightest. She was almost entirely insensible to pleasantries, especially the parentheses of polite conversation, preferring to let the drumroll of her heels convey her hellos and her coattails say her goodbyes.

Her husband, Warren, was a big, squarish man with a tree stump of a neck and a lion's mane of receded tawny hair. He wore unfashionable tweed suits that he hoped had a softening effect on his bearing, but which in fact made him look like a garden wall. Though he was a year younger than Isolde, Warren did not look it, and had been, since adolescence, mistaken for a man laboring toward the promise of retirement. He had a mustache like a boot brush and limpid hazel eyes whose beauty was squandered on a beetled and bushy brow, an obstruction that often rendered his expressions unfathomable, leading some strangers to assume he was gruffer than he was. In fact, Warren was a man of tender conscience and emotional depth, traits that came in handy when Isolde's brusque manner necessitated a measure of diplomacy. He was considerably better groomed that morning only because he had risen early to greet the veg man, who unfailingly delivered the freshest greens and gossip in all of Berbiton at the unholy hour of six.

Seeming to wither in the silence, Mr. Alman repeated, "I said, the king wishes to be baked into a ca—"

"Intriguing," Isolde interrupted in a tone that plainly suggested it was not.

Iz did not particularly care for the nobility. She had accepted Mr. Horace Alman into her home purely because War had insisted one could not refuse a royal visitor, nor indeed, turn off the lights and pretend to be abroad.

While War had made tea, Iz had endured the secretary's boorish attempts at small talk, made worse by an unprompted confession that he was something of a fan, a Hexologist enthusiast. He followed the Wilbies' exploits as frequently documented in the *Berbiton Times*. Mr. Horace Alman was interested to know how she felt about the recent court proceedings. Iz had rejoined she was curious how he felt about his conspicuous case of piles.

The royal secretary had gone on to irk her further by asking whether her name really was "Iz Ann Always Wilby" or if it were some sort of theatrical appellation, a stage name. Iz patiently explained that her father, the famous Professor Silas Wilby, had had many weaknesses—including an insatiable wanderlust and an allergy to obligations—but none worse than his fondness for puns, which she personally reviled as charmless linguistic coincidences that could only be conflated with humor by a gormless twit. Only the sort of vacuous cretin who went around asking people if their names were made-up could possibly enjoy the lumbering comedy that was the godless pun.

Though, in all fairness, she was not the only one to be badgered over her name. Her husband had taken the rather unusual step of adopting her last name upon the occasion of their marriage. He'd changed his name not because he was estranged from his family, but rather because he'd never liked the name Offalman.

Iz had been about to throw the royal secretary out on his inflamed fundament when War had emerged from the kitchen pushing a tea cart loaded with chattering porcelain and Mr. Horace Alman had announced that King Elbert III harbored aspirations of becoming a gâteau.

His gaunt cheeks blushing with the ever-expanding quiet, Mr. Alman pressed on: "His Majesty has gone so far as to crawl into a lit oven when no one was looking." The secretary paused to make room for their astonishment, giving Warren sufficient time to post another sandwich. "And while he escaped with minor burns, the experience does not appear to have dissuaded him of the ambition. He wants to be roasted on the bone."

"So, it's madness, then." Iz shook her head at War when he inquired whether she would like some of either the lemon sponge or the spice cake, an inquiry that was conducted with a delicate rounding of his plentiful brows.

"I don't believe so." Mr. Alman touched his teacup as if he might raise it, then the fire behind him snapped like a whip, and his fingers bid a fluttering retreat. "He has long moments of lucidity, almost perfect coherence. But he also suffers from fugues of profound confusion. He's been discovered in the middle of the night roaming the royal grounds without any sense of himself or his surroundings. The king's sister, Princess Constance, has had to take the rather extreme precaution of confining him to his suite. And I must say, you both seem to be taking all of this rather in stride! I tell you the king believes he's a waste of cake batter, you stifle a yawn!"

Iz tightened the knot of her crossed arms. "I didn't realize you were looking for a performance. I could have the neighbor's children pop by if you'd like a little more shrieking."

War hurried to intervene: "Mr. Alman, please forgive us. We do not mean to appear apathetic. We are just a bit more accustomed to unusual interviews and extraordinary confessions than most. But, rest assured, we are not indifferent to horror; we are merely better acquainted."

"Indeed," Iz said with a muted smile. "How have the staff taken the king's altered state of mind?"

Appearing somewhat appeased, the secretary twisted and shaped the points of his mustache. "They're discreet, of course, but there are limits. Princess Constance knows it's a secret she cannot keep forever, devoted as she is to her brother."

"Surely, you want physicians, psychologists. We are neither," Iz said.

The secretary absorbed her comments with an expression of pinched indulgence. "We've consulted with the nation's greatest medical minds. They were all stumped, or rather, they were perfectly confident in their varying diagnoses and prescriptions, and none of them were at all capable of producing any results. His condition only worsens."

"Even so, I'm not sure what help we can be." Iz picked at a thread that protruded, wormlike, from the armrest of the sofa.

The secretary turned the brim of his hat upon his knee, ducking her gaze when he said, "There's more, Ms. Wilby. There was a letter."

"A letter?"

"In retrospect, it seems to have touched off His Majesty's malaise." The royal secretary reached into his jacket breast pocket. The stiff envelope trembled when he withdrew it. The broken wax seal was as sanguine as a wound. "It is not signed, but the sender asserts that he is the king's unrecognized son."

Warren moved to stand behind his wife's chair. He clutched the back of it as if it were the rail of a sleigh poised atop a great hill. Iz reached back and, without looking, patted the tops of his knuckles. "I imagine the Crown receives numerous such claims. No doubt there are scores of charlatans who're foolish enough to hazard the gallows for a chance to shake down the king."

"Indeed, but there are two things that distinguish this particular instance of blackmail. First, the seal." Mr. Alman stroked the edge of the wax medallion, indicating each element as he described it: "An *S* emblazoned over a turret; note the five merlons, one for each of Luthland's counties. Beneath the *S*, a banner bearing the name Yeardley. This is the seal of Sebastian, Prince of Yeardley. This is the stamp of the king's adolescent ring."

"He identified it as such?" Iz asked.

"I did, at least initially. Of course, I like to believe I'm familiar with all the royal seals, but I admit I had to check the records on this occasion. Naturally, there is much of his correspondence that His Majesty leaves me to open and deal with, but when something like this comes through, I deliver it to him unbroken."

"The signet was no longer in the king's possession, then?"

"No, the royal record identified the ring as lost about twenty-five years ago, around the conclusion of his military service, I believe."

"That's quite a length of time to sit on such a claim." Iz reached for the letter, but the secretary pulled it back. She looked into his eyes; they glistened with uncertainty as sweat dripped from his nose like rain from a grotesque. "What is the second thing that distinguishes the letter?"

"The king's response to the correspondence was...pronounced. He has thus far refused to discuss his impressions of the contents with myself, his sister, or any of his advisors. He insists that it is a hoax, that we should destroy it, though Princess Constance won't hear of it. She maintains that one doesn't destroy the evidence of extortion: One saves it for the inquiry. But of course, there hasn't been an inquiry. How could there be, given the nature of the claim? To say nothing of the fact that the primary witness to the events in question is currently raving in the royal tower."

"The princess wishes for us to investigate?" she asked. Though Isolde held little affection for the gentry, she liked the princess well enough. Constance had established herself as one of very few public figures who continued to promote the study of hexegy, touting the utility of the practice, even amid the blossoming of scientific discovery and electrical convenience. Still, Isolde's vague respect for the princess was hardly sufficient to make her leap to her brother's aid.

Mr. Alman coughed—a brittle, aborted laugh. "Strictly speaking, Her Royal Highness does not know I am here. I have taken it upon myself to investigate the identity of the bastard, or rather, to engage more capable persons in that pursuit."

"I'm sorry, Mr. Alman, but what I said when we first sat down still holds. I am a private citizen. I serve the public, some of whom come to me with complaints about royal overreach, the criminal exploitations of the nobility, or the courts' bungling of one case or another. I don't work for the police—not anymore. Surely you have enough resources at your disposal to forgo the interference of one unaffiliated investigator."

"I do understand your preference, ma'am." The royal secretary rucked his soft features into an authoritative scowl. "But these are extraordinary circumstances, and not without consequence. The uncertainty of rule only emboldens the antiroyalists, the populists, and our enemies overseas. You must—"

Isolde pounced like a tutor upon a mistake: "I *must* pay my taxes. I *may* help you. Show me the letter."

Mr. Alman tightened like a twisted rag. "I cannot share such sensitive information until you have agreed to assist in the case."

"There is another way to look at this, Iz," Warren said, returning to the tea cart. He poured water from a sweating pitcher into a juice glass and presented it to the dampened secretary, who readily accepted it. "You wouldn't just be working for the Crown; you would be serving the interests of the private citizen who has come forward with the claim...perhaps a *legitimate* one." The final phrase made Mr. Alman nearly choke upon his thimble swallow of water. "If the writer of this letter shares the king's blood, and we were to prove it, I don't think anyone would accuse you of being too friendly with the royals."

Isolde bobbed her head in consideration, an easy rhythm that quickly broke. "But if I help to prove that he is a prince, I'd just be serving at the pleasure of a different sovereign."

"True." Warren moved to the mantel to stir the coals, not to invigorate them, but to shuffle the loose embers toward the corners of the firebox. "But if you don't intervene, our possible prince will remain a fugitive."

"You think we should take the case?"

"You know how I feel about lords and lawmen. But it seems to me Mr. Alman is right: If there's a vacuum in the palace and a scramble for the throne, there will be strife in the streets. We know who suffers when heaven squabbles—the vulnerable. Someone up on high only has to whisper the word 'unrest' and the prisons fill up, the workhouses shake out, the missions bar their doors, and the orphanages repopulate. And when the dust settles, perhaps there'll be a new face printed on the gallet bill or a fresh set of bullies on the bench, but the only thing of real consequence that will have changed is the number of bones in the potter's field. Revolution may chasten the rich, but uncertainty torments the poor."

Isolde patted the air, signaling her surrender. "All right, War. All right. You've made your point. Mr. Alman, I—"

A heavy, arrhythmic knock brought the couple's heads around. The Wilbies stared at the unremarkable paneled door as if it were aflame.

Alman snuffled a little laugh. "Do knocking guests always cause such astonishment?"

"They do when they come by my cellar," Warren said.

The door shattered, casting splinters and hinge pins into the room, making all its inhabitants cry out in alarm. It seemed a fitting greeting for the seven-foot-tall forest golem who ducked beneath the riven lintel.

Its skin, rough as bark and scabbed with lichen, bunched about fat ankles and feet that were arrayed from toe to heel by a hundred gripping roots. Its swollen arms were heavy enough to bend its broad back and bow its head, ribbed and featureless as a grub. The golem lurched forward, swaying and creaking upon the shore of a gold-and-amethyst rug whose patterns had been worn down by the passage of centuries.

"A mandrake," Iz said, tugging a half stick of chalk from her khaki breeches. "I've never seen one so large. But don't worry. They're quite docile. He probably just got lost during his migration. Let's try to herd him back down."

With hands raised, Warren advanced upon the mandrake, nattering pleasantly as he inched toward the heaving golem that resembled an ambling yam. "There's a sport. Thank you for keeping off my rug. It's an antique, you know. I have to be honest—it's impossible to match and hard to clean. I haven't got one of those newfangled carpet renovators. The salesman, wonderful chap, wanted three hundred and twenty gallets for it. Can you imagine? And those suck-boxes are as big as a bureau. I have no idea where I'd park such a—"

The moment War inched into range, the mandrake swatted him with a slow, unyielding stroke of its limb, catching him on the shoulder and throwing him back across the room and violently through his tea cart. Macarons and petits fours leapt into the air and rained down upon the smashed porcelain that surrounded the splayed host.

The mandrake raised the fingerless knob of one hand, identifying his quarry, then charged at the royal secretary, who sat bleating like a calf.

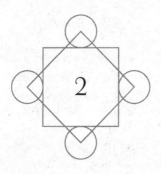

THE PORTALMANTEAU

The analogy most often used to explain *magic* to the children of Berbiton was that it was like a mountain spring—a thing that burst from the earth, emerging from mysterious depths but producing a reliable flow. The cascades that leapt from magic's fountainhead were full of bounties and hazards, both of which were perfectly indifferent to the scholars and fools who frolicked along their slippery shores...

The truth, of course, was far less elegant and more frightening. But schoolchildren did not need to learn about the death of the Yoked God, the Great Putrefaction, and the Transmutation of Spleen. Suffice it to say, those who knew of the visceral origins of Magic's Bubbling Font generally wished they did not.

Four primary streams split from magic's ancient wellspring: wizardry, necromancy, alchemy, and hexegy.

Wizards were powerful conjurers that, among other wonders, were renowned for calling lightning from the unexcited air, immolating careless apprentices, and reading themselves to a state of near blindness. Necromancers, who communed with the dead in ways that unsettled the living and departed alike, were broadly untroubled by morality and sentimentality, a quality that served them well in their efforts to breathe new life into old bones. Alchemists, emerging from a tradition of chemistry and metallurgy, bent the physical laws to their wills, which more often than not were financially inspired. Alchemists could puncture the skins of dimensions and harvest the coals from hell—a chancy though profitable business model.

Of all the brooks of magic, hexegy was but a runnel, a shallow rill that contained a multitude of practical, if not awe-inspiring, functions. The hex-caster, whose power lay in the drawing of complex rosettes, could ease ailments, improve environments, facilitate studies, and assist births.

Wizardry and necromancy, whose practitioners were once considered magic's upper crust, had since the conclusion of the Meridian War been regulated into obscurity. Wizards had been reduced to stage entertainers who pulled strings of scarves out of a variety of orifices, and necromancers had reinvented themselves as behaviorists who treated the ill-tempered pets of the aristocracy. The students of those who'd once animated armies of fallen soldiers now found themselves tasked with discouraging Miss Mittens from eating (and subsequently coughing up) the house plants.

In the boom years that followed the war, alchemy had ascended as the dominant form of magic because of its industrial applications. The lights of the nations were fired by fuel pulled from the alchemists' halos. Several of the alchemists had more money than the monarchy, which was a growing point of royal concern. But while alchemists rose to prominence, and wizards and necromancers had been all but mandated from existence, hex-casters had been allowed to continue to practice because they were benign—and increasingly irrelevant, as they were, bit by bit, being obsoleted by technological innovation. The call for practicing hexegists, which had once been considered a craft as prestigious as lutherie, had been answered by a host of emerging gimmicks and medicaments. The financiers and bourgeois of the capital city of Berbiton increasingly looked to the pioneering efforts of engineers—who had already supplied the city with the miracles of motorized jaunts, electric lights, voxboxes, and hyaline receivers that piped news, melodramas, and music into the nation's parlors and cabs.

The only professions that still commonly employed the delineation of charmed patterns were midwives and dentists, and even they were beginning to swap out their hexes for opiates.

The essential trouble with hexegy was this: The art was unforgiving and often ineffectual. A hex, whether done in the air, chalked on a headboard, or carved upon the soft earth, was as impotent as a scrawl if a circlet bulged from its focus or a single cross leaned one degree this way or that. Even a perfectly traced hex could fail for any number of reasons: an intolerant environment, an unsettled practitioner, or a disinclined subject, to say nothing of interference from other wards, jinxes, and spells.

So, when Isolde Wilby drew before the charging woodland golem a knot of circles and chevrons that colored the air like a sunbeam, she was hardly surprised to see the mandrake dispel her Hex of Tranquility like a runner snapping the ribbon of a finish line.

She would've been trampled by the enchanted creature had she not thrown herself over the ottoman that supported a carefully squared stack of letters. She had been studiously ignoring them for weeks even as her husband found increasingly inconvenient locations to place her looming obligations. It was with some satisfaction that she observed the root golem kick the footstool full of correspondences, enlivening a blizzard of pages. She might've shaken the mandrake's hand if it had had one, and if it were not plowing onward toward the baying royal secretary.

To his credit, Mr. Alman appeared to be trying his best to get out of the way; to his disadvantage was the significant divot Warren had carved into the seat of the club chair over years of daily possession, which left the secretary in something of a hole.

Warren intercepted the mandrake at speed and an angle, tackling its trunk with shoulder lowered and head turned, a daring stroke that proved only slightly more effectual than tackling an oak. The woodland golem listed a little, staggered a step, then straightened again. It hammered upon Warren's back, laying him out like a bearskin. The mandrake raised the great boughs of its arms high overhead, loading a stroke that would undoubtedly ruin Mr. Wilby's organs and consequently his antique rug.

Iz closed the ring on a second hex, and the budding roots that whiskered the mandrake's bulbous hands shot outward, upward, tangling and growing, piercing the plaster of the ceiling and blowing out leaves along the way. The same Hex of Fecundity that made her droughted flowers stand up in the window box now made the mandrake's roots snake from its feet and worm into the hand-knotted rows of the antique carpet.

Seeing that the golem was stuck, at least for the moment, Iz thought to interrogate it. Though mandrakes possessed no vocal cords, they could still communicate a range of emotions to an attuned ear. Plucking another half stick of white chalk from the pocket of her breeches, she rushed forward to draw upon the golem's warted ribs, which were only accessible because its raised arms were presently entangled with the lath in the ceiling. As she formed the first figure of the Hex of Empathy, she wondered if mandrakes were ticklish, though the idle thought was quickly pressed aside by a glimpse of something strange: A colorful rope banded the golem's waist. It appeared to be some sort of belt, one that was almost entirely obscured by the creature's overgrown bark.

Clambering to his feet, Warren swayed like a man straddling a sea-thrown raft. His tumble had tussled his pomaded hair, which now stood out like a witch's broom. "Perhaps we should give our guest a little more room, Iz," he said thickly.

"Just a moment. I want to see what's got it so riled up." Isolde continued to scratch a ring of arcane figures upon the creature's ribs, even as it twisted and writhed with mounting impatience. "Hold still."

Flakes of plaster snowed down upon their shoulders, as the mandrake's branches began to dislodge from the ceiling. It strained its mighty legs, and the dozens of roots that had drilled into the floorboards began to snap, one after another, like brittle wicker.

"That's it. I'm fetching Grandad." Warren rushed to the mantelpiece: an ornate arch crowned by an elaborate bas-relief. The carved scene depicted a many-armed leviathan overwhelming the deck of an ocean liner. With one hand, War hauled the petrified royal secretary up from his eggcup of a chair; with the other, he knocked upon three distinct spots on the mantel's right pilaster. The center tablet of the decorative frieze slid down, making the monstrous squid appear to sink into the sea. In the uncovered alcove there stood a carpetbag—unassuming, and seemingly unpacked. It had a corroded clasp and cracked leather handle. Dozens of patches colored its sides. War extracted the unhandsome bag in the same instant Iz piped a single note of surprise. The mandrake, having freed itself amid a helter-skelter of gypsum and wood, turned to embrace her. She ducked its grasp and ran toward her husband, who stood with his arm deep inside the carpetbag. Chin dimpled from the effort of his concerted rummage, Warren said, "A bit sticky today."

The woodland golem lunged, shedding its roots and canopy as it came. Though the loss robbed it of a little height, it did not appear to diminish its resolve in the least: The mandrake shambled toward the royal secretary, who cowered at Warren's hip.

"Ah, here we are!" War said, grasping something from the purse's impossible depths. With a graceful stroke, he drew forth a claymore, some six feet in length, veined with a fuller that shone like sheet lightning. "Catch, dear!" He tossed the carpetbag into the air to free both hands to better manage the blade. Iz caught the bag and sprang to one side, diving for the sofa, even as War raised the Archsword of the Cloven God and brought its blazing steel down.

The blessed blade carved the storming mandrake from neck to crotch, robbing it of momentum. In the exposed wound, Iz saw what seemed a boiling swarm of luminous mites, blue sparks that crazed between the golem's internal fibers. Cocking the sword to the right, Warren swung again, nearly severing the creature's arm at the joint, and knocking it over into the iron cradle of the fire grate. Even as they collapsed into the blaze, the mandrake's limbs and trunk shriveled. Those diminished logs burst into embers that fled up the chimney and out into the parlor. With toes upon the hearth and head among the coals, the mandrake burned quick as straw. Even as Iz called to her husband to save some part of it, the rapid spread of the flames resisted Warren's efforts to save even a twiglet. The golem's cremation, utter and entire, was scored by the whistle and pop of boiling sap.

Squelching with his heel a cinder that had fallen onto the rug, Warren surveyed his devastated parlor with slouching resignation. He fortified himself with a deep breath and looked to his wife, who sat with the patched carpetbag in her lap and a look of consternation on her face. Still in a thoughtful daze, she opened the bag's clasp to assist Warren as he returned the long blade to its unlikely sheath. He shut the case and, repeating the sequence of probing several discreet switches embedded in the mantel, Warren returned the unnatural luggage to its cloistered shelf.

He righted the chair the royal secretary still cowered behind and invited him to resume his seat before the fire. The quaking, blinking Mr. Alman was quick to answer: "I think I'll stand."

The fire snapped like a party cracker, and the secretary gave one final squawk.

*   *   *

It came as some surprise to discover that mandrake wood smelled remarkably like clove.

While the golem cheered the parlor with fragrance and dancing shadows and Warren excused himself to prepare a tray of gin fizzes, Mr. Alman sat in silence—the result of shock, it seemed—while Ms. Wilby inspected the remnants of leaves and roots that littered the floor and examined what remained of her cellar door that had been so roughly blown out. Eventually, the royal secretary remarked, "I thought it would be a bit grander... the portalmanteau. I always pictured a leather satchel."

Gathering some of the letters that lay strewn about, Iz replied, "We're lucky the bottom hasn't fallen out."

"Does it have a bottom?"

"No," she murmured.

The portalmanteau—which the Wilbies sometimes referred to as "Grandaddy Long Arms" or simply "Grandad"—was a piebald bag that originally belonged to Iz's grandfather, a piano tuner who once upon a time loaded it with the trappings of his trade, though that was before Iz's father had inherited and filled the bag with more curious accessories. Now, the bag's inauspicious exterior concealed a portal that led to an apparently boundless storehouse. That vault was filled to the rafters with the magical artifacts and charmed relics that Professor Silas Wilby, Iz's father, had collected over the course of his life. The physical location of that depot was a secret that Professor Wilby had taken with him to his untimely grave. The "portalmanteau"—another of her father's puns that Iz detested—served as a sort of dumbwaiter to Professor Wilby's fabulous collection of magical esoterica, the extent of which remained largely a mystery. Over the course of years, Iz had only managed to familiarize herself with a fraction of the depository's objects, many of which were as dangerous as they were undocumented. Still, she and Warren borrowed the portalmanteau's treasures as their adventures required, much to the amazement of their admirers and the envy of their enemies.

Warren arrived with two tall glasses of effervescing forgetfulness, the first of which he offered to his wife, the second to the secretary, who still bore the rumple of their ordeal. One wing of his detachable collar had lost its stud and now stood out at a rakish angle. A thorn of his mustache bent downward as if in commiseration. The knee of his trousers was dark with damp, presumably from the contents of his teacup, which had been reduced nearly to its atoms during his efforts to escape his rutted chair.

Equipping himself with a tumbler of ice water, Warren joined his wife on the sofa, and said, "That was a close shave."

"I suppose it's about time we beefed up security around here," Isolde said, eyeing the windows speculatively. "A couple more defensive wards, I should think. Maybe a boobytrap or two. How do you feel about a guillotine over the door?"

"I've always been partial to scimitars myself." Warren chuckled, then snapped his fingers. "Oh! Remember that trap at the Temple of Kordi? What about an axe-headed pendulum?"

"A classic," Isolde agreed.

"Hardly seems like the time for jokes." Mr. Alman's inconsequential lip jutted with bemusement.

Iz hardly broke the sparkling surface of her drink before depositing it upon the now barren ottoman. "Who said we were joking? And what gives you the right to critique our behavior in our own house? First, we didn't shriek enough for your liking and now we're laughing too much. See, this is what I don't like about you lot—you're presumptuous and bossy and boring on top of it. And let me remind you, we weren't the ones cowering and screeching just now. That's because we don't throw up our hands when we're blindsided. We punch back. Now, show me the letter, or go away."

The royal secretary lightly smoothed the waxed furrows of his hair. "Yes, of course." He extracted the missive from his side pocket where it had been incautiously crammed amid the assault.

Isolde accepted the letter. "Who has seen this?"

"His Majesty, myself of course, and his sister."

"What did Princess Constance make of it?" Isolde asked.

Mr. Alman bit his lip. "I know she, as the older mother of younger children, is sometimes presented to the public as an unflappable maternal force, but she has been quite upset by her brother's illness. The letter, the possibility of an illegitimate prince—none of it seemed to concern her as much as her brother's fragile state."

"Says a lot about her priorities. Family over reputation. Can't say I disagree." Isolde inspected the broken seal of the letter with squinting attention. "While at university, I attended several of the princess's orations on the place of hexegy in a mechanized world. She had that famous speech . . . what was it called?"

"Hex to the Future," Mr. Alman supplied.

"That's it! She made quite an impression." Isolde unfolded the stiff sheet and, leaning toward her husband, read the missive aloud:

Sir,

You may have cast my mother aside, but you cannot so easily dispose of the blood that boils in the cauldron of my heart.

We are an avaricious line, Father, and so in keeping with tradition, I shall neither surrender nor be dissuaded from my claim to your attention, recognition, and crown.

Irrefutably Yours,

X

Isolde made a face as if she were tugging a hair from her dinner. "A touch melodramatic, but it does get the point across." She held the page up to the light of the chandelier, searching for a watermark but discovering none. "I presume it arrived in an envelope."

"It did."

"May I see it?"

"I'm afraid I threw it away." Mr. Alman's receded chin retreated further into his neck as Ms. Wilby arched a reproachful brow. The secretary hastened to add: "There was no return address, of course."

"Did you note which post office canceled the stamp?"

"I did not."

Isolde scowled at the secretary. "In the future, should any further evidence fall into your lap, please try to keep it out of the waste bin."

Alman's shoulders slouched. "Yes, ma'am."

Isolde brought the letter nearly to her nose, then stretched it out to the limit of her arm like someone playing a trombone. "So, we have a theatrical threat, a signet that's been missing for twenty-five years, and a regent who wishes to pop himself into the oven. I suppose the list of suspects is myriad."

"I'm afraid so. Since the king has no heir, there are any number of nobles who would like to see the line of succession reconsidered: the Evanhams, the Waterlies, the Clarks, the Attertons...There's his sister of course, but she effectively took herself out of contention when she married a Belloc Islander."

"Ah, the tireless bigotry of those whose greatest accomplishment was being born!" Warren said.

"Sir, you understand, these are not my own judgments. I'm just repeating what has been widely said. Personally, I believe a more likely culprit would be a member of some antiroyalist faction who got their grubby hands on the king's old ring." The secretary sucked his teeth in anger. "Those malingerers! They witness the prosperity of our nation from the horizons of their neglected fields and shake their fists at any mention of the king, who—for *shame*—has failed to rain jewels down upon their naked children and faithless wives!"

"That's quite an unkind characterization of your fellow Luthlanders." Warren's smile stiffened into a polite grimace. "Not everyone who dislikes the royalty is a sluggard or a traitor."

Seeing that his outburst had not found a sympathetic audience, Mr. Alman recovered his temper. "Yes. Well. The point is, there are any number of persons who'd like to see the king humbled. What I would ask is that you discover the identity of the cad who penned this outrage and prove the illegitimacy of his claim."

"You think the signet is a fake?"

Mr. Alman put his hands together as if in prayer. He pressed the steeple of his fingers to his chin. "Perhaps. But even if it is the genuine article, it proves nothing. The ring may have been lost or stolen or—"

Isolde interjected: "Or it may have been given as a gift, a token of affection. The king's behavior seems to indicate both shame and guilt, does it not?"

The royal secretary seemed to inflict his frustration at Ms. Wilby's point upon his cocked-up collar, though the article rebuffed his taming. "So, we're entertaining wild speculations, are we? Well, then perhaps he gambled the ring away in an alley or pawned it for a new jaunting carriage or—"

"Perhaps he did exactly what the author of this letter asserts. You're asking for proof and assuming it will exonerate the king, but what if I prove the bastard's claim?"

A sort of defeated calm washed over Mr. Alman's face: an impression of poise. "If that is the case, then we will deal with the consequences."

"And Princess Constance—she is against this investigation?"

"No. Not against, not opposed, not at all. She is just unconvinced of the urgency. Or perhaps I should say she is more attuned to the urgency of hope. Her Royal Highness would prefer to wait for the claimant to come forward, to announce himself, and let the burden of proof fall upon him. But what she does not appear to understand is that though he—or she— may not present inarguable proof, they will most certainly introduce doubt, and that misgiving will spread through the nobility—and quickly. There is a ready audience for this sort of scandal. The accusation does not have to be true to torment the king, and he is already in such a diminished state. No, I believe we must confront the villain head-on, Ms. Wilby. We must expose the fraud. I don't think the king's sister will resent being presented with a solution to her brother's crisis."

Isolde tapped the edge of the folded letter upon her knee. "As far as I'm concerned, the most compelling argument for my involvement in this case climbed out of my root cellar. Someone, it seems, disapproves of your effort to engage my services. I don't respond well to intimidation. So, I will help you, but all my usual fees and provisos apply: I won't tolerate interference from my clients; I am not responsible if anyone is inconvenienced by the facts I uncover; and I will not, under any circumstance, appear before a judge, cooperate with the police, or accept questions from the press. I deliver answers, but I answer to no one."

Isolde Wilby picked up her gin fizz and sipped it as she strode from the room.

Mr. Alman observed her departure with an expression of amazement, which he turned toward a beaming Mr. Wilby. "I suppose she's keeping the letter, then?"

"So it would seem." Warren slapped his thighs and stood with an avuncular grunt. "Well, sir, I don't wish to keep you. I'll fetch your hat. It must be around here somewhere...ah!"

Warren stooped to retrieve the article from among the smithereens of his tea things. It had been such an august chapeau before someone had trampled it. War dusted the porcelain shards from its crimpled brim and dashed a blotch of egg salad from its caved-in crown before presenting it to the secretary. "There we are. It really was a pleasure to meet you. Let me get the door."

SOTTO VOCE SNIPER

T rolley rails, power lines, and overflowing gutters stitched the capital city together with all the forethought of a field surgeon. As is often the case with so many old towns, Berbiton seemed to have been assembled by accident and as an afterthought. What had three hundred years ago been the desire path of goats being herded to market had been transformed by ensuing generations into a cockeyed boulevard. Horse stables had been retrofitted to accommodate tram cars and rubbish trucks, though neither quite fit. The family plots of original settlers had been buried under malls, theaters, and cafés. The sidewalks, which had in bygone years been scantly delineated by rows of hitching posts, had been fortified with curbs to spare pedestrians the meat grinder of modernizing traffic.

Complicating this thoughtless patchwork were the strata of neighborhoods that often bore inappropriately grand or jolly designations. It was telling that the street most riddled by violent crime lay at the heart of Dove Town. The oldest and poorest neighborhoods, those identified by shipyards, tar-paper roofs, and blight, lay bunched along the river docks. As one ascended the watershed, the treeless blocks began to bloom with grocers and tearooms. There, the middle class in their mid-terraces put out window boxes, which they called gardens, as if those fragile roots could keep their homes from sliding downhill. Above those modest rooftops, the city's towers swelled along the ridge, their golden shoulders pressed together in huddled opulence.

The Wilbies' abode stood out from the colorless mid-hill rowhomes like a painter's signature—a thing at once incongruous and essential, over-shadowed and emphatic. In keeping with the interior, the facade was a fussy oddity amid the bluff of somber dwellings. Crimson shutters brightened white cedar shingles like a pinched cheek. The eaves were numerous, severe, and embellished with bargeboard. A precarious widow's walk soared over the home's roof, affording visitors a cramped platform to enjoy the agoraphobic view. From there, one could see the three foggy bridges—each higher and broader than its forerunner—that spanned the River Zimme. Assisted by a pair of field glasses, one could peer past the eastern bank, cluttered with mills, and make out the distant blue thread of the Garrean Sea, or one could just as well drop their binoculars and marvel at the poisoned clouds that roiled over the storied city.

Mounted beside the Wilbies' front door, innocuous as an earthquake bolt, was a plaque of greening copper. That unremarkable shingle was emblazoned with two words: one simple, the other strange: THE HEXOLOGISTS.

Something like snow clung to the city's streets, the sidewalks, the lamppost hoods, the roofs of the parked jaunting cars. Though it was chilly enough for some form of frozen precipitation, the snow that coated the city was in fact an exotic type of ash, the pollutive silt of the alchemist mills. Individually, the flakes resembled fish scales—they were lucent, opalescent. The resemblance also carried over to their fishy odor, a quality that inspired the colloquial name "carp snow." The air fairly shimmered with the regular morning shower.

Warren shut the front door, locked it, checked his work twice, and snuggled Grandad firmly under his arm. Scowling and stamping a waterlogged shoe, Isolde emerged from the slim alley on the north side of their house. "Downspout came loose again."

"Nothing amiss, then?" War asked.

"The basement windows are unbroken. The storm door is still rusted shut. The chain on the coal chute is intact. You'd be hard pressed to squeeze a spud down it, never mind a golem. What about the cellar? Did you find any turned earth, any holes?"

"I'm sorry to report our cellar is in fine shape. I wish I could say the same of our parlor."

"Then someone must've pushed the mandrake through a portal. It would be tricky to open one of those, sight unseen, underground, and through all my hexes. We're not dealing with an amateur." Iz stomped up the three steps to their front door, removed her stick of chalk from the brocaded pocket of her gray wool coat, the lapels of which ran to the hem, making it look a little like a formal bathrobe.

She drew upon the door a Hex of Aegis—a florid maze like a cross section from an artichoke. It gleamed briefly, then turned dark as a brand. "I suspect we may be dealing with an advanced alchemist. Perhaps a wizard."

Warren shook loose the carp snow that had already gathered on the broad shoulders of his overcoat and tipped his bowler hat down against a gust of river wind. The cap, like his tweed coat, was twenty years out of fashion, but he thought the popular boaters made him look too much like a butcher. "Aren't all the wizards dead?"

"I'm sure that's what they'd like us to think." Stepping toward the street, she raised a hand to hail a jaunt. The horse and cart had been banished to the countryside decades ago, making way for electrahol-fired jaunts: four- and six-wheeled, long-hooded cars with profiles as svelte as a slipper. They produced a pearlescent vapor and a steady stream of grievous injuries to pedestrians, passengers, and chauffeurs alike—a fitting if tragic tribute to the grim bargain the city had struck to dress itself in lights. A straight line could be drawn between the refinement of electrahol from thalanium and the bilious snow that rose in drifts about the town.

Out from the purring blur of traffic, a black stoat of a jaunt braked and cocked toward the curb, leaving its rear bumper to block the lane. Over the blat of horns, the capped driver called through his lowered window, asking where they were heading.

"The Cardinal Library," Iz answered, opening the door for Warren, whose weight made the jaunt's shocks dip and squeak. Following him in, Iz snatched the cloche from her head, shook the shimmering flakes from it, and raked her fingers through her short curls. "Me, working for the Crown again. God. I'm going to get an earful."

Warren rocked to one side so he could lightly pat his coat pocket, "Don't worry, dear. I packed a peace offering."

From the street, the Cardinal Library resembled an alien crown. Crossing peaks ringed the white facade, golden rays thorning each summit. In the expanse between arches, tapered windows punctured the marble, suggesting the organic perforations of a dried sand dollar. It was at once striking and estranging, a common impression that had prompted an early review of the architecture to coin the phrase "pitiless magnificence."

As the Wilbies exited their jaunt onto the forecourt outside the library, Warren continued his train of thought. "It was just *odd*. I reached for the Archsword of the Cloven God as I've done a hundred times before. Then there was this sort of—I don't know what to call it exactly—reluctance? Stickiness?" He paid the driver, patted the roof of the cab, and jogged to catch up with Iz, who'd already begun her march up the wide, curling steps. "Do magical portals need to be oiled? Perhaps we should seek out an interdimensional chimney sweep."

"I wouldn't worry too much about it, War. Sometimes a door sticks; doesn't mean the house is going to fall down. I'm more interested in our friend Mr. Alman. I had the impression that he wasn't telling us everything. He seemed nervous."

"I think he has every right to be on edge. He came with a monster on his heels. He's obviously ruffled someone's feathers. Besides, you make everyone nervous."

"I don't make you nervous."

"That's because I'm too busy being smitten."

"Shh," she said, barring her lips with a finger. She pointed to the sun-curled, hand-drawn sign taped to the outer door, which read: PATRONAGE ENCOURAGED; FOOD FORBIDDEN; QUIET ENFORCED.

The Berbiton Cardinal Library operated under the formidable covenant of "perfect preservation." All materials scrawled, printed, published, or distributed found a home upon the stately shelves and voluminous drawers of the nation's greatest library. The archive's interior was a soaring rotunda, pierced by embrasures that spoked sunlight upon the stacked mezzanines. The layered floors teemed with browsers in search of diversion, scholars scrounging for vindication, indigents seeking comfort, novelists hunting for reclaimable material, and burgeoning adolescents diligently sifting for any reference to the carnal act in verse, narrative, or diagram. And at the focal point of this kaleidoscope of desires and book spines rose the archivist's desk: a round battlement defended by a woman who wore a black shift, a monocle on a gold chain, and her white hair in a sharply angled bob.

As Iz and War crossed the expansive sea of zigzagging tile, they marked the distant echo of a young man's voice, barking and cracking over some unaccountable hilarity. Warren tut-tutted under his breath as he scanned the upper floors in search of the poor fool. The circulation librarian spotted him first: He lurked on the third level, prodding a peer with a newspaper pole. The librarian drew from behind her desk a blowgun that was as long as she was tall. Clinching the monocle between brow and cheekbone, she climbed atop her desk and sighted the unsuspecting nuisance. The blown plug of hard wax struck him squarely on the back of his neck, eliciting first a squawk and then silence.

The librarian was in the process of dismounting her desktop when she spotted Isolde and Warren. She addressed them in hushed tones that they returned in kind.

"It's Sunday. Must be something important to get you out of bed." Raising her eyebrow to release the monocle, the librarian puffed into the blowgun to dislodge the residual crumbs of wax, then returned the weapon to a rack that was crowded with barrels of varying lengths.

"Mother," Iz said, sharing a twitch of a smile with Dr. Luella Timmons-Wilby. "I need your help with something." Isolde placed the folded letter upon the desk, holding it closed, but so that the seal showed. "I've had an inquiry from the royal secretary to look into a delicate matter of—"

Luella Timmons-Wilby gave an arid little cough of surprise. "The *royal* secretary? What happened to all your convictions, your tender conscience that absolutely could not abide a compromise?"

"These are extenuating circumstances."

"They often are, and that's the point. Society is built upon the currency of concession, of give and take, of small sins for greater triumphs. You could be running the institutions you abhor, reforming the very failing agencies you could not abide. You could've been the chief of police by now."

"And you could've been a politician."

"Oh, they don't read enough." Dr. Timmons-Wilby tidied her station as she spoke, though there was very little that required straightening. She squared a stack of new acquisitions, recentered the pot of paste on her caddy, and drawered the bathroom key with its bulky fob.

Iz cast an eye about to make sure no one was lurking within earshot. The main floor of the library was all but deserted. "Anyway, you have Warren to thank for my change of heart, which is *temporary*. He convinced me."

"Where were you, my dear boy, for all her youthful mistakes?"

"Out making my own," Warren said with a wink.

The librarian snatched for the letter, but Iz whisked it back to her chest. Her mother squinted at her. "You know how the Cardinal Library feels about secrets. If it's written down, it should be part of the record."

"I'll have to plead royal privilege, I'm afraid."

"Look at you. You're a natural functionary." Dr. Timmons-Wilby turned to address her son-in-law. Her bobbed hair provided her probing expression with a silvery frame. "So, what is the general subject of the inquiry, Warren? International espionage? An assassination plot? Where there are royals, so follow harangues over money or sex or both."

Warren's hazel eyes rounded and fluttered as he choked on a reply. Iz interjected, "Naturally, we can't share the details, but at the moment, I'm treating it as a case of missing jewelry—specifically, a signet ring. We believe it was lost approximately twenty-five years ago. I need your help looking into King Elbert's time in the military."

The two women stared at each other with a level intensity that might've wilted a flower. Clearing his throat, Warren relieved his coat pocket of a delicate parcel: a crumpet nestled between paper doilies and done up with a bow of silk ribbon. He set the offering on the counter between the ink-stained DUE DATE stamp and a stack of bookmarks that contained a short verse on the terrible fate that awaited readers who dog-eared the corners of pages.

Dr. Timmons-Wilby palmed the crumpet, secreting it beneath the counter with all the dexterity of a card sharp. "You're as cagey as your father. You can wait in the Caffery Room. I'll see what I can find."

Isolde's father, Professor Silas Wilby, had been the world's foremost explorer. He was famous for excavating ancient tombs, uncovering lost cities, and cataloging new species of behemoths who prowled the oceanic gorges. These gleaming accomplishments were somewhat tarnished by his penchant for losing interest in his own expeditions, often mid-voyage and without apparent cause. He'd once exited the search for a northern passage, an undertaking that had been years in the staging, with all the fanfare of a man announcing that he was popping off to the shops for a beef pasty. Professor Wilby had disembarked upon an ice floe saying, "It's pretty much straight on from here, boys." He waved gaily to his partners, who scowled down from the stern as their vessel steamed away. No one had the slightest idea how he got home.

He again made headlines throughout Luthland when he abandoned the hunt for the hollow biome that lay beneath the earth's crust—the legendary lithoverse—where ancient creatures and primitive peoples were believed to thrive. The professor surrendered the effort mere hours from their anticipated destination, citing as the cause the party's shortage of mustard. He quit mountains with the summit in ready reach, exited jungles with sketches of temples he had not bothered to breach, and departed uncharted islands without plotting the longitude and latitude of his discoveries. While the cause of his fickleness was never publicized, it could not be attributed to the melancholic urge to see his wife and daughter, who saw less of the patriarch than the train station's baggage carriers. No, if anything, Isolde's father seemed to abandon one adventure only to make room for the next. Professor Wilby was perennially restless and seldom at home.

When his wife and daughter did see him, he was elusive about his travels and underlying motives. Often, Isolde's mother would mark his homecoming by asking him if he'd found what he was looking for. In answer, the professor would only shrug, wink, and kiss her cheek.

As a girl, Isolde had thought her father a romantic figure: a fearless, enigmatic genius who served the call of adventure. He certainly looked like an adventurer: Long exposure to the sun had only deepened the hue of his russet skin; his hair was untamed; his beard unruly and stripped like a badger with white. He was long of leg and broad of shoulder and did not carry on his bones so much as a pinch of fat. He struck Isolde as heroic, though it was an infatuation that dwindled as she matured, and discovered that her mother's patience was not as effortless as she made it seem.

They had learned of Professor Silas Wilby's death from his banker, Mr. Ecklous.

A tall man with milky hair and watery eyes, Mr. Ecklous sat in their kitchen, looking wrong in his three-piece suit seated upon a spindle-backed chair. Both Isolde and her mother had been perplexed to see the banker come with an article of old familial luggage: a carpetbag that had belonged to the professor's father, and which they assumed was still moldering in the attic above.

Mr. Ecklous had looked neither of them in the eye when he'd said, "I'm very sorry to report that Professor Wilby is dead."

Isolde, who was sixteen at the time, had been sure there'd been some mistake. Her father's untimely demise was often speculated in the papers. The professor had the distinction of seeing his obituary printed on no fewer than three occasions over the course of his stubborn lifetime, the cause of his death having been attributed alternately to disease, disembowelment, and disintegration.

"You have proof? Who was the source?" her mother asked.

"No, in fact, I have the opposite of proof. I have an absence. You see, he left me with a device—a sand clock, a very curious one." Mr. Ecklous peered at the small glass of grapefruit juice he'd been offered and accepted, and now ogled as if it were a rare gem. "The clock never needed to be turned. The sand flowed down, made a hill of an hour, and then when the last grain had rattled from the bulb, the flow reversed: the sand poured upward into an upside-down mound—a stalactite, if you will." He looked at them finally, seeming to expect some glimmer of commiserative wonder, a shared awe with the oddities that seemed to orbit the professor. He flinched when he saw their unreadable owlish gazes. He continued: "The hourglass has sat on my bookshelf for more than a decade. Silas told me that as long as the sands continued to run, I'd know he was alive. Yesterday evening, I found the clock motionless, the sands frozen. I sat vigil all night waiting for the clock to drain again. I am sorry to be here, to have come with this news."

Isolde looked to her mother to see if she appeared concerned. Dr. Timmons-Wilby looked bewildered but not despondent when she said, "I'm going to need more proof than a broken clock, I'm afraid."

Isolde took consolation from her mother's measured response: Her father was not really dead. But, as is so often the case, the bloom of hope was quick to wilt.

In the Cardinal Library's Caffery Room, Warren stood by the window clucking affectionately at the starlings perched on the rounded sill outside. A flock wheeled through the haze beyond, stretching and gathering, mounting and breaking like surf.

Isolde sat at the stately table that dominated the small reading room with an expression of hazy consternation, a look that Warren recognized at once. He touched her shoulder, and she reached back to pat his hand.

"You all right?" he asked.

"I liked the diagnosis of madness for the king more before a golem appeared in our basement."

"What are you thinking now? A curse? Poison?"

"I don't know."

Dr. Luella Timmons-Wilby entered the room talking, much in the style of her daughter. She came relatively unburdened with tomes and documents. Iz had hoped to see her pushing a returns cart full of material. Instead, her mother bore only a pamphlet and a folio, though the librarian seemed sufficiently delighted with her retrieval.

"I think I know when he lost his signet. Or at least approximately so," the librarian said, setting down her light burden and leaning upon the tabletop with the straightened arms of a general looming over a battle plan. The posture was one of such domination that Iz felt compelled to rise. It had been Dr. Timmons-Wilby who'd first introduced Iz to hexegy, and though the daughter quickly outshone her mother's own talent for the craft, there were few in Berbiton who could fashion a more effective Hex of Acuity.

The librarian drew a circle of inverted ankhs upon the tabletop with the nail of one finger. Watching from her side, Isolde smiled at her mother's intricate work. "How do you do that? Anything more than two rings, and I want my chalk."

"Repetition. Also, someone's always nicking my pens. I had to write a note to the director this morning with a crayon! Holding on to a writing implement in a library requires darker magic than I've mastered. All right, there we are." The daedal lines of the librarian's hex began to shine like moonlight through a dormer window. Setting aside the pamphlet for the moment, Dr. Timmons-Wilby opened the folio to reveal velum sleeves containing carefully cut rectangles and *L*'s of newsprint that had yellowed with age. "Of course, the library would never butcher its collection of newspapers like this, but these were donated by someone who was an enthusiast of the royal family. She collected and filed every story, picture, or bit of gossip about the royals for nearly fifty years." Extracting one clipped column, she smoothed the brittle paper over her hex. The faded text and picture spangled and dithered like a mirage. Then all at once, the article snapped into perfect clarity.

Warren whistled softly. "That's the king? So young! What year was this?" Though the header of the clipping lacked a date, the original collector had noted it in the side margin in a thin, slanting cursive. "June 12, 4032. Rather dapper, wasn't he? Whenever I see his picture in the papers now, his face is all puckered up and sneery. He always looks like someone just stepped on his toe."

Isolde read the copy for War's benefit, as he stood peering over the crowded shoulders of the two women. "Captain Sebastian, Prince of Yeardley, to be honorably discharged from the Luthlandian Armed Forces after an extended medical leave. Captain Sebastian was awaiting deployment to the front lines when he was seized by a blood infection that nearly robbed him of his life. After convalescing at Winterbourne Military Hospital for three months, Captain Sebastian is expected to be released later this week. Though he will not have served in the Meridian War, the captain's brief military career was not without distinction..." Isolde trailed off as she read ahead. "The rest is just a summary of his time at academy."

"Now, look at the picture." Dr. Timmons-Wilby pointed at the row of four young men in parade dress uniforms. They were smiling, at ease, arms draped upon each other's shoulders, a pose that brought into ready relief a particular hand and a familiar ring. Isolde's mother presented her with her monocle, and Iz bent to inspect the ring more closely.

"It certainly appears to be our ring." She turned her attention to the prince's face: His knocked-back cap, full cheeks, and saucy simper made him look like a boy playing soldier. He bore the dimpled chin and sparkling eyes that were common among Yeardley men.

"Six months later, we have this." The pamphlet, which commemorated the opening of a new speedway, featured a picture of Prince Sebastian and Lady Mary Soames, whom he would marry two years later. Behind them stretched the long bonnet of a black racing jaunt. The prince and lady were similarly posed; in one hand each held a large pair of tailor's scissors, and in the other hand, the cut end of the ribbon. Here again, the prince's signet was visible with the help of the librarian's hex. The seal was quite obviously not the same as before: The oval shape had been replaced by a rectangle. "A new ring," Dr. Timmons-Wilby said, her voice bright with triumph.

Warren sighed. "They made quite a fetching couple, didn't they?"

"Did they?" Iz mused, reexamining the prince's aloof expression. Gone was the playful smile. Though it would be years before he was crowned King Elbert III, already Prince Sebastian seemed to have embraced the solemnity of his future.

"Oh, I think you can tell they were already in love." Warren reached between them to tap the bannered wreath that hung from the jaunt's fender, which read: TO THE STARTING LINE! DECEMBER 11, 4032. "And it was, let me see, four years after this that she passed away. I don't much care for the man, but the fact that he never remarried always seemed to me a testament to the depth of his heartbreak. What did she die of... the pox, wasn't it?"

"A fever she caught from swimming in the Zimme," Dr. Timmons-Wilby corrected in the sort of automatic drone one used to bless a sneezing stranger. Mother and daughter bore mirroring pensive scowls. "You would've had more opportunities to help with this sort of critical work if you'd not quit the OEI." The Office of Ensorcelled Investigations had operated under the city police. Isolde had served as its inaugural and terminal head. Though her tenure at the OEI had occurred nearly a decade prior and not lasted a year, it still seemed fresh in Luella's mind as she rarely allowed a visit to go by without mentioning it to her daughter.

"I didn't quit," Iz corrected. "Well, I *did*, but only because they forced me out. My superiors didn't take me seriously."

"Do you really think the board of directors that oversee this library hold me in perfect esteem? Hardly. Administrators are oblivious and generally get in the way; effective employees learn to work around them. That's how it always is. Besides, it wasn't really your commissioner's approval that you wanted, was it?"

"This isn't about Dad."

"If you say so. But then, why do this? Why investigate this case? Is it that you're flattered the Crown came to you instead of the police? Are you hoping to trot this coup under the noses of the old brass?"

Isolde straightened, bucking against Warren, who'd been leaning over her. "Someone put a monster in my basement, Mother. They invaded my home. They attacked Warren. All to discourage me from getting involved. This isn't about Dad or my disappointing career. This is about uncovering who is behind the assault on our sanctuary, and the blackmailer seems the most likely culprit. I intend to hold them to account."

"And make them buy me a new rug," Warren interjected in an effort to cool the rising temperature of the room.

Moderating her tone, Isolde composed a peaceable smile. "Exactly. This is about a carpet."

Luella shrugged. "If you say so, dear."

Iz sighed. "Thank you, Mother. You've been very helpful—as always."

"I'm sure I could be more helpful if you'd share the contents of that letter."

"I have no doubt about that," Iz said, and snatched up the newspaper clipping even as she turned on her heel and stamped for the door.

"That's not in circulation," her mother said in a hoarse stage whisper.

"Call it a royal dispensation." Iz raised a declarative finger to punctuate what her restrained volume could not.

"I'll call it theft," the librarian replied.

"I'm sorry, Luella. I'll make sure you get it back." Warren picked up her hand and squeezed it. "Seeing you is always my favorite part of any case."

Dr. Timmons-Wilby smiled thinly, her thoughts obviously still with her daughter. "Elusive and inclined to abuse of power. She would've made a fine commissioner."

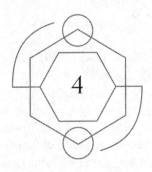

4

BLESSED TO DEATH

There was but one undebated truth in the colleges and lecture halls of Berbiton, a fact settled so comfortably among the scientific community as to have ascended from hypothesis, to theory, to law, and that law was this: Whenever one was in desperate need of a hirable car, every jaunt in the city was instantaneously engaged. It was a truth proved once more on the library's shallow forecourt where Warren flagged desperately at each passing cab while Iz found herself accosted by the person she detested most: Lorcan Magnussen, celebrated columnist and accomplished rabble-rouser.

Mr. Magnussen seemed to materialize from behind a lamppost, which was not particularly impressive given his bantam size. He wore a khaki-colored trench coat on his slight shoulders and yesterday's stubble on his more considerable chin. Before a less jaundiced judge, Mr. Magnussen might've passed for good-looking, with oil-black hair and high cheekbones. But Iz only saw his eyes, flat as coffee rings, and his ever-active mouth from which spewed an unending geyser of mischaracterizations, exaggerations, and libels. At the moment, his maw was occupied by the contents of a paper trumpet full of caramel corn, which seemed at odds with the hour. He devoured the treat with mechanical, joyless efficiency.

He smiled when he saw her frown. "Thought I'd find you here. This is where they all begin, isn't it?"

"Where what begins?" Iz craned her neck in sympathy with her husband's hailing attempts as if she might will a taxi into existence.

"Those fiascos you call investigations." He dug a stubborn kernel from the crown of one molar, scrutinized the offender, then returned it to his mastication. "Did you see this morning's edition? Your case was dismissed."

"It wasn't *my* case. I didn't present the evidence."

"No, you just invented it. And what does that make now—three in a row?" He had sidled up beside her in a confiding way that made her dream of shoving him into traffic. "Funny how your hoodoo never holds up in court. But I suppose that's the trouble with magical entrapments, undead witnesses, and spellbound confessions. In the cold light of day, on the level scale of the judge's bench, it almost seems like you're just making things up, doesn't it?"

Iz had, in fact, skimmed the weekend edition of the *Berbiton Times*, and so had unfortunately been exposed to Mr. Magnussen's gleeful account of Friday's disastrous proceedings. The case against the suspected art forger, Jonathan Reames, which she had been instrumental in assembling, had been thrown out after it came to light that she had used a charmed relic, the Demiurge's Brush, while endeavoring to lure the felon out. The Demiurge's Brush was capable of reproducing any stroke, medium, or pigment. It was, admittedly, a counterfeiter's ideal instrument, a fact that had not escaped Mr. Magnussen's notice, and he had frittered a considerable amount of ink musing upon the diabolical crimes that Ms. Wilby herself might have undertaken while armed with such a wicked brush.

In fact, Iz had only used the Demiurge's Brush on one occasion: to alter a forgery before Reames presented it to an auction house for authentication and sale. The painting, which purported to be an original Arcadi, was deemed a flawless example of the master's style . . . except for his misspelled signature, which had been Iz's insidious addition. Reames was so incensed by the gaff that he had been goaded into shouting before a crowded room that someone had tampered with his work because he "would never make such a stupid mistake."

Seldom had a statement been more swiftly refuted.

But, despite the confession, the magistrate had concluded that Isolde Wilby and her magic brush might as easily have been the source of the forgeries as Mr. Reames. And so, the scoundrel would soon walk free.

All of this, Magnussen had presented to his readers in vivid and humorous detail. Which was his way of punishing Isolde for steadfastly refusing to grant him the exclusive right to dramatize her adventures for the grasping public. For years, Magnussen had hounded Iz for the chance to tag along on her investigations. Each time he asked, Isolde had answered she just would rather the criminals get away.

She raised the lapels of her coat and tucked in her chin, ostensibly to block the icy draft, but actually to see a little less of the reporter's smug face. "I divine the *truth*, Mr. Magnussen, an ideal with which the law appears to have but a passing interest and your publisher a vigorous rivalry. You could be reporting on the plight of the factory worker, or our impotent Parliament, who seem to have confused gridlock with stability, or the worsening carp snow, or any number of other subjects of public interest. Instead, you are lurking behind lampposts and pouncing upon private citizens as if you had any claim to their time."

"I go where the story takes me, Miss Iz Ann Always, and for whatever reason, you never seem far afield of the fracas. These are tumultuous times. I'm sure you've heard the rumors: The king is unwell. His sister is trying to hush it up, but he hasn't made a public appearance in weeks. There's a lot of jockeying going on behind the velvet curtain. I suspect alliances are shifting. There are some nobles who do not wish to see the line of succession go through Princess Constance and her brood of Belloc mutts. And the Soames line still feels cheated by the death of Queen Mary. I suppose they will have the support of the Attertons when they make their play for the throne."

"Why investigate, when you can suspect, suppose, and speculate? Saves on time. And cab fare."

"All truth is born from the womb of rumor," Magnussen sniped, and before Isolde could reply, veered into non sequitur. "I've written a book."

"I'll have to dust off my crayons. Or does your publisher plan to include a box with every sale?" Isolde took a step back to get out from under the power lines that crossed over the sidewalk and which had dripped slush on her shoulders at the gust of a passing lorry. The city's cat's cradle of strung wires seemed to grow more convoluted every day. The Wilbies were still without a voxbox because Isolde did not want to install in her home another way for journalists, prospective clients, and investigators to contact her. Still, she knew her luddism was impractical and could not last forever.

Mr. Magnussen hopped again to her side to continue his uninteresting boast. "My book is called *The Hexed Court: A Rationalist's Critique of the Gray Arts*. You see, my thesis is that when the law consecrates experts who can manipulate the evidence, influence witnesses, adjust memories—"

"That's police procedure you're thinking of," Isolde snapped.

He pressed on: "When you render unreliable the jury's own senses, you no longer have a legal system: You have a stage upon which people like you can incriminate the innocent and exonerate the criminal at will. You have ensconced yourself as the magistrate over us all."

"Believe me, Mr. Magnussen, if I had one quarter the influence you think I do, you would be writing ad copy for splinter-free bog roll."

He touched his chest lightly, affecting theatrical fright. "My goodness, is that a threat?"

Isolde shrugged. "More of a dream, really."

"Are you planning to contribute your bitters to the punch bowl of Victor's soiree this month, or are you going to let the old boy twist in the wind again?"

Isolde cringed. Her middling fame as a sleuthing hex-caster had brought with it a certain pull with the social elite who wished to gather to themselves as many celebrities as possible in the hopes that such brilliant company might bathe them in a flattering light. There was no worse, nor more determined offender in this regard than the industrial alchemist, Mr. Victor Cholmondeley.

Isolde answered, "I'd rather have my ears peeled from my head than waste an evening on one of Mr. Cholmondeley's routine orgies."

"No, I can't make it either," Lorcan answered with droll glumness.

From the culvert, Warren gave a hurrah as a jaunt finally broke from the indifferent stream of cars. Opening the door, he waved to his wife, who charged forward, though not quickly enough to knock the reporter from her heels. His caramel corn leapt from his paper horn as he jogged to keep up. "Come on! Can't you share anything about this latest inquiry?"

"I'm sorry, Mr. Magnussen. I'm still waiting to read about it in tomorrow's edition. I look forward to learning the facts once you've had a chance to birth them."

The gauzy sun shone behind the Winterbourne Military Hospital, dressing it in a flattering corona that was still not enough to make the ruin seem any less dire. In the twilight of the unlit derelict, Iz waited amid the sticky lace of overgrown catchweed while War paid the driver. A passing flock of chattering birds filled the low clouds with coarse laughter. The barren hills that vanished into the snowy haze seemed a fitting cradle for the abandoned facility.

Slapping the cab's sleek roof affably, Warren said, "Thanks again, John!"

Iz smiled inquisitively at her husband as he trotted across the overgrown roundabout, Grandad bouncing at his hip. "So, he agreed to wait?" she said.

The long-hooded jaunt snorted nacreous smoke from its vents as it reversed back down the shattered drive and was swallowed up by the fog.

"No. Just seemed a likable fellow."

"I suppose we have a long walk home to look forward to."

"No walk feels long when it's with you!" Warren said, offering her his arm. They strode toward the buckled doors of the hospital's receiving bay.

The lobby appeared to have spent many years serving as a dustpan to the broom of the wind. The thin sunlight at their backs lit the dry soil, seedpods, and leaves of dead grass that coated much of the floor. Beneath this natural debris lay file sleeves and strata of paper, all in the process of melting back to pulp. Dozens of gurneys and carts stood in the tracks of old patterns of traffic that led to the check-in desk, the dingy east wing, the stairwell, and a doorless elevator shaft. These queued cabinets and rolling beds suggested the remnants of an exodus that appeared to have happened long ago.

From just inside the doorway, Warren knelt to inspect the layer of dirt that hazed the checkered floor tiles. He set his fingertips to the heel of an animal track. "Looks like the only thing to have passed through here lately is a raccoon. Otherwise, the place seems deserted."

"Does it? Look at the gurneys—no wheels. No casters on the carts, either. Someone removed them."

"Scavengers?"

"Maybe." Iz climbed onto the nearest bed, employing its side guard as a rung in her ascent. She stood, arms out to balance herself on her wobbly perch, and surveyed the placement of the cots and cabinetry from that higher vantage. "I think these are footpaths. Someone set this up to cover their tracks—or rather, to avoid leaving any."

Warren frowned at the murky recesses of the adjoining wing beyond the welcome station, reconsidering shadows that had seemed harmless a moment before. "Probably just some enterprising raccoons."

"Or a gang of murderous thugs." Iz held out her hand for Warren to grasp, then hopped down from the rattling bed.

"Shall we proceed with caution?"

"Now, where's the fun in that?" she answered, still holding his hand at a formal height as if she meant to lead him onto a ballroom dance floor.

As they approached the entrance to the east wing and the gloom that lay beyond, Iz drew in the air a Hex of Radiance—a name that was somewhat ambitious considering the effect. A dish of bluish light formed before her palm, casting just enough light to keep them from stumbling, but not so much as to intimidate the roaches, which were legion.

A miraculous number of the hospital navigational plaques remained affixed to the walls. They followed the signs for THE ARCHIVES down to the basement where the air grew increasingly heavy and the smell of rot more pronounced. They soon discovered the source of the rank humidity: The basement stood flooded nearly to the ceiling with dark water. They had come with the hope of discovering some remnant of Prince Sebastian's lengthy stay at the hospital. A manifest of Captain Yeardley's personal items that he had arrived and departed with would've been particularly convenient. Isolde was disappointed to see that all had been swallowed by a lagoon fed by rainwater and broken plumbing—disappointed, but not surprised. Easy answers were rare in her experience, if for no other reason than they were readily discovered by her cheaper competitors. Iz had long ago decided to be flattered by the fact that she was usually not a client's first choice. If a mystery could be unraveled by a quick trip to a basement—well, why not let someone else make the boring trek?

Thwarted and a little intrigued, she followed Warren back to the main level and its scarcely less offensive atmosphere. They were bound for the exit when a thought struck her and she convinced him to join her in the exploration of a cleaning closet. There, they found a surprisingly well-preserved stock of solvents, mops, and buckets, and upon the wall, a hanging clipboard clasping a number of curled but intact papers. She thumbed through those records to learn the last date the halls had been mopped, an event that would've coincided with the hospital's decommission. Discovering that the facility had been shuttered four months after the end of Captain Yeardley's stay renewed Iz's optimism: Perhaps not all of the prince's records had been consigned to the archives.

Guided once more by the lodestar placards, they surmounted guano-spattered stairwells to the fifth story where the Convalescent Ward was housed. Thanks to several heavy doors and the continued integrity of the floor's windows, the area was somewhat better preserved than the lower levels. The nurse's station, though sheeted in dust, bore the order of its former use.

Taking advantage of the light of the nearby plate windows, Iz dispelled her illuminating disc. Though not the most taxing, the hex required concentration and effort, an exertion not unlike doing sums while pedaling a bicycle uphill. It was a manageable strain that grew more demanding the longer it went on.

Both hands now free, she opened the ledger set prominently on the nurse's desktop. She flipped through the visitor registry, hunting for the approximate dates of the prince's recuperation, which she soon found. When her eye settled upon the name "Captain Yeardley," she enjoyed a fleeting thrill of discovery. A few minutes' perusal revealed that the royal family had not been to see the mending prince, excepting his sister, Princess Constance; she had looked in on him several times. Otherwise, his only regular guest was L.Cpl. Rudolph Atterton, who called upon him almost daily.

The name struck her as familiar. Extracting the rumpled newspaper clipping from one of her coat's deep pockets, she read the caption that accompanied the picture of the smiling soldier. There, L.Cpl. "Rudy" Atterton was identified as Captain Yeardley's orderly.

"Seems the prince had quite a devoted batman," she remarked to Warren, who stooped over an open binder at the desk's elbow.

"And a favorite nurse." He tapped a page of the duty roster. "Jess Blessed. An unusual name. Quite nice though." Iz asked to have a look, and found her husband was right: Whenever Nurse Blessed was on duty, she was frequently assigned to Captain Yeardley, especially later in his stay. Flipping backward several months, she found a variety of nurses had at first shared him as a patient, though there was no sign of Jess Blessed. The closest was a Jessamine Bysshe. Then, she found the prince's name, and beside it, two scotched words that had been assiduously blacked out. Next to one redaction appeared in quotation marks the word "Blessed."

With her nub of chalk, Iz began to draw a Hex of Palimpsests on the countertop, an activity that took several minutes, a period Warren spent surveilling the abandoned halls for any sign of marauders or raccoons. The intricate hex had been all but forgotten before Iz rediscovered it while perusing an unexpurgated copy of the *Hexod Florilegium*. The hex's construction was a test of her abilities, and there was a moment following the closure of the last circlet when the ward appeared to be but a convoluted graffito. Yet, even as she scoured her work for mistakes, the counter's cracked lacquer began to shine with ghostly letters and digits penned by innumerable hands. The strings of numbers and words drifted up from the nurse's desk, distinct as smoke from an incense stick and just as fleeting.

She dismissed the linguistic mist with a swat of her hand and lightly settled the duty binder over the heart of the hex. Almost at once, the inked-out letters surfaced like bodies from a foundered ship. And the next instant, they beheld the words that someone had attempted to blot out: *Jessamine Bitched.*

It seemed someone had coined a scathing nickname that another had softened to "Blessed," an appellation that had evidently stuck as Nurse Bysshe was Jess Blessed thereafter.

"What do you make of that?" Warren asked.

"Petty envy, perhaps. There was a prince in the ward, but he had a preferred nurse."

"Doesn't seem fair she gets called names when it was the prince who must've done the complaining."

"Unfair—but unsurprising. It does make me wonder, though, whether Nurse Jessamine Blessed was really so fortunate in the end. How often does a tale of a bastard begin with a woman in a vulnerable position?"

A banging gate at the end of the corridor brought their heads up. Five men and three women trooped in with military poise, though their clothing was anything but uniform. They were outfitted like field hands and armed like a militia with an array of antiquated weapons. They clutched hunting rifles and rusted revolvers. Their target was as unquestionable as it was disappointing; they converged upon Iz and Warren's position as if they meant to take it.

Five strides out from the nurse's station, the company halted. The foremost, a tall woman who wore her belt cinched under her ribs and a straw hat tied up like a deerstalker, leveled her revolver at the frozen couple. "What's your business?" she asked.

Iz answered, "We're criminal investigators. We're pursuing a case for the Crown."

The tall woman spat on the ground. "I told you they looked like royalists. Get your hands up."

Raising her hands but allowing them to hang slack at the wrist, Isolde appeared to have struck a theatrical shrug. "A royalist? My god, did I leave the house with my jewels on again?"

"What's in the bag?" A red-haired man wearing denim and a rope belt nodded his field gun at the portalmanteau, which appeared rather deflated on the counter before Warren. "Valuables?"

"One or two," Iz said.

"You, toss it over," he said to Warren, who stood with raised hands crowded about his face like a father playing peekaboo.

War's voice rumbled with laughter. "This seems an unfortunate misunderstanding! We're not royalists. We don't like the Crown, either—do we, dear? No! We think they're a bunch of golden ticks latched upon the hunkers of the poor. We only took the case for the good of our fellow countrymen. We are here to serve you!"

"Is the Crown paying you?" the tall woman asked.

Warren sucked his teeth. "They are."

"If the king fills your pockets, then you live in his."

"Throw me the bag," said the red-haired man.

With the practiced rapidity of a busboy, Iz snatched Grandad from the countertop, gathered up the duty roster and the visitor log, and ducked down behind the station. Warren continued to stand, smiling and stretching his stout neck as if it were being chaffed by his collar until Iz reached up, gripped his cuff, and pulled him down.

Crouched behind the bulwark of the nurse's desk, Iz pushed the portalmanteau into Warren's hands. "Why don't you dig around for something helpful while I conjure up a diversion."

As Iz began carving the air with a finger, War thrust his arm into the mouth of the magic carpetbag. He groped and delved and grunted like a man attempting to put a sham on an overstuffed duvet. "Bad news. It really seems to be stuck this time."

From the other side of the desk, the tall woman's voice rang clearly when she said: "I'm going to count to ten. Then we're going to start shooting."

Iz's finger twitched, and the hex failed with a cough of wind and a muffled clap. Iz cursed under her breath, even as the commander of their firing squad counted down.

War stopped struggling with the portalmanteau, his gaze drifting to the corner of the plate window that was visible from their refuge. "Do you remember when I lost my ring?"

Isolde scowled with ready comprehension. Some years prior, Warren had been rummaging around Grandad's bottomless bellows when his wedding band had slipped from his finger. The ring was in every way unremarkable. It was not a cherished heirloom, nor uncommonly arrayed, nor expensive to replace, and yet War had been devastated by the loss because what distinguished the modest band was its history of contact with his wife: The ring was suffused with tender caresses, clasped hands, and stroked hair. As such, he believed it the rarest metal in existence.

Stirred by her husband's romanticism, Iz had volunteered to venture where Warren's girth would not permit him to go—into the portalmanteau to retrieve the ring. And so, she had gone exploring with a lamp on her head and a lifeline around her waist. She did not tell Warren that her father had warned her about entering the portalmanteau; it was, he'd said, a place that was safe for hands and arms, but not for heads and minds. She had stepped into the old carpetbag as if it were a bath and vanished as if she'd fallen into the sea.

She had found War's ring easily enough. It lay centered in a wide aisle upon a smooth pad of stone that stretched beneath soaring iron-backed shelves, slatted with walnut, and crowded with crate, rack, and urn. At a glance, the space resembled the warehouse of a museum of antiquities. The soft, cool air was redolent with the mineral aroma of stone and the exotic musk of preservatives. And yet, the moment she stooped to grasp the ring, a feeling of overwhelming dread gripped her by the heart. It was a sensation as potent as vertigo, as inescapable as a night hag. Intellectually, she knew her father's treasury must be under the protection of some powerful curse; but physically, animalistically, she wanted to shriek and retreat. She pinched Warren's ring, clenched her eyes shut, and shouted for him to pull her home.

Crowded together behind the nurse's station, Iz looked him in the eye when she reminded him: "You said never again."

"Once is almost never."

"Said the bullet to the head."

As if hearkening to her call, the guns roared and lead bombarded their shelter, shattering wood and reanimating the dormant dust.

War opened the portalmanteau, his pleading expression made more compelling by the violent confetti that erupted about them. She kissed him deeply, her hands gathered to his cheeks, then climbed into the carpetbag with the nurse's registers clutched to her chest.

As the top of her head vanished into the impenetrable darkness, Warren secured the case's clasp and inhaled a polluted breath. The air was sharp with gun smoke. A plangent ringing congested his ears. He rocked his wedding band against his knuckle with his thumb, a consoling fidget, then tucked the portalmanteau under his arm.

When a break in the onslaught came, he charged at the plate window and the ashen sky beyond.

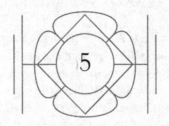

TURDUS FELIVOX

N ineteen years earlier, when Mr. Ecklous had called upon Isolde Wilby and her mother to inform them of the patriarch's passing, the rheumy-eyed banker had presented Iz with her material inheritance: a piebald carpetbag and a sealed letter from her father. The letter, which she read while her mother stoically pondered the kitchen window, accomplished two things: It introduced Isolde to the arcane magic of the portalmanteau and its fabulous holdings, and it convinced her that her father was truly gone.

In the letter, her father described the original relic that had instigated an obsession that would dominate the remainder of his life: a modest plumb bob that had been given to him by an unknown benefactor who only identified themselves via a glyph resembling a dead tree. Mr. Snag, as her father called him, had shipped the plumb bob to his old offices at Wynn University of the Thaumatic Arts with the explanation that the instrument, forged from some extraterrestrial material, was bodily drawn to charmed relics, even very distant ones, and so could be used as a sort of divining rod for fabulous artifacts. Mr. Snag went on to remark how unwise it would be to leave such potent tokens lying about for any old fool to find. And so Iz discovered that her wayward father was not the indecisive adventurer he'd seemed, but was rather a man driven by the desire to collect as many magical objects as he could and stash them inside a mysterious vault that had but a single remaining entrance—the mouth of the portalmanteau. Professor Silas Wilby's famed expeditions had been but a smoke screen for his curatorial efforts, and that was why he quit so many excursions with little explanation and less forewarning: He had, as Luella was often informed upon his sporadic homecomings, *found what he was looking for.*

Much of her father's final letter occupied itself with advice for safeguarding, maintaining, and accessing the portalmanteau. These sections, though they contained crucial warnings, were worded blithely enough. In those lines she heard echoes of the way her father had spoken to her as a child, often in a conspiratorial whisper, always with a smile, as if they were partners in some scheme. He cautioned her that many of the relics were touchy and fragile and dangerous, and he revealed his (ultimately inadequate) effort to create an index for the collection, and the depot's protective pall.

But the letter also veered into advice and encouragement that seemed oddly trivial at first blush. Her father shared a trick for vanishing unwanted peas from a dinner plate, a reminder to put her socks on before her trousers, and directions for making "special milk," a warm drink tinctured with vanilla, cinnamon, and sugar. *Special milk,* her father wrote, *is a powerful potion in the battle against the dark. And it is perfectly all right, my dear Iz, to be afraid of the dark. People who tell you not to be afraid of things are usually the first to get eaten by tigers. Fear helps us to prepare. I say, gather your supplies, arm yourself, and make the dark afraid of you.*

Isolde returned to the date at the head of the letter, a thing she had initially overlooked in her haste. She realized with a start that he had written it ten years ago when she had been six years old.

Reading those paragraphs, she felt her father's presence more intensely than she had upon his recent whistle-stop visits when he'd seemed so harried. Yet, it was the letter's conclusion that convinced Iz—in a way that no magic hourglass could—that her father was not coming home. Professor Wilby closed his letter by saying:

I'm afraid my calling will keep me from you and your mother more than it should, will replace our intimacy with secrecy, and our affection with confusion. I will, I fear, fail to know you as I should, as I *would*, and I will excuse this failure with appeals to the "greater good," though they in fact may be neither. I can foresee a day when the only balm for my guilt will be further absence and a more fanatical commitment, and the only acknowledgment of my failings will be made posthumously.

I leave this bizarre and unsafe collection and its humble gate to you, Iz Ann Always, because you will know what to do with it and, more importantly, what *not* to do with it.

Do not neglect to live your life. No cause, no matter how noble, will ever love you.

Your Loving, if Undeserving,

Dad

On the cold stone floor of her father's reliquary, Isolde Wilby lay in an inglorious heap.

She groaned, regained her feet, and flapped the dust from her long coat.

She was about to cast a Hex of Radiance when she realized there was already some light to see by. She turned to regard the way she had come— a view she'd not had the opportunity to absorb on her prior visit. Then, she had been too busy suffering the effects of the dreadful melancholy that protected the archives, a foreboding that was now notably absent. Something had changed. Something was different.

The source of light was a lozenge-shaped picture frame. A battered leather-clad book swung by a cord from the lowest point of the gilded border. The frame itself stood unfilled—no canvas nor mirror plugged its center. The crowded shelf behind it was clearly visible. Still, the frame's radiance was sufficient to reveal that it hovered midair, free of wire or support. Iz stuck a finger into the opening, felt nothing, and so deepened her exploration to include the rest of her arm, wiggling her fingers in search of the telltale frisson of an illusion or hex. She felt nothing.

Deducing that this aperture was the entrance she had lately tumbled from and the unseen reverse side of the portalmanteau's mouth, she gripped the frame and gave it a tentative tug. It submitted as gamely as a balloon on a string. She wondered if her somersaulting passage had dislodged whatever obstruction or force had been thwarting Warren's recent attempts to access the storehouse.

War had long ago proved to have the greater facility for retrieving objects from the portalmanteau. It was a talent that he attributed to a youth spent working in the family butchery, from which the surname Offalman was naturally derived. He had found the work of dressing the slaughtered animals so repellent that he had learned to sort the organs of the dead with his eyes closed and entirely by feel, a talent that his father liked to boast of, though the praise only made his son blanch. Though the portalmanteau was more cavernous and complex than the innards of a hog, War had a knack for navigating by touch, and having larger hands and longer arms certainly helped.

Even so, after years they had cataloged only a fraction of the contents of the cache. That was partly owed to the groping nature of their explorations, partly to their natural trepidation in the activation of charmed and enigmatic artifacts, and partly attributable to Professor Wilby's deeply unhelpful index that hung from the aperture like a hound-chewed pheasant from a hunter's belt.

Isolde shivered at the thought of the tight spot she'd left War in— under fire and cornered. She had only agreed to his suggestion because she trusted he had an exit in mind. The daily mechanism of their marriage was powered by reflexive faith rather than constant reassurance. In their line of work, they had little time for doubt and misgivings. Trust was quicker, and survival so often came down to a matter of seconds.

Warren was all right.

She had to believe so.

She took her bearings to give her mind something else to focus upon. The nearest shelf to eye level behind her contained an antefix of a lion's face (probably plucked from the roof of some vine-swallowed temple), a bejeweled spiraled tusk (presumably taken from a narwhal, though she could not rule out the possibility of a unicorn), a mummy's mask bearing a mischievous expression and sloe-black eyes, and—the only artifact she recognized on sight, though she'd never used it—an unassuming clay lamp with a handle as dainty as an infant's ear. That relic bore the rather ominous moniker the Caldera of Vitis.

The fore edge of the shelf presented a series of bronze placards, embossed with a sequence of digits and letters, which provided each object's catalog number and a means for navigating the collection by feel. Ideally, these codes would be clearly and reliably reproduced in her father's index and paired with an evocative name, an account of the relic's origin, and any warnings regarding its deployment. In actuality, Professor Wilby's index was full of incomplete and half-legible catalog numbers, uninterpretable handwriting, and notations to refer to the primary index, a work which they had never found. More irksome still, her father's weakness for levity rendered many of his decipherable descriptions less than helpful. He had, for example, described the Archsword of the Cloven God as "a cumbrous letter opener," while the Caldera of Vitis bore the considerably more daunting note: "Contents: one volcano."

Isolde was about to once again peruse her father's exasperating index in search of something useful (especially since she felt so useless trapped in here while War was caught out there) when she saw the distant golden glimmer of a pair of cat eyes.

The slitted orbs stared from some way down the aisle—blinking, squinting, watching.

Her first instinct was to rub her fingers together, kneel down, and call the kitten with the universal feline greeting of "psst-psst." It was an urge she suppressed. While she did not know where her father's treasure house existed in the universe, she doubted very much that it was the sort of place into which stray cats could freely wander.

Seized by an unpleasant premonition, she ducked under the shelf, wedging herself between a tar-sealed crate and an immense amphora. From there, she observed the animal or at least what she could see of it by the aperture's subdued light.

As she watched, the cat's eyes began to rise some six feet into the air and grow larger as they ascended. It took her a moment to discern that their growth was the result of the rapidly shrinking distance between her and those beaming medallions, which suddenly seemed considerably less feline.

The dragon emerged from the gloom like a fish from the deep. It was similarly lithe but long as a train car. Mantled in copper-bright scales, it flew through the air with the grace and urgency of a ribbon being torn along by a gale. Thick whiskers rippled from its jutting chin and embellished the bony crest that framed its head. Its eyes were luminous, its nostrils smoking, and its protruding teeth as orange as a mole's.

It pounced upon the aperture, took its edge in its considerable jaws, and shook the frame so violently, Iz thought it would break, a development that would doom her to an eternity inside the portalmanteau—or however much of an eternity starvation and dragons would allow her to enjoy.

With no clear sense of what she would do immediately afterward, Isolde leapt from her hiding place, bellowing an emphatic *"No!"*

Releasing the aperture, the dragon bucked high into the murk, then dove at her, its mouth open and brightened by the fire that rumbled in its belly.

Shattered glass followed Warren through the air like the icy tail of a comet.

Before leaping from the fifth-story window, he'd felt almost entirely certain that the roof of the fourth floor was adjoining and waiting to receive him. When he'd admired the hospital's crumbling facade from the head of the driveway, he'd noticed the tiering of its north side, where he believed he now was. Unless he'd gotten turned around while climbing all those flights of stairs. Perhaps this was east. If that was the case, he would have a second or two to chastise himself before he cratered the overgrown lawn.

And if he perished, what of Iz? Would she be trapped inside the portalmanteau, or would some unsuspecting thief discover a very unhappy hex-caster lurking inside a dead man's bag?

The appearance of the graveled rooftop inspired a triumphant hoot from Warren, which was soon curtailed by his indelicate landing. He skidded from his leather soles, fell upon his hands and knees, dropping and retrieving Grandad along the way. He discovered the next instant that his dramatic exeunt had surprised a resting flock of starlings. They flew up before him with such intensity that he was, for a moment, driven back by the force of the feathered blizzard. He clasped the carpetbag to his face to save his eyes from being pecked out and to muffle the homily of profanity that poured from him.

Though the very next instant, he was grateful for the confusion of down and thorny beaks.

The crack of a scattergun above him felled half a dozen birds at a stroke. They bounced around his feet. He did not pause to thank them. He took to his heels, running for the far end of the roof along a winding path. He dodged vent hoods and jinked about chimneys, doing his best to present his assailants with a crooked target. Yet it was the flock, buffeting him from every angle, that proved his greatest defense. Lead and dead birds continued to rain upon the gravel as he fled.

Through the frenzy, he saw the abutting wing of the hospital rise up before him, and the rusted lintel that stood half-buried beneath a sheet of ivy. He gripped the knob and pulled. The door cracked an inch, then caught fast. The ivy was stubborn, but he was more so. He felt in that moment he could yank the plug from the bottom of the sea. The old vines snapped and shed leaves as the gap slowly widened. Mortar dust and the smithereens of bricks burst on either side. Birds clapped him on the back. Warren bared his teeth, showed his strength, and broke the ivy's hold.

Diving into the breach, Warren tugged the beset door shut behind him. The slab dampened the drum of bombing birds and the distant pop of guns.

Breathing hard, he turned to discover he stood in a better-preserved wing of the hospital. The carpet was stained, but swept; the furniture ramshackle, but upright. Here, the reek of mildew was sweetened by pipe smoke.

The person who puffed upon the pipe had graying temples, polished spectacles, a clean white shirt with sleeves rolled, and a kindly face that seemed at odds with the trumpet-mouthed blunderbuss he leveled at Warren's head.

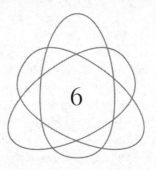

6

AN ALTERNATIVE TO
INFINITE GOAT

The dragon reared before Isolde like a rampant horse—his short, muscular arms scrabbling upon the empty air with the talons of a raptor.

She held the brittle earthen lamp cocked behind her ear as she shouted for a second time, "No!" A command to which she added, "Stay back or I shall unleash a flood of molten rock upon you!"

Naturally, she had learned about dragons while at Wynn University of the Thaumatic Arts. The course Advanced Basilisks and Behemoths had included a lengthy lecture on dragons. Though the formidable creatures were generally shy of civilization, they were not unknown to the modern world. Her instructor, Dr. Margaret Tamm, had been preoccupied with the elaborate courting rituals and reproductive practices of the species, which was how Iz had learned that dragons were ostensibly monogamous except during the spawning season, an event occurring every thirteen years and best described as a month-long orgy. Dr. Tamm's two-hour diatribe strayed frequently into the intimate details of her own life, particularly her unhappy marriage, information that had been awkward in the moment and infuriating upon the occasion of the exam, which had included not a single question about the minutiae of dragon coupling but had featured an essay prompt on the physiology of the fire gizzard. Half the class had failed.

It had been with evident exasperation that a student—deep into Dr. Tamm's explication of dragons' surprisingly small gonads—had interrupted to ask the question: "But what do I *do* if I bump into a dragon? How do I chase it off? And if I can't frighten it, how do I get away? Aren't there any hexes you could teach us?" To which the doctor had replied, "Dragons are immune to hexes. Rifles work a little better, but only on the juveniles. No, if you're ever careless enough to wander into a dragon's territory and find yourself confronted by an adult of the species, speak loudly and with authority. Make yourself look as large as possible and pray to god it has eaten recently."

And so Iz menaced the dragon with every atom of her being.

To her surprise, the beast hesitated.

When it did, she saw the golden lorgnette that dangled from a thin chain about the shelf of his shoulders.

She jeered, dropping the angle of her cocked arm a degree. "You dirty thief! What are you doing with my polyglottal specs? I've been looking for those for *years.*"

"What are you doing in my home?" the dragon asked in a voice as deep and resonant as a mineshaft.

"This is not your home." She thought better than to add that this was, if anything, the beast's prison. The span of his bony crest would obviously prevent him from passing through the narrow frame. Which seemed no small mercy. She wouldn't want a dragon popping out of her purse while riding in a jaunt or sipping tea in her kitchen. Though, upon further reflection, she could scarcely imagine an opportune time for a jack-in-the-box dragon. "This is my father's vault, and you are trespassing."

The serpentine leviathan arranged himself into an ampersand, an imperious posture that allowed him to both cross his comparatively insubstantial arms and tower above her, though she did not flinch. "I was hatched here. If a nest is not a home, then no beast belongs anywhere, and we are all vagrants in the world."

"Hatched? How old are you?"

His tar-black tongue flicked out, passing across his haphazard teeth. "Six."

Isolde nearly choked. "Six! *Six?* You're very eloquent for a six-year-old."

"Most animals cannot afford to be as slow as your race to mature."

Isolde realized that as long as she could keep the beast talking it would delay any chewing. "You have a lot of experience with people, then?"

"Most species just leave footprints. But you lot, you leave libraries. I've read one or two shelves of your formative myths. Dreadful, dreamy, self-important twaddle!" The dragon laughed, the sound as sonorous as a collapsing bridge. "And far-fetched! So many ambivalent parables about clumsy gods and little men knocking titans on their ears." His undulations made the scales of his armor shimmer in waves. He seemed to be enjoying himself. "What fabulous fantasies!"

"You're a reader, then?"

"Self-taught." With impressive deftness, the dragon pinched the dainty arm of the spectacles that hung about his neck and brought one lens of the lorgnette to his right eye. "These helped, of course. They make any language understandable, even to an illiterate. They really are wonderful."

"My name is Isolde Wilby. And who might you be?"

The dragon drew himself up to make space for a bow, an unmistakable gesture that still seemed ill-suited to a form that could curve but not exactly bend. "I am Turdus Felivox."

Isolde hummed a single quizzical note. "An unusual name."

"A considered one. I named myself after the scientific coinage for the cat-bird, because I am flighted like a bird and clever like a cat."

"Well, Felivox, are there any more of you?"

"Oh, I ate my siblings long ago. I hatched first, and with no one to feed me, I had to forage for myself. I'm a bit ashamed to admit, I ate my siblings still in their shells. Later, I did wish that I had spared one or two of them. One does get lonely rattling around in such a chasmal den." He surveyed the darkness with a deliberation that Iz found sympathetic, though his reverie was brief. He swung back around to face her, his eyes shining like an alligator's in the moonlight. "But then, perhaps we wouldn't have gotten along, my siblings and I, and I would've had to eat them after sharing some months together. That seems worse, doesn't it—having to pick your brothers from between your teeth? And I would've had to share the Infinite Goat."

"What on earth is that?"

Despite his hard scales and beak-like procheilon, the dragon still managed to curl his mouth in a display of haughty disbelief. "You don't know what a goat is?"

Isolde ground her teeth. "Of course, I know what a *goat* is. What is an *Infinite* Goat?"

"It's a goat that grows back as long as you don't eat the horns. For someone purporting to be the master of this castle, you certainly don't seem to know much about it." The dragon wound and knotted in the air before her, as if he would snuggle down into a nest of himself—or perhaps it was just the coiling of a pit viper preparing to strike.

"How did you defeat the defensive pall?"

The dragon's length kinked in surprise. "The what?"

Isolde attempted to cross her arms, bumped the fragile Caldera of Vitis against her elbow, and thought better of the pose. "The last time I was here, I suffered a sudden and intense sensation of impending doom. The feeling was accompanied by a crippling headache. I nearly vomited. As I should have. That was the purpose of the vault's defensive measures. You've sabotaged it somehow."

"Oh, you're referring to the Iron Nanny." The dragon's tongue flicked out to clean the bare sphere of one eye. "I had to do something about that. I understand it was built to cause psychotic breaks in humans, but it also, perhaps inadvertently, prompts indigestion in dragons. It gave me terrible gas."

"Is the Iron Nanny a person? Did you murder someone?"

The dragon scratched his throat in slow thoughtful strokes, looking nonchalant and also strangely guilty. "Oh, no, no, the Iron Nanny is a clock. Just a run-of-the-mill six-foot-tall clock. It looks a bit like...well, I suppose, a bit like you. But lumpier. You're not very lumpy. You look crunchy." Felivox's lips tightened toward his earholes, baring tooth after tooth.

"I'm very crunchy. What did you do to the clock?"

"I stopped it. Though, in fact, I hardly touched it. I mean—the thing about clocks, even cursed ones, is that their natural state is one of non-function. A clock is just an ambitious doorstop. They wind down, they can be overwound, you have to oil them, but not too much. No, no. It's frankly incredible the lengths you humans go to just to avoid looking out a window and guessing the time. Oh, but you think your time is so precious, don't you? It used to be 'I'll see you tomorrow' and that was good enough, and then you all got a bit busier with, I don't know, building trebuchets or printing presses, or whatever, and then it was 'I'll see you in the morning.' Then along comes the Industrial Revolution, and now, *oof*, now it's all 'I'll see you at 8:15 sharp, or you're fired.' "

Isolde cocked her head—first one way, then the other—like a baffled museum-goer straining before a new installation. "How do you know all of this?"

Felivox twisted into a shrug. "I read the paper."

"What do you mean, you *read* the paper?"

"I mean, sometimes there's a copy of the *Berbiton Times* kicking about on the floor, and I pick it up and read it."

Isolde attempted to pinch the bridge of her nose, bumped the clay lamp that contained "one volcano" against her chin, and marshaled her arms into a shot-putter's pose once more. "Let's leave that for the moment. You were attacking the aperture. Why?"

"Aperture? You mean my gold hoop?" Felivox blew a puff of cinerous smoke from a single nostril. The plume formed a ring that passed through the weightless frame. "I wasn't attacking it; I was giving chase. Look at it! Doesn't it just cry out to be pounced upon? Don't you just want to take it in your mouth and shake the light out of it? It's always flying about, springing this way and that!"

"You think it's a toy. And you never thought to bite the arm that appears inside it?"

The dragon laughed: a chug that called to mind a knocking motor. "I *did* consider it. But then, if I ate the arm, that would be the end of the game, wouldn't it? No more zipping up and down the aisles; no more tug-of-war."

The mention of War sent her thoughts dashing back to her husband. What had he done? What was keeping him? Was he hurt? A vortical despair stirred within her as her imagination embroidered a pageant of suffering with merciless detail. She saw, in a heartbeat, her husband perish in a hundred horrid ways.

Iz lowered the clay lamp, her arm feeling suddenly leaden.

"Decided you're not afraid of me, then?" Felivox asked, a note of exhilaration in his voice. He threaded nearer, bringing his considerable snout closer to her unimposing nose. "Or are you just giving up?" His breath smelled like a crematorium.

Iz pulled off her felt hat and stuffed it into her coat pocket. She scratched out her curls as if she would itch away her morbid thoughts. "I'm worried about my husband, Warren. That arm you've been tormenting—it belongs to him. I left him in a bad spot."

"Only to find yourself in a worse one."

Iz turned her back on the beast, though it made her shiver to show him her nape. Carefully, she set the Caldera of Vitis back in its spot upon the shelf. "You're not going to eat me."

"I'm not?" The dragon gave a chuffing laugh that sounded like a steam engine leaving the station. "Are you sure? I'm rather fed up with goat."

"You won't eat me because my husband is a very good cook."

"Oh, I don't need any help cooking you; I can handle that perfectly well myself." He breathed in deeply, and she heard the fire within him rumble. She wondered if he would immolate her, then and there, but the next instant, his long mouth lifted in an unsettling, craggy grin. "Though, if I'm honest, I've developed something of a taste for raw meat."

"You won't eat me because I'm not infinite. Two gulps and I'm gone forever. But if we are friends, then I can promise you more and much better cuisine." She stuck out her hand, and he ducked in close to inspect it. "I'm not offering you a snack. We'll shake on it. You help me explore my father's trove, and my husband feeds you as much as you like."

"Oh, now I'm *helping* you, am I? I'm your assistant?"

"Not an assistant—a colleague. You've spent years exploring the corners of a repository that I've only explored by fingertip. You're right: It might be my legacy, but it's your home. I'm sure I would benefit from the expertise of such a scholar."

"Flattery, is it? Well, well, I do like how that feels. Yes, I'll have more of that, please." He reached for her small hand with his four-toed claw, the back of which flashed like a copper pot. He paused. "Not table scraps, though. Actual meals."

Iz gave a single categorical nod. "If you're disappointed with the fare, arm is always on the menu."

"Ah, then I believe we have a deal," Felivox rumbled.

The dragon gripped her palm with observable care, and still it felt to Isolde like she was shaking hands with a bear trap.

It was not the first time Warren had been tied to a chair. And judging by the quality of the knots, it was not the first time that the man with a pipe had lashed a person to one, either.

Warren complimented him on his work, and expanded his praises to encompass the room, which was admirably tidy and arrayed with a few luxuries—a coat tree, a walnut ashtray, a stately desk, and a view that must have been spectacular once, before the old forests had been razed and the alchemist mills had spread their poisonous cloak over the nation.

War suspected this had been the chief physician's office: a spacious, sunny sanctuary for receiving deep-pocketed patrons and esteemed members of the board. Now, pans caught drips from the ravaged ceiling and cracks marbled the windows. Eight armed louts crowded about the pipe smoker, who looked like an accountant, though he had introduced himself as Nurse Percy Slorrance. He sat with one leg hooked on the corner of his vast desk, exuding a measured calm that was not shared by his compatriots. The red-haired man, who had seemed particularly keen to shoot, was now shifting his concerted glare from Warren to the portalmanteau.

"Where did your associate go?" Nurse Percy had a light voice and a face as golden and full as a dinner roll.

Warren scoffed. "You mean my wife? I'm not sure where Ms. Wilby disappeared to."

Percy puffed thrice on his pipe, producing a little ellipsis of smoke. "Are you alchemists?"

"Goodness, no. My wife has a talent for hexes and mysteries. I mostly just carry her bag." Warren resisted the urge to look at the portalmanteau, which sat next to Slorrance on the desk.

"Your wife said you were here on the king's business." Slorrance knocked the bowl of his pipe against the ashtray's cork ball, then dug into the pocket of his vest to retrieve his tobacco wallet. "Are you pension ratters?" He watched Warren carefully for his reaction to the phrase.

"I must admit, Percy—I'm familiar with both of those words, but I've never heard them pressed together before."

"The Crown does not like to pay for the care of its inactive military persons, particularly the aging survivors of the Meridian War." The war had ended a generation ago. And though it was still fresh in the minds and memories of its veterans, the citizenry and nobility of both Luthland and its once mortal enemy, Intarsia, were in a hurry to move on, focusing on the new battlefront of trans-Garrean commerce.

Warren answered in solemn tones, "There's nothing more shameful than shirking one's commitments, especially to those who've already sacrificed so much."

"Yes, but pensions are expensive and life is cheap, at least according to the royal actuarial tables. So, the king has on retainer a troop of investigators whose sole purpose it is to uncover—or contrive—evidence of malingering or abuse that can be used to dismiss the claims of impoverished soldiers. 'Pension ratters,' we call them. They used to come here to scour the archives for disqualifying evidence: psychological problems, narcotic abuse, suspicion of self-inflicted wounds..." Nurse Percy bobbed his head with the tempo of his words as he finished packing his pipe. It seemed a well-rehearsed speech. "The vast majority of these purported crimes and acts of cowardice were in fact only the debilitating wounds of war and the Crown's neglect. Still, the ratters have succeeded in voiding the pensions of thousands of men and women who served honorably. That's why I flooded the basement: to foil the king's rats. I'm sorry to say, I didn't think to check the nurses' stations for unfiled records. We'll have to correct that oversight." Slorrance puffed upon a new coal as he shook out a match. "So, tell me, Mr. Wilby, what were you looking for?"

Warren sighed as if he were puffing out a candle. "I'm afraid I can't share the details of our investigation without betraying the trust of our client, *despite* my personal uncharitable feelings for the man. I can, however, promise you this: We were not looking to discredit any pensioners. In fact, I have a cousin who is a veteran of—"

"I suppose you expect me to take you at your word?" The nurse clicked his teeth upon the stem of his pipe. The red-haired man, who'd shifted around the desk to be within reach of Grandad, gave the carpetbag a tentative poke.

Warren coughed dryly, then shrugged, or rather shrugged as much as a man could with his shoulders trussed to a chairback. He was trying to conjure up some compelling defense, which was really more of Iz's forte, when a foggy memory presented itself. "Slorrance. Slorr...That name is familiar. *Slorrance*. You don't have a relative on a merchant ship, do you? I knew a CO named Slorrance. Wonderful fellow. I was a boatswain. I had my first voyage under Mr. Slorrance. He kept a close eye on me. I think he was afraid I'd trip on my mop and fall overboard. I nearly did a time or two. That man loved candied orange slices. And chops! My god, I had never seen such whiskers before! He had to turn sideways to pass through a hatch. Oh, but this was—what—fourteen years ago? I'm sure he's retired by now."

"Only just." Nurse Percy's mouth puckered with amusement. "He's my uncle."

"No! Isn't that wild? And *retired*? He always said the tides would retire first, but good for him!" Warren wagged his head like the tail of a happy dog. "I bet he taught you how to tie a knot, didn't he? That man could pretzel a plank! Oh, did he ever tell you about the time the albatross got into his cabin? It was the orange slices that lured the devil in, you see, and..."

Before he had met Isolde, Warren had been possessed by a rash tendency to rush out and embrace the agenda and habits of the first stranger who'd speak kindly to him, often to disastrous effect. His deep-seated need for comradery had, among other youthful calamities, driven him into the criminal arms of bootleggers, seen him hired on by a traveling circus as a strongman, and had signed him on for a six-month stint at sea on the occasion of his twentieth birthday. War's mother liked to say he would gladly befriend a hungry cannibal if it saved him from that most dire of all fates: solitude.

Solitude, at least in her formative years, was Isolde's preferred state. Left to her own devices, Iz would forgo meals, sleep, and commitments, electing instead to sit in isolation before a window, where she would gaze not out at the world but inward at landscapes all her own. Though such bouts of introspection often began with some intelligent purpose, they soon lapsed into a sort of fatalistic exposition as one bleak observation led to a darker question that begat a whole abysmal inquiry.

As overeager as Warren was to embrace the world, Isolde was wont to shun it.

Between the two of them, the Wilbies clasped an unlikely middle, a fulcrum of moderation that suited them both. Still, Iz would sometimes tease War about his inexhaustible manifest of acquaintances, saying he had probably played billiards with the creator's cousin and shared a cab with the reaper's niece.

And yet, it was an inclination that served him well now. His yarn about the albatross with a sweet beak had been met with laughter, which necessitated an encore and a few more anecdotal tangents, besides. One by one, Nurse Percy's militia shouldered their shotguns and holstered their pistols to free their hands to clap each other's backs and wipe away tears of merriment. All except the red-haired man, who sneered at Warren's efforts to entertain.

At some point in Warren's regalements, Slorrance appeared to have been gripped by a sudden embarrassment. He untied the prisoner with the same speed he'd bound him up. As he undid his work, Nurse Percy explained how he'd grown disenchanted with his beloved profession after watching too many of his patients suffer and die from needless privations. His current band of antiroyalists was largely composed of disaffected nurses, former patients, and their children. He considered himself a reluctant revolutionary, but a determined one. He had seen too many unlucky persons ground down by avaricious royals and finicky bureaucracy to sit idly by. Now, he ran an underground clinic in a wing of the forgotten hospital where he labored to soothe the ailments of persons who the state would prefer to expire *patriotically*—meaning, quietly and out of view of the royal château.

When Nurse Percy brought the conversation back around to Warren's unfortunate client, War hurried to clarify his position: "We were less than keen to take the king's case. In fact, I had to talk my wife into it."

For the first time in some minutes, a frown darkened the pleasant dinner roll of Nurse Percy's face. "Why did you do that?"

Though unbound, Warren saw no reason to give up his seat. He did take the opportunity to cross his legs at the ankles before answering: "I'm a reader. I prefer biographies, but I do like a good history. Have you read *The Second Kingdom's First Victim* by Sir Dudley Foster? No? He wrote about a particularly rough transition of power that occurred nearly two hundred and fifty years ago, during a time when two prominent families sparred over the throne. There were disagreements, betrayals, scuffles—the sort of petty antics that serve as fodder for uninspired playwrights. Eventually, a new rump landed upon the throne. It went generally unnoticed—especially among playwrights—that the backdrop to the royal squabble was widespread misery. Nearly half a million commoners died of gutter fever and famine and crime. It was the common man who paid the bill for the royal recital. Dudley Foster put the situation rather succinctly when he said: 'When the palace smokes, the slums burn.' "

Slorrance wore the taut face of a man who'd just had his expertise explained to him. "They're already burning, Mr. Wilby. A revolution is inevitable. Delaying it only punishes one side."

"You may be right about that, Percy, but I'd like to think there's still a chance to change the course of our nation without flooding the streets with blood. Yes, the palace is rotten, and the royal ratters are unconscionable, but I think that King Elbert's laissez-faire tendencies have provided the country with an opportunity. The middle class is growing, the influence of the Court of Commons swells, and its members grow more diverse. Women have the vote; they hold office. Our children are more literate than our parents, and far fewer of them are being thrown into the sausage maker of war. Personally, I think Elbert has been too permissive with the alchemists, but his broad tolerance has left room for us plebs to assert ourselves—too slowly, perhaps, but steadily. The time of royals is passing; I would not like to see it reinvigorated. There are members of the nobility who don't like our soft king. They see him as yielding too much power to the masses. They would like to shuffle the deck, change the sovereign, and return to the old game, I think. Elbert may be an ineffectual king, but I fear his successor more."

"My opinions regarding the status quo and the middle class are less charitable than yours. But we seem to share a similar goal in mind, if not the means of grasping it." Nurse Percy's teeth clamped upon his pipestem in a manner that seemed conclusionary. "Mr. Wilby, I trust that we can rely upon your discretion regarding our present encampment."

Warren slapped his tweeded thighs. "Percy, I would sooner pull out my own tongue than wag it. You are doing good work here. Admirable, necessary work. And if, in the end, my assessment of the state of our nation is proven wrong, I will be honored to set my shoulder next to yours."

The redheaded man swept up the portalmanteau before Slorrance or his former prisoner could move to stop him.

"Would you please return our guest's bag, Mr. Darlington?" the nurse asked in a weary tone.

Warren detected barely contained contempt in Mr. Darlington's reply: "You can't go on giving away opportunities that fall into our lap, Percy. I haven't been paid in weeks."

"The cause is our compensation. We are not mercenaries."

"No, mercenaries get wages! I said I'd serve. Never said I'd starve." Darlington clutched the portalmanteau all the tighter as he backed toward the open entrance of the room. Warren rose to keep track of the man, who had the bearing of a cornered rat. "The lady said there were valuables. That geezer left his wife behind and took the bag, which says to me they're very valuable, indeed."

"They may be valuables to us, but believe me, my friend, to you they would be a hazard," Warren said, rounding his chair. He could sense Slorrance's company tensing at his back, heard the rustle of holsters, the clatter of forestocks.

Darlington snapped the bag open and threw his hand in without taking his eyes off the slowly advancing Wilby. His smirk creased first one cheek, then the other, as he dug deeper and deeper into the carpetbag.

"Please, be careful," Warren said.

Darlington dropped the bag and himself with it. His arm buried to the shoulder, his ruddy cheeks turned peaked as boiled eggs, and his eyes bulged with uncomprehending horror. He drew a breath to scream and was the same instant tugged farther into the gaping luggage. Head vanishing after his shoulder, his remaining arm hooked over the bag's lip and clawed desperately at the bald rug. His search for a grip was short-lived as he was snatched farther into the portalmanteau. His legs, now standing straight in the air, jogged and kicked like a logroller. A geyser of blood erupted from the mouth of the carpetbag, splashing the ceiling, as Darlington's knees and quivering boots were gulped into the mouth of the bag with the finality of a drain.

The remaining crowd stared at the deflated bag, now cinctured with gore. The pointed silence was only broken by the blood that dripped from the ceiling and thumped upon the rug. At the fore of the stunned group,

Warren stood frozen with both hands on his high forehead and his hat knocked back, his hazel eyes round.

A slight hand gripped the side of the blood-ringed purse. All gasped as a dark brume of smoke escorted the appearance of a thin face under a laurel of twisting hair.

Isolde Wilby climbed from her grandfather's satchel. Wiping the corner of her mouth, she smiled and said, "What a fine canapé! Now, who wants to be the main course?"

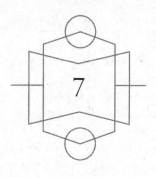

7

BIRD BRAIN

I n recent years, the study of magic had been recast by the culture as
a singularly dreary endeavor. The wizards that flowed from the car-
toonist's pen were uniformly aged, disheveled, and huddled in musty
libraries. They had birds in their beards and rats in their heads. The formerly dignified calling had fallen out of fashion for reasons inexact and
inexplicable, though the result was clear enough: The study of ephemeral
arts was for the anemic, the bookish, and children who picked their nose
in class.

And yet, nothing could've been further from the truth.

At its core magic was expressive, artful, even theatrical. All magic
included some performative aspect. Alchemists had their stances, wizards
their orations, necromancers their songs, and hex-casters their illustra-
tions. Indeed, Isolde's mother had once described the study of hexes as
"minoring in magic while majoring in art."

Though, to be effective in any of these fields required more than a
knack with poses, words, melodies, or figures. The mastery and practice
of magic, like so many other professional crafts, required stamina: men-
tal, physical, and psychic—a complex matrix of strengths that were often
gathered up and stuffed inside the insufficient envelope of "talent."

Naturally, there were those who demonstrated an aptitude for one charmed pursuit or another, and as with every art, there was an immense range of capacity among magic's practitioners. An amateur hex-caster might, over the course of their life, come to grips with only a handful of lesser hexes. More advanced operators might specialize in one or two major wards, which once had been sufficient to establish and support a career. But whether one dabbled in the foothills or stood astride the peak of the craft, all had to grapple with the sacrifices necessitated by the ascent.

Hexes gathered their power from their surroundings, sapping from the world whatever air, moisture, heat, light, and life their size and purpose required. And yet, the principal source of energy came from the practitioners themselves.

When Isolde had started out as a girl, it had taken her half a day to recover from casting even a moderate hex. Luckily, she had demonstrated a talent for both bearing and sharing the burden of her designs. Some novices never managed to advance to a point where they could draw a major ward without succumbing to a vomitous migraine. Now, in her prime, Iz could fashion numerous hexes before feeling the onset of exhaustion.

And she took some pride in the fact that she had begun to supplant the bearded wizard in the daily funnies. When the cartoonists wished to mock magic or its proponents, they called upon her. They presented her as a waif in men's trousers that were too large and always falling down. She wore her hat pulled so low on her head as to render her virtually blind. In those editorial cartoons, she was constantly bowling through people and knocking things down. Chaos followed on her heels as crowds fled before her.

All of which suited her just fine. Let them run; it only cleared the way.

The freshly fallen ash leapt before Isolde's feet like kicked-up goose down. To her left flowed an unbroken procession of blocky electrahol refineries with blacked-out windows, barbwire perimeters, and well-staffed guardhouses. Cannon-like smokestacks bombed the pearly scud with more of the iridescent murk. To her right, the barren rolling hills bore the filet of dry stone walls—an irregular grid of forsaken farmsteads and pastures, empty now except for the occasional shambles: a gutted cottage, a listing silo, a barn roof tented over rot-buckled walls.

And straight ahead in the middle of the empty road trudged her husband. He seemed a man in a trance. He had said little since they'd been released by the antiroyalists, who'd expressed a strong aversion to keeping the company of a slender woman who belied a monstrous appetite. As soon as they were free, Iz told Warren of Mr. Felivox's existence, and the arrangement they'd come to regarding the redirection of his diet away from people—in particular, *her*—toward War's pantry.

It was a bargain that was quickly amended to exclude the arm that intruded upon them through the aperture, a limb that Iz had not recognized. Fearing the worst, she had asked Felivox to, just this once, indulge his epicurean curiosity. (Iz could only hope that she had not instilled in him a taste for man.) When she had emerged from the portalmanteau into a bloody quiet, Iz had soon learned that her husband was not in so dire a position. He had made friends with their firing squad. It seemed lucky for all involved that Felivox had eaten an unpopular fellow. Still, Nurse Percy and his gang were eager to see the back of them. With no hope of hiring a jaunt, the Wilbies had begun the long walk back toward the River Zimme, its trinity of bridges, and the city beyond in the compounded silence of a new snow.

After a speechless mile, Warren at last stopped, turned, and embraced his wife as entirely and snuggly as a wet robe. He kissed her neck, her ear, her mouth and said with a tear-brightened gaze: "Never, never again. I can't believe I put you in a sack with a dragon! When I saw all that blood, I wished it was mine. It felt like mine! I thought I was dead, and then you climbed out, and..." He repeated his kisses and she returned them. Had they been home, and not posted in the road, she might've invited him to greater expressions of his love and relief.

"I didn't mean to scare you, War."

"That always happens when we split up."

She took his hands in hers and rubbed the walnuts of his knuckles with her thumbs. "The only thing I like about our separations is the reunions." She patted his cheek and then resumed her march back to Berbiton. "Come on. The faster we go, the faster we're home and out of these clothes. There's still a little Sunday left, and I don't intend to waste it!"

As they strode past the steeples of industry and the bones of homesteads, Iz took the opportunity to review what they had learned. The military hospital was as far into the war as Prince Sebastian, king-to-be, had ever progressed. It seemed reasonable to assume that his ring was lost (or just as likely *given*) there. They now needed to discover the fates of the prince's batman, L.Cpl. R. Atterton, and the royal's suspiciously devoted nurse: Jessamine "Blessed" Bysshe.

It was clear to them both that though a faction of antiroyalists could be behind the attempt to blackmail the king, those persons squatting in the blown-out hospital were not the perpetrators of the plot. Percy Slorrance seemed entirely devoted to the present emergency of caring for the forgotten and abused veterans, and Warren's conversations with the nurse had convinced him that if the band of antiroyalists were goaded into violence, it would not be the subtle sort. They would attack the king in the streets, not through his mail slot.

"I only wish I could've done a better job of patching things up with Percy. He seemed a good sport doing good work. But I was just so flabbergasted by the whole fountain of blood that I..." A bird alighted on his shoulder, and Warren cricked his neck to get a better look at the starling. It had the coloration of an oil slick: a lavender-blue sheen over a black base. Its irises were sulfur yellow and probing. "Hello, again."

To his surprise, the bird answered "Hello" in a voice that crackled like burning straw.

Iz was squinting at the bird and raising her finger to draw a hex over it when the murmuration of starlings descended upon them. The birds covered the rustic wall to their right, bellied the electrical wires that swooped between poles on their left, and carpeted the silvery snow in every direction about them, leaving the Wilbies with little room to turn, much less escape.

Warren said in a sidelong whisper, "I think I ran through this very same flock on the hospital roof. I wasn't sure then whether they were trying to peck me to death or cover my flank."

The flock began to speak. The sound was so disorienting, Warren had to resist the urge to plug his fingers into his ears. The words emerged separately, at a variety of volumes, and from every direction and range. The speech leapt from one side of the road to the other, cawed down from the wires, and chirped up from the street. Each bird appeared to be the master of but a single word or syllable, which they dutifully contributed as needed. The result was a little like being heckled by a very organized audience. Neither Iz nor Warren knew where to look, though their gazes naturally darted around in search of the ever-shifting speaker, who was still—incredibly—of a single mind. The messenger was a confusion, but the message was not.

The flock said, "Is and War-ran Will-be, you are only do-ing harm. Your help is not need-ed here. Your in-diff-er-ence is pre-ferr-ed. Let the dead rest."

"Who are you?" Iz asked.

"We are bird brain. We are the speak-ing flock."

"Who sent you? Who do you serve?" In the air, Iz drew a sigil that whorled like a fingerprint—a Hex of Conviviality that encouraged if not compelled oblique speakers to be more forthright. She'd scarcely finished the effort before the flock began to laugh, the sound riotous and withering. The multitude of iridescent hoods rippled in flashes of purple and green. The blazon of Iz's hex turned gray in the air and crumbled like cigar ash.

The cackling ended as abruptly as it had begun. "We are a pa-tron of the race, Miss Will-be. We know you are a kin-dred spirit. You serve the mas-ter of civil-ity."

"If you knew me at all, you'd know I don't take discouragement well. I am at present working at the behest of King Elbert III. If you feel any loyalty to him, you will not attempt to impede my work further. And if that is not the case, then I'll have no choice but to consider you a suspect."

"You have been warn-ed. The dan-ger you face is both con-sider-able and un-for-give-ing."

"Oh, I collect grudges for a living. One more can't hurt. Speaking of grudges, I don't suppose you'd like to confess to portaling a mandrake into my cellar, would you?"

In answer, the flock lifted into the air with a susurration of beating wings, gathered into a black, billowing mass, and surged over the thinning snow toward the teeming slope of Berbiton in the middle distance.

Observing the recession of the bird brain, Warren drew a small silver comb from his jacket's inner pocket and applied it to his mustache. "Not a particularly helpful lot, were they?"

"Oh, I don't know. I thought they were quite obliging."

"How so?"

"We don't have to wonder whether we're on the right track. You don't send a flock of spies to discourage the hopelessly lost. And whoever is behind those birds is practicing some rather impressive magic."

"More wizards?"

"There aren't any more wizards, remember? But it could be someone is using something else to control the birds. An artifact perhaps. Something outside our collection. Whatever the case, our feathery friends have given us our next step."

"The pet store?" Warren suggested.

"What?"

"For birdseed."

Iz laughed at her husband's simpering. "No. The flock told us to 'let the dead rest.' So, it would seem our batman or our nurse or perhaps both are no longer among the living." The hidden sun had begun to set, adding its rust to the gunmetal sky. The wind changed with the latening hour, blowing in the sweeter smell of the River Zimme and its sharper cold. Iz pulled her cloche down and hiked up her collar, leaving little more than the tip of her pointed nose showing. "We'll have to pay Old Geb a visit."

Warren's smile wilted. "Do we have to?" A shudder sawed his considerable shoulders. "Don't you remember last time? He was so vicious! I didn't sleep well for a week. Can't we just go to the morgue? Doesn't that sound so much nicer? I could pack us some goat cheese, a summer sausage, a crusty loaf, and a flask of lemon squash. We'll have a picnic at the city mortuary!"

She began to walk, and he pocketed his comb as he followed. "There are lots of mortuaries, and boneyards, and shallow graves. We can't inspect them all, War. For now, we have a dragon to feed, and an evening to salvage, but I'm afraid there's no getting around it: Tomorrow, we'll have to go see the imp."

AN INVETERATE INCUBUS

The next morning, Warren Wilby hummed in his kitchen as he arranged sprigs of parsley about a cake of butter-capped goose liver. He was in a superior mood having spent the main of the previous evening sequestered in the bedroom with Iz.

War was well acquainted with people's biases against his wife. They assumed that the coolness of her facade seeped up from a frozen core. Much as an underground stream chilled the hams of a springhouse, so did the famous Hexologist's public reserve ensure a private frigidity...

The fact was, Isolde was a passionate lover, as the Wilbies' infrequent houseguests soon discovered upon sharing a wall, floor, or indeed a roof with Isolde and Warren during their evening congresses. The pair were as vocal as macaws and immune to any effort to shame them. Should a guest over breakfast be so bold as to broach the topic, albeit via oblique reference to screech owls or rusty shutters or other things that cry out in the night, Isolde was quick to point out, "No one has any compunction about shouting their heads off at the racetrack, and they're not even the ones in the saddle." Insensible to the discomfort the statement caused, Isolde would go on to explain in explicit detail how the marital act stimulated the mind and carried in its ecstasies epiphanies that could not be summoned in the library or laboratory. *Sex helped her think.*

Their intimacies had a very different effect on Warren. He found their pairing to be akin to an emotional exorcism, as all the tangled and unsettled feelings—the anxiety, frustration, and dread—that had gathered in him over the course of the day was all at once blown to the ether, as undiluted serenity rushed in to fill the void.

And in those unguarded moments, War perceived in his wife's flushed skin and thundering pulse, feelings that she could not always articulate with such fervor or eloquence. But then, what were words but the surrogates of sensation, the emissaries of feeling?

Nine years of marriage had not subtracted so much as a sigh from their lovemaking; if anything, their ardors had only grown more passionate.

Warren opened the portalmanteau where it sat on his kitchen table and reached in with the dish of pâté. His shoulder shuddered with the passing of some force amid a scrambling sound like an iron rake being dragged over cobblestone. Neither jolt nor screech appeared to concern Mr. Wilby. He smiled when he withdrew the empty plate.

"How was that, old sport?" Warren called into the yawning purse.

Felivox's voice made the teacups hanging under the cupboards chatter and ring. "Revelatory! Absolutely divine! Do you have any idea how much goat hair one must choke down just to get even a hint of liver? Yes, yes! More of that, please."

Warren chortled at the dragon's enthusiastic reception. He snatched the towel from his shoulder and used it to open the door of his porcelain-clad oven, extracting a baking sheet bearing a pair of roasted hens. He was blowing through a week's worth of groceries, but it seemed a bargain considering the alternative. "I feel quite the incentive to serve only my best. I'm cooking for my life, after all!" He slid the pan and the two golden-skinned birds into the portalmanteau.

A sound like snapping kindling followed as Felivox devoured the offering in two bites. "Oh, there's nothing enjoyable about eating a man! You're all bones and squeals! To say nothing of all your accoutrements—I had a bootheel stuck between my teeth for hours."

Shuddering at the image, Warren doused the hot pan under the running tap, raising a blast of steam. "Same reason I don't eat clams! They're just ocean-flavored gaskets. They exist purely to lodge themselves between your molars."

"Ah, I've read some favorable accounts of the ocean! What does it taste like?"

Warren threw open his pantry door and ducked past the hanging nets of onions, shallots, and gourds. "Briny, weedy, fishy...it's hard to describe." He rummaged a little deeper into the recesses of his shelves. "Ah, here we are! Smoked trout. Here's your fruit of the ocean, your sip of the sea. Trout on toast points with triple cream—how does that sound?"

"Essential!" Felivox boomed.

Iz found her husband washing a reef of dishes and chatting with a dragon as casually as neighbors over a garden hedge. The air was laden with a great muddle of aromas, the sum of which reminded her that she was hungry. She had elected to pay the Cardinal Library an early morning visit and had left the house at the wretched hour of seven with nothing more than a sip of tea in her stomach. Warren identified this fact at once, saying, "You haven't eaten. Sit down. I'll whip something up."

As he laid bacon in one pan and cracked eggs into another, Iz reviewed the discoveries that the morning and her mother's help had brought. The military career of Prince Sebastian's batman, L.Cpl. Rudolph Atterton, ended shortly after the prince's release from hospital. L.Cpl. Atterton was deployed to the southern front on the Intarsian mainland. Weeks later, he was declared killed in action, a designation that was soon revised as more facts emerged. Though the man killed in the trenches was found wearing Rudolph's uniform and carrying his personal effects, the corpus was, by all accounts, at least sixty years old. The army appeared to try to sweep the scandal under the carpet, but the press perused the story, theorizing that the noble son had paid an old man to take his place, allowing him to desert his post, change his name, and vanish into the countryside of the enemy's lands. The army eventually updated their classification of the lance corporal to *Missing in Action*, which struck many as overly charitable. The Atterton family, a long and noble line, expended considerable resources in a two-year effort to uncover the true fate of their vanished son. The course of that inquiry was a minor, though regular feature in the *Berbiton Times*. The search was at first hampered by the war, but in the clearing of peacetime, some progress was made on retracing the lance corporal's steps to either clear his name or discover his circumstance. It was a scandal that continued to frequent the back pages of the paper until the Atterton family quietly concluded their fruitless investigation, presuming (or perhaps preferring) to believe their wayward son, Rudolph, was either dead or determined not to be found.

Sitting in his apron across from his wife, Warren pulled on one earlobe and squinted at the mazes of his tin-tiled ceiling. A sound as deep and regular as ocean surf rumbled from the open portalmanteau. The overfed dragon had fallen asleep. "That's quite a tawdry little tale. And what about the prince's nurse, Miss Jess Blessed? What happened to her?"

Iz wiped her mouth with her napkin and rose to wash her plate, though Warren attempted to intercept it. She drove him back to his seat with the snap of a tea towel. "There's not a single record of Nurse Jessamine Bysshe after the summer of the prince's hospital stay. No marriage announcement, no births, no further notices of employment, no obituary, nothing. She seems to have simply disappeared. It's not a particularly unlikely end for someone without distinction, but if she was the one to end up with the prince's ring, we're no closer to finding it."

"Seems quite a coincidence that Rudolph and Jessamine both dropped off the map in such quick order. We thought that it was the prince who was requesting Jessamine's presence in the hospital, but it could just as well have been his faithful orderly. She might have run off with Rudy." Warren closed Grandad and hooked the ancient clasp. The silence was jarring but not unwelcome.

"It's certainly possible. Elopements aren't unheard of between nobles and commoners. And if it's a case of forbidden—or at least inconvenient—love, then perhaps someone from the Atterton clan is responsible for sending the discouraging flock to accost us on the road. We could be dusting off embarrassments they'd rather keep in the attic." Iz balanced her clean dish upon the summit of the overfilled drying rack and wiped her hands on her blouse.

"The Attertons have some pull. They had a queen for a short time, after all. Poor dear." Warren pushed back from the table and slapped his thighs.

She hooked her arm around his neck as she sat upon his lap. "Do you want to stay here? I can handle Old Geb on my own."

"Oh, I wouldn't dream of it! I still owe him for the last outrage. I mean to give him a piece of my mind!"

Iz kissed him on the nose. "It would be poetry wasted on an abyss. You might as well try to duel with a hole."

The proprietor of the Spillway Public House, Mr. Pyle, wore the raddled look of a man who'd been disappointed to discover he'd survived another night's sleep. His teeth, bared by a perpetual grimace to sharpen his dwindling vision, were as brown as the petals of a pine cone and similarly arrayed. Snowy forearms, swollen by years of wrangling taps and kegs, bore the blue-and-purple badges of recent altercations with patrons who had once again confused his barroom with a boxing ring. The mirror behind him was more crack than glass. All along its great length, the dark backing showed through where projectiles had, over the years, contributed to an increasingly elaborate archipelago of absence.

Mr. Pyle had learned long ago that the tidal lunacy of paychecks was stronger than the madness of the full moon. He had also been taught that last call was not an ultimatum but a bugle call to battle. And he had been ruthlessly schooled that playing the confessor with no power to absolve only left him with a bevy of received but unanswerable sins.

Though it was a quiet, desolate Monday morning, and the smell of sage soap masked the previous day's debauchery, Mr. Pyle still clung to the warped wood of his bar with the grim fatalism of a man cleaved to a drifting plank upon a rolling sea. He seemed, in every way, the embodiment of despair.

But his melancholy broke the moment he saw Warren Wilby fill his doorway. All at once, Mr. Pyle straightened and began whistling an old shanty. Rounding the empty benches, Mr. Wilby undertook a formal dance that resembled a waltz but with himself as a partner. Pyle took down his best pewter mug from the highest shelf and evicted the spider that had died there. Filling the vessel with milk from the chiller, he only smiled more broadly when Warren signaled for him to pour a second dram for himself. He came bearing gifts!

Hipping aside the vacant barstools, Warren laid a small parcel of ribboned parchment on the spot that Mr. Pyle had polished especially to receive it.

"Ginger?" Pyle clasped his hands together like a child in prayer.

Warren hoisted his eyebrows and unwrapped the packet, revealing a stack of plump, dark biscuits. "Molasses."

The men each took up one of the sugar-glazed cakes and bit with savoring deliberation. There was no conversation during the ritual, which lasted a full minute and concluded with the downing of half a mug of milk. Only then did Mr. Pyle ask, "Where's your bride?"

"Outside. She's drawing a fresh hex in your alley."

"She doesn't give up."

"No, she doesn't."

"What's this one supposed to do?"

From the open doorway, Iz clapped chalk dust from her hands as she answered, "It's a Hex of Tranquility, one I've tailored especially for spirits. If we can't drive him out, perhaps we can at least make him less torturous of his hosts."

"Thank you for trying, Missus Wilby. Care for a cookie?" Mr. Pyle asked.

"No." She dug into the pocket of her coat, extracted a large blue bill, and slid the ten-gallet note across the warted bar. "Is he here yet?" Iz scanned the humble barroom, central to which was a massive hearth and a smoldering fire. The river-stone chimney seemed both too large for the space and also its only redeeming feature. In a city of ever multiplying brasseries and gin joints, the bucolic ambience of the Spillway seemed an anachronism, though a welcome one.

"Never left." Mr. Pyle rattled a crowded steel hoop as he fit a single key into a locker under the bar. He returned with a handblown bottle shaped like a dancing woman in a twirling skirt. A yellow-green liquor sloshed beneath the stopper that was her painted head. "He's in the inglenook. Has a new skin, I'm afraid."

"What happened to Joshua?" Warren asked, suddenly concerned. Mr. Pyle pointed to a crimson tobacco tin sitting on a shelf behind him among bottles of half-done spiced rum. "Cremated. Always said he wanted to rest among friends."

Looking pale, Warren bundled the remaining biscuits and slid them toward the publican, who appeared to have recovered his saturnine mood.

Iz led the way to the unlit snug beside the chimney, bootheels knelling the floor planks like a fist upon a door. The small table set in the lee of the hearth was attended by three rundlets, though only one of the barrels was presently occupied. Stockinged legs poked out from the deeper shadow. The torn hosiery laddered over one raw knee. A pair of T-strap heels lay in a tangle nearby.

Iz switched on the inglenook's sconce, spotlighting the tragic figure who appeared to have collapsed there. The young woman lay with her head back, resting in the corner between panel and chimney. Her mouth hung open; her disheveled black bob resembled a chimney brush. The smell of urine competed with the vapors of alcohol. Vomit stained the neckline of her beaded shift. A full glass of rum sat on the leather-topped table beside her waxen curled hand.

"So young," Warren said from Iz's shoulder.

"And already as old as she'll ever be." The voice that croaked from the woman's open throat sounded like a hoarse child whispering through a tin horn.

"Old Geb," Iz said.

The mischievous imp that occupied the Spillway made a habit of possessing obstinate alcoholics. The incubus took up residence in its victims' throats, where it clung to their vocal cords, sipping their tipple and needling them into gulping down more and more poison until they lapsed into a stupor. Once they were comatose, Old Geb would employ their arms to drink its fill, emptying their wallets along the way. In this manner, the spirit abused its hosts until they sickened, suffered, and died. Then, it leapt to a new mark, traveling into their bodies upon the vespers of consumed spirits. One could only safely address the incubus soberly, and even then, with great caution.

Old Geb was, without a doubt, the most hateful spirit Iz had ever encountered, but it was not without talent.

"Iz Ann Always," the devil in the drunk sang back. "Thought I felt a little something on the back of my neck. What was that—a sleep hex? On me? And here I believed we were well acquainted. Friendly. Kindred." The young woman's arm jerked, fingers clutching the rum-filled tumbler as if piloted by a clumsy puppeteer. The hand poured the liquor down the sot's throat. Some slipped over her chin and ran down her stretched neck, but much of it flowed past her teeth. What might've drowned the unconscious woman was intercepted by the demon lodged in her gullet, who exhaled in satisfaction before stamping the empty glass upon the table. "You can't resist me, can you? Iz Ann Always finds an excuse to visit, but never listens to the answers she comes for. *Daddy.*" The juvenile voice dragged out the final word, turning it into a harrowing moan.

Isolde sniffed. "I visit the privy frequently, too, but it's not because I enjoy the smell. I have need of your services."

"And you know the price."

Iz lifted the bottle of absinthe and gave it a gentle shake. The enlivened green fluid made the dancer's skirt seem to flare. Iz poured a finger of the expensive spirits into the incubus's empty glass. Again, the unconscious arm animated with a jerk, snatching up the tumbler, and tipping its contents past the young woman's lips. Old Geb sighed, and the body of its host shivered and convulsed. "So, Iz Ann Always, you're looking for a corpse?"

Isolde flipped open her notepad to make sure she recited the full name correctly. "Lance Corporal Rudolph Elias Atterton. Is he known to you?"

"Let me see, let me see." The voice of the incubus seemed to withdraw deeper into the core of the young woman. Iz waited motionlessly as Warren shuffled unhappily behind her—muttering and punching his fists into his coat pockets as if warming for a fight.

Old Geb's only gift, besides squandering livers, was scouring the unwritten inventory of the interred. If there were bones in the ground, the incubus knew them, knew the name that had once belonged to them, and could often guess what had caused the skeleton to surface from their skin. It was a skill the imp was loath to share, especially with the police or anyone who'd like to see it become an institutional instrument. Incubi were famous liars, especially to those they disliked, and Old Geb was elusive when cops were around. The imp was a useful fount of information for Iz purely because it liked her. It was an admiration Iz preferred not to dwell upon.

"I do not know a Lance Corporal Rudolph Elias Atterton. Pity. I always enjoy worming through the bones of a soldier. They leave behind such fascinating puzzles. Though sometimes, a battlefield mills a man so well, not even I can put him back together. And they call *me* a fiend."

Iz did not reward the incubus by squirming at his horrible ruminations. "I have a second name for you. Do you know—"

The incubus grunted, a sound that apparently engaged the gears of the young woman's voice box. The imp's host laughed vaguely like a dreaming sleeper. Old Geb thumped her arm upon the tabletop. "Another name, another pour!"

Again, Iz tipped the voluptuous bottle. Again, the shot was lifted and drained into a mouth gory with smeared lipstick.

"Jessamine Rutha Bysshe. Do you know where she rests?" Iz asked.

The incubus did not deliberate long before answering. "She is known to me. Jessamine Rutha Bysshe is in a pauper's plot."

"Which one?" Iz asked quickly.

"Honewort."

"How did she die?"

"Hard to say. Bones are in good order. Strong. Young. Full of life. But she tastes . . . she tastes of the pox."

"I see. All right. That's enough. Now, perhaps you can let this young lady rest. It won't do to kill another one so soon after the last."

The incubus giggled, the sound like a drowning child. "You are so thoughtful, my dear, dear Iz Ann Always. I will give you one more for free. Professor Silas Roner Wilby—the man himself, or what is left. So widely known. So thinly spread! I have seen such spectacular ends, such theaters of expiry, but his torments were operatic, a veritable showpiece of suffering."

The floorboards creaked with the sound of Warren's shifting weight. Iz plucked from her coat pocket a stick of chalk, which she held up to stay him. She began to draw a hex on the wall, haloing the cocked-back head of the imp's host.

"Get a bucket," she whispered to War, even as Old Geb cackled on.

"How he cried out for his mother, your mother, for you, Iz Ann Always never there. No one came as he wept and was ripped apart by the ravening angelic gyre. Alone, alone! How bitterly he sobbed!"

Iz closed the Hex of Disgorging, and the thatched circle turned as black as a firepit. She stepped back, even as the young woman lurched forward, gagging. Warren got the pail under her just in time to catch the violent ejection of her excess.

Warren placed the somewhat revived young woman in the back of a jaunt as gently as he could. While he asked the driver to deliver the beset tippler to a friend at a recovery house and paid the fare and gratuity, Iz spoke to Old Geb's now awake but still bleary-eyed host.

"You will feel a powerful urge to come back here. Do not. The incubus is slow to give up on a comfortable perch once it's been chosen. If you stay away for a few nights, it will forget you and find another to torment. But if you come back, this will happen again—and worse." Iz presented the young lady with her calling card. "If you need assistance with the symptoms of withdrawal, come see me."

With a tormented expression of shame, the young woman accepted the card, studied it, and said in a rough and husky voice, "Thank you, Ms. Wilby. I will pay you and your husband back for the fare."

"If you like. In the meantime, find something better to do than this. Pretend that you are worth the trouble until you convince yourself that you are."

BODY SNATCHING DILETTANTES

Warren Wilby had never been overly fond of cemeteries. Though he did not feel superior to those who took solace in visiting the graves of loved ones, he could scarcely imagine a gloomier setting for celebrating the lives of those who had passed. He did not understand the appeal of headstones or marble vaults, both of which seemed primarily an obligation requiring maintenance. Nor did he enjoy epitaphs, which often struck him as rote, or ostentatious, or uncomfortably intimate. A crowded graveyard made him feel like an unwilling voyeur.

Unfortunately for him, Honewort Cemetery had the doleful distinction of being Berbiton's most congested boneyard. Because the headstones of the interred were paid for by an ancient (though evaporating) trust, and burials were financed by the Crown, there was never a shortage of interested tenants. For Berbiton's poorest, resting in the bosom of Honewort was the preferable alternative to being tilled into the public pit.

Honewort, which lay just off High Street, was hemmed in on all sides by soaring apartment high-rises. Despite its enviable address, the cemetery could hardly be described as posh. The graves were so tightly packed that if a stiff wind were to blow through and knock all the markers down, the headstones would've fairly paved the ground.

The sun had set, and the ashy snow abated, making room for a cataractous moon to rise. The stately tombs of the now-extinguished Honewort line stood out like wedding cakes in a bakery display. Even so, decades of corrosive precipitation had blunted their gables and melted the inscriptions on their once-proud lintels to the point of illegibility. The rest of the cemetery's markers were uniformly modest but cut from a hodgepodge of stones, a fact that reflected the board of trustees' willingness to purchase remnants from quarries and construction sites.

The Wilbies picked their way through the headstones by the weak, stuttering light of an electric torch. It was impossible not to tread on the dead, and still they tried their best to be respectful, or as respectful as one can be while leapfrogging about a cemetery after hours.

They were both a little surprised to discover they were not alone: A new plot was being opened in the overloaded ground. A pair of fossors animated the side of a crypt with their shadows. The younger worked to deepen a hole, while the elder oversaw from the fringe. A sleepy mule hitched to a cart nosed a feedbag. The mournful drone of a rusted music box accompanied the young man's labor. Warren switched off his torch, hoping to skirt the attention of the gravediggers, whose voices carried better than his light. Hunkering behind the inadequate cover of a headstone, Warren held his hand behind him, signaling Iz to duck.

The youth in the hole—who presented nothing more than a pair of active shoulders, the flag of a shovel head, and a head full of sweat-deflated hair—spoke first: "Another lead box! Poor Murph! That mule's too old to be dragging around so much weight. Why do they have to make them so heavy?"

"It's precautionary," the gray-haired fossor said. By the light of a kerosene lamp, Warren watched the elder crouch upon a rolled length of sod beside the deepening grave. He had a beard like a dandelion gone to seed and a black suit that was split at the knees and thready at the cuffs. "This man was a Flail. Evidently, an unlucky one that nobody wanted to take responsibility for."

The youth paused his digging long enough to reset the braces on his shoulders. "What's a Flail?"

"A kind of alchemist—not the rich sort. The kind who works down on the line." The elder opened his pocket watch, appeared to note the hour, and snapped it shut again. "A Flail gets teamed with a Haloist, and the pair of them pull thalanium out of a hole in the universe."

"A what?"

The elder, rather than sigh and grouse and tell the youth to let him be, seemed eager to answer. There was something of the professor in him, it seemed. He hugged a clipboard, overburdened with forms and smudged carbon copies, and answered with one eye winked in thought. "You know where electrahol comes from, don't you?"

"A pump?"

"No, not a pu...I mean, *yes*—the bus driver gets it out of a pump, but electrahol is *made* in a thalanium refinery. Thalanium is a sort of charcoal-like byproduct that comes from the Entobarrus. And it's the alchemists who retrieve it. You ever get a peek inside an alchemist's mill—those blacked-out buildings on the far side of the river that shriek and smoke all day and night? Well, I have. Terrifying places. Absolutely uncanny. Don't recommend it." The fossor fiddled with his nose with a series of practiced if impolite strokes. "Inside those mills, there's a conveyor belt that the alchemists load with lumber or reeds or whatever organic stuff they can lay their hands on, and they ferry it through a portal that's maintained by a Haloist, whose whole job is to keep that door in space and time open."

The youth set the handle of his shovel into his armpit to free his hands. He rewound the sluggish music box on the graveside as he asked, "Open to where?"

"Open to hell. The Entobarrus is like a neighbor you can hear screeching through your apartment walls but hope to never meet in the lobby. It's a fiery place full of all sorts of monsters and plagues. But years ago, some genius figured out that if you truck timber from our world through the fires of the Entobarrus, it comes out the other end as fuel. That's the stuff that lights your apartment, and powers the hyaline towers, and makes the taxis run."

"And smells like dead fish." The youth scraped the earth again with his shovel.

"Quite right. Anyway, so this poor sod here was a Flail. It was his job to beat back the beasts that try to squeeze through the halo while his partner was pushing wood through it. I'm sure he had an iron rod and some fiery bolts and all sorts of wards to keep his guts from getting baked by those devils on the other side. I've known Flails. Good people. Family men. It's not a bad living, but it is a terrible way to die."

"So, what happened to him?" The youth hiked his chin at the lead-cased coffin.

"Well, let's see." The old fossor consulted his board of rumpled papers. "Cause of death, cause of death, cause of . . . hmm. Seems something from the other side grabbed him."

The regular crunch of the shovel stalled. *"Something?"*

"They didn't include a name or a genus or what-have-you. Probably anyone who got a good look at it isn't around anymore. I'm sure it was something awful and slobbery and full of teeth or tentacles or . . . Wait, there's a note here." The elder cleared his throat as he straightened his arm to assist his effort to read the lines before him. "This something appears to have turned him into lava."

The shovel rattled to the floor of the hole. *"Lava?"*

"I'm paraphrasing—the technical term they have here is 'irradiated plasmatic silicon.' But I saw inside the coffin for one of these poor sots years ago, and I thought, *That's lava. That's just a trough full of lava.* So. The point is, there's not a body in there, per se. It's more of a puddle of fire that doesn't ever really cool off. It's not safe to keep around. So that's why he goes in a lead box and that box gets buried here."

"And we are all very grateful for your service," Isolde said, standing on the orange shore cast by the fossor's lamp near the foot of the open grave.

Still squatted behind his macabre cover, Warren turned to discover that his wife was no longer behind him. Feeling silly, he stood and dusted the snowy ash from the legs of his trousers.

"Body snatchers. Aren't you getting bold!" the elder fossor said, rising with some difficulty from his perch on the sod. "As the groundskeeper of Honewort, I am placing you under arrest for trespassing and interference with a corpse."

"We are not resurrectionists. We are investigators," Iz said, gesturing to her husband as he gingerly stepped over a tilted tombstone to join her.

"You look like snatchers to me," the elder insisted, observing with some confusion as Warren introduced himself and reached down to shake the hand of the young gravedigger, who said his name was Lenard Joyns, though everyone called him "Len."

"My name is Isolde Wilby." She drew a card from her coat pocket and presented it to him. "We are the Hexologists, and have been engaged by the Crown to investigate a matter of a pressing nature, which has led us here, to your grounds. We are looking for a grave. Perhaps, you—"

The youth once again reached over the lip of the grave to grasp his music box. He blew the loose earth from the barrel of the caseless instrument and began carefully churning its minute crank. The music box began to play again. The simple, brief melody was brash and uneven, evoking nothing so much as an infant banging upon a toy piano.

Appearing to interpret Isolde's inscrutable expression as a critique of his box's music, the youth said, "It helps to keep me from getting the creeps."

The young fossor's voice broke when he spoke, betraying the extent of his youth. Warren supposed he could be no more than fourteen or fifteen years old.

War said, "It's not a bad little tune. Reminds me of a shanty. Something to get the elbows up." Warren raised his arms to posit the semblance of a dance.

The young gravedigger seemed to relax a little. "Lady visiting her son gave it to me. It was his, but then he killed himself. She was going to leave it on his stone, but I said I thought it was a nice song and asked if she'd mind if I visited to listen to it once in a while, and she said I should just take it before the carp snow did."

Seizing upon the break in conversation, Isolde addressed the groundskeeper again. "I'm just looking for a grave. I know we should've come during regular hours, and we apologize for the inconvenience. But, as I said, we are pressed for time. We are looking for Jessamine Bysshe."

The groundskeeper scratched his beard with her calling card. "You're the one from the papers, aren't you? The ghost whisperer, the monster tracker. That you?"

"More or less." Isolde shrugged.

"They call you spooky in the papers—witchy, weird."

Warren had the face of a man about to rise to his wife's defense, but Isolde cut him off before he could. "None of those sound like insults to me."

The tatterdemalion gentleman slipped her card into the breast pocket of his shaggy coat. "Didn't mean it as a criticism, Ms. Wilby. You should hear what they call us: bone moles, headstone humpers...as if we're not out here doing the city a service."

Warming to the man, Isolde said, "But we don't do it for the praise, do we? We do it because we can, because we have the stomach for it. Civilization is not carried on the backs of the squeamish."

"Quite right. Jessamine Bysshe, you said? All right. Let me see..." The groundskeeper scrubbed his nose as his eyes rolled to one side. After a moment, he announced, "I have no one here by that name."

Isolde twisted her head to one side. "Are you sure? You've memorized every marker? There must be thousands."

"Nine thousand two hundred and eighty-eight, which should be ninety-one by morning. I know these souls, madam, and there's no Jessamine Bysshe here."

"That rat!" Warren all but spat. "I can't believe Geb would lie to you. I mean, I can, of course, but still, that's an imp who's really earned its horns."

"What about a Jess Blessed?" Isolde asked.

Again, the old groundskeeper's eyes whitened with his sidewise gaze. "I have a Jess Blessed."

"Could you take us to her?" Isolde asked.

The elder clicked his teeth together, seeming suddenly uncertain or perhaps embarrassed. "I can't let you dig her up. I do like you, madam. You seem like good people, but there are laws, and I must abide by them."

"Of course. No one's snatching any bodies tonight. You have my word. We will not touch Ms. Blessed's body nor her ghost. Things would go very poorly for us if we did."

The groundskeeper, who introduced himself as Arnold Hollins, paced through the graveyard with lamp hiked and watch in hand, his stride turning sharply and frequently as if following the track of an invisible maze. His path meandered, doubled back, and crossed itself until Isolde began to suspect the old man was lost. Then Arnold Hollins explained that he was engaging his version of a filing system, a pattern he had memorized to help him recall not only the names of his residents, but their resting places as well. That knowledge was partly held in the registries of his feet.

Soon, Isolde discerned that what she had previously mistaken for a pocket watch was in fact a compass. The instrument appeared to be part of his memory retrieval ritual. She'd always found compasses to be such a funny instrument. Whenever you raised a compass to refer to its wisdom, the needle would first swing and saw, seeming to dither with self-doubt and indecision. But then it settled into itself; it found its north; it resolved into fixed confidence. Even if its instincts were skewed by the presence of another magnet, even if it was wrong, the compass was quickly resolute. It seemed such a human sort of magic.

Giving him the benefit of the doubt, the Wilbies were soon rewarded as Hollins came to a halt and lowered his lantern to illuminate the front of a rounded stone. The groundskeeper swiped the ash from the tilted marker, revealing its simple inscription: JESS BLESSED, MARCH 8, 4008–JUNE 11, 4034. She had died at the age of twenty-six, not even two years after Prince Sebastian had convalesced in her hospital wing.

Warren removed his bowler and wiped his tall brow, which despite the cold had collected a little sweat. "I wonder why she changed her name— and to that, of all things!"

"Perhaps she was living under an assumed name to protect herself from someone. She might've chosen 'Jess Blessed' to preserve a thread to her former life. Or maybe it was done in a fit of irony. It might've been like most last words: just blurted-out garbage. It's silly how much significance the living love to heap upon final utterances and acts. As if no one was ever hit by a train or died in difficulty or was befuddled by delirium. Our culturalized avoidance of death makes us tend to ennoble the transition itself in a way that is frankly—"

Warren performed a brief but communicative cough.

Iz bit upon a smile and took a breath. "Anyway, I suspect that if Ms. Bysshe did indeed succumb to the pox, as our imp suggests, then she might not have had the opportunity to correct the record before she died. Back in the '30s, the heads of Health and Safety were especially quick to whisk away anyone who showed symptoms of plague. For all we know, she checked into a hotel under a false name, woke up with a fever, and was shipped off to a pox camp before sundown."

Mr. Hollins hummed his agreement. "The state was not particularly interested in the rights of plague patients. Most of them died alone and unattended. It's a miracle she ended up here and with a headstone. She could've just as easily been cremated."

Iz knelt on the sparse grass of the nurse's grave. She wondered how many years until the caustic snow would scour her name from the world. "Are you ready, War?"

"Wait! I shall gird my loins." He drew the small piston and drum of a tin atomizer from his coat pocket, sprayed a little cloud before himself, and stepped into it. "There. All girded."

The Wilbies had elected to leave Grandad secreted in its cabinet in the mantelpiece at home. The majority of the portalmanteau's magical artifacts would be useless where they were going, and if they were separated from it during their explorations, the entrance to her father's vault would be lost forever.

Yet, they had not come unequipped. In the back pocket of her knickerbockers under her long coat, Isolde carried the Sepulchral Spade, a powerful relic that looked more like a silver cake server than a tool designed for tillage. She had wielded it on two previous occasions, experiences which had inspired Warren to arm himself with the bug sprayer full of rosewater, which was the only known deterrent of nithe-grims.

Nithe-grims, or nithes as they were more often called, were spectral creatures that fed upon the haunts of the departed. Parasitic by nature, nithes were drawn to the residues of tragedy, misfortune, and misery—emanations that they greedily consumed. When they fed upon the shadows of the departed, the result was similar to that of moths: They chewed holes through that ghostly cloth. But when they supped upon the living, the outcome was much different. Rather than destroy, their feeding inspired an incapacitating euphoria—a lethargic bliss so entire, so thorough, it caused the body's autonomic processes to falter. The woman or man bitten by a nithe-grim perished from a perfect tranquility of the heart.

A spritz of rosewater might discourage an idle nithe from investigating them in passing, but Warren knew that once the blighters started to swarm, there was really nothing for it but to run.

When Iz unsheathed the cake server from her trouser pocket, Groundskeeper Hollins was quick to protest. "Ah-ah-ah, I thought we agreed: no digging."

"It's not for digging. Not into the physical earth, anyway," Iz said, holding the tool up for Hollins's inspection. The thin and finely filigreed blade certainly didn't look like much of a shovel. Except for the irregular serration along its tip and edge, it looked like a polished-up showpiece reserved for New Year's Eve.

"Seems a little worse for wear," Warren said from over her shoulder.

"I'm sure it'll be fine."

"What does it do, exactly?" Arnold Hollins asked.

As she began to draw a rectangle of fizzing yellow light in the withered winter grass over Jessamine's grave, Isolde explained, "The Sepulchral Spade was originally a gift from a necromancer to his wife, an ardent gardener who was also ardently dead. This was centuries ago, so the details are a bit garbled, but the necromancer intended for his wife to use the trowel to create a secret garden in that liminal space between life and death where they could meet and canoodle. What she actually did was repeatedly stab her husband with it, thereby solving the whole problem of commuting back and forth between here and the hereafter."

Warren lifted his shoulders as if fending off a shiver. "Well, you can't spell 'necromance' without 'romance,' I suppose."

Isolde rolled her eyes and carried on: "The spade can be used to scratch out a doorway to the afterlife, or rather its waiting room. Between our world and the Gray Plains of the Unmade lies the Nethercroft. It's an interesting spot. There, each soul is given a sort of gallery of memory to populate as they see fit. The exhibits that inhabit the Nethercroft showrooms are called 'haunts': staged recreations of the most important moments from an individual's life—the sort of stuff that flits through your head when you die."

"Seems fairly grim," the groundskeeper said.

"Not really. We living have our monuments and the dead have theirs. The Sepulchral Spade is our ticket to take a look-see at the shrines that Ms. Jess Blessed raised on her way out."

Mr. Hollins's beard swallowed his mouth as he frowned. "So, you're going to peep about this young woman's memories? Seems a bit...I don't know... *tawdry.*"

Finishing the frame of her sigil, Iz continued to draw a series of cursive glyphs; the addition of each made the scintillating light brighten and shed more sparks. "It's really no different than performing an autopsy on a murder victim; a small amount of privacy is sacrificed in search of superior justice."

"It does seem a *little* different," Warren said, and Iz paused to regard him over her shoulder with an expression of amused surprise. "Oh, don't give me that look, Iz. You know this makes me a little queasy."

"I know, darling. And I am sorry. But just remember, we didn't come here to pant upon the windows and peep through the keyholes of Jessamine's life. We will not see anything she did not wish to share. These spectral scenes serve a purpose, and it isn't to titillate; it's to give loved ones a way to find each other on the other side. And sometimes to settle scores. If Jessamine wished to set things straight, she may have enshrined the truth in one of her haunts." Iz resumed her work, crawling out of the rectangle as she closed the last figure of her hex. The beaming light flashed like a lightning strike and vanished just as swiftly.

The rectangular hex had been replaced by a flight of earthen stairs leading down into darkness.

Pocketing her cloche, Iz removed her wool coat and draped it over Jess's headstone. Warren did the same with his jacket and bowler, then balanced his unreliable torch atop their pile. He slapped his arms and rubbed his hands to dispel the cold and his apprehension.

Staring wide-eyed down into the abysmal cellar, the groundskeeper gradually swung his lamp toward Iz. "You'll need this, I imagine."

"It wouldn't help, I'm afraid. Lamps don't work where we're going."

"How do you see?"

Iz descended onto the first step, and turned again, her eyes sparkling, her dark hair frosted with hoary moonlight. "That's what the ghosts are for."

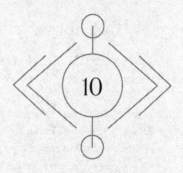

10

A JOLLITY OF GHOSTS

rm in arm, they descended into a perfect dark.

Isolde knew that when robbed of stimuli the mind did not gladly submit to the vacuum—an indignity too like death to pass unchallenged—but rather, the deprived senses adorned the void with consoling fantasies. Much as a lonesome child soothes herself with her thumb, so did Isolde's vision embellish the abyss with nervous fireworks.

Had she been able to summon one, the wan light of a Hex of Radiance would've beamed forth like a channel buoy in contrast to the oppressive gloom. But she might as well have attempted to strike a match amid a monsoon as cast a hex in the Nethercroft. This is when knowing a necromancer would have been particularly useful. But of course, they had all been culled from society after the Meridian War as part of the armistice. Isolde found it strange to think that her grandmother would've been able to take an Introduction to Basic Necromancy at university, because by the time Iz entered academia, even speaking the name of the magical order aloud was considered gauche, like a child shouting anatomical euphemisms to excite the attention of adults. She'd even known a student who'd been expelled for expressing too much curiosity in the verboten art. In the years following the war, the texts and fetishes that orbited necromancy had been studiously gathered up by the state and locked away or destroyed.

Iz gave her husband's abundant forearm a squeeze. "No wandering off this time."

Warren snorted—a playful show of pique. "I didn't *wander* off. I was investigating."

"You were attempting to steal a book."

"I was not! I was just trying to get a peek at the table of contents." Warren's cavalier tone broke when the darkness suddenly seemed to breathe through them, puffing upon the untested instruments of their skeletons. They were crossing a threshold, one the living were not meant to traverse. Above them, the preserve of mortals moaned, a complaint hastily swallowed by the spheres of the dead.

It took another step or two for Iz to recover her voice. "What was that book about...puddings?"

Warren blustered at the affront. "*Puddings?* It was Chef Benoit's *Anatomy of a Sponge Cake*. It's been out of print for nearly thirty years. It's a lost treasure!"

"Cake is cake, darling. It's just a delivery system for frosting."

Warren gasped. "Heretic!"

They nattered on to assuage their nerves as they continued to descend. Though it was not long before they found they had run out of things to say. Searching with their bootheels for each invisible step, they fell into a regular rhythm of pausing and probing and descending as one. The cadence reminded Warren of their wedding recessional, yet brought to Iz's mind the deliberative pace she had struck as a girl while sneaking out of the house at night. So it was, lost in their own memories, that they discovered the dead end together when their toes thumped against the wall of stratified clay.

By feel, Isolde once more employed the Sepulchral Spade, scraping out the shape of a door. The lines of the jambs and lintel sparked like an arc weld, making them squint, and somehow deepening the darkness above and behind them. The moment she closed the portal's frame, the earth fell away, revealing a peculiar blue glow that seemed to fill the chamber beyond.

The assault upon their senses was like stepping through the entrance flaps of a carnival tent. Overlapping chatter, cheers, and laughter vied for their attention even as the noisy confluence made it impossible for the Wilbies to focus upon any single source. Like a carnival, it was not immediately apparent which way they should go, or indeed if there was even a path to pursue. The spectral fairgrounds before them were crowded with phantasmagorical clumps of commotion, discrete as the stalls of a barker's alley. Each lit-up block of activity contained a single vignette: a preserved moment of Jessamine's existence. These brief plays were enlivened by blue ghosts whose shine was sufficient to light the pounded field, the muddy sets, and the Wilbies' way. Narrow murky lanes snaked between the dramas, providing gutters for the specters to vanish into as they broke the invisible limit of a scene. The set pieces and props that anchored each performance were fashioned out of earth. Barn doors, hedgerows, draperies, and bric-a-brac—all appeared to have been composed of compacted potting soil, interlarded with rootlets, worms, and beetles. The neon ghosts before them appeared to play upon a jungle gym of alluvium.

While the denizens of the Nethercroft were spectral beings that could no more be embraced than the morning fog, the earthen objects that populated the sets were tangible enough. This, however, did not mean these props were perfect reproductions. Warren could no more have cracked a book found in the Nethercroft than open the door of a sandcastle. Both were pleasing shapes devoid of internal detail. Though, the Wilbies had learned, interaction with either ghost or their loamy possessions had a way of attracting the attention of the nithe-grims, who hastened to such disruptions as if summoned by a huntsman's horn.

The scenes before them were not true memories, as none of them were from the perspective of the original witness. Rather, they were Jessamine's own creations, impressionistic renditions of events that had been colored by her own anxieties, hopes, and loves. It was a spiritual theater that reflected the biases of its director.

The first vision they encountered was of a young girl in a flour sack dress—though to call it a "dress" was to flatter its lumpen maker who appeared to have done little more than to cut holes for a head and a pair of arms. The girl shinnied out on the main tie of a rough barn, high above a hay-strewn floor. In the bubble of the play, the beam had neither a beginning nor an end, but hung unsupported in the air. Beneath the girl, a crowd of children, small as figurines, shouted through cupped hands, *You can do it, Jessamine! Go on, Jess! Almost there!* But the girl's progress had been arrested by the snagging of her dress upon a nail head.

In the Nethercroft, sometimes inconsequential things—rather than receding into the soil of the background—would appear as luminous artifacts, distinguished by their importance. The golden bell that hung from the center of the tie was just such an object. The adventuresome young Jessamine reached for the bell, and as she did, her arm and fingers began to stretch like wax running down a candlestick. Her distended fingertips grazed the gilded bell just enough to stir its clapper, yet she was rewarded with a knelling better suited to a clock tower.

Isolde studied the girl's features, marveling at this first glimpse of the young woman who'd been knocking around in her imagination. Jessamine's brows were straight and thick, her cheeks round, her mouth enlarged by prominent teeth she was just beginning to grow into. But it was her look of determination that made the greatest impression: Jessamine seemed a tenacious soul.

Then the scene reset, and the girl's inching progress along the rafter was undertaken once more. She scooted out, snagged on a nail, and rang the bell—then scooted, snagged, and rang again.

Knowing that disturbing the haunt would attract the attention of nithegrims, which were elsewhere for the time being, the Wilbies carefully skirted the moment of triumph, only to find themselves ducking beneath the festooned gate of a secluded garden, fashioned from compacted peat. Nestled against an overgrown boxwood, between a tangle of morning glories and a cracked birdbath, sat a vaporous Jessamine Bysshe dressed in what seemed the remnants of a curtain. She shared a rotting bench with a boy who wore the cap and coat of a delivery service. The pair leaned toward one another with sleepy gazes and unsealed mouths. When their lips met, diaphanous flowers untwisted from the vine as a geyser of warblers, feathered in light, spouted from the arid basin.

Iz observed these proceedings with all the bashfulness of an astronomer peering through the lens of a telescope. Warren, meanwhile, shielded his eyes and sidled past the hedge, murmuring, "Excuse us. Pardon me. Carry on."

The next haunt was larger in scale, encompassing a buckling front porch and a rutted yard. A hollow-backed mule chewed weeds beside a rustic plowshare. Jessamine and what seemed her entire family had congregated to stare at something on the invisible horizon. Her brothers and sisters, seven in all, were all similarly emaciated. Her mother clutched her thin throat as if she would strangle herself. Her father was as grim as a gibbet. An open-air jaunt, surely a novelty at the time, materialized from the edge of the haunt. A well-dressed couple clambered out. They addressed Jessamine first, introducing themselves as Val and George Larkland. The surname made Isolde's ears prick up. Val and George Larkland claimed to be her distant relations, obviously much more prosperous ones. Isolde surmised that they were in their fifties, urban, middle class. They asked Jessamine if she would like to come and live with them. The offer seemed prearranged. The gentleman presented Jessamine's father with an envelope, and the half-starved man cracked it open and counted the gallets within.

Though she bore the awkward lank of a twelve- or thirteen-year-old girl, Jessamine appeared worldly enough to understand what was happening. She was being sold to a childless couple by parents who could no longer afford to feed her. It was a tearless goodbye. Jessamine climbed into the back seat of the jaunt and stared straight ahead as Cousin George turned the car around and piloted them to her new life.

Though George and Val Larkland bore little resemblance to their new charge, they doted upon her like a daughter. In the ensuing haunts, the Wilbies observed as the delighted couple poured their not inconsiderable resources into dressing, educating, and socializing Miss Bysshe, who seemed to be living up to her *Blessed* appellation. In Iz's experience, the story of a poor girl being resettled with more affluent relations rarely had such a glad result. But in scene after ghostly scene, Jessamine basked in her adoptive parents' delight. They cheered as she pirouetted on skating ice, applauded her performance as the bob-haired prince in a play, and gasped in delight at the lopsided cake Jessamine uncovered with a laughing *ta-da!* at the dinner table. As Isolde observed the apparitions of the Larklands sitting with clasped hands upon a lawn at Jessamine's graduation from secondary school, she perceived in their beaming faces a pride so pure and thorough, she wondered if it wasn't exaggerated by Jessamine's recollection. Much as the garden flowers had unfurled in honor of a first kiss, so too had the proud faces of her cousin-guardians been romanticized.

Yet, even as Iz pondered the ulterior motives of Jessamine's cousins, she had to admit there was a possibility she was projecting her own familial disappointment upon more attentive parents. It was, after all, not impossible for a father figure to be present and demonstratively pleased with his child. Happiness did not necessarily denote gullibility.

Having wended their way through scenes of first dances, boat races, choral performances, holiday dinners, and afternoon truancies to the boardwalk, the gallery of haunts began to thin and the grave-like scarp that enclosed them grew nearer.

"Not a single nithe," Warren remarked, though he still held his rose-water atomizer at the ready.

"Why should they come only to starve? There's not a crumb of misery except for her farewell to her family, and even that seemed full of antic-ipation. She had such a happy adolescence," Iz said, wondering if their snooping would only expound upon the tragedy of a young woman being whisked from history by the indifferent broom of disease. She knew not every tragedy secreted a mystery.

Nestled against the verge of the root-lathed soil was a final tender scene between a fully grown Jessamine and Cousin Val. Jessamine stood before a floor-length mirror studying the angles of her nurse's uniform while Val knelt and tugged at her hem with a needle and thread. "Nearly finished!" she said, stitching with practiced efficiency.

Jessamine smoothed the long, broad wings of her collar. Her starched nurse's cap was as tidy as a halo. Cousin Val was dressed for an evening out. A fur stole lay on the earthen bed behind them. "There we are!" Val began to stand, her skirts hampering her ascent. Jess bent to help her rise. "Oof! Can't sit on my knees for long anymore."

"You really didn't need to go to the trouble, Mum."

"Good luck is never any trouble!" She brushed the creases from her blouse, and recentered the thin tiara on her head. "On my first day at school, my mother sewed a penny into my hem, and you know what happened?"

"You met Pa."

"I met Pa. Now, let's have a look at you." Cousin Val set her chin upon Jessamine's shoulder, and the two women stared into the looking glass. "You look as smart as you are." Jessamine kissed the back of her mum's hand where it rested upon her shoulder. "I do love your pa, but sometimes I wish I'd finished school if only to prove to myself that I could."

"Of course you could've!"

"But here you are. No mights or maybes. You did it! I couldn't be more proud."

Cousin George strode into the room, appearing from a doorway to nothing, and nearly clipping Isolde as he came. She had to hop aside to keep from disturbing his passing vapor. A scarf hung over his neck, and he gripped a pair of gloves in one hand. He stopped short at seeing Jessamine in her uniform. "My god, where did my little Jess go? Who is this poised professional before me?"

Laughing, Jessamine embraced the man she now called Pa. The two squeezed one another and rocked back and forth. He said, "I keep thinking that I can't possibly be more proud of you, and you keep wringing out just a bit more pride! What am I going to do with you out of the house? I'm going to get fat and drive your poor mum crazy moping on the patio."

"No, you're not," Jessamine replied. "You are going to finish your greenhouse and fill it with flowers, and when I come home, I'm going to smell each and every one while you tell me their names." Jessamine kissed him on the cheek. Then the scene reset and Cousin Val was kneeling with her thread again.

Warren Wilby blew his nose into his handkerchief. Daubing his brimming eyes, he said, "I don't know how much more of this I can take!"

"Lucky for you, it seems this is the last of the haunts." Iz stepped around the women to inspect the loamy boundary behind the standing mirror, which seemed the limit of Jessamine's memorial. "I suppose we might as well turn ba—" Her gaze caught on something, a figure in the soil. The earth bore a small impression, no larger than a pocket compact. The design was immediately recognizable.

It was the castle top from the prince's signet ring.

As Mum repeated the phrase, "Good luck is never any trouble!" Iz set the Sepulchral Spade to the earthen wall and carved a new door around the prince's crest. Seething sparks rained upon the toes of her boots as the edges of light blazed, then cooled.

She had just connected the four sides of the portal when the relic in her hand gave a little shriek. Iz inspected the charmed artifact. A sizable splinter of the blade had sheared away, leaving behind a somewhat diminished instrument.

From over her shoulder, Warren said, "Well, that's not particularly promising."

"I'm sure it'll be fine."

Gathering his lips into an incredulous pout, Warren raised the flit-gun and sprayed his wife with rosewater.

Passing through the door Isolde had opened, they discovered a space unlike the rambling carnival behind them. The secret chamber was close, almost cramped, though still inhabited by ghosts. They were in a hospital room. The crank-operated bed stood partially raised, propping up the occupant who was in the process of having his whiskers shaved. Nurse Jessamine Bysshe rang the sides of a kidney pan with a safety razor, then dragged the blade down one lathered cheek of her comatose patient. In a chair at the foot of the bed, a man in a half-buttoned military jacket read from a book of verse, or attempted to around a series of extravagant yawns. The drowsy orator was immediately identifiable from his picture in the *Berbiton Times*: It was Lance Corporal Rudolph Atterton. Which could only make the gaunt man half-hidden under lather none other than Prince Sebastian.

As Iz and Warren intruded upon the scene, the specter of Atterton made a great show of licking his thumb to turn the page of his book. When he did so, Nurse Bysshe piped a small cry of surprise. The razor clattered to the bottom of the kidney pan as she startled to her feet.

"He's awake," she whispered.

Scowling in disbelief, Atterton peered over his book to discover that the prince's eyes were indeed open, and his gaze was roving the room. Rudolph sprang from his seat, nearly unsettling it, and rushed in behind Jessamine. He might've pounced upon the prince if his nurse had not held him back.

"Give him room," she said.

"Give him whiskey," the prince croaked and then coughed, spattering both nurse and batman with the lather that had melted over his lips. The ejection appeared to stun them all. The prince said, "My god—am I frothing at the mouth?"

Then their amazement broke. Jessamine clapped her hands together in delight, and Rudolph let out a great whoop of joy. When she moved for the door to fetch the doctor, the prince's batman grasped her by either wrist and carried her into a romping two-step about the room. He laughed as they galloped and Jessamine beamed. Her cap came unpinned and floated down to the floor.

Then the scene reset, and the tapping of Nurse Bysshe's razor gave tempo to the lance corporal's renewal of yawns.

Warren smiled, partly at the gaiety of what they had just witnessed and partly with relief that there were no more haunts to explore.

"They seemed a merry pair, didn't they?" Careful to avoid the nurse's elbow, Iz leaned about her to inspect the IV stand and the labeled bag that dripped into the prince's vein. "I had been operating under the assumption that the prince was the one to have sired an unexpected child with Miss Bysshe, but perhaps it was his orderly. After all, if Prince Sebastian was in a coma, it couldn't have been he who requested the presence of Nurse Blessed."

"But then, why would he give her the ring? Or did he give it to someone else?" Warren asked.

"I don't know," Iz murmured, turning her attention to the chamber's boundary. She pointed at the wall and the familiar welt in the soil: a second impression of the prince's signet. "It seems there's more to see."

Warren's momentary optimism clouded. "Come on, Iz. Haven't we wandered far enough from the exit?" He stared back through the way they'd come, and the boisterous haunts that lay beyond. The stairs that led back to the living already seemed uncomfortably distant.

"Think about it, War, these markings that she left—they weren't for us. They were meant for the prince, or rather King Elbert once he passed on. Jessamine Bysshe had something she wished to say to him, something she wanted to remind him of. Perhaps it's an absolution, perhaps it's an accusation, but either way, it will likely put a bow on this whole mystery. We could be done with the case tonight. We're just a slice away from all the answers." She raised the ragged Sepulchral Spade and gave it a tentative shake.

With a brave smile, Warren nodded his assent.

As she edged a new door about the prince's seal, Warren backed up to give her room to work and himself a little space to mutter through his nerves: "One last haunt, quick march back, up the stairs, and home again by sunup. I bet old Felivox is famished! I'll be lucky if he doesn't chew off my—"

He felt a fluttering sensation, like an unanticipated drop, a missed step on the stairs, and in the same instant, he saw the dancing orderly and nurse burst from his chest and continue their gambol about the hospital room.

Iz turned just in time to see her husband's accidental commingling with the specters. They shared an apprehensive grimace, before looking about for any sign of nithe-grims. The ringing of the safety razor on the surgical pan made them leap, then relax. The contact had been too brief to rally the ghouls.

"You sure about this?" Warren asked, crouching before the newly open portal. The chamber beyond seemed gloomier than the one they occupied.

"Absolutely," Iz said, sticking out her hand for his.

With interlocked and whitening knuckles, they advanced upon the gripping cold of the blue-black. It felt as if they were leaving the safety of a diving bell to explore a sunken wreck.

It took a moment for their eyes to adjust to the deeper gloom, and a moment more for them to comprehend the confused spectacle before them. The floor of the hollow was no larger than the last, but the ceiling was considerably higher. Two of the compacted walls bore the stamp of brickwork, the sills of windows, and rainspouts. A bank of firewood shored up one side. From the upper limit of the cavity, a goat-headed grotesque leered down at them. The ground underfoot resembled uneven cobblestone; a gutter split the center of the lane. Isolde discerned they were standing in a cross section of a city alley.

Yet, it was what lay at the heart of the backstreet that captivated them most. A collection of disembodied limbs, each flashing like spilled mercury, grappled about an erasure. The sparring of the tattered body parts was accompanied by snatches of a scream and pinched-off shouts, none of which were intelligible.

"This is the work of nithes," Iz murmured as she circled the nearly erased fray. She observed a hand and a shirt cuff ball into a fist, then vanish as it punched. The heel of a shoe appeared, splashed through the water in the gutter, and evaporated again. If she squinted, it did not so much seem a collection of disorganized anatomy as a squall of glowing rubbish. The nithe-grims had gnawed the specters nearly from existence, feeding off the obvious grief of the occasion. Though Iz knew that Jessamine must've been present because these were the annals of her remembrance, there was no sign of her ghost. The nithes had eaten her right out of memory.

Iz knelt to try to catch a better glimpse of one of the brawler's shoes, even as it popped in and out of being. "Something awful happened here."

"Nithes," said Warren.

"I know. I just said that." Iz looked around to find Warren spritzing the portal they'd lately come by. A pair of willowy-limbed wraiths flowed into the room. Their movements were considered, unhurried. They resembled in hue and shape a plucked wisdom tooth—pale, headless, top-heavy things, with spur-like legs reaching, pulling, searching blindly as a starfish.

"Looks like they've got us cornered." Warren worked his atomizer as he retreated. The wheezing flit-gun of rosewater seemed to discourage the ghouls only vaguely. War felt as impotent as a man ordering a cat to do this or that. The nithe-grims paused to consider (or perhaps disdain) the injunction of his perfume, then continued on their way. He strained onto toe-point to peer over their empty shoulders. "More behind these two. A lot more."

"All right. Let's try to keep calm. Panic will only whip them along." Isolde turned her attention to the wall opposite the congested entrance. The texture of the masonry made the prince's seal more difficult to find, and yet she did. His insignia puckered the drawer of a basement chute. She scowled at her fractured artifact, then began to cut into the soil with her spade once more.

This time she drew a smaller window, one that they would have to crawl through. She hoped its modesty would deter the nithes or at least conserve her blade. She had nearly finished cutting her quarter door when the blade sheared again with a screech of abused metal and a spurt of livid embers. She inspected what was left of the Sepulchral Spade, which had been reduced to something closer to a stiletto.

"We seem to be going the wrong way, my love," Warren said at her back, his voice pitched with fear. "The stairs are that way."

Iz was a little consoled to see that the nithes had taken an interest in the remnants of the specters that whirled at the heart of the haunt behind her. She ducked her head to peer through the tunnel she'd cut. The light seemed a little brighter in the adjoining alcove, even as it dimmed behind them. "If we can draw them out, we may be able to slip past them," she said, and scurried like a mouse into her hole.

Sighing resolutely, Warren put the barrel of his bug sprayer between his teeth, got onto his belly, and wriggled into the breach.

The trunk of a yew seemed to brace the room's ceiling like the pier of a bridge. At the foot of the tree, centered upon a park bench of mud and clay, sat the ghost of Jessamine Bysshe, shoulders draped with a heavy cloak. Her drawn expression loosened a little when the prince appeared—or rather the remaining half of him, his legs having been consumed by nithes at some point in the past. He came alone and dressed plainly in a cape and cap. It struck Iz as a clandestine meeting.

Jessamine stood at his approach, and her shroud draped in such a way as to conceal a subtle swelling that might've passed unnoticed in the world of the living. Here in the Nethercroft, the life nestled within her ghost shone softly as a koi in a pond. She was pregnant.

By way of greeting, the prince presented her with a large wallet, saying in a solemn, sympathetic tone, "There's enough to keep you comfortable for a while. Let me know when you settle and where, and I'll send more when it's safe to. We don't want to draw attention."

"What if I'm caught?" Jessamine asked, her brow beetling with anxiety.

"They're coming through!" Warren shouted, backing against his wife, pressing her toward the dramatic scene. The nithe-grims seemed to float to the surface of the soil like bodies after a flood. Warren continued to assail them with flower water, and the wraiths, bland as grubs, slunk forward undeterred.

"You're too clever to be caught," the prince said.

"But if I am, they'll never believe me. I'm no one," Jessamine said, as Iz skirted the edge of her bench and fled to the limit of the chamber.

"You are *not* no one." The prince raised his hand, and the signet ring upon his finger shone like a filament. Observing in snatches and over-the-shoulder glances as the prince pulled the ring free, Iz scoured the wall as much by feel as by sight, searching for a sigil, the next marker of escape.

Prince Sebastian pressed the ring into Jessamine's palm, and said, "Only in case of emergency."

"But where should I go? What should I do?" Jessamine asked.

"My thoughts exactly!" Warren shouted as he ducked a nithe's languid reach. The parasitic specters had at first seemed as closed up as umbrellas on a sunny day, but presumably the weather had turned because now they began to open. More limbs emerged and spread out from their base as their legs shifted to become grasping arms. His atomizer finally spent, Warren hurled it at the growing crowd of nithes. The canister passed harmlessly through them and thumped dully upon the banked soil.

The prince said gently, "Be patient. Avoid your family. Send them a letter. Tell them you are going abroad to study the architecture, or learn the language, or whatever you like. Remember, time is our ally, and the world's memory is short. Atterton has been deployed. I'll never forgive what he did to you, what he *made* of you. But you will have your day, yet, Lady Larkland." The final endearment made Jessamine beam and the life inside her luster like the heart of an opal. Even as Warren dodged the growing horde of wraiths, Iz gaped at that fetal crucible, shining brighter than anything in the other haunts.

Her hand brushed a familiar pattern, and she looked to discover the prince's seal under her fingertips. She drew the Sepulchral Spade from her pocket, scowling at the sliver that remained of the relic. She wondered how much farther they could run.

Warren gave an aborted squawk.

She turned in time to see the nithe-grim follow its probing arm from the floor. It seemed to be pulling itself up by Warren's hand. Its ghostly feeler wound up his wrist, snaking under his shirt cuff. War looked to his wife, who felt her face loosen with the torpor of dread. His mustache twitched, and his eyes grew bright. He grasped his belly as if he'd been gunshot, collapsed to his knees, and roared with euphoric glee.

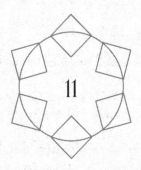

11

A RISIBLE RESURRECTION

Isolde Wilby had discovered her parents' small collection of erotic etch-ings at an age when the depictions successfully answered one or two lingering questions she had about certain aspects of the carnal event. It also introduced her to the beginning of a distinction that would take another decade to fully develop: the hazy but not insignificant difference between eroticism and pornography. She would come to believe that the former was an homage to the union, a celebration of the act entire—spiritual, libidinal, and emotional. The latter was merely an aggrandizement of the parts, divided for scrutiny and consumption like cuts of meat in a butcher's window. Pornography was parody without a greater purpose. It turned tender intimacy into an eerily detached ritual; it transformed the human body into alien anatomies. It made the familiar utterly inexplicable.

And so did her husband's sudden mirth seem false and frightening. His laughter—that sacred melody that she had always delighted in—ground upon her eardrums like the mechanical cackle of a buzzer. He arched his back and writhed upon the ground, clawing at his clothes as if consumed by invisible flames. More nithe-grims gathered around him, probing him with the languid tenderness of morticians laying out a body for burial. Their lurid tentacles caressed his flushed cheeks, tickled his throat and the jutting cords of his tendons, drawing from him all sorrow, loneliness, fear, self-loathing, and anger.

Isolde's instinct was to fly to his side, to throw herself between the nithes and his too-gentle heart. But joining him in his terminal bliss would only doom them both.

The way they had come was entirely obstructed by the headless humps of emerging nithes, summoned to the site by their feasting brothers. Iz looked to the shard that remained of the Sepulchral Spade, and knew at once there was not enough of the blade left to delve them a new route back to the stairs.

"You're too clever to be caught," said the disembodied head of the prince, whose neck was being devoured by a hungry nithe.

"Don't be so sure," Iz murmured, pulling off her boots by the heel, and her socks by the toe. She was not concerned that her close contact with the trunk of the yew would summon more nithes to their location, much as one did not dread a riot while being trampled by a mob. Disaster had already found them. Things could scarcely get any worse.

Barefoot, she sheathed the spade in her back pocket and leapt upon the yew's ropey trunk. She began to climb. What should've been a quick scrabble was complicated by the friability of the material that Jessamine's spirit had bashed into the shape of a tree. It was like attempting to ascend a desert dune. Each foothold inspired a little avalanche. Branches crumbled beneath her grip. The nithe that had finished consuming Prince Sebastian's ghost seemed to detect her presence, her apprehension, her misery, as she breasted her way up the crownless tree. It reached for her with elongating tallow-white limbs. Between those tentacles, she saw Warren, waving at her like a signalman. He shouted through joyful tears, "Come, join me, Iz! This is rapturous! I have never felt so splendid, so light, so empty! Come! Come to me!" Grasping the placket of his shirt, he pulled, inciting a spray of buttons and the baring of his broad, woolly chest.

Hair matted to her forehead by a cold sweat, Iz straddled the rotund bough that vanished into the earthen vault. She raised the broken relic, set its needle point to the ceiling, and began to carve a hatch. Golden sparks rained upon her turned cheek. Below her, Warren moaned, and the nithe stretched for her dangling ankles.

The Sepulchral Spade shattered like a droplet of toughened glass:

abruptly, violently, entirely. Isolde shouted in surprise and frustration. Then it felt as if she had dipped her toe into sparkling wine, and she looked down to see the nithe's pale spur snake over the arch of her foot.

A veil of gray light fell upon her shoulders. She looked up to see the moon framed by the ragged square she had cut. Grasping the grassy verge of the hole, she pulled herself up into the night air. Through the maze of headstones, she saw the young gravedigger, Len, pulling the reins of his mule, who was presently refusing to tow a tub-cart. Iz shouted for help. The young man leapt and screamed, startling poor Murph. For a moment, Isolde feared they might both bolt off into the night, but then the gravedigger gentled his braying beast.

Len gawped at the wild-eyed woman, caught mid-resurrection. She supposed she must look like a ghoulish jack-in-the-box. Taking advantage of his astonishment she said, "Fetch a rope. My husband is stuck. We must pull him out."

Arnold Hollins, the elder groundskeeper, appeared from behind a mausoleum, his lantern swinging in sympathy with his quick, uneven gait. "How'd you get all the way over here?" he asked.

Iz pulled herself up, but kept her hands posed on either side of the ethereal door, as if could hold it open. Through the shining frame, she watched as the nithe that had pursued her now lost interest and began to descend. Warren's laughter had turned to gasps. "A rope! Quick! My husband is in trouble!"

Mr. Hollins handled the news better than his apprentice had. He roused his understudy from his stupor with several sharp claps, commanding him to fetch as much cord as he could quickly find.

But before Len could fly upon his errand, Iz called the youth nearer, saying, "That music box—do you still have it?"

Len rummaged through his dungarees and extracted the small, naked crank and drum. She snatched it from his open palm. "When there's rope, tie one end to your mule and send the other down. I expect we'll need a quick extraction."

Holding her breath, she lowered herself back through the trapdoor into the underworld. She did not know how long it would remain open, and she did not linger upon the point because worry would only beckon the nithes back to her. Amid the breathless wheezing of her ecstatic husband, she had no choice but to smile, to call to mind the gayest days of her life. She had rarely sung since she was a girl and the neighborhood children told her she had the throat of a raven and the ear of an ash bin—an injunction that had initiated a lifelong insecurity in her voice. Yet, she began to sing now. As she slid down the crumbling trunk of the sunken yew by the light of a pregnant nurse, she warbled Warren's morning song that he sang to the kettle as he made their breakfast. It was a silly song full of obvious rhymes that meant nothing to anyone, but which was a symphony of comfort to her. The backs of the nithes that blanketed her husband bulged like feeding ticks. For the moment, those feasting parasites did not appear to notice her return. Still, she knew her song was a paper armor. They would sense her before long.

With her feet on the ground, Isolde began to turn the music box's crank while arresting the progress of its thorny drum with the side of one finger. She wound until she thought the spring might break, then cast the little instrument into the farthest crook of the tomb. It bounced and rolled like a thrown die and was, for a horrible moment, silent.

In the stillness, Iz listened to Warren's breathless rasping.

Then the mechanism came unstuck, and the skeletal toy aired its miserable tune.

The nithes that huddled about Warren twisted their barren chests toward the corner, their interest aroused by the lullaby of a suicide. Their last banquet all but finished, the nithes slouched toward the wretched diversion.

Still humming the happy morning tune, Iz cocked her head, marked the distant smudge of moonlight, and was disappointed to find no sign of a rope.

With furtive steps, she crept to her husband's side. His hands had seized into claws; his mouth was gaping and dry. His eyes, still wide, were as dull as unpolished pewter. He looked like a poisoned corpse. Isolde's warbling melody caught in her throat, and the rearmost nithe slowly turned to regard her.

Putting her ear to War's chest, she marked the lethargic drum of his heart. One beat was enough to give her strength. She looked upward again to the hatch to the living and felt her hope falter. The moonlight had been expunged. They were cut off. There would be no resurrection. She draped herself over her love like a shroud.

Then, what had seemed a caved-in exit changed into a skylight, silhouetted by straining figures. The moonlight flickered over the shoulders of the gravediggers. The rope trickled down the tree trunk, and the song that had dwindled in Isolde's throat found a second and stronger chorus.

Untying the line from around Mr. Wilby's unconscious form, Mr. Arnold Hollins deflected Isolde's expression of gratitude. "Murph did most of the work. Should we fetch a doctor?"

"There's nothing they could do. There's no antidote for nithes but hope, misery, and time. I'll take him home and put him to bed." She spread her reclaimed coat over her husband's legs as he loosed a great snore. "I could use some help with that. I'll pay, of course."

"We'll help you get him home." Mr. Hollins looked up at the sky that had begun to change with the tides of the rising sun. "First time in sixty years I've pulled a man out of the ground. It goes against the grain, you know, but I can't say I minded it."

Isolde straightened her arm, proffering her hand to shake. "Mr. Hollins, I am in your debt. When my husband revives, he will repay you in pastry, and I will compensate you with my own talents. If ever you find yourself faced with a quandary or in need of a hex, you have my card."

Isolde leapt at the knock whose authority was palpable even from the kitchen. Though it was nearly noon, her head still buzzed with the events of the night before. She had not eaten. Not slept. And yet, rather than exhaustion she felt like a racehorse bucking up to the starting gate. She needed activity, release, escape. She dried her hands on Warren's heavy apron, which she'd had to wrap three times around her waist until it formed a sarong, and went to greet her caller at a march.

Throwing the door open, she heaved a great sigh in the face of the petite man posted upon her doorstep. He looked like a jockey in search of a horse. "I came as quick as I could. Irmmie wanted to come along, too, of course, but she's still got her ankle up, and I told her to stay put. Which means she's probably running around pulling up the floorboards." He wore his baldness like a crown, fringed by an ermine ring of dense white hair. His hazel eyes, capped by the black dashes of his brows, shone with constrained emotion. He had the bearing of a working man dressed in his best clothes; his brown suit seemed the sort of thing a man of modest means might save for birthday parties and court appearances. A well-used wicker basket dangled from the crook of his arm. He opened the parcel for her inspection. Gleaming links of strung sausages lay over the foggy wax paper wrappers of cutlets and shanks. Even at a glance, Isolde saw that the hamper represented a day's wages at least. "I didn't know what to bring. So I brought a bit of everything," Warren's father said. "How's our boy?"

"He's..." She searched the air over his head for the right words and, finding none, said, "Thank you for coming, Morris."

Isolde ushered her father-in-law to the second floor via the claustrophobic servants' stairs: a dim, uneven, complaining flight that seemed designed to make a mountain goat stumble. The stairs continued on to her attic laboratory, though they did not follow them to their end. Beyond the spongy landing, the walls of the long, slim hall were shingled from wainscot to molding with picture frames that featured ancestral silhouettes, amateur watercolors of holiday sunsets, photographs of faded pink and ghostly sepia. Newspaper clippings, yellowed as a pipe smoker's wallpaper, curled from the stays that attempted to contain them. Amid this assembly of the Wilbies' lives, fortunes, and diversions—an exhibition that spanned five generations—there hung a photograph of Warren and Isolde, arm in arm and thundering down the broad steps of a courthouse. Warren, dressed in a white-and-blue seersucker suit, had his head thrown back in laughter as Iz smiled through a paper doily that she had pinned to her fringe—a mockery of a veil that only came down to her nose. She looked more like a lunatic than a bride, and Warren, caught midleap, seemed as weightless as a cloud. The photojournalist who had startled them with his flashbulb had intended to peddle the image to the papers since Isolde Wilby was already a minor celebrity. Warren had charmed the man into selling it to him instead. It was the only image they had of their wedding day.

Inside the adjacent bedroom, Warren lay like a corpse under a tortoise shell of quilts.

The sight made his father cling to the doorframe like a man gripped by a sudden spell of vertigo. Striding in, Iz rested the back of her hand against her husband's pallid forehead.

"How long has he been like that?" Morris peeped.

Isolde crossed her arms, uncrossed them, tussled her hair, and stuffed her hands in her pockets, all in the span of a heavy breath. "Since about midnight. He's not always so still. He clenches his jaw—moans and shivers. It's hard to watch, but there's nothing to do but try to keep him comfortable."

Shaking off his momentary shock, Morris crossed the room to the small fireplace opposite the heavily draped windows and opened the kindling crate to take stock. Satisfied with his materials, he rattled the grate to dislodge its cold cinders, shoveled the ashes out, and arranged the fatwood on the iron cradle. Striking a long match, he said, "Warren was kicked by a horse when he was seven years old. Doctor took one look at him and said he wouldn't last the hour. He told Irmmie to call the cousins. We'd be having a funeral. Three days later, Warren sits up, and says he's hungry. If he can shake off a kick to the head, he can shake off this. Whatever this is. A snake bite?"

"Ghouls. They sapped away every last drop of misery."

Morris rattled the chain to the chimney's damper. "That doesn't sound so bad."

"It nearly stopped his heart. And now, all that was taken from him is flooding back. You're seeing the suffering of a lifetime squeezed into one night."

"That sounds worse." As the pine wood sizzled and snapped, Morris threw open the drapes and cracked the window to draw a draft. "Any chance those ghouls will come back to take another shot at him?"

"No." Leaning over her husband and focusing upon the headboard and the open space beneath the scrollwork of two kissing swans, Isolde chalked a flawless hoop. She filled the hex with intersecting hatches. "This won't help much, but it's all I can do for him now."

"Where are you going?"

"Somewhere he can't."

"Is it safe, or are you running off to find more trouble?"

"It's a bit of both, I imagine. I heard a name last night. It made me remember someone I haven't seen in many, many years—someone who might be able to help us." Iz scrawled the final petal on her Hex of Tranquility. She stooped to kiss her husband on the cheek. The slight warmth she felt there reassured her. She stroked the rough bristles at his temples. "And, Father Morris, there's someone else I need you to feed."

He laughed. "You finally let him have a pet?"

Isolde replied with a tucked-in smile, "Not exactly."

Morris Offalman absorbed the revelation that his daughter-in-law was now keeping a dragon in her magic purse with remarkable aplomb. When she introduced Felivox, the diminutive butcher stuck his arm into the bag to shake the hand of the beast. Though the act made Iz catch her breath, she was relieved to see Morris's arm jostle but not detach while the dragon complimented him on his grip. Warren's father seemed as eager to share some of his wares as Felivox was to receive them. The last she saw—over her shoulder and from the doorway—Morris was rooting through his picnic basket and the open portalmanteau was smoking at the foot of Warren's bed. The butcher chattered on about the ideal proportions of fat, meat, and rusk. "And don't get me started on breadcrumbs! It has to be quality rusk! You want breadcrumbs in your meat—eat a pigeon!" Morris's voice carried so well, Isolde could hear him boom from the foot of the main stairs.

Seizing her coat, still dusted with grave soil, and her increasingly formless cloche from the coat tree, Isolde approached the escritoire near the front door, and flung open one of the drawers banked there. A black-handled switchblade rattled inside. She slapped it shut, and cracked a second, revealing a small-caliber pistol with a nacre handle. This, she also smacked closed. Directing an obscenity at her elusive quarry, Iz snatched open several more of the secretary's drawers until she at last found what she was looking for: a stick, some six inches long, roughly broken at one end, and warted with the nubs of pinched-off buds. "There you are."

Pocketing the twig, she hurried out the door before second thoughts or her conscience could stop her.

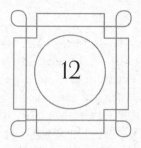

THE LUCKLESS *SANGFROID*

———◆———

Warren would never have left her side. He would've loomed over her day and night, yielding his post only to bolster her spirits with the smell of cardamom tea or lemon cake or frying back fat. He would've made himself her blanket, her bolster, her mattress; he would've summoned every doctor, quack, and conjurer in a hopeless effort to assist her revival. He would never have accepted that there were some wounds that only time and the spirit could heal.

If they could be healed.

Whatever happened, and for however long it lasted, War would've carried on reading her the morning edition, and mocking the book reviewer who never liked anything, and filling out the daily puzzle with exaggerated dramatism, and invigorating his culinary incenses while he slowly but surely lost his mind.

She had been much quicker in that regard.

After mere hours alone with his alternately wheezing and moaning form, she had begun to follow the furrows of thought that flowed down the byzantine clefts and ravines of her active mind, all draining down to the same hole: *If he were already walking the Gray Plains of the Unmade, should she not join him? Should she not greet him there? Should she not hurry out ahead?*

It was a character flaw—one of many—that she loathed in herself, but she was not equipped for vigils. She had to *do* something.

When she had told Morris that she was leaving to find "someone who might be able to help," Isolde had left it to her father-in-law to suppose she alluded to assistance for his son rather than the advancement of their ongoing investigation—which was the truth of it.

If Warren awoke, and she were not there, he would understand. Isolde wondered if Morris, who was a good and decent man, would feel as charitably about his son's wife abandoning him to chase down a lead.

A droning vacuum truck plodded down the street, sucking icy thalanium ash from the gutter. The carp snow had broken at last. After many days of estrangement, the sun was reacquainting itself with the dusty gullies of the capital city, whose inhabitants rushed out to catch the light like droughted farmers spreading pails and pots and teacups to collect a long-awaited rain. The ladies of the nursery down the street from the Wilbies' house had pushed all their bassinets onto the sidewalk, exciting mewls of pleasure and yowls of confusion from those squinting passengers. Young men tipped their spring boaters, banded in black and red, while young women, having swapped their fur stoles for bare shoulders, aired their hair and best perfume. The staffs of cafés and delicatessens dug out their terraces, opened variegated umbrellas, and dragged seating up from the basement. The legs of cane chairs clattered like a drumline as Isolde found herself shouldering through an impromptu parade as the roads emptied and the footways filled. Chauffeurs parked their jaunts and sunned themselves on their long bonnets. The blither of laughter and conversation rang from salons and boutiques, as hundreds of thousands of windows were hurriedly unstuck and flung open after weeks of being allowed to swell against the elements—seasonal and industrial.

The revelry was squandered on Isolde, who found her coat too heavy and her head too full. Warren would never have let her waste such an extraordinary noontime. He would've made her hire a tandem bicycle or take a stroll down the alameda, one of the only places left in the city that sustained trees. He would've made romantic observations about how sunlight looked better when sieved through a poplar, even a winter one, and then kiss and cuddle her until they were compelled to run home to finish what they'd begun.

All Iz wanted at the moment was a hirable car.

The few chauffeurs who had not been lulled to sleep by the dazzling sun were disinclined to waste the miracle of a clear day in a stuffy cab with a scowling fare. A particularly indolent chap, who had the brim of his cap pulled low over his eyes and his back propped upon the angled windscreen of his car, did not even look up when he asked Iz where she wanted to go. She answered that she wished to visit Gambler's Kedge. The mention of the riverboat casinos made the driver pop up like a mousetrap, his eyes shining with pleasure. "You know, miss, that's not a bad idea. Hop in."

As she rode, Isolde ruminated upon the revelations of Jessamine's haunts. The prince's orderly, Rudolph Atterton, had seemed to have shared some intimate moments with her, and was the most obvious candidate for having requested her presence to the exclusion of other nurses. By the time the prince awoke, Jessamine might've already been carrying Atterton's child.

During their clandestine meeting in the park, Prince Sebastian had reminded Jessamine of Rudolph's deployment, which may have been scheduled or hurried along to save the noble Atterton family the embarrassment of a cherished son siring a bastard by a nurse with a questionable pedigree. Clearly, the Prince of Yeardley both blamed his batman for Jessamine's condition and harbored some sense of responsibility for it. He'd said, *I'll never forgive what he did to you, what he* made *of you.*

But it was the prince's final promise that struck Isolde as the most interesting: *You'll have your day, yet, Lady Larkland.*

The Larklands were a formidable clan, both in quantity and preeminence, counting among their number nearly a dozen knights, three earls, and a duke. The Larklands were not known for being especially warm toward outsiders. Which made George and Val's decision to adopt a country waif all the more remarkable. And still, despite the obvious affection they held for her, Cousin George and Val had not given Jessamine Bysshe the great gift of their surname.

Isolde wondered how Prince Sebastian had planned to interject Jessamine into the celebrated Larkland line. By marriage? Fiat? Based on Prince Sebastian's somewhat recondite instructions, Isolde presumed that the bargain required Jessamine to bear Atterton's child in seclusion, wean it, and surrender it, either to a willing family or the state. Thus freed, Jessamine could return to claim her reward for her discretion: the title of Lady Larkland.

Though plausible, the explanation didn't sit right with Isolde. She was filling in too many holes with assumptions and guesses. And what exactly had happened in that city alley that the nithes had nearly gnawed from existence? Something traumatic, something violent, something Jessamine had wished to show the prince...

The hired jaunt barreled down the winding incline of Abalam Street through increasingly charmless blocks of workhouses, depots, and sweatshops. The sun, blocked by the chasm of the soot-cased buildings, seemed to lift her golden skirts to avoid dragging them in the murky streets that flowed like a lahar with the alchemists' ashes. Then the ground leveled, the aroma of algae pervaded the air, and the river district broke open before them like a clandestine speakeasy, and all was bunting and lights and music.

The moored riverboats were like a chorus line that stretched down the length of the boardwalk. Appropriately enough, the aging wooden vessels, which featured four and five tiers of railed galleries, evoked nothing so well as the fragile perfection of a house of cards. Tone deaf calliopes made strangers of familiar melodies under smokestacks that flowered like a fool's cap.

Iz was not surprised when her driver tried to gouge her when it came time to pay. Citing an out-of-zone fee, he quoted her a figure twice what the meter showed. Rebuffing his attempt at extortion, she said, "You just want a little more pocket money for the tables." She paid what she owed and climbed out into a crowd, half of whom appeared blotto on sunshine, the other half, drunk on the usual stuff.

There was a hierarchy to the gambling boats that pitched upon the River Zimme. The smaller crafts with peeling hulls and paper windows contained rickety tables, sticky cards, and an abundance of bathtub spirits—features that appealed to old pikers and skint students. As one's fortunes improved, one might graduate to the intermediate ships that boasted floor service, dealers in shirtsleeves, and functioning washrooms. But Isolde knew the man she had come to see would be on one of the finer boats that catered to well-heeled tourists, industrialists, professional card sharps, and the monied class who had already won the lottery of a noble birth.

Most majestic of the gambling fleet was the *Sangfroid Hand of Heaven*, a gold-wheeled, six-decked floating temple of vice.

Though no tickets were ever issued to the passengers of the permanently anchored *Sangfroid*, one of two things were required to board her: extravagant attire or an extravagant bribe, of which Isolde had neither. In her felt flowerpot of a hat and mud-spattered breeches, she looked more like a gardener in her bathrobe than a lady of Berbiton. The gatekeepers at the top of the gangplank seemed to think so, too, halting her march with raised hands and laughter.

"Think you want the barge second from the end, milady." The muscular porter in a gilt peaked cap leered down at her.

"Tell Captain Dursun that Isolde Wilby has come to call in a favor."

"No, I don't think I will." The larger porter clasped his hands behind his back and looked out over her head to signal the conclusion of negotiations.

"All right." Rummaging through the voluminous pockets of her coat, which increasingly looked like the sloughed skin of some colorless divan, Iz produced a small pad and black wax pencil, which she applied with a series of vigorous strokes. She tore the page free, folded it, and presented it to the porter, who accepted it with the pompous amusement of a man humoring a child. When he opened it, the scrap ignited like flash paper, leaving him shaking his hand in alarm rather than pain at the heatless explosion. Inspecting the hand, he discovered that the fire had left a mark: an octagonal hex of golden light consumed the breadth of his palm.

Stowing her pad and crayon, Iz said, "That is a Hex of Woe. Its bearer will suffer from insomnia, vertigo, tremors, impotence, styes, tinnitus, and galloping flatulence."

In a voice stripped of its former surety, the burly porter said, "I'll have you arrested."

Crossing her arms, Isolde shrugged. "As you please. But the only one who can remove the hex is me. And I want to see Captain Dursun."

The trim man who trotted down the gangplank wore an expression that vacillated between ebullience and exasperation. The gold braids on his shoulders looked more like a curtain tie back than an indication of rank.

The captain's cream-colored uniform, like those of his porters, had a touch of the cabaret to it, an effect increased by the tilt of his cap and his voluminous muttonchops, which swooped out from his temples and joined under his nose, a style which Warren had once described as resembling two kissing squirrels.

"What are you doing here? Where's Warren?" Captain Dursun asked.

His man answered, "She's hexed me, Captain. A Hex of Woe!" The porter swiped tentatively at the gilded polygon on his paw like a man trying to shoo a wasp.

"What is that, Isolde?"

Iz extracted a crumpled tissue from her pocket and blew her nose. "It's a Hex of Deplaquing. Dentists use it during cleanings."

"Take it off, please." No sooner was the request made than Iz grasped the porter by the wrist and, holding her hand several inches over his, enticed the hex up from his skin and into the air where it floated a moment like a ruck of light before evaporating amid a crackle of static.

Nursing his naked palm, the porter eyed Isolde as if she were a grumbling dog.

Captain Dursun smiled at the gawping couple making their way up the gangplank who'd witnessed the magical transaction. The paunchy lord and his much younger, suppler companion, who appeared to have been battered in quicksilver and dredged in sequins, shared nothing in common physically except for an open-mouthed expression of horror.

With a reassuring grin, the captain said, "Just a sample of this evening's light show! We have a celebrity aboard. Come, Ms. Wilby, I'll show you to your dressing room!"

Though what he actually did was pull Iz into the first unlit compartment they passed and lock the hatch behind them. In the gloom, they stumbled upon the ring buoys and boathooks haphazardly stowed there. When they'd found sufficient footing by the meager light of the imperfectly painted porthole, Dursun said, "All right, Iz. What on earth was all that about?"

"It's good to see you, too, Emin. Your doorman was being rude."

"They're supposed to be! Their job is to put off people who look like they just...rolled down an embankment into a ditch. Look at you! Where's your better half?"

"At home. Resting. Recovering."

Captain Dursun, who had seemed to be taking it all as some ill-conceived but merry prank, sobered at the word *recovering*. "From what? Is he all right? What's happened?"

"He will be. We had a run-in with some ghouls underground. But he's out of the woods—at least, I think so. His father's with him. I've come to impose upon you for that favor."

What lay on the other side of the favor was an event that did not need to be rehearsed. Four years prior, Dursun, then a first mate, had called upon the Hexologists to find his daughter, Sema. The police had spent the two days since her sudden disappearance in the night doing nothing but developing a theory that either Emin Dursun or his wife, Nimet, had murdered their child and staged a kidnapping to cover it up. But the Wilbies believed Dursun's account of the night in question, and their investigation eventually led them to the nest of a vampiric chimney wraith and a depleted, but still living, Sema. When the Wilbies returned his daughter to him, Dursun had been unsatisfied by their modest fee. He'd insisted upon the standing debt of an unspecified favor, which they could call in at any time. Thus far, Warren had used the "favor" as a pretense to invite the Dursuns over to dinner once or twice a season. They had become one of the Wilbies' good friends.

"Anything you need. Is it money? Are you in some sort of trouble?"

"No, no, I'm just chasing down a lead in a case. I need to speak to someone, and I suspect I'll find him aboard."

"Is that all? Well, tell me who it is. I'll drag him down by the collar right now." His smile lifted his cheeks and his magnificent slate-colored whiskers along with them. He seemed relieved by the modesty of her request.

"I don't think he'll cooperate if he knows I'm coming."

Emin's momentary joviality drooped, as did his chops. *"Cooperate? What do you intend to do to him?"*

"Just talk. A short conversation that he may or may not wish to have." Iz had little facility for putting others at ease. Her effort to reassure only served to make Emin frown.

"All right, who is it?"

"I believe he's currently operating under the name Obelos."

He rubbed his mouth and worked his jaw as if he would spit out a piece of gristle. "He's a whale, Iz."

"I know."

"And you also know I don't own the ship, and my employer would be very displeased if I were to upset the man who had paid for his house."

"I'll be discreet."

"Oh, good. I'll call the fire brigade."

They mounted the service stairs at the heart of the ship to save time and also the tender sensibilities of persons who were unaccustomed to rubbing elbows with someone who looked like a ragpicker. Even the staff in starched dickeys were taken aback by the sight of their captain sneaking in an obvious stray.

The high rollers congregated on the exclusive sixth deck of the *Sangfroid Hand of Heaven*. Though the reclusive sun shone outside, one would never know it from the insulated ebony penthouse, which would've benefited from a window or two as the reek of cigars and ambergris cologne weighted the air like gun smoke.

The sixth deck was split into a series of three spacious dens, each of a theme, none of any subtlety. The primary materials employed were brass, crystal, lacquer, and glass, all wrought in service to the contemporary style that critics liked to describe as "lithe" or "sleek" or that most slippery of adjectives, "modern." Isolde had always found the aesthetic impersonal and sterile. While her home could absorb clutter with aplomb, contemporary decor would be entirely spoiled by the presence of a dropped scarf or abandoned saucer. Its beauty relied upon its emptiness, and so followed its soul.

The first den was a tribute to big-game hunting, though the designer seemed poorly acquainted with the anatomy of any animal. The beastly pillars that cornered the bar and legged the tables and backed the chairs were all distended, their prominent features flattened, leaving the gilded rhinoceroses, antelopes, and leopards to look less like something plucked from a savanna and more like something peeled from the road. Lording the heart of the room was a seven-sided felted table occupied by a stately dealer and six players of varying degrees of sobriety and dismay. The clatter of clay chips landing upon a central pyre accompanied the stirring of ice at the bar. Captain Dursun needn't have worried about Iz's presence exciting the offense of these noble guests, who were so absorbed by their game they would have, in all likelihood, overlooked the tromping passage of a hippopotamus.

The second den was a tribute to the intricacies of industrial machinery, or rather what the designer knew of those marvels, which apparently began and ended with the cog. Everywhere she looked, the room humped with the round backs of gears and their toothy crenelations. And again, everything focused upon an immaculately groomed gambling table attended by somewhat more rumpled guests. A pair of bored young women with ostrich feathers in their headbands danced to the admirable efforts of a four-piece band.

"He's in there," Captain Dursun said behind a cupped hand inside the short corridor that joined the dens. "Should I introduce you, or do you want to just slip in?"

"I can see myself in from here. Thank you, Emin."

"I know Nimet will want to bring Warren soup."

"And I know he'll want to eat it." Iz smiled tightly.

The captain of the *Sangfroid* touched his cap and left.

The final den provided what seemed the most fitting subject for the designer's dubious talents: an ode to space. An excess of wenge wood panels flattered the brass planets and crystal stars in orbit about the central table. The dark floor and low lighting gave one a sense of what it would be like to toe the edge of infinity. The sublime effect was only a little tarnished by the pair of crescent moons that framed the bar like celestial parentheses.

Decor aside, the tenor of the room was palpably different: The air was clearer and the ambient noise more subdued. Isolde had to hunt for a view of the gaming board, which stood hidden by the backs of whispering spectators. Raising herself on the footrail of the bar, she glimpsed a lustering black-and-gold roulette wheel. A snowy-haired croupier stood over the glamorous dial. The table's lone gambler, who sat with his back toward her, clacked together a stack of ivory betting plaques. The chips rang out like a guiro.

"Would sir care to place a bet?" The croupier posed the question almost casually.

"*Luck*," the faceless bettor intoned, his voice like warm water funneled into the ear. The bartenders stilled their swizzles. The whisperers swallowed their tongues. "It is luck that hobbles the general's horse and aims the errant shot. Luck is love's pander, its broker, its pimp. Luck rules on a golden throne under a mantle of rags. Spendthrift and skinflint is luck." Again, he drained his stack of plaques into his palm. "Luck is the universe's thumb placed upon the unequal scales of history. Luck is the primordial sea from which all magic—coherent and entire—once sprang. It is not upon providence but the pivot of misfortune that all existence turns."

His betting chips repeated their tattoo. "Equalizer luck, judicious luck, objective luck: We sit here today to worship you, to lay our offerings upon your altar—god maker, bone breaker luck. You do not smite us for our misdeeds nor exalt us for our noble efforts. You do not favor the lord over the lout or the saint over the cretin. You are the manifestation of righteous ambivalence. Forgetful, omniscient, ungrudging luck. You make wizards out of babblers, and cinders of empires. Hearken to me, unhearing luck!" His voice rose as if lifted by ecstasy.

"Would sir care to place a bet?" The croupier asked with undiminished nonchalance.

"Should I place my bet or should I retire? What do you think, Wilby?"

Still on her perch at the bar, Iz's gaze darted about, searching for what had given her away. And then she found his face, reflected and distorted in the polished planet that hung over the wheel of chance. From that heavenly orb, Obelos stared back at her, eyes blazing like boiling craters on an alien moon.

13

UPON THE HIPS OF MARTYRS

A peace offering." Isolde presented the broken twig through the allée of the parted crowd.

Rather than turn to face her, Obelos beckoned with a raised and curling hand. "Put it on the board."

"I don't gamble," Iz said.

"If you win, we will talk. If you lose, you will wish you had not come. Or you may turn around and go home, if you like."

Screwing up her courage, Isolde marched to the table. The crowd in their spangling shifts and bespoke suits made room for her as if she were a mud-bellied dog. She positioned herself behind an empty chair and sized up the betting board. She glanced at Obelos, who continued to monitor her with unnerving intensity; she returned his stare in kind. His poreless ocher skin looked as incapable as a soap bubble of holding a wrinkle. His eyebrows were as brief as hyphens; his dark eyes deep as verse. His cheeks were clean-shaven, and his black hair lay slicked to his head, choices which complemented his meticulously tailored tuxedo. He didn't appear to have aged a day since the last time she saw him. He still looked like an upperclassman.

And yet his voice was as resonant and commanding as a magistrate when he said, "Would madam care to place a bet?"

"Fine," Isolde snapped, stamping the twig down on the golden six.

The gallant croupier glowered at the twig on his board as if he expected it to leap up and bite him on his nose. In a strained voice, he said, "If madam would care to visit the cashier's station, betting chips may be acquired in exchange for gallets or certified check."

"Do they accept kindling?" Iz asked.

"No." The croupier pushed his gold-plated rake across the felt, preparing to brush the lady's rubbish from the board when the handsome gambler intervened.

"I'll vouch for her, Shelley. Let the lady's wager stand as played, please. I'm all in on seven." Obelos slid his betting plaques across the grid until they shared an edge with Isolde's square. The decision elicited titters from the ladies at Isolde's back.

Announcing an end to betting, the croupier turned the wheel in one direction and spun the ball in the other. Isolde ignored the black-and-gold blurring wheel. The crowd oohed in anticipation. The ball rattled over the deflectors and clattered across the pockets. Still, Isolde did not look away from her former classmate's face. His mouth moved, animated by the inaudible patter of a gambler begging the universe for a win, or so it would likely seem to those who didn't know him as well as she did. Iz suspected what the result would be, but she wished to watch the cause of it. She wanted to see him cheat.

A blue spark flickered deep within Obelos's eyes.

Their audience gasped and laughed incredulously, then erupted in a triumphant cheer as the croupier announced: "The winner is six. Congratulations, madam. You've won a stick."

The wizard looked at Isolde and smiled like a man rousing from a beautiful dream.

They walked along the top tier of the deep boardwalk on dark and pitted ties. Obelos strolled with his hands clasped behind his back and a distant expression on his face.

"You knew where to find me," he said at last. "You've been spying."

"Not really. We have a mutual friend in Captain Dursun. A while ago he mentioned a whale: a patently wealthy and fantastically unlucky gambler; a man who never won. Not once. This whale never showed a hint of frustration. Emin said the gambler sat calmly through it all as if he were a coachman, snapping the reins of the earth. It all struck me as less than unlikely. It was obvious his whale was a cheater. I asked Emin the name of his impossibly unlucky gambler. When he told me, I knew it was you."

"You did, did you?"

"Yes. Obelos was the name of your left shoe. You had such a silly habit of naming inanimate things. Left shoe Obelos, right shoe Angelos, and a hat called Frank. You still have them?"

The gambler smirked. "I do. Your memory was always incredible...and exasperating."

"Thank you. What I don't know is why you've staked yourself upon the lap of luxury just to bleed your treasure."

Obelos paused to let a scrum of reveling students in flat caps cross ahead of them. The beardless lads carried one of their own upon their shoulders, though it wasn't clear that he was enjoying the ride. "Did no one ever tell you it was unseemly to gloat? You won, Wilby. You always did seem to be touched by luck."

Isolde was quick to reply: "That wasn't luck. You did that. And what was all that nonsense back there about primordial magic and babbling wizards? Skating a little close to the truth, aren't you?"

"Not at all." Burying his hands in his pockets, Obelos watched the pod of students hurl their peer into the chilly water. Thrashing in the less than pristine river, the youth bayed like a hound. "People enjoy seeing an over-confident man disappointed. They like to see a braggart humbled. It fills them with such self-confidence. If you are willing to fall off a horse at a dead gallop, the public will clap you on the back and let you fish through their pockets."

"And yet, you do not. You gain nothing. You only lose."

"What's your theory, Wilby? You always have a theory."

"You manipulate the roulette ball—when necessary—to ensure that you don't win. You're laundering money for someone. Obviously, the owner of the *Sangfroid* is invol—"

Obelos threw back his head and laughed with seemingly genuine delight. "Oh, Isolde! You really think I'm such a tawdry fellow? Money is so dull."

"Said the man with too much of it."

Isolde had been so focused upon the wizard, so bewildered by his shuffling dispassion that she hadn't noticed he was not strolling idly but was leading her away from the pandemonium that surrounded the docked casinos. Already the bunting, vendors, and opportunistic pigeons were behind them. Ahead, the underside of the Vaward Bridge loomed. That famous stone roost for bats cut a swath of midnight across the dazzling sky. As they stepped into its shadow, Isolde suffered a flicker of foreboding, a misgiving that was not improved when Obelos turned and began to trudge up the paved cant toward the cleft of the immense abutment. And still she followed, holding the hem of her coat balled in one fist, laying her other hand upon the lichen-slicked slope to assist her scuttling ascent. The wizard appeared not at all inconvenienced by the climb. He scaled the slippery embankment in his black-and-white wingtips with all the surety of a funicular.

Isolde was relieved to crest the summit, but less pleased to see they were not alone. Against the cleft of the buttress, squatting among the dayless murk, was an enormous figure dressed in a much-abused gabardine cape. An oilskin hat drooped over his face. The stench of urine was unmistakable, and yet it was the reek of goat that made Isolde lift a knuckle to shield her nose. The titanic beggar who sat under the slow drip of weep holes was quite obviously a thinly disguised troll.

Isolde could not see Obelos's expression when he asked her in a neutral tone, "Why did you come?"

She gripped the stick of chalk in her pocket, more for its familiar reassurance than the protection it promised. "Perhaps I came to apologize."

"No." The wizard made a quick beckoning gesture to the troll. The creature stood with the slow and sawing difficulty of a rising elephant, stretching to a height of some nine or ten feet. The insufficiency of its apparel was equally conspicuous. A considerable gut, bristled as a boar's, pooched from the bottom of the tattered rain slicker. Its knees protruded from torn trousers like burl from a tree trunk. The new angle afforded Iz a clear view of a row of unpaired tusks.

Wordlessly, the troll stepped to one side. Obelos stalked into the masonry and vanished.

Alone with the troll, Iz asked, "Am I allowed to follow?"

The troll drummed the ground with bloated, lard-colored toes.

"All right," Iz said, and pulling her cloche snug on her head, strode into the stonework.

It felt a little like passing through an energetic curtain, but one that first warmed the marrow of her bones, then swept upward through the layers of her muscles, fat, and skin, finally stirring the follicles of her hair as it dissipated.

She stood upon the wide sill of a bay window facing a deep, sunny tract of polished travertine. The vaulted hall was split into several levels. A breezy mezzanine, freighted with crowded bookshelves, crossed above a capacious water feature—or was it a lap pool? Around this tiled oasis, colorful rugs, ottomans, and pillows softened the veinless pale stone. Gold-footed pillars, stout as elms, partitioned a gallery of glass cabinets and posed garments. Suits of armor and brocaded robes stood wired in heroic poses. Something verdant, like the pseudo-spearmint aroma of ripening peaches, perfumed the dustless air. The space evoked a resort, a manor, and a museum all at once.

Isolde looked over her shoulder through the grandiose window's grander view. Outside, a sapphiric sea billowed and foamed.

"I never asked for an apology," Obelos said. She turned again in time to see him pass behind one of the ostentatious columns. She climbed down from the sill and stamped after him. Her heels rang like gunshots through the wizard's vast home. Around the pillar, she found him loitering over a glass box set upon a soapstone plinth. At first, she could only see the velvet cushion inside, but not what sat upon it. "I asked for privacy. I asked you to leave me alone." Drawing nearer, Isolde saw what occupied the pillow: the thicker end of a stick of hazel wood, neatly pruned on one end and roughly snapped at the other. Opening the hinged top of the display case, Obelos withdrew Isolde's twig from his pocket and set it alongside its other half. "You know what I am. You know what they would do to me if they found me."

"I regret breaking the wand. It was a gift. A rare one. I was...rash."

"I think 'deceitful' is the word you're looking for. I trusted you. I more than trusted you."

"And I could not follow where you wished to go."

He shut the case gently. "Yet, here you are again. What do you want, Wilby?"

"My husband—"

"You're married. Yes, I know. I've read the papers. The Hexologists—hunters of wraiths, slayers of bugbears, champions of the common pleb, determined sleuths in search of the truth—at least, when the truth pays the fare." Returning to the central hall, Obelos rounded the pool, and Iz followed, inspecting the tiled basin, whose waters were darker than they had first seemed. She could neither see its bottom nor guess its depth.

"Last night he was bitten by a nithe-grim. Several of them, and—"

Halting, Obelos regarded her with an expression of surprise. "What were you doing in the Nethercroft?"

"Pursuing a lead. Being reckless. We escaped, and Warren is recovering at home. I hoped you might have an unguent or talisman or—"

"I'm a wizard, not a necromancer. There's nothing I can do. And you know there isn't."

Obelos positioned himself beside a tall, felt-topped table, the surface of which was hardly bigger than a dinner plate. Upon this disc of green wool sat a pair of age-yellowed dice, one slightly larger than the other. Obelos shook and threw the dice with automatic proficiency, as if it were a nervous or unconscious compulsion. He scarcely marked the outcomes of his rolls, though Isolde did: The result was always an unlucky one and two. She supposed they were loaded dice, though on further study, she saw that sometimes the smaller die came up one and the larger two, and other times the reverse. If they had been rigged to always come up as one or two and no other number, she would've expected to see a thrown pair, but the dice steadfastly refused to match.

"Is it a trick of the throw? Something in the wrist?" she asked, unable to contain her curiosity.

Obelos presented her with the dice. "See for yourself."

She accepted the warmed cubes with cupped hand. Rattling them thoroughly, she threw them on the table, and snorted in bemusement to see the same result: a one and a two. She tried several more times as Obelos wandered nearer the reflection pool that dominated his palatial home. Answering her question before she could pose it, Obelos said, "They're cursed. They were made from the hip bones of a pair of martyrs who lived under the Felpurian Empire nearly two thousand years ago. Marcus and Evanne were husband and wife and practitioners like us. By all accounts, they were harmless and well liked. But there was a drought and the lords of the land decided that Marcus and Evanne were responsible for it. They ordered the pair stoned to death in a dry riverbed. The drought continued for another two years. At some point, their bones were collected and turned into a number of holy relics, though the ones in your hand are all that remain."

Isolde studied the tragic objects with new eyes. "Why have them?"

"Because they're bad luck. Wilby, why did you really come?" He removed his tuxedo coat, halved it, and lay it upon a velvet pouf. He began unfastening the links on the cuffs of his starched white shirt. Isolde wondered if he meant to go for a swim.

"Before you were Obelos, you had another name: Alexander Larkland."

"Oh, you've come to remind me of the relations I disappointed? How kind!" As he rolled up his left sleeve, she saw the top of his forearm, just beneath the elbow joint, was encased in what seemed a vambrace of gilded wire. The openwork cuff came to a point just above his wrist, concluding in a round electrum stamp that called to mind the mouth of a lamprey.

She supposed it might be some sort of arcane weapon. If he wished to intimidate her, Isolde refused to give him the pleasure. She carried on: "No, I wanted to ask you about someone. Did you ever hear of a relation— an adopted one—named Jessamine Bysshe."

He frowned. She had surprised him again. She knew that if there was one thing a wizard did not enjoy, it was surprises. He recouped his implacable calm with a cursory sigh. "I remember Jess. Rather, I recall hearing about her. She broke my great-aunt and uncle's hearts. Lady Valerie and Lord George Larkland could scarcely believe it when their darling Jessamine abandoned them. As I recall, she sent them a letter or two saying that she had soured on her profession and had decided to see the world, seek her fortune, chase the winds."

"Lady Valerie and Lord George loved her, then?"

Obelos ran his cupped hand over the curious brace on his arm, exciting, or perhaps revealing, a green miasma that roiled from the wire like steam from a sewer. "Loved her more than anything, I think. After she left, they talked about her for the rest of their lives. Uncle George died a decade ago, and Aunt Val wasn't far behind him. Couldn't survive another heartbreak, I suppose."

"Do you really think Jessamine gave them up just for a change of scenery?"

"Most of my relatives believed that Jessamine had gotten herself in a family way and had run off with a handsome vagrant."

Isolde cocked her head. "From what I understand, she didn't change her surname after the adoption. She was always Jessamine Bysshe, never Larkland."

"My kin did not exactly welcome her with open arms. They would not allow her to take our hallowed appellation, so she kept her birth name. The Bysshes were purportedly second or third cousins of ours, though there was some argument about that. Most of the family believed that George and Val had run out and snatched a field mouse off the side of the road. Of course, when Jessamine went missing, my aunt and uncle wanted to involve the police, hire investigators, bleed dry every account in search of her. The elder statesmen of the family wouldn't hear of it. They said it would be unseemly; it would only compound the family's shame. I imagine my brethren were just relieved she was gone."

"And George and Valerie consented? If it had been my daughter, I would've—"

"Noble families are strange, Wilby. There are certain pressures that are hard to explain to someone who hasn't grown up with them. Suffice it to say, the royal court is full of prisoners. I'm fortunate to have escaped. I can't imagine how it all affected Jessamine. I always wondered if she didn't run away just to be rid of us." He shook his head lightly, dispelling long unexplored memories. "But why are you asking about her? Is she part of your investigation? Did you find her?"

"I'm sorry, I can't say."

"Ah, yes! I forgot, you're 'One Way Wilby.' For all your philanthropy, you're still quite a stingy little girl."

"And I suppose you consider yourself a patron of the race?"

Obelos peered at her, the distant thunderclouds behind his eyes flashing with lightning. "There it is! There it is at last. The real reason you sought me out. You could've interviewed another Larkland about Jessamine. But you wanted to know about this 'patron of the race.' Who is it? What have you seen?"

Isolde crossed her arms, irked at just how easily he had discerned her motives. "Someone portaled a mandrake into my cellar, and a flock of talking birds has been harassing us. Seemed like the work of a wizard. I only know of one."

"Birds, you say?" He grimaced with disgust. "Filthy creatures." Approaching the edge of the abysmal pool, Obelos held his gold-braced arm over the still expanse. A green smoke began to seep from the alloyed medallion and drift downward. When the vapor touched the water, it broke and bled along like morning fog. "Whoever this *patron of the race* is, whoever is pestering you, it isn't me. I consider myself more of a reluctant neighbor of the race. But why are you doing this, Wilby? You don't care about the peerage or their dirty laundry. Why stick your neck out?"

"Oh, you know me—can't leave well enough alone."

He rolled his fingers, animating the rills of mist that fell from his hand with helices and purls. "That's the sort of excuse you trot out when you overwhip the cream. Doesn't seem quite sufficient for someone who nearly fed her precious spouse to a pack of nithes."

Isolde felt a great warmth flood her face. "That's not what happened. And I think a much more fascinating question is why a man in his prime would choose to live alone under a bridge."

"Because it's preferable to having lunch with his mother." Obelos smiled thinly. "I do understand a child cannot avoid facing their parents, either in person or in absentia. Really, the only question is whether the confrontation will be aired as words or forced underground as deeds, impulses... obsessions. One way or another, we all address our makers."

The wizard had succeeded, perhaps intentionally, in putting together two uncomfortable thoughts that Isolde had been doing her best to keep separate in her mind: the fear that her doggedness was a danger to Warren and the fact that she had dedicated so much of her life to solving other people's mysteries while doing so little to investigate her own. What was she trying to prove? That she was capable of unraveling any knot? That she could find her father, or at least discover his fate, if she really wished to? But then why search for a man who was so determined to be lost? He didn't just vanish. He had escaped, bit by bit and over many years. As far as Iz was concerned, there was no mystery about who he had wanted to get away from.

"This isn't about my father," Isolde said.

"I was talking about my mother, Wilby. You're showing your hand."

"And you're leading the conversation. Let's get back to my original question. If it's not you behind the birds and the mandrake, who could it be? One of our old dons? A foreign power? The military? What about—" Before Isolde could press him further on the question of who else might be behind her recent bedeviling, the obsidian water began to boil.

The tentacle that broke the surface resembled a fleshy spearhead, one padded in a hundred suckers, each big as an eggcup and all pulsing as one. That terrible palm was nearly as large as Isolde herself. Curling into a bowl, the tentacle caught the dripping green vapor. The creature's proximity appeared to excite the relic on the wizard's arm, or perhaps Obelos merely opened the mystic tap. The trickling gas turned into a cascade. As the mist fell into the leviathan's eager pores, Isolde inquired in a voice cinched by fear: "What is it?"

"A sink of bad luck. A hungry curse. An awful pet. It is the *Exoris uthidae*."

Though it seemed taxonomical, the name did not inspire in her recognition. This was a behemoth outside of her knowledge. "Why do you have it?"

He looked over his shoulder at her as the green fog continued to flow. "Oh, Wilby, you remind me why echoes make the best houseguests: They only answer, never ask." He closed his fist, concluding the misty dribble. "I trust you shan't call on me again."

He twitched his finger, and the tentacle sprang from the water. She scarcely had time to gasp. The monstrous arm wrapped around her, jerked her into the air, and dragged her into the fathomless deep.

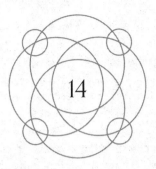

14

AN ENUMERATION OF SINS

⬡

The crush of water, compounded by the tentacle's vicious grasp, left Isolde feeling like one of Morris's sausages. As the light above faded to a dusky hue arrayed with the bubbles of her final breaths, she wondered if she weren't mostly filler: a person-shaped assemblage of breadcrumbs with just enough flesh and blood to hold her together. Warren possessed so much humanity and stood in such proximity to her that it was sometimes easy to imagine his ample compassion was her own. But seeing Alexander again after so many years, and perceiving the resentment that he obviously still carried, reminded her that one could not be human by association nor live with a borrowed heart. Were this the end of her, perhaps a sea monster was the confessor she deserved.

The leviathan released her as suddenly as it had snatched her up. Isolde found, amid her disoriented relief, that she was now squeezed inside some sort of tube, evidently one that had been capped. Probing and scratching the algae-slicked blockage, she opened her eyes upon an imperfect gloom. In that thin light, she could just make out wooden staves. She opened her mouth and screamed with the effort of trying to break them. The bubbles ran down her neck rather than up from her head, alerting her to the surprising fact that she wasn't fighting her way to the surface; she was clawing her way down.

Then the world began to teeter.

The rain barrel toppled, unsettled by her flailing, and vomited her onto the floor of the alley. Water slapped upon the wall behind her, carrying the silt of carp snow off toward the street. On hands and knees and through the limp fringe of her hair, she stared back into the tipped cask. A tangled sigil shone upon the slimy base. The pattern darkened rapidly, leaving behind the blaze of a squid with knotted arms.

Isolde spit to clear the taste of stagnant water, even as she absorbed her surroundings. She recognized the rubbish bins, the zigzag of empty clotheslines, the dented rainspout. She was standing in her own alley.

Rising, she opened her fist to regard the objects that dug into her palm. She had not meant to take them. The cursed dice carved from the hip bones of martyrs had still been in her hand when Obelos's pet had seized her. Slipping the tragic relics into her pocket, she discovered her sodden cloche.

"Not the worst ride home I've had," she said, and twisted out her hat.

In undershirt and boxer shorts, Warren lay sprawled upon the living room sofa displaying all the poise of a fallen tree. His arms and legs were spread to better absorb the draft from the vacant fireplace. He felt the sort of emptiness that follows a concerted weeping—one that did not so much run its course as run dry. At the same time, having split a hamper of meat with a dragon, he felt a terrible fullness. Warren longed for the relief of one good belch followed by the more generous embrace of death.

The back door banged and Isolde squished in from the kitchen dripping like an overwatered window box.

"You're up," she said. Warren could tell by her rounded shoulders she was exhausted. Still, she rallied a thin smile for him. "How are you feeling?"

"Half-dead and overfed. You've gone off and had an adventure without me. No fair."

Isolde asked if Papa Morris were still about, and when Warren said that he'd just sent him home to look in on his mother, Isolde began to strip.

"If I had the strength, I'd join you," Warren said.

Relieved of her drenched attire, she snatched up the blanket draped across the wingback chair. Making a little cocoon for herself, she said, "Probably for the best. I smell like a pond."

"Should I make a fire?"

"No. I'm warm enough."

"Should I ask where you went?"

Isolde snuggled her chin into the woolly mass. "I wish you would. I'm tired of carrying this millstone around by myself. I could use a little help with it, honestly. But I know you're completely spent, and I don't want to—"

Warren interrupted her by raising a heavy hand and letting it drop again. "As long as you have something to say, I am ready to listen."

The Wilbies kept few secrets from each other as a matter of preference, habit, and convenience. Secrets were burdensome and demanding of regular attention; a secret had to be nursed at odd hours and dandled in the night. Still, Isolde had always been forthright with her mate that there were things she was obliged to keep to herself—secrets that were not hers to share. Warren knew that his beloved carried around a mystery or two.

And yet he could not conceal his astonishment when Iz began by confessing that not only did wizards still linger in the world, but she knew one, and had been to see him that very afternoon.

She admitted it all plainly, taking care to articulate her new discoveries regarding Jessamine's experience with the Larklands. It did not escape Warren's notice that, though she began with the shocking admission that she shared a private history with a wizard, she quickly retreated into the impersonal details of their investigation.

Isolde concluded: "What I still don't understand is why the prince promised Jessamine a title and the Larkland name. Strikes me as an elaborate reparation for a sin that wasn't his own. And why did Rudolph Atterton desert his post only to engage such an unconvincing stand-in? Cowardice? Shame? The Attertons are rich; he gave up a fortune when he ran off. If he really did run. I'd like to talk to his family. The papers made it seem like they gave up searching for him out of embarrassment, but maybe they found out exactly what happened and suppressed it."

"It wouldn't be the first time a noble family sat on the truth. Still, the Attertons aren't exactly a friendly lot. If you want to talk to them, we'd have to call in a favor, maybe hand a few out." Warren rolled his head, exciting a series of pops from a neck that had spent too many hours propped in bed. "Would you like to tell me about the broken wand?"

Isolde sighed into her throw. "The short version of the story is that there was a period of time while I was at university when I . . . dabbled."

Warren's brows rose with surprise. "Perfectly natural! Why, there was a young lad in my third year—"

Isolde huffed a dry laugh. "Not like that. I dabbled with magic. Wizardry. Off-limits stuff. The administration at Wynn University of the Thaumatic Arts were always banging on about the institution's absolute intolerance for banned magic. The state had them under a magnifying glass, looking for any excuse to shut them down, which of course they eventually did. We all knew if you were caught fooling around with the taboo stuff, the university wouldn't protect you. No, they'd march you down to the police station and drop you off. Due process for people caught trafficking in illegal magic was said to be a midnight hearing and a morning hanging."

"Forbidden fruit, secret courts, risk of death—how could you resist?"

Iz smiled, the expression quickly shifting from puckish to wistful. "Alex caught me trying to summon an efreet."

"A fire jinn? Aren't those dangerous?"

"Wildly. But I was naive. I wanted to sling fire, and for that, you need an efreet in your pocket. Luckily, I failed. Less luckily, Alex caught me in the act. I thought that would be the end of me. But, no. He was fascinated. He wanted in. He did not feel particularly at home with his family. He longed for a different path; he was incautious, restless, ambitious—all my favorite things. He was also, it became quickly apparent, far more talented than I was with conjuring and spell craft." Iz looked upward at distant memories. "I went from being the tutor to the tutee in a matter of weeks. We had such a way of egging each other on. We went deeper and deeper. It was intoxicating."

"And intimate?" Warren asked, being careful to keep his tone light.

Isolde shrugged beneath her pile, bared a shoulder, and raked the skin with her nails. "Not in the way you might think. Part of Alex's trouble with his family stemmed from his perfect indifference to weddings or christenings or any of that. He was married to his mind. And happily so. He was a brother to me. As an only child, that was something I'd always wanted."

"What happened?"

Her methodical itching shifted to the tops of her arms. Warren couldn't decide whether it was a ritualized sort of self-consolation or flagellation. Isolde's voice was flat, her expression slack as she answered, "For a time, I tried to follow him, I tried to keep up. I didn't have the same facility or control that he did. He gave me a gift—a wand. He had pared it from the Hazel of Want, at great risk to himself. He didn't know it, but even then, I was realizing that I was out of my depth and ready to swim back to shore. But I . . . I also loved him, and I wanted to impress him. We had always said that if there were only two wizards left in the world, at least we wouldn't be alone."

Isolde seemed to realize she was scouring herself. Clasping her hands together, she continued on more quickly, as if she just wanted to be done with it. "There was an accident. I hurt him. I could've done much worse than hurt him. I broke the wand he'd gone to such pains to retrieve. I told him that I was finished with wizardry, and so he said he must be finished with me. We did not part on good terms. I promised to keep his secret and my distance, and that was the end. He left school, left his family, and vanished from the world."

Warren leaned forward and capped both her hands with one of his. "I'm sorry, Iz. What a torment. What a burden. But I'm glad you didn't go any deeper. I'm glad you swam back to land, even knowing all that you had to give up to do it."

"I couldn't take you with me today, but I still felt like you were there."

He sat back with a grunt of satisfaction. "Oh, I am everywhere! I am a vapor in tweed." His cheeks plumped; there was some color in them at last.

"Your undershirt is on backward." She sketched a six-pointed hex in the air with her finger—a Hex of Reversion. His shirt spun on his torso, the sleeves briefly dissolving to accommodate the passage of his arms.

When the collar realigned, he stretched his shoulders appreciatively. "That is better. Of all your hexes, I think that is the one I love the most. So, any chance your wizard friend likes to potter with mandrakes or talkative birds?"

"No, he's not our man. He just wants to be left alone, especially by the likes of me." Dragging her blankets along like an unwieldy cape, she crawled onto his lap. "How are you feeling? Still overfull?"

He smiled. "Oh, you know me, dear—always a little peckish."

THE SYREN AND THE HARBOR SEAL

It was nothing short of a miracle that Warren had been able to secure a brief audience with Duke Atterton the very next day. Though Isolde's name carried some cache, the nobility did not particularly like her, nor did they wish to appear to hearken to a commoner's whim. In order to secure the afternoon appointment, he'd had to plum several wells of goodwill, promising (among other things) that the Hexologists would attend and bless the duke's sister's biannual séance. Lady Lily's gatherings were a well-known social affair that mostly involved sitting around a table, holding hands, and speaking in quavering tones.

Warren was waiting for the right time to break that undesirable news to Iz.

At the moment, though, he was consoling himself with the strains of the spirited combo playing over the hyaline of their hired jaunt. When they had originally boarded the dusty vehicle, the driver had asked if he should turn the music down. Warren had consulted his wife, who was so lost in thought, she only replied, "I already had one, thank you." Seeing it would not bother her, he adjured their chauffeur to let the band play on, then sat forward to enjoy the racket through the little window in the privacy glass.

The rollicking music broke off abruptly. The station announcer spoke in a rush. "Pardon the interruption to our usual programming, but we go live now to the royal château in anticipation of an announcement from Princess Constance regarding the condition of His Majesty King Elbert III."

The mention of the princess and the king snapped Isolde from her reverie. The driver lifted his hand to the hyaline's knobs. Fearing he would switch it off, she intervened. "Leave it, please."

"I'm turning it up, miss. I like the princess. She has a voice like warm custard poured right down your neck."

Before Iz could answer, the broadcast crackled with an excess of applause. A moment of reverent silence ensued, a quiet punctuated by the princess's full, dulcet tones. "Citizens of Luthland, I come to you today not as a daughter of the House of Yeardley, nor as a princess of the realm. I come to you as my brother's sister. It is a familial bond many of us share. And is not family the basis and inspiration for all governance? We are blessed by the brotherhood of the House of Peers and its sister, the Court of Commons. Our magistrates, our institutions of order, our armed forces, our leaders of industry are cousins to one another and kindred to us all. We are joined by birth and bound by a shared devotion to this land and the love of its parentage.

"My brother, King Elbert, is well and improving every day. But he has, it must be known, recently endured a resurgence of the ailment that afflicted him during his military service many years ago, wounds that he bore in uniform. Suffering—but far from surrendering—my brother now gathers his strength to continue his unremitting stewardship of Luthland.

"There is no doubt: Members of the House and Court, patriots, veterans of the Meridian War, and the nation's leaders of industry all continue to stand behind our king, much as my brother stood before our enemy upon our darkest hour. King Elbert shall address the nation in the coming weeks to express his gratitude to his faithful servants, his countrymen, his cousins. Mine is but a prefatory expression of thanksgiving, a tribute to the civility and steadfastness of the people of Luthland, who once again have rejected the hysteria of the rabble-rouser who would seek to make us all victims of their churlish cowardice. Luthland stands united, unwavering, and firm."

As the drone of applause was gradually overtaken by the announcer's artless rehash, Isolde assessed the speech. She thought it savvy enough. Princess Constance had stuffed patriotic devotion into the mouths of the national institutions, making it difficult for them to spit out. She had reminded the nation of her brother's military service but chosen her words carefully enough to not have to dicker with those who would point out he'd never seen combat. And the princess had defused with her ruminations on family the one point that made native institutions the most nervous: the specter of change. She'd confirmed King Elbert was still king.

"And all the nation sighed," Isolde murmured.

The Wilbies arrived at the soaring apartment tower where the Attertons kept a penthouse uncharacteristically early, only to be met outside the turnstile door by a blue velvet wall in a gold braided cap. The large doorman rebuffed them as if they were children attempting to sneak into a burlesque.

"The Saffoi Towers have a dress code." He surveyed her from cloche to clodhoppers. "And, madam, this is not it."

Iz tightened the lapels of her tatty overcoat. "We've come on the king's business, and Duke Atterton is expecting us. Surely, it doesn't matter if we've left our dickeys at home."

"I'd say royal business is all the more reason not to leave the house looking like a wet possum and..." The doorman scanned Warren, who wore an unrequited smile. "And a corduroy couch."

The Saffoi's gatekeeper proved immune to War's niceties and briberies, leaving the Wilbies with little choice but to leave. Determined to keep their appointment, they sought out the nearest boutique. Isolde introduced herself to the proprietor of Hymn of Hems by saying, "Hello. We would like to purchase your cheapest finest clothes."

Though initially appalled by the aggressive request, the couturier, one Mr. Alfred Dansby, soon perceived the identity of his customer. Brightening at the presence of the world-famous investigator in his establishment, Dansby inquired after an autograph, which Iz supplied. After some discussion of budgets, sizes, and time constraints, he presented them with two unclaimed custom orders.

Mr. Dansby asked if the Wilbies wished for him to donate their street clothes to the local shelter, an innocent offer that made Warren gasp on the man's behalf.

Isolde's overcoat was, to her mind, the perfect article of clothing. Its shoulders beaded the rain, its lining blunted the cold, its pockets were as numerous and voluminous as the drawers of a desk, its plump collar did not chafe her neck, its knee-length did not impede her stride, its drab coloration (which Warren called "dove" and she "gray") vanished into crowds and sank into shadow. Iz *loved* her coat.

Or rather she loved her rack of (formerly) identical coats that she had commissioned a seamstress to make nearly a decade ago. Iz's habit of soiling and drowning her clothes made having ready backups a must.

Since their delivery, those six coats had accrued a number of stains, burns, and stitches that now distinguished them, inspiring Iz to invent a name for each. There was Tabby, Splodge, Notch, Fussock, Reef, and Poppy, the last of which bore a small bloom of blood on the breast pinned by a knot of dark thread that sealed a bullet hole she had only just survived. Her admirers, those who read of her exploits in the Sunday rags and unauthorized pulps, believed her shabby coats were a sort of boast—an exhibition of her battle scars. For a time, Warren had assumed she continued to darn them out of thrift and a general indifference to the impression of her appearance. The truth was more eccentric: Her coats kept her company. To Iz, each had its own personality and temperament. She muttered to them when she was worried or perplexed. They were a balm to her thoughts. Her father had had a similar crotchet: He talked to the ornamental heads of his canes. When he was in a jolly mood, he would make his cane handles talk or, in the case of his oriole-headed walking stick, sing. Isolde's coats seemed a natural continuation of the familial quirk.

While the proprietor of the Hymn of Hems apologized for what he now saw was a grave insult, Isolde smoothed her treasured overcoat, Fussock, on the sales counter and drew in chalk upon its back a Hex of Aegis. "Wrap them all up, and send them to our address. If this coat is not waiting for me when I arrive home, I will return with questions. And hexes."

Ten minutes later, a very annoyed Isolde minced up the sidewalk of High Street in a spangling gown while Warren creaked along behind her in a very snug tuxedo.

The doorman at the Saffoi's gold-framed turnstile gloried in their transformation. With a shallow bow, he presented the door. "Madam, sir."

In passing, Isolde pressed something into his palm, saying, "For your trouble."

It was only after the Wilbies had cleared the revolving door that the doorman opened his hand and beheld the crumpled tissue he'd been given.

The Wilbies sat upon the Attertons' backless purple-and-gold divan as if it were a courtroom pew. Their humiliated expressions seemed at odds with their extravagant clothes. Isolde wore a sleeveless floor-length green dress that looked like a fishtail and was just as constricting. She would've liked to see the thing ripped up and repurposed as a horse blanket—a feeling that the mirror-clad elevator they'd lately ridden in had not amended, as it displayed in infinitely repeating iterations just how unflattering the cut was to her slight figure. Warren's tuxedo was so tight that he looked like a harbor seal in a bow tie, though one in relative good health: The long night's sleep he'd recently enjoyed had all but banished the symptoms of the nithe-grims.

The Attertons' penthouse was as airy as a marble quarry, and scarcely better furnished. The colossal curtainless windows showcased a milky vista. The alchemists' snow had reasserted its dominion over the city's skyline. Upon the glass coffee table before them sat a dish arrayed with two crustless sandwiches with fillings so stingy as to be indiscernible from the side. Though these morsels had been provided for the Wilbies, they seemed a pro forma expression of hospitality. Warren imagined that if he were to peel the white triangles apart he might find a hastily scrawled IOU.

Duke Florian sat in his driving clothes with his legs crossed, playing with an unlit cigarette. His hair was gray, his frame thin, his skin tight from the application of a variety of tonics that appeared to slowly be turning him into some variety of expensive leather. His eyes were as closely set as his nostrils, and nearly as small. A pair of goggles hung about his thin neck. He had lately come from the racetrack and appeared to be in no hurry to change. He'd not gone for the races but rather for their absence; on off days, he liked to drive the empty track in a private racing jaunt, of which he owned thirteen, information that he shared without provocation and expounded upon without pity.

Indeed, the first fifteen minutes of their audience with the duke had been absorbed by a recitation of his vehicles' technical specifications that might've gone on forever if Lady Lily Atterton, Florian's younger sister, had not brashly interrupted him with a reminder that they had a function to attend that evening and perhaps he should let his guests speak their business. Lady Lily, who was a little person with an imposing stare, sat before an enormous taut screen sewing a needlepoint pastoral scene. She wore cherry-red rouge on her puckered lips and a lacy boudoir bonnet on her head. Her slippers, which just peeked out from the bottom of the screen, were petite, heelless, and scaled in silver.

As Iz briefly explained the reason for their visit, she did her best not to stare at the smudge of oil or soot on Duke Florian's cheek, which surely he must've noticed in the mirrored lift. She suspected it had been purpose-fully applied as an indicator of his prowess with engines: He was not just a body in a bucket seat. No, he liked to pop his head under the bonnet as well.

The duke had a tendency to bracket his dialogue with a scornful huff, a small exhalation that seemed to dismiss what you had just said and refute any rejoinder to his own statement. "I haven't thought about ol' Rudy in years, Miss Wilby. And he relates to your investigation how?"

"Only tangentially, sir. The Crown has asked us to find a missing heirloom, and our search has carried us back to Prince Sebastian's brief conscription. Your brother served, did he not?"

"The military had no need of Rudy, but my brother had need of the military." The duke lit his cigarette with a little silver lighter he drew from his vest pocket.

"An orderly to Prince Sebastian. It seems something of a modest post for the son of such a storied family as yours."

"I would like to say it was a modest assignment for a modest soul, but the truth is, it was considered a plum post at the time. The prince got to choose his batman—royal privilege and all that—and he chose Rudy. Heaven knows why. They met at the academy and hit it off, I suppose." He tapped his cigarette over the armrest with such purpose one would think an ashtray waited to receive the deposit, though one did not. The little crown of ash fell upon the pristine floor.

Warren pulled on his lapels to give his pinched underarms some relief.

"I attended the military academy for a year after my first failed run at secondary school. My father hoped it might instill in me a little purpose. All it did was ruin mornings, marching, and mashed potatoes for me."

"Mornings, marching, and mashies. Yes, that was about the sum of it."

Warren's already cheery expression brightened. "You served?"

"Of course. Discharged honorably and with the rank of captain. I only caught the tail end of the strife, but I was on the line."

"We're all glad you came home safely, Captain." Warren's comment appeared to please the duke.

"I was told your brother was listed as missing in action during the war." Isolde omitted the fact that she'd also read in the archives of L.Cpl. Atterton's dereliction of duty, a scandal that had come to light after his initial disappearance from the battlefield. "I'm sorry for your loss."

A course of emotions sped across the duke's face: embarrassment, disgust, and anger. He appeared to chew and swallow each before finding his composure with a sharp drag upon his cigarette. "I would not speak ill of the dead, but since I have no doubt he's out there stinking up an opium den and planning his untimely return, I'll be frank: I fully expect him to pop out from under my death bed to ask for money. He never seemed to have any. But *really*, I don't know what concern this is to you or *His Majesty*." The phrase was punctuated by a particularly ironic snuffle. The duke tugged his goggles from his neck, seeming to suddenly find their presence irksome.

"We are, of course, quite hopeful that the rumors are not true and King Elbert is happy and well." Lady Lily glared at her brother as sharply as a pinch.

The duke harrumphed and fidgeted in his seat unhappily. "Do you know I was sixth in line to the throne before Princess Constance popped out her autumn pair? Unfair to think that either one of those two—" The lady coughed, and the duke reconsidered his next words. "Those two young men have been given such a step up on my sons. You know, my eldest will be graduating top of his class later this year, and . . ." As the duke went on to elucidate the technical specifications of his paddock of children, Isolde patiently waited for an opening and pondered the noble's obvious ambitions. What would Duke Florian Atterton, sixth-in-line-no-more, have done if Prince Sebastian's signet ring had fallen into his lap? Was he bitter enough to torment the king with idle threats? Perhaps they were less than idle.

"He's dead," Lady Lily said sharply, her strained diplomacy spent at last. The words were so striking, they muzzled her brother entirely. This time she did not look up from her needlework. Isolde saw in her lowered head the corking of a vintaged anger.

"Who's dead?" Duke Florian asked.

"Who do you think? Rudy. He didn't run away from home; he's not out there living in debauched exile. If he were alive, he would've come back for her funeral," Lady Lily said, and the duke scowled.

"Whose funeral, ma'am?" Isolde asked.

"Queen Mary's. Rudy was very close to his cousin, at least while she was still Lady Mary Soames."

The duke crossed his arms like a pouting child. "Always pawing and passing notes to the girl. It was unseemly."

"It was perfectly innocent," his sister rejoined.

"*Nothing* Rudy did was either perfect or innocent. Have you forgotten what happened the last time I let you talk me into sending investigators to snoop around in his wake? The boy was without shame."

"Then it must be something in our blood because I think it's shameful how quickly we abandoned him. He was still our brother, and we failed him." Upon her screen, Lady Lily stabbed a woolly lamb grazing in her pasture with a needle.

An unpleasant silence descended upon the room as the two aging siblings ground a little deeper into an ancient rut.

Sensing a rescue was in order, Warren strained the seams of his suit as he rocked forward to retrieve one of the two sandwiches. He pressed it into his mouth with admirable enthusiasm, though he regretted it almost at once as the dry sponge adhered itself to the roof of his mouth, leaving him to spade it out with his tongue. Stretching his neck to assist his swallow, he smiled and said, "I always enjoy a bit of potted herring."

"It's egg salad, I believe," Lady Lily replied vaguely.

Warren coughed. "Delicious."

Sensing that the nobles were beginning to tire of their company, Isolde instead asked the most critical of her remaining questions, one that might supply her with what she lacked most: physical evidence. "Do you still have any of your brother's effects, Your Grace? Diaries, letters, that sort of thing?"

The duke looked at her as if he were only seeing her for the first time. The smut on his face darkened with the sudden purpling of his gaunt cheeks. "How dare you. You come into my home, rake up the coals of a very personal—a *private* difficulty, and then have the nerve, the absolute gall to ask whether you can rifle through my brother's things? I should have you arrested!" He came to his feet with impressive swiftness, and the Wilbies dutifully popped up with him. He raised a finger and swung it from one of their faces to the other and back again. "You finger-wigglers are all the same! Magic, my eye! You're charlatans—plain and simple. You're swindlers! And if I discover that Elbert sent you here to stir up trouble, or if I find out that you're working for one of those tawdry rags, I will see you both in chains! Now, get out. Get out!"

THE ANSWERS
UNDERFOOT

Isolde teetered down the sidewalk like someone who had their shoe-laces tied together. Having lately been unceremoniously ejected by a delighted doorman, she was in the mood for a good stomp. And yet, the idiotic dress forbid it. How could she be expected to think while wrapped up like a mummy? She turned to complain to Warren—intending to say that they would either have to visit another clothier or join a nudist colony—just in time to see him dart into the mouth of an alley.

She hurried, as well as she could hurry, to pursue him, only to find him bellowing violently into a dust bin. He vomited, gasped, and repeated the ordeal as she patted his rounded back. When at last he righted himself, he announced through teary eyes, "That was not a sandwich; that was a booby trap! That was a devil dressed in white bread. That was—" He broke off as he was compelled to answer the call of the bin once more.

Feeling helpless and frustrated, Isolde stooped to grip the narrow hem of her ridiculous dress. Meaning to rend her mermaid tail, she began to tug and pull. As she did, she glared down at the cobbled alley floor, congested with the usual urban compost of newsprint, ashes, and scraps. The bricks flowed out from a central vein like the idealized barbs of a feather. She considered the mason who had proudly poured their artistry into this alley, creating a distinct and unappreciated work of art, a single ridge in the city's sprawling fingerprint.

Gripped by an epiphany, Iz straightened like an exclamation point. She reviewed her memory to make sure that the details were sufficiently clear, then announced to her panting husband, "I know where the alley is, or at least how to find it."

Warren spat heavily and shivered while he answered: "Darling, we are in an alley. I found it. I am not enjoying it."

Isolde rubbed a circle on his back. "No, no—the alleyway from Jessamine's haunt, the one that the nithe-grims ate down to the bone. If we can locate it, perhaps we can wring out some of its secrets."

With a trembling hand, War mopped his mouth and mustache with a handkerchief. "Splendid, Iz. Splendid. But first, let's find me a new stomach. I'm finished with this one. God, I'll never eat eggs again."

It took them the better part of the day to recuperate from their morning interview with the Attertons. A trip to the apothecary went some way to alleviating Warren's gastronomic distress, and a stop at home liberated him from his seal-skin suit and Isolde from her fish-tailed dress. Arrayed in a fresh overcoat from her rack, Iz felt much more herself as the two of them skulked the verges of High Street amid the twilight hour.

While she ducked in and out of alleyways, Warren availed himself of the food carts that congested the gutters and impinged upon the sidewalks outside the neon fluted playhouses and overlit dance halls. To the confusion of the vendors he patronized, War stowed the fruits of their chaffing dishes and woks—each kabob and dumpling, each sausage roll and gyro—into his carpetbag after first shouting tasting notes into its recesses. He'd square his face within his unclasped purse and bawl over the squall of traffic: "Notice the spice! That's turmeric. Stains the fingers but tickles the tongue!"

On the one occasion that a vendor was brave enough to ask why he was roaring into his luggage, Warren gaily replied, "Because that's where the dragon is!"

High Street ran down the long ridge that creased the city, marking the divide between the River Zimme's watershed and the dells that rolled off to the west. While many of Berbiton's cobbled streets had been paved over with bituminous cement in recent years to accommodate the delicate suspensions of electrahol jaunting cars, High Street remained a warty vein of uneven, hump-backed stone, spanning some two and half miles. The nature of High Street's lessees evolved over the course of its length, changing from dilapidated rowhouses to plate-windowed boutiques to high-rises and exclusive clubs. It was said there were two of everything on High Street, which made finding one alley in particular rather a chore.

Fortunately, Isolde's detailed recollection of the earthen stage from the Nethercroft provided her with some useful parameters. She knew the passage abutted High Street because of the distinctive shape of its cobbles, and knew it lay on the east side because of the central gutter that funneled runoff down to the river, a feature that was absent on the west. The modest coal chute she'd carved an escape hatch through in the Nethercroft identified one of the buildings as a rowhouse because skyscrapers with multiple tenants had their fuel delivered via underground bays. There were other clues as well—from the presence of earthquake bolts, to the dearth of telegraph wires—attributes that helped her remove from consideration entire eras of construction and, consequently, whole city blocks. Finally, there was the goat-headed grotesque; if she could find it, she would know she had found the fateful scene of the spat.

Yet, after hours of trooping about and poking her head into dim and noisome backstreets, Iz began to wonder if she'd not overestimated the genius of her sleuthing. Perhaps the clues were good, but simply out of date: in the ensuing decades, the buildings might've collapsed or been refaced; the ill-fated alleyway might've been dug up or repaved. Privately, she began to doubt.

But then she saw the horned beast leering down at her from the second-story ledge. When she stepped into the alley, the eerie light of the nascent night seemed to paint the edges of everything in the ghostly tones of the Nethercroft. At her side, Warren was quick to bolster her tentative triumph with his own confidence. "Excellent work! You've done it! Now what?"

She turned in a slow circle, absorbing her surroundings, which were disappointingly ordinary. There was no speakeasy entrance nor crumbling shrine—only lidless bins, the stripped carcass of a rusted bicycle, and termite-drilled crates. "I thought I might try my luck with the Conch of Enoch."

Warren smiled, though his brows seemed to frown. "Again? Are you sure? Didn't your ears ring for a week?"

"I've refined my technique."

"I don't doubt that you have, darling, but your last attempt was to eavesdrop upon echoes that were only days gone. Do you really think you can tune the conch to sounds that have rattled around for, what, twenty-five years?"

"There's only one way to find out."

With an assenting shrug, War undid the clasp on the portalmanteau. "We should ask Felivox if he knows of any magical earplugs or—"

Isolde stayed his search with a touch of his elbow. "Wait a moment. Look." She ticked her chin upward, and Warren followed the understated signal to the dimly lit window and the woman peering down at them through a gap in her drapes. The moment she discerned she'd been spotted, the spy dropped her curtain and switched off her lamp. "There may be a simpler way."

They returned to the public walk and climbed the steps of the voyeur's home. The lintels and cornices of the three-story brownstone were handsome enough, lending the construction a stately aura, but one that could not entirely compensate for the neglected mortar, cracked windows, and weedy gutters that sprouted like a window box. An empty sign bar rusted above the door. Iz asked Warren to retrieve a relic called the Stare of Ancients from the portalmanteau. After a moment's rummage, he presented her with a jade mask, or rather the serrated remnants of a statue's head that had been chiseled down to a ragged domino. Iz raised the mask to her eyes and turned her attention to the empty bracket above the front door. The Stare of Ancients, while incapable of seeing the transitory elements of the past, could reveal long-standing features of the bygone world. With some squinting, the lost shingle reappeared, though with the flickering translucence of a train window at night.

The sign read: DE LEE & GWATKIN: MIDWIVES AND MONTHLY NURSES.

Sharing this revelation with War, she added, "A woman, pregnant at the time, is scarred by a kerfuffle in a midwife's alley. Seems an unlikely coincidence."

"You think De Lee and Gwatkin were looking after Jessamine?"

"One way to find out." Isolde took the knocker in hand and gave the door three sharp raps. Sweeping the cloche from her head, she unplastered her curls with clawed fingers. "Have you noticed we've attracted an entourage?" Her gaze flitted toward the roofline along the far side of the street. The round heads of hundreds of starlings beaded those darkened peaks. "They've been converging on us since midtown."

"How auspicious." Facing the peeling panels of the midwife's front door, Warren removed his bowler and smoothed back the threads of his hair. "What are you planning to say?"

"To the birds?"

The vestibule light came on. "To the woman rattling her keys."

"I'm going to appeal to her as a professional."

Warren's expression bloomed with disbelieving surprise just in time to greet the woman who opened the door.

She held her housecoat closed under her tucked chin. The pair of white brows that peeked out from under her terrycloth turban stood out against her dark skin. Her gaze was elusive, her voice rusty with age but still forceful as a bugle: "There's a flophouse down the way if you're looking for more privacy than my alley. Don't forget to put a helmet on your little soldier, young man."

She made to close the door, but Iz spoke quickly, "I'm looking for De Lee and Gwatkin. I need their help."

The woman looked Iz up and down, her practiced squint foiled perhaps by Iz's formless coat, then she scowled at Warren, who could only blush in his own defense. "I'm retired."

"Please." Iz laid her hand over the fingers that held the door cracked. "It's rather urgent."

"It always is." The turbaned woman appeared about to punctuate the statement with a slammed door, but then she huffed and waved them into the vestibule.

The ground floor, what had served as the midwives' office in years past, was dark, its furnishments draped in dusty sheets. The woman, who introduced herself as Charlotte De Lee, led them up a creaking and unswept stair to the upper level and the modest apartment it contained. The small sitting room was rendered as crowded as a jungle floor by no fewer than eight footstools, each occupied by a cat, seemingly of every color and age. Two excused themselves upon the arrival of unexpected guests, but the rest merely blinked or snored in greeting. Only the adjoining kitchenette was lit. A low-slung shade hung over a small table that held a green glass ashtray, a silver cigarette case, and a box of matches. A ribbon of smoke rose from the notched cigarette. Several chalky frames decorated the walls; a black shawl sashed one among them.

"I'll put it out," Charlotte De Lee muttered as she tapped the cigarette against the ashtray's clean basin.

"Don't trouble yourself on my account," Isolde said, glancing about.

"It's not on *your* account." De Lee sat down with a grunt and invited them to sit, though she soon flagged her hand at Iz when she touched the chairback to her left. "No, no. You here, you there." They dutifully took their appointed seats, or at least Warren tried to. When he put his weight on the diminutive wire chair, it raised a squealing protest that made the feline hosts raise their heads and Warren reverse his descent. Clutching the portalmanteau to his considerable chest, he said that he preferred to stand. The midwife shrugged and turned her attention to Isolde. "How far along are you?"

"I'm not."

"You're not pregnant?"

"No."

"Right." Charlotte De Lee broke open the cigarette case, selected a round from the chamber, and lit it off a match with two prim puffs that she drew into her cheeks but not her lungs. She placed the cigarette in the ashtray, directing the unlit end toward the empty chair on her left. "Come to rob an old woman, have you? Is that why you brought the empty bag?" She glared at Warren, who coughed and spluttered in protest.

Isolde pressed on: "We're here to ask about someone else, a client of yours, I believe. Jessamine Bysshe, or she may have come to you under a different name: Jess Blessed." She watched De Lee's expression closely, and observed something like the twinge of a toothache crimp the corner of the midwife's mouth. "We suspect that about twenty-five years ago, she witnessed some sort of commotion in your alley, one that seemed to make a profound impression upon her. I'm curious to know if it made one upon you, as well."

De Lee smacked her tongue against her lips as if to clear the lingering taste of tobacco. "That doesn't sound like any of my business. It doesn't sound like any of yours, either."

With her finger, Isolde drew a simple ten-sided hex upon the table, one of the first that she had ever learned, a Hex of Declaration, a sigil which served two purposes: first to identify the creator as a student of the art, and second to call into relief any other hexes in the vicinity. The moment Isolde closed the boxy circlet, a half dozen wards began to glow on the walls about them. Hexes of protection, of restfulness, of anti-somnambulation, and of deodorization glinted from over the doorways and peeked out from under the faded curtains. Apparently offended by the display, three more cats padded off to hide in the apartment's back rooms.

By the colorful light of these sigils, Isolde fixed the midwife with a concerted and forthright stare. "I'm a hex-caster, like yourself. We are not thieves or journalists. We're investigators. I am here in service of the Crown, but my sympathy at present lies with Ms. Bysshe. I think she found herself in some trouble. We are not here to judge. I only wish to get to the bottom of what happened to her."

De Lee, whose mouth had rounded with momentary surprise, pinched off her astonishment. "I never had any talent for hexes. My partner was our resident practitioner. Beatrice drew all that stuff on the walls years ago. Years and years. I'd forgotten they were there, to be honest."

Iz canceled the declarative hex with a twist of her fingers that resembled a voiceless snap. The piebald glow dwindled as the symbols faded back into the shadows.

Warren stooped to get a better look at the photograph whose frame was draped with a ribbon of fading sable. He cast his eye back and forth between the two posed women. The taller of the pair had blond ringlets and an open-mouth smile. She stood with one foot cocked behind her other knee and her elbow propped on her partner's shoulder. Though age had softened the shape of her face, War saw in the second woman's lopsided smile a clear resemblance to their host. The image seemed so joyous, and its washed-out mourning sash so dejected.

"I'm sorry for your loss," he said, then turned to fill the bellows of his lungs with a great sigh. "I never let myself forget what a privilege it is to have someone I love to share my life with. We bear it all together— the beauty, the difficulties, the cumbersome things that you never asked to carry but life lays upon your shoulders anyway. Without my wife to confide in, I think I'd fall flat under the weight of all those promises and secrets. It's too much."

The second cigarette having burned down untouched, Ms. De Lee set about lighting another. As she angled it toward the empty seat, she said, "I admit—I am tired of hoarding other people's sorrows."

Iz slid her hand across the table, not as one looking for embrace but as a bank teller discreetly tendering the details of an account. "I give you my word, we are here to see the truth exposed and justice done. Two days ago, we visited Jessamine's grave, and we—"

De Lee sat back heavily, her arms falling from the table to hang by her sides. "She's dead."

"Yes, I'm afraid so. She passed away twenty-three years ago. She's buried in Honewort."

"I never knew what happened to her. She disappeared after that night. Never came back." De Lee rocked forward in her chair, suddenly keen. "Do you know if she kept it—the child?"

"Not for certain, but I believe so." Isolde had draped her coat over the back of the chair, and now twisted to delve its pockets. When she turned again, she had a pad and pencil in hand. "And we might be able to discover what happened to the child for certain with your help...assuming you have any memory of Jessamine or, particularly, what happened in your alley that night."

All at once, De Lee's expression softened with introspection. "I can't recall the final time that I lay my head in my mother's lap and she stroked my hair, but I know it must've happened. And I don't recall the day I first saw Beatrice or held her hand. Either moment would be such a comfort to me now. But they're gone. All gone." Her nares flared with sudden loathing. "And yet I cannot forget that retched night, hard as I've tried."

Iz set her pencil tip to paper. "Please, tell us everything."

She answered with the clipped urgency of a confession. "Beatrice had gone to see her mother that afternoon. I'm glad she did, glad she wasn't here to see it. She hated the papers—everything except the society page. Oh, she'd sit up half the night telling me all about the royal family, their antics and scandals. The rest of it—all the politics and news of the war— she'd scale fish on it. She loved to listen to the hyaline. There was always music and dancing and carrying on. She liked to keep the curtains drawn. 'We see enough grief during the day,' she always said. 'No need to go looking for it at night.' Me, on the other hand..." An old tabby with a low, swinging stomach nosed about De Lee's ankles. She bent and gently lifted the cat, installing it upon her lap.

Knuckling the cheek of the purring tabby, the midwife said, "Cats are funny. They get embarrassed. They'll stumble or get stuck or do something silly, and then they'll straighten up, look about—act like they meant to do that. Even when they don't think anyone is watching, they'll put on a little play of competency and grace. I don't know, maybe they assume someone is always watching. They do have a vain streak. Or maybe cats don't need a witness to feel embarrassment. Maybe they're better than us in that way.

"Because people...people are shameless. We are different beasts when we think no one is looking. We are strange and frightening things."

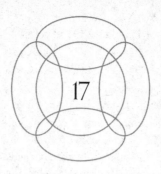

17

UNCERTAIN WAS THE NURSE

Charlotte De Lee described Jessamine Bysshe as having an air about her. Conversing with Jessamine was like strolling a boardwalk in summertime. She was dazzling, unceremonious, and wholesome. In her memory, De Lee saw the young woman in the washed-out pinks and pellucid blues of a seaside watercolor. Jessamine Bysshe smiled often and with such disarming bonhomie.

At the kitchen table, mummified in strands of cigarette smoke, the demeanor of Charlotte De Lee's oration shifted, gradually changing from an impatient staccato to a murmur befitting one caught in a trance. Isolde noted the alteration, but chalked it up to the effect of an oft revisited trauma. "She was my last patient that night. It was her second visit. She was about eight weeks along—healthy and happy, all the things you'd hope to be. A little trouble sleeping, a touch of indigestion, but nothing serious. Which she knew, of course. She was a nurse herself, but she said she took comfort in hearing it from 'a more reliable source.' She was funny. She asked me two or three times if I was absolutely sure about the moratorium on soft cheese. I told her butter was just as good and better for the baby.

"I remember watching her put on her summer bonnet. She was almost glowing. She was so happy. She promised to return for her next appointment in a month. She said we'd ask the baby then how it felt about a mild bleu.

"I turned the lock after her, doused the office lights, and climbed the stairs. I had to feed Pitter-Pat. I went to the cupboard for a tin of fish. Then I heard something. Raised voices, unhappy ones. I went to the window and looked into the alley. The shadows were thick, but I could see them all perfectly well. A pair of men stood nearly nose to nose beside the neighbor's firewood. They were arguing. I couldn't understand what they were saying at first.

"Jessamine stood at the mouth of the lane not far out of the streetlight. She was holding a sheathed sword, belt and all. That seemed very strange. She looked frightened.

"The men, the ones arguing, they were obviously drunk. They seemed to have just been passing by, probably crawling from one bar to the next. They were dressed for a celebration. There was a big deployment ceremony in the mall that afternoon. Another battalion being shipped out.

"One of the two was in uniform, the sort of braided gaudy thing they wear for coronations and such. I didn't recognize him, but I recognized the other gentleman right away. He was dressed in a black suit—a fancy thing. I'd seen his picture many times in the papers. It was Prince Sebastian. He'd been ill recently, and I was surprised to see him out and about again.

"Since it was summer, my window was open. I could hear what they were saying when they got louder, and they did—much louder. That's when I figured out who the other man was. Prince Sebastian called him 'Rudy,' short for Rudolph, Rudolph Atterton. I put it together because that was the name Jessamine had given as the father of her child."

The scratch of her pencil abruptly halting, Isolde and Warren shared a glance but did not dare to interrupt the woman, who seemed to be narrating a vivid dream. Charlotte De Lee stared at the cold ashtray, the burned-down cigarette, and the higher corner of her mouth pinched tighter as tears glazed her eyes. "You did warn me, Bea. You did. I was always too nosy." She lightly stroked the back of the cat in her lap, who seemed to have fallen asleep.

War and Iz waited for De Lee to continue, and when she did, her voice was leaden and low. "Mr. Atterton didn't want her to go through with the pregnancy. He said that such a birth would disrupt his military career and pose a great hardship to Jessamine. He said, and I won't ever forget this, 'You can't expect me to be the patron of every bastard that gets fumbled into existence inside a mop closet.'"

Warren made a sound of disgust. "If I'd been there, I would've been tempted to pop him on the snout."

"Funny you should say so because that's exactly what the prince did. He hit Mr. Atterton on the nose. Hard.

"I think everyone was surprised. And then it was war. The two of them were on each other like a couple of dogs. I thought someone on the street would see, would run in to stop them. But everyone was stumbling around, getting one last drink in before shipping out. Everyone was smashed. You know how those things go. Once the city tucks into the bottle, it all falls apart. I read the next day, there were dozens of brawls that night. Hundreds of arrests. The cops had their hands full. And yes, I know I could've done something. I *should've* done something. I wanted to ... but. Jessamine was caught down there, stuck in the thick of it, watching the father of her unborn child and a prince of the land doing their best to wring each other's necks.

"It seemed to go on forever, but I'm sure it wasn't a minute before Mr. Atterton got the upper hand. He got hold of a stick of firewood and was swinging it around like a club. He clipped the prince a time or two. I thought he might kill him.

"Jessamine was shouting at them to stop. When they didn't, she pulled the sword. I don't know what she was trying to do. Maybe get their attention. She waved it at them. It's hard to say what happened next. It was dark. Maybe the prince pushed him, maybe Mr. Atterton stumbled, maybe Jessamine took a step forward. But Jessamine was holding the sword when the officer fell on it. It was so quick. He just turned, fell, and died. The blade went right through his heart. It was the first time I ever saw someone go. I wish it had been the last."

De Lee had shifted her hands from the sleeping cat in her lap onto the tabletop, where she squeezed and kneaded them with trembling intensity. Warren explored the kitchen cabinets until he found a glass. He filled it from the tap and set the tumbler before her, though she did not touch it, nor even seem to know it was there. The more she spoke, the more she seemed to recede from the room. Warren looked to Iz and with an animation of his mouth and brows communicated his concern. Should they stop her? Should they spare this poor soul the remainder of her nightmare? Isolde shook her head once and definitively.

Charlotte De Lee heaved a great sigh, which seemed to steady her. She discovered the glass of water and sipped it. "The rest is a bit of a muddle, I'm afraid. Jessamine found me and asked if they could call someone on my voxbox. I hardly knew how to use the thing, it was so new. Of course, I said yes, and then the military police came—I think they were MPs. There was an ambulance or a transport of some sort blocking the alley, keeping out any prying eyes from the street, and there was a very kind nurse who came to check on Jessamine and myself, though I felt silly to have been affected by something I just watched. It hadn't been me down there. I was safe. I was way up here. But the nurse—what was her name? I feel like she told me her name. Or maybe she wasn't a nurse. Maybe she was a nun. Either way, she was very nice. She had a mask like we were in surgery; honestly, it felt like we were. Everything was so split open. So pulled back. So bloody, so—" Charlotte De Lee stifled an unanticipated sob, and as she choked upon her distant grief, Isolde raised a finger, loading a question. War touched her shoulder, and she looked up to see him give a small discouraging frown. Isolde put her finger down and knitted her brow as Warren murmured a string of sympathies.

After a moment and the dispatching of several tissues, De Lee was ready to continue. "The MPs, or whoever they were, cleaned up the mess and took away the body. Jessamine left—I don't know when exactly. I feel like I just turned around, and she was gone. Then everyone was gone. I went to bed. Tried to sleep. Didn't have much luck with that. The next morning I found a bunch of royal lawyers standing on my doorstep—all of them very concerned about what I might say and who to. They gave me money, a lot of it, and I signed my name on what seemed like a hundred papers, all of which said the same thing in one way or another: I would take the money and keep my mouth shut. And I have. I never told anyone. Not even Bea.

"Soon as I had the money, I had to get rid of it. I told Bea I'd inherited it from a rich cousin, and I took her on a cruise. We sailed the world three times round. She danced on every ocean, drank every glass of wine. I was so miserable. I told her I was just seasick, but I couldn't stop thinking about that man dying in my alley, the look on Jessamine's face. I kept telling myself it was an accident, but sometimes when I think back to it, it doesn't seem like an accident. But even so, I can't bring myself to blame her for holding the sword or the prince for pushing his friend on it, if he did. That man, that Atterton, he was crazed. The things he said to her—there's no telling what he would've done if they hadn't stopped him."

Isolde could hold her tongue no longer. "These attorneys, I suppose they confiscated all your papers related to the pregnancy?"

Charlotte sucked in a breath and shook her head. She seemed to recover some of her former spirit. "As if I would've handed over a woman's medical records to a solicitor! They would've had to throw me in jail. Maybe they suspected as much because they didn't even ask."

Isolde closed up her notepad and slipped it into the breast pocket of her blouse. "Then you still have them? May I have a look?"

"You must have wax in your ears. I said my patients' files are private." De Lee rose with a grunt and a complaint from the tabby who'd been asleep. She swept up the cigarette purse and stowed it in a kitchen drawer. Emptying the ashtray, she briefly soaped it in the sink, then set about drying it on a tea towel, turning so that she could fix Isolde with a defiant stare.

Isolde folded her arms. "You wouldn't release those records to those attorneys because you suspected they'd only use them if it were to the prince's advantage. I'm sure you were right in that regard. But I want to use them to hold the Crown, the courts, and the Attertons accountable. If there is a child and they are still alive, your documents are perhaps the only thing that remains to support their petition to be recognized by their family, should the child desire it. I only want to see that they receive what they are owed."

"And Jessamine? Do you mean to out her as a killer and drag her memory through the mud?"

"Ms. De Lee, you said yourself it was dark. What transpired was almost certainly an accident that resulted in a violent man reaping his violent end. My concern here is for the child. I do not mean to be cruel, but when you die and all your records are gathered up and carted off to the incinerator, that child will be left without recourse. They will be twice orphaned:

once upon their mother's death, and again upon yours. But that does not have to be the case. I believe that with your help we might yet squeeze a drop of charity from that awful night. Perhaps we can provide for Jessamine's child what she always wished for herself: the recognition of her disinclined family."

Riding in the back of a hired jaunt, Isolde leaned against the window and let the strobe of the passing streetlamps comb her tangled thoughts. The privacy screen was up, and still she could hear the faint squawk of the hyaline broadcast and the jivey rag that seemed at such odds with her mood.

On the far side of the plush bench, Warren snored softly, his chin rolling upon the knot of his necktie, his head bobbing with the rhythm of the seams in the street. The late hour and his recent needling by the nithegrims had left him drained. Scant minutes after their driver had pulled into traffic, he'd begun to doze. She saw no reason to wake him.

In her hand, she held a thin dossier that contained the records of Jessamine's brief tenure under De Lee's care. One page included a single line that appeared to resolve the Wilbies' royal investigation. In the blank that followed the question of the father of Jessamine's child was the clearly drawn name: Rudolph Atterton.

During their farewell in the park, when the prince had bestowed his signet ring upon Jessamine, he'd said that he could not forgive what Rudy had done to her, what he had *made* of her. Isolde had assumed that he was merely referring to the pregnancy—Atterton had made her an unwed mother. But now it seemed more likely the prince was referencing the lance corporal's death. Rudy had made her a killer. Isolde tried to imagine how she herself would've approached the dilemma Jessamine had faced in the alley. Choosing between the unwilling father of one's own child and the prince of a nation seemed an impossible quandary, one that forbade the possibility of a happy ending.

It seemed to his credit that the prince felt responsible for shielding Jessamine from the consequences of that evening. Perhaps he had felt on the hook for his orderly's predaciousness, or perhaps he was merely grateful for her intervention in the alley, which might well have saved his life. In parting, Prince Sebastian had called her Lady Larkland—a promise, it seemed, that he would see that her extended family welcomed her to the fold, a prospect rendered moot by Jess's untimely illness and death.

Iz had more than a few lingering questions. De Lee had said the military police had collected the body, but why? As a favor to the prince? Weeks later, a stand-in would die in the trenches in the lance corporal's uniform, and both the press and the extended Atterton family would assume Rudy, ever the roguish lad, had deserted his post and paid off a patsy. But it couldn't have been Rudy who'd organized the ploy; he was already dead. It had to be someone in the military or some noble hoping to secure favor with the king-to-be. Whoever it was, they might've gone so far as to load the corpse onto the transport ship, then throw it overboard once they were underway. Not even Old Geb could sniff out what became of those who were lost at sea.

Still, it seemed such an elaborate ruse for what amounted to a drunken fight and an accidental death, albeit a noble one. Was that really cause enough to indebt a prince to a pregnant nurse? Was the prince's gratitude sufficient to launch such a grand conspiracy? Or had something else happened, something Charlotte De Lee did not see? Perhaps it wasn't an accident at all. Perhaps it was—

"Ah, the basking of a woman who has solved another case!" Warren said.

Having not noticed him stir, Iz turned to consider her groggy husband with a distant and disorganized gaze. "So it would seem."

Sitting up, he stretched his neck and smoothed his mustache. "Whoever it is that has that signet ring is barking up the wrong tree. He's got no more of a claim to the throne than I do. Lucky thing we weren't hired by the Attertons! They're in for a rude surprise." War snuggled back into the cab's generous padding, his cheeks balling about a smile. "Oh, how I'd love to see Florian's face the day Rudy's long-lost son knocks on his door! Though it seems, the Duke of Rotten Eggs was right about one thing: Rudy was the bad sort. He was— Why the frown? You're not content?"

"In the alley, Charlotte De Lee quoted Rudy about not being a patron of unwanted children. *Patron*. Why does that word keep popping up?"

"Coincidence? Perhaps you keep hearing it because you're listening for it."

She rallied a smile for his benefit. "Perhaps."

Warren laid his hand upon the gulf of stitched leather between them, and she took it. "Are you feeling up for an evening celebration?"

"You're not tired?" She scooted to his side as he raised his arm to receive her.

"Darling, I am only tired of sharing your magnificence with the rest of the world. I want you all to myself for a moment."

"Only a moment? Can't even pencil me in for half an hour?" She crossed her leg over his knee.

Curling his arm around her, he squeezed her close and touched her nose with his own. "I could pencil you in for the rest of the night."

"All right, but I'd hardly call it a pencil..."

18

THE END AND ITS
ANTIPODE

The next morning, Warren put on his paint-speckled overalls,
retrieved the stepladder from the tumbledown garage, mixed a fresh
batch of plaster, and with trowel in hand, climbed toward the crater in the ceiling of his parlor. He had been ogling the hole ever since the
mandrake had opened it, promising himself daily that he would tackle its
repair in the morning, only to find himself staring at the ragged gash and
renewing his vows in the evening. At last, the nightly chore of glaring at
the damage had grown more strenuous than the specter of patching it. He
could bear it no longer. The hole had to be closed.

The moment he surmounted the top step, the doorbell rang. It seemed
ill-timed but inevitable. There was no surer way to make a caller materialize on your doorstep than to climb a ladder. He looked about for any sign
of Iz, but supposed she was either in her laboratory or the bath.

He answered the summons to discover a gentleman with russet skin, a
navy uniform, and a matching peaked cap. War might've mistaken him for
a member of the constabulary had he not been holding a vase containing
an eruption of violet delphiniums.

"I have a delivery for Ms. Isolde Wilby," the courier said with the depleted
enthusiasm of one nearing the end of their shift and perhaps their career.

Isolde ducked past Warren even as he prepared to receive the vase. She spotted the card attached to a metal trident near the heart of the fragrant arrangement and plucked it free. Fingering the envelope open, she read its handwritten contents aloud. "Dear Mrs. Wilby, I hope you are able to come to my shindig and tow along that famously loquacious spouse of yours. Sincerely, Victor Cholmondeley."

"Isn't that nice!" Warren said, accepting the green glass vase. "First time he's sent us flowers. Really upping the ante, isn't he? Makes a boy feel special! Maybe we should go."

Isolde looked over the man's shoulder at his idling box van as she extracted a rumpled gallet from her pocket. Presenting the tip, she asked, "How many of your deliveries are from Mr. Cholmondeley today?"

"All of them, ma'am."

Isolde patted her husband on the chest. "Special, eh?"

The royal secretary, Horace Alman, seemed in a good mood when he met the Wilbies at Aster's Tearoom that afternoon. The gingerbread-styled cottage trembled upon the hump of Muir's Cross, the central bridge that spanned the River Zimme. The café was one pastel link in a chain of slightly built gracile boutiques. A determined wind rattled the picture windows that squared the room. The tea maid wore mittens when she brought out the pot, an imposition she appeared to resent. The other six tables stood empty, which the maid emphasized by shifting the vacant chairs about, making them squeak upon the parquet. Mr. Alman tipped her lavishly and suggested that she close shop for half an hour and perhaps avail herself of the alehouse down the way. No sooner was the offer made than the front door banged open and shut and the shop bell tolled its farewell to the tearoom's only staff.

Outside, the street rippled with blown carp snow, thin and fragile as the shed skin of a snake. And how adder-like was the chill! It rose from the snow-swollen river, slithered up the piers, slipped under the door, ascended the cast iron table legs, coiled about their saucers, and nested in their cups.

Still, the secretary radiated sublimity. His blue suit and vermilion pocket square were as bold as a naval flag. Were it not for the lingering bruise on his jaw, a souvenir of his tumble with a mandrake, Isolde might

not have believed he was the same man as the sweating, nervous functionary who'd come to her with an unwelcome proposal and his hat on his
knee.

Mr. Alman cocked his chin in that particular way that signaled some
mannerly jabbering was imminent. Isolde recognized the affectation and
had to bite back a groan. "I hope you haven't had any more unexpected callers since our last meeting, Ms. Wilby. Did you ever get around to installing
that guillotine, or did you decide to go with a pendulum in the end?"

Iz smiled as if she were attempting to chew through a gag. "Neither. We
secured a guard dragon instead."

"Quite a pleasant chap!" Warren beamed.

The royal secretary grinned uncertainly. "Yes, of course."

"I take it the king's condition has improved. Has he surrendered his
aspirations of baking himself?" Iz sipped her cold tea and resolved not to
revisit it.

Mr. Alman sobered at once. "I'm afraid not. No, his condition is
unchanged. But the nation's greatest medical minds are still in attendance,
and Princess Constance continues to apply her own abilities in the effort to
heal her brother."

"Then the king is in good hands. Princess Constance's talent for hexegy
is formidable. I have no doubt she'll divine a cure soon enough."

"Yes, we certainly hope so. And please excuse my demeanor. I'm merely
relieved that you called with news that you've concluded your investigation.
And so swiftly! You mentioned evidence. Does that mean you have proof,
proof that the king is uninvolved, proof that would stand up to scrutiny?"

Reconsidering her decision to remove her long gloves, Isolde wriggled
her fingers back into the kidskin sleeves. "Yes, but first I must introduce
you to our players and the playing field. We begin our tale in the flooded
archives of the Winterbourne Military Hospital..."

As Isolde rehearsed the events of recent days and the convoluted epiphanies of imps, headstones, and nithes, the royal secretary's early cheerful-
ness curdled into baffled disquiet. When he learned that the giving of the
prince's signet ring—a pivotal event in the case—had been observed by
the Wilbies on a spectral plane and was supported by no further substan-
tiation, he was clearly perturbed.

He pecked the table with his finger forcefully enough to rattle their teacups. "You said you had proof, Ms. Wilby. This sounds suspiciously like the evidence of a séance!"

"But we don't need to *prove* the prince gave the ring to Jessamine Bysshe. We only need to know that she received it. The illegitimate child, when he or she comes forward, will corroborate the connection. The only piece of proof that we really need is a document where Jessamine Bysshe shares the identity of her child's father. And that we have." Isolde nodded to Warren, who opened the paper dossier that rested before him. He extracted a time-yellowed sheet and slid it across the table. He held the page with his finger, which stood pinned just above the name Rudolph Atterton. "And if need be, we have a witness to the signing: Ms. Bysshe's midwife. Which brings us to the unfortunate events of a certain High Street alley." Isolde succinctly recounted the scuffle between the prince and his orderly, who lobbied for the pregnancy's termination, and the uncertain if bloody conclusion that followed Jessamine's intervention. Iz described how she believed the body had been disposed of at sea after Rudolph's uniform and personal effects had been removed. Though she could not prove the details of the conspiracy that would make it seem that Atterton had died on the battlefield rather than by his own sword in an alley, she was quite convinced of the impossibility of the story as reported by the press. Rudolph Atterton had not deserted his post, nor had he been the one to secure an unconvincing stand-in. Those actions could only have been carried out on the Crown's behalf and at the military's behest.

As Mr. Alman absorbed all of this with an increasingly astonished expression, Isolde continued: "Here's my theory: Jessamine and Rudolph's child discovered the prince's ring sometime after their mother's untimely death. Understandably, they took it as proof that their father was Prince Sebastian, who appeared to have gone to some trouble to both conceal their kinship and still leave behind a tendril of connection. The child would have had no way of knowing the ring was a token of the prince's gratitude to Jessamine for saving his life. I'm sure you can imagine what sort of fancies such a series of events might've excited in a young person, especially one who'd been orphaned. Here was proof that their noble father loved their mother, and by extension them as well."

"My god! Why on earth did he sign on for such a conspiracy if the child was not his and the death was in self-defense?"

"Guilt?" Warren suggested. "It was his orderly, after all, who had taken advantage of his nurse during his hospital stay. Perhaps the prince felt responsible for exposing her to such a rotter. And she might've ended up in prison. I imagine the Attertons' lawyers would've dragged her through the mud. If the prince was grateful for her having saved his life, perhaps this seemed the best—the *only* time to intervene."

"Or it might've been panic." Isolde shrugged. "You'd be surprised how many conspiracies begin, not with a grand design, but a simple desire to make the trouble go away. The prince called for help; the machinations began; and there was no easy way to stop them once they did. And my husband is absolutely right about the Attertons' response. They didn't like Rudy, but they hated the king more. Given the chance, they would've driven a wedge between the noble families. Sides would've been chosen; the course of history would've been changed.

"The point is, this was never about hiding the existence of a child. No, this was about obfuscating the violent death of a noble son and the ill-advised cover-up that ensued. King Elbert is sitting upon a conspiracy that, if revealed, might even now tear the nation apart, and I imagine that's a very uncomfortable cushion to sit upon."

The secretary moved to lift the sheet that had been pulled from Jessamine's medical record, but Warren whisked it away before he could grip it. Mr. Alman looked up, bemused. Iz tightened her lips in an apologetic smile, though neither the apology nor the smile were very convincing. "I'm sorry. I promised I would only release that to the child in question, should they ever announce themself."

"Of course. Poor bastard." The formerly puffed-up secretary suddenly seemed as empty as a shirt on a clothesline. The specter of a renewed feud between the Yeardleys and Attertons appeared to trouble him as much as the possibility of an unexpected sire. Isolde had resolved one tribulation only to enliven another.

And yet, she did not care about the embattled Crown. At the moment, she only felt impatient with the secretary's stupor. Clearing her throat, she asked, "Would you like us to attempt to discover the identity of the child or whoever sent the letter?"

The question appeared to rouse Mr. Alman from his ruminations. "No. No, if the wretch wishes to be pilloried, let him announce his claim and out himself. And if he chooses to take his threats no further, then I imagine the Crown will not try to punish the miscreant any more than fate already has."

Isolde cocked her head. "You're hoping this will all blow over?"

"The king is gravely ill. The pillars of Berbiton are quivering. No need to hasten their collapse by starting a noble war behind closed doors." The secretary stood and practiced a formal bow to them both in turn, an extravagance they politely endured. "If there's nothing else, I will consider this the conclusion of our affiliation. Thank you for your assistance, Ms. Wilby, Mr. Wilby. You are as good as your reputation. Please send me your bill. I shall ensure remittance is prompt."

As they watched, the secretary stepped into the wind, leaning as if scaling a steep incline. Warren clucked his tongue as he squared up the loose pages and returned them to the dossier. "Another dissatisfied customer! Though, I have to admit, I'm a bit disappointed, too."

"Oh?" Iz murmured without breaking from her contemplation of the emptied street.

"I was hoping we'd find someone to invoice for a new rug."

Isolde shook her head as if rousing from a trance. "Yes, that's gnawing at me, too. Not the carpet—the mandrake, or more specifically, the person who put it in our basement. It had to be someone with foreknowledge of the case."

"Any guesses who that might be?"

"I suppose it might've been the Attertons. If anyone has the means to hire an enchanter, it's them. They also have plenty of ears in the king's court. Word of the king's true condition might've gotten back to them easily enough. Perhaps they feared renewed interest in the black sheep of the family and took steps to intervene. Though of course that's assuming they knew the whole truth of what happened in the alley all those years ago, which seems unlikely. Rudolph's siblings seemed genuinely caught off guard by my questions. It felt like I was reopening an old wound, one they hadn't considered in a while. And I doubt the duke, who called us . . . what was it? 'Finger-wigglers'? I doubt he would've secured the services of a practitioner. If he wanted to spoil our investigation, I expect he would've just hit us with a lawsuit—or a racing jaunt. Which leaves us with a less likable suspect, I'm afraid."

"Less likable than the duke? Impossible."

"It could be the military. If anyone would have knowledge of the king's private correspondence, it would be the War Department. I wouldn't be at all surprised to learn that they still have one or two magical assets lurking around, off the books and out of sight. The military appears to have signed on for a criminal cover-up, which is something they'd probably prefer not to see the press rake over."

"That *is* an alarming thought. Do you think this military magician is responsible for the talking starlings, then?"

"Sending a flock of birds to scare off a couple of private investigators doesn't really strike me as a military response. Would they put a mandrake in the cellar of a private residence? Perhaps. But a bunch of yapping birds? No. It doesn't feel right."

"Whether it was the military or the Attertons or someone else, do you think they'll leave us alone now? After all, the case is closed. Surely, whatever threat we posed has passed. What more could they want from us?"

"I don't know." Isolde made a steeple of her gloved fingers and pressed the point against her chin. "But I think Mr. Alman was right to be unsettled. An illegitimate child might've been dispatched with a lump sum or, if the blighter were too greedy, a lump on the head. What we have here is a conspiracy, one that seems to involve a powerful family and the military. The best we can hope for is that the parties involved will prefer just to move on—let the silence resume."

"Bah! This whole case was more trouble than it was worth. We ran three circles around the city, hopped up and down on one foot for five days straight, all just to see the whole affair papered over. I suppose that's what we get for serving at the Crown's pleasure."

Isolde stood and marched to the door, stopped and came around, opening her mouth to speak. Warren watched her expectantly, but she only swallowed the thought and shook her head.

"What is it?"

"I don't know. But this doesn't feel settled. It feels...*arranged*. It feels as if we were trying to solve the wrong mystery. I was looking up, when the road turned down." She squinted and worked the fingers of one hand as if twisting an invisible thread, a speculative gesture that made the furrows on Warren's brow multiply. He saw in her musing the looming specter of obsession.

He decided to introduce a distraction. "Did I mention we received a copy of Mr. Magnussen's new book in the post this morning? The publisher sent it over for comment or endorsement, should you feel so inspired."

Isolde's cheeks brightened with amused umbrage. "Oh, *did* he? Did he really? Well then, I simply must write Mr. Magnussen an approbation, one that will make the angels sing! His editor will weep tears of gratitude! The Publisher's Guild will declare a moratorium on publication to give his magnum opus room to breathe! Now, what rhymes with piss pot?"

AN ATOM OUT OF PLACE

Despite her lingering doubts about the results of her royal inquiry, Isolde found herself quickly absorbed by the piles of correspondence she had so long deferred. There were the usual armchair experts who came to quarrel over some aspect of her more famous investigations, or rather the erroneous version of events that appeared in the papers. More interesting (if depressing) were the letters from children who came with mysteries that ranged from banal noises in the night to missing parents, nearly all of whom had departed either with a suitcase in a jaunt or with flowers in a hearse. Requests for lectures and other public appearances were ever in profusion, though seldom entertained, as were the invitations from galleries wishing to display for public perusal the portalmanteau's many treasures. She had offers from would-be coauthors, occasional felicitations from fans congratulating her on another untangled plot, and an unending parade of pleas for help from the desperate victims of all manner of exploitation, misfortune, and barbarity—the vast majority of whom she could not help and yet hated to reject. Which got to the heart of why she detested her correspondence so deeply: It was full of refusals—full of ritualized and automatic and painful "noes." Few understood that while she was often brusque, she was not callous. Her affect was cool, but her heart was warm.

When she could bear the labor no longer, she turned to Warren for diversion. He soothed her with walks and theater tickets and outings to bookshops, museums, and restaurants where he confounded the staff by pouring entire boats of gravy into a tattered carpetbag that vented fire like a steak flambé.

So the days flowed, and the memory of the unsatisfying case of Jessamine and her misbegotten child began to fade from Isolde's thoughts, eroding like the clues to last week's crossword, until the evening edition of the *Berbiton Times* brought it all flooding back again a fortnight later.

In dishabille with legs tucked under her, Isolde sat in their living room before the cold fireplace, which had remained unused since their encounter with the mandrake. Not wishing to have the remains of a woodland golem in their parlor, Warren had swept and sponged the hearth and firebox until both were as clean as the day of their construction. So restored, he was reluctant to sully them again.

As the room's radiators ticked along with the patter of sleet upon the windows, Magnussen's manuscript lay open on the rug beside Isolde. She peered down at it with an expression of patent glee. Intermittently, she barked a laugh, then read aloud a particularly hilarious passage to her husband, sprawled upon the couch. On each occasion, Warren lowered the partition of his newspaper to better enjoy his wife's jubilation. He wore a matching set of striped pajamas that made him look a little like a sailor and somewhat like a convict—associations that he had taken advantage of in the playhouse of their bedroom.

"Here's another one," she said, clearing her throat to better affect an imperious tone that was somewhat undercut by her guffaws: " 'The hex-caster is also prone to libidinal disfunction. The stick of chalk—or alternatively the index finger—used to fashion hexes is an ancillary phallus, representing either the hex-caster's deficient virility or a latent envy of the organ in question, as is the case with many female practitioners.' "

"I think Magnussen is revealing more about himself than his subject." Warren chuckled as he uncrimped his paper. He had just resumed his reading when his merriment abruptly soured. "Oh, this is sad. Charlotte De Lee passed."

Isolde she sat up straight. "What?"

"She's listed in the Police Blotter under MISCHIEF AND MAYHEM."

"How did she die?" Isolde rose and rounded the couch to look over her husband's shoulder, even as War read aloud:

"'Ms. Charlotte De Lee was discovered partially immolated in a sitting chair in her home. Though the constables on the scene initially attributed her death to spontaneous combustion, the head investigator, Detective Aloysius Smud, suspects a less fantastic cause. An ashtray was discovered on the armrest of the burned chair, suggesting De Lee fell asleep while indulging in her vice.' The police have listed the cause of death as *accidental*."

"I don't believe that for a second. We know De Lee had her ritual, but she didn't smoke. She would never have fallen asleep with a cigarette in her hand. Of course, an intruder wouldn't have known that." Iz pinched the corner of the page, pulled it free, and read the remainder of the brief item as she paced. She murmured, "No tampered locks. No upturned furniture. No one reported any disturbance before the appearance of smoke..."

Arm hooked on the back of the couch, Warren observed her stormy patrol. She strode from the fir-wood spinet on the north wall to the framed tabula of a Hex of Vigilance on the south. On her third circuit, she choked the page at its middle and clasped her hands behind her back, inadvertently affecting a papery bustle.

"You think she was attacked, and the scene was staged to look like an accident? But by who? Someone from the palace? Someone trimming up the loose ends from the whole alleyway incident?"

Paper rustling as she trooped, Isolde wagged her head, not in disagreement but in deliberation. "Perhaps, perhaps. Or maybe she was killed by whoever is behind the bird brain. Remember, we led the flock right to her door."

Warren winced with guilt. "That poor woman. And her cats! My god."

"They'll be all right. Smud may not be the best investigator I ever met, but he is an animal lover. Always had a soft spot for strays."

Warren cupped his hands over his mouth as he grappled with sorrow for a woman he scarcely knew but immediately liked. He consoled himself with the thought that Charlotte was probably walking through the haunts of her beloved Beatrice in anticipation of their longed-for reunion. "What should we do? Go to the police? You're still on good terms with Smud, aren't you?"

Isolde paced faster. "And say what? That he got it all wrong? An old midwife who lived alone was not the victim of a smoldering cigarette but the target of a concerted plot, an assassination! You know how popular I am with the chief. He'd call me in just to bawl me out. And when he asks me to speculate on a motive, do I expose the king to ridicule and ourselves to retribution—now without a witness for a murder without a corpse? No, we can't pawn this off on the police, I'm afraid. I knew this case wasn't finished with us. I left the truth half-bared, and Ms. De Lee paid the price for my bungling!"

Warren grasped her swinging hand, bringing her increasingly frantic gallop to a halt. "You can't blame yourself for a lack of omniscience, Iz. You did your best. You did good work. You are not to blame."

Cheeks flushed, she raised his hand and kissed his round knuckles. "But I still accept responsibility. We must correct our mistakes, and find those who are guilty and hold them to account. We need to find the child—Rudolph Atterton's unacknowledged heir. I suspect they're either behind this or in danger themself."

Relieved to see her self-recriminations interrupted, Warren pounced upon the suggestion. "All right! Where do we start?"

"The orphanages. Jessamine was still in hiding when she died. We can assume so because her adoptive parents never found her. Her child would've almost certainly gone to the state, if it survived and the ring was not stolen by a— What's wrong? What are you doing?"

Hopping nimbly over the ottoman, the remainder of the evening edition drifting to the floor, Warren strode to the mantel. "It's nearly 9:30, now. If I work through the night, I can be ready by morning."

"Ready for what?"

"I can't very well go to an orphanage empty-handed!" He probed the pilaster, making the whittled sea monster in the oceanic frieze descend and the patched end of the portalmanteau appear. Snatching the case from its furtive cache, Warren undid the clasp and shouted into the recesses of the charmed satchel as he tramped toward the kitchen. "Wake up, Felivox! We're baking biscuits!"

Any other man with such a hulking build and bearing a wicker basket large enough to swallow a small child would probably have excited mistrust roaming the grounds of an orphanage. But Warren Wilby was as menacing as a panda bear. With one youngster sitting on his shoulders and another hanging from his neck, War doled out tissue-paper bindles bound up with red string, each filled with an assortment of lemon shortbread, sugar wafers, chocolate drops, and coconut bars.

As he filled mouths with baked goods and the yard with laughter, Isolde explained to the children's caregivers that she had discovered a familial connection to an orphan who would now be twenty-four years old. She came bearing the name of the deceased mother, Jessamine Bysshe (who also went by Jess Blessed), in hopes of learning the fate—or at least the name—of her child.

At best, Isolde's line of inquiry was met with exhausted reluctance to take on another chore, but more often, her questioning engendered disbelief among the custodians, who marveled at the Hexologist's naivety. Did she truly believe in the endurance, the accuracy, the perfect inviolability of the records of such underfunded, fragile institutions? Two decades ago, half of the staff were in pinafores themselves! Were they expected to know the names of wards who were old enough to be their own sibling? Still other staff members were stridently suspicious, speculating that her snooping was not inspired by an excess of charity but by the promise of an undisclosed monetary reward. While her husband gave away biscuits by the dozen, Ms. Wilby distributed calling cards like confetti to a procession of incurious persons.

The first day they managed to visit four orphanages and had nothing but crumbs and cool assurances that the matter would be looked into to show for their trudging. Their second, third, and fourth outings bore similar results. Isolde conscripted her mother into the effort, tasking her with scouring the records that had been surrendered to the Cardinal Library by the institutions that had been retired in recent years, of which there were nineteen in total. These, combined with the thirty-eight extant orphanages—to say nothing of the private charitable missions whose number was roughly twice that—presented the Wilbies with a task that was at first daunting, but soon virtually hopeless. By midweek, Warren was buying flour and sugar by the twenty-pound sack, and Isolde was searching for a printer who could produce a run of calling cards on short notice.

In the end, the epiphany did not leap from the dusty memory of an aging custodian or the fusty file drawer in the basement of an orphanage, but fell from the Lifestyle section of an old newspaper into the lap of a librarian.

Answering her mother's summons, Isolde and Warren once more gripped the imposing lip of the circulation desk amid the enforced hush of the Cardinal Library. Rays of whittled sunlight branched overhead, fine and dim as spider silk. A patron near the rail of the lowest atrium laughed, gasped, and clapped their hand over their mouth in anticipation of the dart. They were spared the blowgun's wrath. For the moment, the sentinel was distracted.

As an unabashedly smug Dr. Luella Timmons-Wilby recounted how she had come by her revelation, she teased Isolde with a folder that she whisked back and forth as if to discourage a stubborn fly. "It was all that combing through the files of orphans that brought it to mind. I hadn't thought about it in years, though there was a time when it was as common a topic as the weather. No one could decide whether it was a scandal or a social experiment, and it just went on and *on*."

Isolde pursed her lips, determined not to reward her mother with either a hint of curiosity or impatience. She refused to ask the obvious follow-up, a query that another person might've considered merely a polite demonstration of conversational interest. Iz thought her mother was enjoying herself a little too much, having once again proven a point the archivist loved to repeat: *More mysteries were solved from the shelf than on the street.*

The silence might've stretched on into a snit if Warren had not intervened at a whisper. "Sounds fascinating, Luella." He deposited a sachet of lavender macaroons on the illustrious ledge of the archivist's desk. "What sort of social experiment was it?"

Dr. Timmons-Wilby smiled at him appreciatively. "The fact that Victor Cholmondeley was young was part of the scandal. Scarcely thirty years old and adopting ten children. *Ten*. It raised a lot of eyebrows."

Keeping her eyes on the file, Isolde turned her face toward Warren, hunched beside her. "And you wanted to go to his party."

"I like parties. And flowers."

"I know, darling. I'm sorry."

Squinting at the couple's obscure exchange, Luella continued: "At the time, Victor Cholmondeley was a rising potentate of industry. An alchemist by trade, Mr. Cholmondeley was not content with generating thalanium. No, he wished to cast himself as a philanthropist, or rather a social engineer who would be embraced by a grateful nation for his innovations in welfare services and early education. At least, that's what he said at the outset. He adopted a cohort of ten young children to investigate the effect that breeding and rearing had on the success of a child. Some considered him a visionary doing legitimate scholarly work. Others marked him as a chauvinist of the poor—a man bent on proving the existence of a genetically imposed caste system.

"Again and again, his 'findings' appeared to confirm the thesis that no amount of education, nutrition, or opportunity could elevate the base intellects of generational indigence. Cholmondeley famously said, and I quote, 'Just as a man can't put a bowler on a chimpanzee and expect it to take tea with the queen, one cannot fill the sieve-like minds of the lowborn and expect them to synthesize genius. The attempt to do so is not only a waste of resources, it is a cruel imposition upon the poor cretins themselves who might otherwise be perfectly happy toiling in the fields,' end quote."

"What a prince," Warren grumbled.

"He wishes. But to your business: I believe that one of his chosen wards might be familiar to you." At last, Luella Timmons-Wilby opened the age-tinted dossier, revealing a newspaper clipping. This, she laid out for her daughter's inspection. The headline read CALL HIM PAPA CHOLMONDELEY. The ensuing article restated the premise of the alchemist's experiment, though in more flattering terms than the archivist had used. Yet, it was the accompanying picture that gripped Isolde's attention. The smudged quality of the image rendered the eleven figures stark as ink blots. Ten children stood in white bibs before a turreted manor that rather resembled a castle. Looming over the row of children was a spruce and smartly dressed Victor Cholmondeley. His striking features were arranged in an expression as soft and paternal as an anvil. The children, all similar in height and scarcely old enough to stand on their own, looked to have been startled out of bed just a moment before. Their names appeared below in accordance with their order in line.

Isolde's eye lighted upon the answer they'd been searching for all week. There, just to Cholmondeley's right, stood a pie-faced little ghost named Henry Blessed.

She moved to pinch the corner of the clipping, but her mother snatched the folder away. Dr. Timmons-Wilby smiled at her daughter's crimped expression. "Warren told me your association with the Crown has come to an end. So, I'm afraid there'll be no more royal dispensations for holdings out of circulation."

Iz turned to find Warren cringing apologetically. "That's quite all right. Thank you. We'll take it from here," she said.

"Everything you need to know about the Cholmondeley experiment is on the third floor." Dr. Timmons-Wilby offered a scrap of paper containing a short list of catalog numbers. "Here are a few titles to get you started, but, as usual, the real cultural dialogue is in the periodicals, which are—"

"Oh, we're not staying," Iz interjected.

"You're not?"

"No, I'm afraid we have a party to attend." The announcement appeared to come as some surprise to Warren, who was still digesting the remark when Isolde turned and advanced upon the exit amid the hammering of her heels.

Iz disliked it when visitors used the word "rambling" to characterize her home. "Rambling" suggested a deficit of purpose or intent. The fact was, every chamber, alcove, and closet of the four-story townhouse served a purpose. There was not so much as an aimless drawer in what her father had called Castle Wilby. The house did not *ramble*.

But it did go on a bit.

And as a predictable result, certain small items—keys, gloves, fountain pens—had a tendency to go missing. There was no more frequent victim of the house's vanishing act than Warren's cuff links, which were often removed in a distracted hurry and in a variety of locations as the Wilbies answered the call of their ardor. Warren frankly resented that he had to fiddle with the articles at all, which had fallen out of fashion years ago, but his size required specially tailored shirts, and his tailor, Mr. Sherman Katsaros, was a traditionalist who believed that buttons on cuffs were a symptom of societal collapse, leaving Warren little choice but to agree. He owned numerous pairs of links and many more partial sets that had been broken upon the altar of the insatiable house.

Which was how Isolde came to be at the rearmost corridor of the third floor, a narrow hall narrowed further by a surplus of wood trim. She seldom visited this corner of her home, and never without cause. But if they were going to at last bend to Victor Cholmondeley's concerted pleas and grace one of his boorish parties with their presence, cuff links were required and, for the moment, elusive.

Even twenty years later, she had to resist the impulse to knock on the door to her father's study. She turned on the light and allowed herself a moment to bask in the past. Above the stately chimneypiece hung a portrait of her grandfather. He had her father's dusky complexion, a tone Iz had not inherited, though they shared the same dark, crimped hair. His expression, which had seemed so imposing to her childish eyes, now appeared a bit startled. Her father's credenza desk, which had once been as tall and vast as a stage, had shrunk in the years since his disappearance. His book-crammed shelves, formerly full of the world's mysteries, now seemed mobbed by expired almanacs, discredited histories, and the indulgent musings of every kook and crackpot to ever have taken up a pen.

Isolde took it all in: the shrunken majesty, the cairns of notebooks, the haystacks of correspondences—all was as he'd left it, save for two additions, the foremost of which was dust. A fine silt fogged every spine, spindle, and panel. While her mother had been in the house, she had not allowed Professor Wilby's study to be cleaned for fear that dusting might lead to tidying, and tidying might invite a purge. Luella Timmons-Wilby believed every shred of paper, every pencil shaving, every crumb of tobacco in the pipe caddy's well was an essential relic in her husband's feretory, which in total represented a powerful beacon. The study was calling out to Silas Wilby. One day it would guide him home...

Though Isolde did not share her mother's delusion, when Luella moved out, it had proved easier to continue the tradition of avoiding her father's study than to address the mess he had left behind.

Other than dust, the only other addition to the room sat on the desktop under a white cotton coverlet.

Forgetting Warren's cuff links, Isolde approached the shrouded capsule. She pulled the hood from the crystalline bell, revealing an hourglass, caged with three turned posts of brass and capped with discs of alabaster. Mr. Ecklous, her father's banker, had sent it over after the fateful visit in which he announced the timepiece evidenced his client's death. The sands inside stood frozen in a cone that clung to the roof of the top chamber in defiance of gravity.

Neither Isolde nor her mother held the hourglass in sufficient esteem as to consider it the authority on Silas Wilby's continued existence. No, Iz let her father's final letter and his protracted absence crack the gavel in that regard, and nothing as simple as an office ornament was enough to dispel her mother's stubborn faith.

Yet, there was something undeniably odd about the hourglass.

Isolde stooped to get a better look at the stagnant funnel of snowy sand. Her gaze caught upon a small interruption on the floor of the lower reservoir. Off to one side of center lay a single grain of sand.

"Hello," she murmured. Had it been there before? She couldn't say for certain. Perhaps it had, but then, why hadn't she noticed it?

Seized by a sudden compulsion, she lifted the protective shell from the timepiece, gripped the gravity clock by two of its pillars, and shook it as if she were salting her eggs.

Raising the hourglass to eye level, she found that neither top cone nor the bottom atom of sand had been unsettled by her vigorous effort.

"You all right, darling?" Warren said from the open doorway.

Setting the timepiece down again, Isolde laughed at herself. "Just trying to shake ol' Dad awake." Before War could answer her glib reply, she hurried to ransack a bank of little drawers near the lap of her father's desk. "I know they're here somewhere..."

Amazed to see his wife riffling through what he understood to be a shrine to the patriarch—a holy of holies upon which only dust could intrude—Warren's voice quivered with uncertain laughter. "What are you doing?" He reseated the bell over the hourglass. Taking up the instrument's dustcover, he unveiled a stack of papers. His eye naturally fell to the signature at the bottom of a protruding page: the hieroglyph of a winter-stripped tree. Seeing Mr. Snag's mark always made him shudder. Though Isolde was more ambivalent on the point, Warren held Mr. Snag and his tempting letters solely responsible for his father in-law's vanishment. "Is this really the time to go searching for more mysteries—what with our full plate and all?" He tugged the coverlet down over the crystal dome.

"I'm just looking for—aha!" She plucked from a minor cubby a little velvet box. She thumbed the clamshell open upon a pair of nacre-capped cuff links. "Here we are." She strutted up to him with the set.

Warren put his hands and dangling cuffs behind his back. "I'm not going to wear your father's cuff links, Iz. You know I'll only lose them."

"And wouldn't *that* be fitting?" Her attempt at humor had a manic edge to it.

Warren frowned with concern. "Are you all right? You never come in here."

Isolde sobered a little, reconsidering the fasteners in her palm. "Maybe my mother is right. Maybe all of this is just a rash and half-hearted appeal to a ghost. Unwilling fathers, orphans, and bastards grasping at straws, vying for recognition, validation, approval. It all cuts a little close to the bone, I suppose." She retrieved his hand, which had fallen to his side. He did not resist when she pressed into his wide palm the cold treasure she'd seized from her father's desk drawer.

"I will cherish them," he said.

She peered at a slip of paper tucked into the lid of the little box. "Says here they were a gift from the bank to commemorate the tenth anniversary of my father's account."

Warren wiggled his brows. "How fancy! Too bad you chucked your mermaid tail in the bin. We would've made quite the stir."

"Oh, but my true tails are still hanging in my closet."

"Gah! That's not fair. I'm going to look like a tarred man waiting to be feathered next to you!"

She pressed her chest to his. "You are the only man I've ever known who wears his suits and not the other way around. Most men wilt into their coats. You bloom." She kissed him on the chin, then charged into the hall, shouting over her shoulder, "And just to prepare you: I expect this evening will be a disaster!"

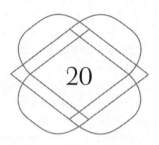

THE INFERNAL HALOS OF INDUSTRY

Three hours later, Isolde found her previous use of the word "disaster" both prescient and perhaps a touch insufficient.

The thrumming conveyor belt at the heart of the industrialist's mill carried her forward at a ponderous clip. She rode scrunched up like a jockey upon a gargantuan sheaf of green trunks that had been stripped of their leaves and limbs, though not their sap. After a moment of thrashing and tugging, Isolde had discerned that this botanical glue was as inescapable as flypaper. She was well and truly caught.

Her sticky mount had continued to crawl through Victor Cholmondeley's backyard factory, though her dawdling passage failed to make the log's destination any less terrifying. The Entobarrus—that tempestuous and fiery realm—blazed before her through a gaping portal of enchanted flame, a coruscating orange ring that sizzled like a quenching vat. The energy that crackled out of that hellmouth was as baffling as it was uncomfortable. Isolde felt its heat pass through her very bones.

At present, her coming damnation was being attended by a pair of alchemists, a Haloist and a Flail, who stood atop rebar minarets on either side of the grinding conveyor. They were arrayed in the traditional black-and-red panoplies of their profession and were so absorbed by the work of keeping the blistering hatch open that neither noticed the woman in coattails riding a log backward into hell.

Isolde's efforts to shout herself into their notice were foiled by the squeals of something that resembled a giant fleshy spider, one that shrieked like a derailing train, and was crowned with thirty-two eyes, all of them iridescent as a pearl. It—whatever *it* was—scrambled about the bound cord of wood as it broke upon the Entobarrus's raging climate. The Flail cast shocks of jagged blue energy at the devil's hooking legs, though the monstrous arachnid scarcely flinched at these repeated assaults. Should those deterrents ever fail, Isolde knew, the Haloist would be compelled to let the gate collapse, interrupting production, saving the nation, and perhaps on this occasion, cutting her in half.

The alchemist's bolts, which cracked like thunder over Isolde's head, began to crash nearer and nearer to her feet. If the lightning spared her, the scab-hided spider surely would not. She couldn't imagine which demise she would prefer, though the point was moot because fate had yet, over the course of her short and foolish life, to ever ask for her opinion.

Two hours earlier, she and Warren had sat cozied together in the back of a hired jaunt, both bedecked in menswear, though to quite different effects. Iz had oiled and pinned her hair, taming it into a coif that resembled a dandy's, parted on the right. The slender lapels and long tails of her coat combined with her talc-white shirt and open collar made her look as svelte as a magpie. She could've high-stepped across the stage of a cabaret and not seemed out of place. War, meanwhile, was arrayed in a maroon-vested pinstripe suit and a necktie that was as lurid as a tongue. The striking ensemble, which he had purchased the previous season and then immediately lost the courage to wear (for fear that it would make him look like a bear tangled up in the drapes) had been recommended that evening by Iz, who confessed she thought it made him appear a little rakish and dangerous and *wasn't that fun*? Riding in the purring vessel, they both felt a bit fizzy in their costumes, which they fought the urge to lustfully remove.

They had been compelled to travel light. Since they could not bear to see the portalmanteau flung into a cloakroom, they were defenseless save for the Umbra Annulus, a small onyx ring that Isolde had squeezed onto her pinkie finger. Warren disliked the mystic trinket and plainly said so when Iz had put it on. She had reassured him that she would use it sparingly. The promise had done little to assuage Warren's apprehensions as he pointed out that one could hardly use a hole to infinity by halves.

Mr. Victor Cholmondeley's manor—in defiance of contemporary tastes—was an asymmetrical, overdecorated country castle that looked radically different from every approach. The abundant, haphazardly placed windows appeared to have been punched by a harried train conductor. The roofline was ragged with parapets and witch's hats and finials. An immense rose window, which locals called the Goat's Eye, beamed from under the brow of the highest eve, its black bar and golden circumference visible from hilltops more than a mile away. When illuminated, many considered that jaundiced iris a harbinger of mischief, and it was almost always lit.

Though the rose window was a more recent addition, the rest of Cholmondeley's abode was a relic of the past that might've easily become a ruin had it not been for the industrialist's intervention. At the ripe old age of twenty-six, the lowborn alchemist Victor Gill had bought the three-hundred-year-old estate (composed of a carriage house, a sprawling stable, a chapel, and a manse) and the family name, Cholmondeley, with it. He'd rescued all from the verge of oblivion and, by dint of will and labor, had raised the crumbling landmark to prominence again.

Though, indeed, there had been a time when the estate had seemed too great a burden for the alchemist. Some years prior, there had been threats of foreclosure and last-minute negotiations with the bank, embarrassments that had not escaped the attention of the press. It was only in the past five or six years that Cholmondeley's fortunes had reversed, a boon attributable to a single technological innovation.

While the rest of the industrial alchemists were forced to go to greater extremes to import lumber from the ever-receding forests of foreign lands, Cholmondeley had devised an as-yet secret method for conjuring enormous quantities of organic material, seemingly out of thin air. While his competitors vied to keep their thalanium mills active, electrahol flowed from his refineries at an unflagging pace. Victor was as rich as a god and more popular.

Yet, for all his accomplishments, Cholmondeley had failed to attain what many suspected he desired most: a title. Despite his successes and philanthropic efforts, the monarchy had shunned him, knighting first his peers, then his inferiors, until it was obvious that he was fighting to overcome an insurmountable debt in the eyes of King Elbert's court. Perhaps his low birth was to blame. Perhaps the regent found the alchemist's past social experiments distasteful. Whatever the cause, Mr. Cholmondeley seemed the principal example of a new breed: the plebeian tycoon.

Ignoble or not, the elite flocked to him and his soirees like flies to a cidery. His parties walked the line between exuberance and excess, revelry and debauchery. Despite the fusty skin of his adopted estate, Mr. Cholmondeley's taste in food, wine, music, art, and guests was positively avant-garde and culturally prophetic. Victor's monthly affairs had established the careers of chefs, debuted once-in-a-generation artists, and launched lines of fashion that would shape the styles of shopwindows and sidewalks for years to come. Conversely, the delirious occasions had also ruined politicians, humbled intellectuals, and nullified wedding vows. His bashes were reliably full of bombshells, the shrapnel of which often punctured the pages of the gossip rags.

Cholmondeley had been mailing invitations to the Wilbies for years, though he might as well have posted his entreaties to the sea for all the attention they received. Iz had no desire to endorse with her presence a man who craved validation above all else. She suspected that the only reason the summonses continued after so many snubs was that the industrialist enjoyed crowing to his guests that the famed Hexologists *might* arrive at any moment.

Iz wondered whether, in retrospect, the industrialist would come to regret both the boast and his persistence.

The black hoods of dozens of luxury jaunts blended with the benighted hills beyond the iron entry gates where the taxi deposited the Wilbies. The manor was as bright as a campfire and similarly remote, though strangely, as the Wilbies crunched up the wide gravel path through an alameda of junipers and luminaria, the impression was not one of finding a refuge in the wilderness but of approaching a new and gaudy wasteland. Merry whoops and trills of elation erupted from the open windows, competing with the dazzling cacophony of a brass combo. A window broke. More laughter flooded out. A muscular bimbo wearing a pink feather boa and nothing else busted from the tree line ahead of them, nimbly pursued by a shimmering lady in a dress of cascading golden tassels. The two crashed through the pencil trees on the other side, the man howling when the branches flayed his nethers. It was balmy for a February night, but not *that* balmy.

"Looks like we're overdressed," Isolde quipped.

Absorbing the upper-class circus with some amusement, the Wilbies were still smiling when they were accosted at the château's soaring front doors by a pair of alchemists in dark leather vestments and raised hoods. The breastplates of those guards were bolted with the medallions of their trade: wards of protection and power. Neither Iz nor Warren resisted the search that followed. Warren held out his arms to assist the blond-bearded alchemist who had the hard look of a man who delighted in making a production of sucking the marrow out of beef bones. He seemed conspicuously mean, which only inspired Warren to chat with him more.

The woman who searched Isolde had a gaze as warm as a morgue and a hood crowded with coils of black hair. She slapped Iz up and down with similarly tenderizing force. She found her eyeliner pencil and bill clip, returning both to the pockets they had come from. When she groped under Isolde's shirt collar, Iz said, "Whoever drew that Ward of Pinions on your left side didn't know what they were doing. They didn't close the rosette. It's useless." Isolde pointed to the spot where the leather stamping broke. "That wouldn't put off a mockingbird, much less a harpy."

"This cuirass belonged to my mother. She made it herself," the alchemist growled.

"Well, at least you didn't overpay."

The alchemist looked as if she might move her wrenching of Isolde's shirt to her throat, when she was interrupted by someone calling her name from above. "It's all right, Silva. Let them through, please."

Flattening the points of her collar, Iz linked arms with her husband, and together, they mounted the steps past the scowling sentinels. As they neared the crest of their ascent, they were met by the one who'd interrupted their frisking. He was shoeless, but well dressed. His mane of iron hair was further embellished by the teardrop chandelier above him. The impression was angelic and, Isolde had no doubt, quite intentional.

He spoke in a torrent: "It's not so bad when you get a little closer, is it? Though I admit it looks a bit grim from the street. But you...you came! I'm so—" He breathed deeply through his nose and ground his palms together as his eyes brightened with rehearsed emotion. "Please—*please* come in. I hope Silva and Mayer didn't bruise you. I tell them to be gentle, but they..." His eyes squinched to abet an exaggerated grin. "They suspect everyone. They think the flies cracking on the windows carry daggers up their sleeves. But, my god! I thought you'd never come. Never! I thought—" He patted the air about them like a museum curator delighting over a new addition. "But how was the drive? How are you? Come in, come in."

Victor Cholmondeley projected the burly vitality and hypoxic cheer of a mountaineer. His beard was sculpted to a wedge, and his copious head of hair stood artfully disheveled. His suit, flouting the current mode, was loosely fitted. An undone bow tie spilled from the breast pocket of his dinner jacket. Peeking out from under the droopy cuffs of his white trousers was a pair of black-socked feet, which the industrialist arched in pleasure. The man exuded charm and an easiness that seemed at odds with his history. Isolde had come expecting to meet an iron rod, but here was a bouncing spring.

Perceiving her surprise, the industrialist said, "A rich man who does not know how to enjoy his wealth is just a pauper with a hoard. I have learned that life cannot be relished in retrospect, nor reveled in by proxy."

"True enough, sir!" War exclaimed, shaking their host's hand with reciprocated vigor. As he did, he couldn't help but gape at the scene over the man's shoulder. The grand stair that cascaded and curled like a velvet avalanche from the atrium above was festooned with partygoers, some seated and whispering, others draped like drowsy cats between risers, still others saddled upon the marble banister and sliding down to a growing orgiastic pile. A shirtless poet stood atop a pedestal over the smithereens of a vase and an explosion of flowers, reading from a chapbook and flogging her back with a birch branch. A pair of barking toucans orbited the chandelier and contributed their own occasional confetti.

Not all of Cholmondeley's guests were in the grips of such wild abandon. The adjacent ballroom was swamped with lords in black ties and ladies in tiaras, who congregated in defensive clumps, sipping dishes of champagne, each doing their level best not to look scandalized. The house's staff, arrayed in immaculate and quite traditional uniforms, wove through the mob—past flamboyant wallflowers and exhibitionist drunks—bearing

great silver dishes of aperitifs and cigar boxes and bowls hilled with colorful pills that pepped you up or tamped you down. It was bedlam, a hedonistic riot, or as Victor described it, "the usual whoop-de-do."

But this was evidently not the scene the industrialist wished to show
the Wilbies, nor the cause of his determined campaign of invitations. With
several quick escalations of his brows, he communicated to Silva, who had
just clapped Isolde from knee to neck, that he expected her to open a channel through the hilarity.

While wizards preferred wands and hex-casters liked chalk, the cus-
tomary implement of the alchemist was an iron crozier. Silva raised her
shepherd's crook over the heads of the attendees, leaving Warren to wonder if she didn't mean to brain someone. But rather than physically beat
a path, the alchemist conjured a static field of yellow sparks that cracked
and leapt like sugar on a fire. This stable wedge of energy pushed into the
crowd, nudging them aside like the prow of a ship.

Arms bent to embrace an absent partner, Victor Cholmondeley waltzed
himself into the clearing. Coming around, he winked at the Wilbies, inviting them to follow, which they did, though with less lively steps.

Though the alchemist's field was ambivalent as to how or where it
shoved the revelers, none of the partygoers seemed much surprised or
alarmed by the displacement. Isolde took this for a regular occurrence—
the host's preferred vehicle for selective mingling. From the center of the
evanescing void he waved with the dreamy automation of a pageant winner on a parade float. They traversed the active dance floor, skirted the
wailing brass band, and arrived a moment later in a short hall that concluded in a tall iron-studded door. Producing a set of keys from his pocket,
the industrialist said, "I love my guests! I do, I do. But I never put anything out for the public that I couldn't bear to see broken."

He cracked the door just enough to allow him to slip into the room
beyond. The Wilbies followed him into the gap with the industrialist's
bodyguard close behind.

A bank of glass doors enclosed the western side of the adjoining salon,
affording a partial view of the industrialist's workshop and the encompassing clear-cut hills. The inky edifice of that structure was interrupted,
here and there, by leaks of light. Eerie rays pushed their way through
cracks in the blacked-out casements.

The salon before them was guarded by no fewer than a dozen custodians, whose cheerful cobalt uniforms and white gloves were a little
annealed by the rifles they clutched.

It seemed to Iz there was something off about the salon's character, its
arrangement, and furnishings. The dark tin ceiling and fulsome moldings,
the stiff tapestries of dragons with serpentine tongues and canine bodies,
the plentiful cases, shelves, and pedestals arrayed with the formal den-
sity of a hedge maze—all together conveyed an ostentation that evoked a
wealthy child's dollhouse rather than an exhibit hall. Everything seemed
a little too large, crowded, and ungainly.

In contrast to this pretentious staging were the objects on display.
Encased in glass boxes and secluded behind protective panes were the
shards of ancient urns, the remnants of deteriorating tablets, rot-eaten
clothes, effaced coins, and a hundred other crumbs of the past, each presented on velvet cushions and under spotlights with all the pomp and
solemnity of saintly relics.

The industrialist beamed as he enumerated his holdings for the Wilbies' edification: Here was the eggshell of a griffin. Here were the stock-
ings of the Arbiter of Romagea—or at least the right one. And here was the
Hammerstone of Knorrl, used to produce the arrowheads that defeated the
Wraith Army of Bosaken, some one thousand years ago.

"It's quite an impressive gallery—a veritable museum," Isolde said
with more charity than was her habit.

The industrialist raised his hands in playful demurral, though her flattery clearly pleased him. "I'd say it's closer to half of one. An indispens-
able wing of a greater hall, perhaps."

Perceiving at last the all-too-familiar cause behind Cholmondeley's
stubborn invitations, Isolde sighed. "My father's collection. I wondered
how long it would take you to get around to that. Certainly didn't waste
much time."

"You know who likes to dally and tease? Uncertain persons. Which I
am not." The industrialist raised his hands to fix the words upon an imaginary marquee. "The Cholmondeley-Wilby Museum of the Magical Arts.
Or perhaps you'd prefer the reverse. Personally, I think that Cholmondeley-
Wilby rolls along better than Wilby-Cholmondeley."

Isolde stopped herself from replying that they both sounded like a euphemism for venereal disease. "I suppose you regard yourself as a patron of the race."

"God, no!" Victor found his reflection in one of the crystal boxes, bared his teeth, and checked his gums. "Humanity is such an unambitious assemblage of tics and vices. People don't want to be patronized. They want to wallow. They want to breed. They want to be affirmed. I'd put it this way: The trees are not the benefactors of the grass. Neither are we the parents of the masses. No, if anything, I want to protect all of this *from* them—from the capricious agendas of the common man. I mean, Izzy, really! We both know the day is coming when they will decide tomorrow doesn't need us, doesn't need magic. The state has already criminalized our cousins—the wizards and necromancers. Surely, we're next! Our days are numbered."

Meaning to goad him, Isolde watched him closely when she answered: "Is that what your adopted children were—*unambitious assemblages of tics and vices?*"

For the first time, Victor Cholmondeley's expression darkened and Isolde perceived in his surprise the annoyance of a man who was unaccustomed to being challenged. Though the industrialist quickly composed himself with a credible hee-haw. "I was naive in my youth. From what I know of your career, you were, too." He dusted the lip of a plinth with his finger. "But look, Izzy, I came from humble circumstances. And predictably, there was a moment when I wondered if I had not, amid my self-education, discovered some secret method for elevating a person from squalor to . . . well, to all of this. I thought I was made of common clay, that we *all* were. But I was wrong. The only thing my efforts did was convince me that I am unusual. I believe exceptional persons find a way to distinguish themselves as a matter of course. The old way of relying on bloodlines to generate our society's greatest assets—our wisest leaders, our most savvy generals—well, I think we've all grown disenchanted with that particular farce. The market is the new court in which a man of sufficient talent may build his throne. Success is its own coronation."

"But a lonely one. What happened to your children?"

The industrialist ducked his head and crossed his hands behind his back, adopting the posture of one bound and pulled along by greater forces. "When they turned eighteen, I saw each of them placed in a profession according to their talents. They are all happy enough and certainly no worse off than if they had passed through the grinder of a workhouse on their own."

Iz considered an encased rusted object, corroded beyond recognition. She stooped to read the placard, which identified it as a hinge from a shutter upon the window of a shrine that had long since collapsed. "So you consider the experiment a success?"

"Those children came to me with empty bellies and cornhusk dolls and washed-out cameos of dead parents and that was it, Izzy. That was it! And you know, I saved each and every one of their wretched little treasures. I kept them locked away, and then on their sixteenth birthday, I gave it all back to them. I said, 'Here are the rags you came with. You can put them on again, or you can let them go. Release them! Burn them! Be free!' And that's just what they did. They put the rags of their past in a crucible, and we burned them together."

"What about Henry Blessed?"

Victor's beard bristled about a confused sneer. "Who?"

Isolde scrutinized him with the same care she'd lately paid a hinge. "Henry Blessed. He was one of your adopted."

The industrialist fussed with his loose cuffs and eyed his posted men, tics which Isolde took were intended to remind himself of his station. His easy air had nearly vanished when he said: "This is starting to feel like an interrogation, Izzy. I've been nothing but cordial to you and—"

"Think of this as more of an interview, Vicky." Isolde stroked her throat as if it were a cat. "I know what you want. I do. But I don't like surprises, and I do my research. So, before I cut the ribbon on a museum with a stranger, I'd like to know exactly what I'm signing on for." Isolde sniffed and paid him a withering smile. "But I understand if you value your privacy more than opportunity. I didn't mean to put you on the spot."

The sock-footed industrialist skated on his polished floor as he hurried to reassure her. "Wait, wait! Come, now! Henry? Yes, yes, of course, I remember Henry. I lov— Henry had such beautiful potential! He was the brightest of the lot. Determined, inventive, unsentimental. But he..." The industrialist gagged his mouth with the cup of one hand and appeared to suffer a flurry of emotions, though he recovered quickly enough and dropped his muzzle. "Henry died, the poor boy. He was sixteen. He set out to swim across the river. You know how capricious those currents can be.

The police never recovered his body. It was a . . . necessary reminder that some losses cannot be recouped. I put his headstone in my own plot. Of all my children, he was the closest to being a son."

Isolde ducked her head in commiseration. "I'm sorry for your loss."

Cholmondeley rubbed his nose and sniffed wetly. "We all soldier on. But I take it, this means you have at least considered melding our collections?"

"Frankly, at the moment, I'm more interested in a lavatory. It was a long drive, and I didn't know we were going to leap right into the thick of things here."

"Yes, of course." The industrialist turned to his bodyguard, Silva, and charged her with escorting Ms. Wilby to the washroom. This was done under the auspice of making certain she did not lose her way, though Isolde understood why Cholmondeley would want to keep an eye on her in his home. She was careful not to advertise she had discerned his distrust.

Silva, however, was not so coy. The moment they were out of the vaulted gallery, she gripped Isolde by the elbow and marshaled her through a series of halls, which included a fair smattering of nodding guests on benches and day sofas. They hadn't progressed far before becoming embroiled in a crowd attempting to press through too small of a doorway and all at once.

"You don't care to plow through with your iron wand?" Isolde said.

"I only do that for important people," Silva answered, appearing to take pleasure in the thought that their delay would be causing the Hexologist some discomfort.

A barefoot gentleman in a feather-fringed domino bumped against the same blockade of guests Isolde found herself caught behind. "This always happens when the kitchen puts out the shrimp. Everybody riots," he muttered, glancing at her. Reconsidering, he surveyed her more pointedly from pant cuff to starched collar. "Ms. Wilby? Is that you?" He pushed the mask onto his brow, where it roosted like a road-flattened bird.

Isolde groaned at the revelation of the reporter's flushed face, his unbuttoned shirt, and the round knuckles of his exposed breastbone. "Mr. Magnussen."

"Oh, please call me Lorcan."

"No."

He laughed. "I thought you said you wouldn't be able to attend."

"Just trying to throw you off the scent."

Her sarcasm was wasted on Mr. Magnussen, who took the comment as praise. "Oh, you know me—tenacious as a tick! So, what do you make of our host? I think he's a pretty impressive fellow. Such an inspiring story! Hustling his way up from beggary, amassing by pure grit all of this... *grandeur.*" Lorcan smiled at Isolde's imposing escort, perhaps expecting her to show approval at his flattery of her employer. The alchemist peered back at him with the passionless intensity of a gun barrel. Magnussen forged ahead: "It makes you think about how much personal responsibility dictates the fate of the poor. Victor is proof that anyone can be rich."

Isolde snickered. "First off, I don't think that's quite the compliment you think it is, and secondly, fortunes are mostly made thanks to a surfeit of luck and a paucity of morals. Tenacity, talent, and principles are all common enough. It's avarice that's scarce."

"You're a believer in the virtuous poor, I see. Seems a trifle reductive, doesn't it?"

"Then allow me to reduce it further. Cholmondeley treated his adopted children as social experiments while exploiting them for good press. And he made most of his treasure by wringing the life from the verdant world. He's a lucky man without a heart."

Magnussen gasped, though he seemed to be enjoying the shock. "He's a pillar of society!"

Isolde locked eyes with the alchemist looming at her side. "He's a fence post in a cow patch."

"Surely, this isn't the time to be stoking the flames of classism! Not while our king's health is so fragile." Magnussen's effort to maintain a confident hands-on-hip pose was abruptly spoiled by the arrival of another wave of guests, come in search of prawns, who rammed against the clog outside the dining hall, driving everyone closer together in body, if further apart in spirit. Now smashed against the grimacing hex-caster, the reporter carried on, though with diminished cool. "I heard the Crown hired you to investigate his affliction. What is it? Evil spirits? A witch's curse? Or has gout finally caught the old boy by the toe?"

"I haven't the faintest idea what you're talking about," Iz replied with convincing boredom. Then the obstruction broke and the bodies began to flow again. Lorcan Magnussen's next remark was overwhelmed by a general cheer. The reporter could not keep from being swept up by the crowd as Iz waved farewell. Leaning toward her escort, Iz said, "I bet you five gallets he tries to leave here with shrimp in his pocket."

Silva jabbed her iron crook into Isolde's ribs, a painful interjection that she still preferred over recent company.

They trudged on through clouds of perfume and smoke as they traveled farther and farther into the rambling manor, compelled by competition (and one instance of clogged plumbing) to consider a number of toilets before at last discovering a vacant washroom beneath a servants' stair.

Standing in the doorway, Isolde turned on her heel, holding up her eyeliner pencil. "This is going to keep me up tonight. May I please fix your ward?"

The alchemist bared her teeth. "My mother was killed by a bane bird. It snipped off her head and carried it back to its nest. I know her armor is imperfect. I'm not willfully repeating her mistake. I'm leaving the door open for retribution. I want it to come back. I want it to take me to its nest. I want to retrieve my mother's skull." Silva leaned into Iz until the brim of her hood nearly knocked against her brow. "This isn't a fault. It's a lure."

"I respect that." Isolde capped her pencil. Turning toward the powder room, she added, "I'll just be a moment," and shut the door.

A colorful leaded window stood over the commode. Climbing onto the porcelain tank, she cranked the window open and briefly delighted in the fresh air. She brushed the dust from the sill outside to make it appear as if she had used it to exit into the garden.

Hopping down, she caught sight of herself in the mirror above the sink. Already her pasted-down curls were breaking free, snaking out, rising up. There seemed no point in trying to tame them. Some things could not be reasoned with. Her hair would always pursue its shape, and she would chase her answers.

She pulled the onyx ring from her little finger, took several deep breaths, and popped the Umbra Annulus into her mouth.

Like a wishing well swallows a coin, Isolde fell into her shadow puddled upon the floor.

21

OVER, UNDER, BACK, AND THROUGH

S hadow swimming was a lost art, or rather a vanished one. Twelve
  hundred years prior, during the plateau of the Second Viruin
  Empire, the Umbrists had been the premier clan of leasable assassins. Having mastered the ability to dive between shadows like an arctic
seal traverses holes in the ice, the Umbrists could pass under the noses of
entire armies, cross moats, and slither beneath barred doors. They seemed
to simply materialize under the beds of their noble quarries, who they'd
strangle or carve open before departing as they'd come.

For decades, the vaguest allusion to the Umbrists was enough to inspire
a merchant or lord to call for more light, and indeed, the more cautious
aristocrats took to sleeping on the bare floor in the center of empty chambers while every torch and lamp burned through the night.

Then all at once and at the height of their terrible sway, the Umbrists
disappeared. They descended into the shadows, never to resurface, taking
with them the secrets of their magic. Their departure was so sudden and
complete, their exploits began to shift from terrible truth to unsettling
myth—melding, as they so readily did, with the lore of frightened children. *There are no monsters under the bed* and no Umbrists, either. No evidence of their existence survived save for a single artifact—long rumored,

long disbelieved—rediscovered an age later by a particularly determined explorer named Professor Silas Wilby.

What happened to the Umbrists was a subject of esoteric debate, the sort of thing that inspired schisms among academics and red-faced arguments over a second bottle of wine—this, despite the fact (or perhaps *because* of it) that the question could never be definitively answered. The two most popular theories were that either the Umbrists had succumbed to internal dispute and backstabbed themselves from existence, or they had been hunted to extinction, falling victim to the tactical placement of light traps.

Isolde was agnostic on the point, though she suspected the truth might be more pedestrian than either theory. The most common cause of lost magic was professional paranoia and the reluctance to share knowledge with a new generation. Iz knew all too well how much expertise could evaporate with even one untimely death.

Still, it was no mystery why Warren did not like the Umbra Annulus. Swimming between shadows was like plunging into an unlit sea, one with a woozy sense of dimension, an indefinite floor and an uncertain ceiling. From inside the veneer of shadow, the lit world appeared as through a warped pane of glass. Wherever light fell, the surface was visible but quite unreachable. And once one dove into a shadow, one could only escape through the hatch of another.

Submerged, Isolde slipped under the bathroom door and flowed under the soles of Silva's shoes. Iz's view was wavering, her perspective confused and truncated. She could see little of the mansion in any direction. Beside the shadows and sheets of distorted light, there were stark absences—inky edges where a wall or a table leg met the floor. It was like navigating a hedge maze or the tread of a giant's boots. It took a moment for her to get her bearings, though she made a point of not looking down at the nothing that yawned below. She focused instead on immediate landmarks. There was the foot of the grandfather clock they had lately passed; there was the square foundation of the baluster. The dim servant stairs rose like a ragged cliff, or perhaps it more nearly resembled a frozen waterfall.

It was called "shadow swimming" because one had to flail their limbs to propel oneself forward, though the medium was thinner than water and somewhat more like air—except there was none of that inside the void, either. A shadow swimmer had to hold their breath and hope to reach the next airhole in time. If they failed in this, they would suffocate and their body would drift from the twilit world, sinking into a gulf that was as thin as a silhouette and deep as the infinite.

Pushing such harrowing thoughts aside, Isolde swam up the stairs as the cuffs of butlers and the hems of maids flashed above her.

Cresting the final step, she marked the mounting insistence of her lungs. She looked for an out-of-the-way spot to emerge, discerning what seemed a long plank of rippling gloom amid the busy corridor. She broke the surface with the slow discretion of a crocodile. When her chin was above the shadow line, she bit the ring and opened her mouth to breathe around it. The strobe of running legs greeted her as the house staff fled this way and that. From there, she could smell the kitchen's aromas and hear the clatter of pans. Glancing up, she saw that she had surfaced under the cover of a bench, which was fortunate, because had the staff witnessed the head of a woman bobbing up from the floor, a panic might've broken out.

Taking the lay of the land, Iz craned her neck until she found the foot of the next stair, which was defended by a leathered alchemist—a positive sign, she thought. Any egress that necessitated a guard (even among the vetted staff) could only lead somewhere interesting. Isolde filled her lungs, moved the Annulus from her teeth to one cheek, and dove again into the shadows.

She carried on diving and surfacing, picking her way onward, always upward through the manor's many levels. When the servants' area afforded her too few lightless recesses, she moved to the main halls, which were even more heavily patrolled and so relatively deserted—though that did not necessarily work in her favor. A head appearing under a chair in a bustling corridor was easier to overlook. Still, she was not roaming idly; she had a destination in mind. She wished to explore what lay behind the Goat's Eye. The stained glass beacon that the locals reviled had excited a very different feeling in her. Even from the lawn, Isolde recognized the colorful window for what it really was: an enormous protective hex.

When Isolde had told Warren that she intended to have a quick look around Cholmondeley's back rooms, he'd asked her what she hoped to find. She'd answered, "Prince Sebastian's ring would be quite a convenient discovery, but barring that, any evidence that would connect Victor to the threatening letter." Warren thought that hunting for such a small object inside a crowded mansion was a hopeless errand. And though Isolde agreed, she believed her odds of unearthing something useful would be much improved if she narrowed her search to Cholmondeley's most well-guarded room.

When Isolde discovered she'd at last run out of stairs to climb, it came as some relief. She lurked in the lee of an alcove at the end of a broad hall that serviced nearly a dozen doors, only one of which was guarded, and by a pair of hooded alchemists, no less. Feeling confident she had arrived at her intended destination, Isolde marked her heading, took in as much air as she could, and dove again into the nihility.

As soon as she was under, she had the queer sense that something had changed. The murk seemed thicker somehow and warmer. Pausing mid-stroke, she squinted down into the black. It looked the same. Or nearly so. Had it developed a subtle texture, or was that a trick of the eye? She considered going back to the refuge of the alcove, climbing free of the shadowy substrate, but then what? She'd be trapped on the top floor and between sentries. No, the only thing for it was to forge ahead. So she did, though the kicking of her feet seemed more laborious, her progress more sluggish. She swam onward. The walls of the hall above, papered in vertical stripes, seemed to vacillate like seagrass. Approaching the pair of guards posted on either side of the door, she was about to pass beneath them when she felt a strange current drag along the length of her leg.

Peering down again, she saw she was not alone in the desolate realm of shadows: a swarm of worms—pressed together and moving in concert—swelled toward her. They were blunt, featureless flails. They spread in every direction beneath her, rising like the hump of a breaching leviathan. Then she understood that what she had at first mistaken for a school of grasping worms in fact shared a common bed, like the tastebuds of a mammoth tongue. The thickening saliva that surrounded her also weighed her down. She had the unshakable feeling that she was being licked from the glass of existence by a ravenous abyss.

Though not predisposed to panic, Isolde had no defense against the dread that surged in her. All her intellectual processes fled before the single urge to escape. She looked up for the nearest outlet as she thrashed her way forward. Her head bumped against the lit floor of the hallway and she continued on under the heels of one guard and the wall he stood against. In the chamber beyond, she was disappointed to be confronted by a swathe of impermeable light. She floundered headlong across it, beating back with each kick the viscid tubes that pressed upon her.

Perceiving a rectangle of gray salvation in the slanted distance, she thew every ounce of strength behind her breaststroke. Even as her throat spasmed with the desire for air and the tendrils pulled at her legs, she reached for her escape.

Isolde broke from the shadows like a fish beached by a shark. The moment she was free, she spat out the ring and gasped, watching as the Umbra Annulus tumbled and began to roll, wheeling from her huddled shade, out across a well-lit carpet.

Bashing her head upon something, she reached up to find the slat of a commodious bed. Feeling suddenly leery of the shadow she lay upon—which seemed too flimsy a barrier between her and that behemoth—she scrambled out from under the mattress.

Straightening her twisted shirt, she sized up her surroundings. The canopy bed behind her occupied the center of the spacious but scantly furnished chamber. Before her stretched the vast black-and-amber dial of the Goat's Eye. Set to one side near a cascade of drawn-back red drapes was a humble desk. It broke the lustering expanse of stained glass like a sty.

Still panting from her ordeal, Isolde looked to the door, waiting to see if the guards without would come charging in. Listening to the chunter of the party below, she was relieved to hear no whistles, or bells, or claxons. She loosened the bow tie that now seemed to strangle her. Stooping to retrieve the onyx ring, she was surprised to see how badly her hand quaked. As a young woman, she used to marvel at how completely and abruptly her father had managed to vanish from the face of the earth, but then when she began to dally with his treasures, his disappearance had begun to seem less mysterious, more inevitable.

Shivering at the thought of returning the Annulus to her finger, where it would pose no physical threat except to her nerves, she sequestered the ring in her jacket pocket.

To hasten the return of her composure, she focused on the enormous hex built of glass and lead. It was an intricate ward, a compound one, with concentric sigils encircling a long-barred Hex of Amplification. She did not recognize every symbol, but she had no doubt about their combined purpose: the inhibition of magic. Her hexes would not help her here.

She wondered how the industrialist could possibly sleep while tucked under the glower of such a potent sigil. Like the heat of a forge saps a blacksmith, so did the hex's presence drain her. Though she was inured to such forces, she was not immune to them. Scrutinizing the curtains that hung on either side of the Goat's Eye, Iz supposed Cholmondeley must close it some hours to blunt its effect, assuming he slept here at all. The bed seemed more a stage than a refuge. Perhaps this was a space intended for more wakeful activities.

The sparsely furnished room offered little to explore, which was disappointing. Given the manor's congested decor, she'd expected her host's private chambers to be full of things to riffle through. Why go to so much trouble to protect what amounted to an empty room? Even the industrialist's desktop was barren. Running her hand over its uncluttered top, Iz noted the gouges and pocks, the ink stains and water rings that muddied its surface. It was not a rich man's desk. Indeed, it seemed like a relic from a different life, a less auspicious one.

She tugged at the desk's only drawer, and was somewhat surprised to find it unlocked. But then, what was there to secure? The drawer contained nothing but a small collection of frayed threads and a pair of schoolhouse snips.

Iz picked up and examined one of the half-raveled cords along with the small steel scissors. She muttered to herself, "Now, would you look at that. Braid magic! Pretty obscure stuff, Vicky. I didn't know you had it in you."

It was unusual for a practitioner of one vein of magic to pursue a second. As a rule, wizards did not putter in necromancy, and alchemists didn't experiment with hexes. This was partly a result of the animus that existed between certain factions and partly a reflection of the immense difference between the various schools of magic. Necromancy required a mastery of song, and alchemy a proficiency with movement and dance. A wizard's power was dependent upon a command of many languages, half of them dead, and hexegy could only be practiced by an accomplished artist. The exceedingly rare practitioners who worked in multiple schools of magic were called pluricians, and their scarcity was usually accompanied by mortal brevity. Pluricians died young as their organs surrendered to the stresses of their powers.

Cholmondeley didn't strike her as a plurician. No, in fact, he seemed like most other industrial alchemists, who were typically lapsed practitioners who had long ago foisted the dangerous work of halos and flails upon younger backs. Perhaps Cholmondeley was something more modest; perhaps he was just a dabbler.

The remainder of her brief search proved fruitless. The only other somewhat interesting feature was a rather garish tapestry of an armored knight riding upon a unicorn that was draped over a floor-length mirror. The rest of the room was unadorned.

And yet, she was left with the troubling prospect of her escape. The door was guarded and she had no intention of returning to the shadows. It was only a matter of time before her absence would pose a great inconvenience to her husband, who'd have to explain why she had crawled out a bathroom window.

Hoping to find an unsecured egress, she slipped behind the curtain, and soon discovered hinges in the glass. The discreet door, which was unfortunately locked, appeared to open onto a shallow balconette.

Returning to Cholmondeley's desk, she retrieved his snips. Their point fit into the lock well enough to force it, though the tip was bent by the effort. Thinking it better to leave Cholmondeley with the prospect of a misplaced tool rather than an obviously abused one, she pocketed the scissors.

The moment she was out, she saw that this was an oft-used spot. A podium ashtray occupied one corner of the wrought iron walk. The cold stubs of several cigars lay like turds in the sand. Before her, an unlatched gate led down to the sliver of a landing, off of which stretched a long catwalk. The bridge, which spanned the gulf between the manor and the gable of the adjoining barn, was undoubtedly the industrialist's private access to his mysterious workshop. Seeing neither alternative nor reason to delay, Isolde crept down to the landing and set out across the narrow beam.

While they waited for Isolde's return, Victor Cholmondeley invited Warren to retire to the loggia to sour the fresh air with a pungent cigar. War gamely agreed, and only confessed that he did not smoke after the industrialist had struck a match.

"Why didn't you say so, man?" Victor asked with a playful scowl as he turned the fire to his own use.

Warren admired his cold cigar, which he held expertly enough, and answered, "I've never wished to frustrate another man's pleasure with my own faults. It's not that I haven't enjoyed a smoke or a drink in the past. Quite the opposite, in fact. Where other men possess a valve of self-control, I have only a levee that, once breached, is quite difficult to rebuild."

Sucking the life from his match, the industrialist spoke around clamped teeth: "There is nothing more admirable than a man who knows his limits—nothing sadder, either."

Warren breathed out and shrugged and looked at the sky and the gossamer shreds stained by the pocketed moon. "I miss clouds."

Cholmondeley laughed with a candor that made him cough and almost choke. "Are you joking? We have nothing *but* clouds!"

Warren twiddled his cigar and bared his teeth with what seemed a smile that desired to clamp upon that wrapper. In fact, he was only chomping upon his worry for his wife. She'd said she wanted to take a quick look about for the prince's ring, but already *quick* seemed too long. The subject of her search was too unlikely, the risk too certain. Still, with feigned humor he said, "Those aren't clouds! That's scum. That's phlegm. That's smokestack soup!" He gave a sideways glance and saw the break in his host's agreeable mood. He bullied on: "I miss *clouds!* I miss lonesome clouds, wispy clouds, and all those fleets of white frigates with pregnant sails that would go coursing across the endless blue—warring, burning, sinking at sunset. I miss the clouds that looked like a freshly tilled field and the great placid mountains that presided over a morning—before turning volcanic in the afternoon. There's nothing like that now. There's just a ceiling. A terribly low ceiling and closed-in walls. It's like we're living inside a collapsed house."

"Those clouds, that *phlegm* as you call it, which swaddles our land like a newborn infant, represents progress, equality, the conveniences and luxuries of an electrified world." The industrialist considered his smoldering indulgence with an oblique expression. "If being a father taught me anything, it was to expect ingratitude. It's difficult for children to understand why they can't have more pudding, or more time to play, or more attention. A little of anything just makes them want more. They understand neither practical nor moral constraints. They only understand *more*. And they call me greedy."

Cholmondeley's pointed rebuke brought to mind Warren's conversation with Nurse Percy in the crumbling military hospital. In answer to Percy's bleak assessment of the state of the nation, War had expressed optimism for the erosion of the old ways and the shoring up of democratic institutions. Now, he wondered if he wasn't being naive. If all the political power drained from the royal château only to flow out to the country mansions, would anything of substance change for the poor, the luckless, the overlooked?

Feeling dispirited, Warren rolled his gaze upward to where the frustrated moon backlit a slender trestle that crossed from the manor to the sizable barn. War's expression stiffened as he focused upon the slight figure that edged along the catwalk. The fog of distance might've made another man doubt, but Warren recognized the slinking specter at once.

"Excuse me, sir," he said, offering the industrialist his unfired cigar. "Might I avail myself of your voxbox? I need to make a call."

The bridge from the industrialist's bedroom to the neighboring workshop ended in a corrugated shell and a door that opened upon an observation platform. From that high perch, Isolde took in the mill floor from end to end. She marked the Flail and Haloist upon their pedestals, holding open a seething halo and beating back the beasts attempting to break through. The alchemists whirled and swayed in forms that resembled a pirouette, a jig, a convulsion. Beyond the halos, crane arms shifted pearlescent logs of thalanium—frail as charcoal—to waiting hopper cars. And nearer underfoot, a titanic viny trunk, some fifty feet long at least, inched forward, carried by a rumbling conveyor that rattled the chains of the rigging above.

It was strange to think that this perilous work was going on while, just outside, the nation's gentry gulped champagne and fell out of their clothes. Every alchemy mill Isolde had ever heard of was planted far afield or in the poorer districts. Having such a chancy production in sight of the owner's bedroom only made sense in the context of Cholmondeley's secret technology, which seemed the sort of generational innovation a wise man would prefer to keep at his hip.

Disappointingly, the viewing deck did not include access to a stair or ladder, though Isolde supposed that made sense. While Mr. Cholmondeley had gone to some lengths to install this private balcony for monitoring his mill, he likely did not wish to supply his workers with easy access to his bedroom. Still, it made her plan of slipping through the mill and back out to the raucous party more challenging.

Which was how she came to consider the chains, chiming like sleigh bells in their tackle block and dangling just within reach. Had Warren been there, no doubt, he would've counseled her to go back the way she had come. Unfortunately, he was elsewhere. So, she grasped the chain and gave it a tentative tug. The din it raised did not appear to attract the attention of the laboring alchemists.

She threw herself entirely upon the mercy of those iron links.

No sooner was her weight upon it than the chain began to run. The floor of the mill, some forty feet below, seemed in a hurry to catch her. She bucked her legs once to gather momentum, then let go.

The result was less of a leap and more of a flap. She landed awkwardly upon the green log, which she only then discovered was covered in fine hairs and a viscous sap. The more she struggled to free herself, the more glued she became. She shouted at the alchemists, but they could not hear her over the rollers and the shrieking spider doing its best to crash Cholmondeley's party.

Then she saw between her elbows the hump of the cord that bound the sheaves of muscular vines together. The thick, colorful rope, which bit deeply into the beryl fibers, was partially obscured, though she still recognized it.

All at once, she perceived Cholmondeley's secret source of softwood, and also she saw her salvation.

Slipping her arm from her cemented coat sleeve, Isolde wrestled the industrialist's scissors from her pocket. She worked the small beak of the snips around one strand in the braid that encircled the timber. As lightning leapt above her and the beast of the Entobarrus gripped the inflamed halo with its barbed legs, Isolde cut the thread.

The wood beneath her seemed to simply vanish, and she bounced upon the now empty conveyor belt flat on her stomach. The abrupt disappearance broke the Haloist's concentration, and the portal to the Entobarrus collapsed amid a thunderclap. A bouquet of dismembered spider legs pelted the tarred belt, even as the production line ground to a halt.

Isolde rolled over and sat up. Along the front of her dingy shirt curled several strands of wilted green. She pulled the catchweed free as the tatters of the shrunken braid fell to her lap.

She looked up. From atop their pedestals, the leather-cowled alchemists regarded her with twisted expressions of surprise.

"Hello. I'm looking for the powder room. I don't suppose you—" The alchemists' croziers began to incandesce with the promise of more lightning as she swallowed the rest of her joke.

Having spent her share of afternoons stagnating in the halls outside the offices of headmasters, provosts, and police chiefs, Isolde was not unacquainted with the limbo of impending punishment. It was not a particularly pleasant feeling. Standing with her hands raised and her back against the wall of Cholmondeley's workshop while the Haloist contemplated her with a crackling staff, Isolde could only wait and stew.

The floor of the mill was surprisingly innocuous now that the violent interdimensional storm had been stanched. The line workers had taken a break, and the custodial staff had emerged. Some removed the titanic severed legs and poured salt on the sizzling green blood; others were absorbed by a still more curious chore.

Isolde knew that the quality, age, and trim of an alchemist's vestments communicated much about their station. So, when she saw the stoop-backed man wearing a cracked and balding apron with crude stitching and no detail, she marked him for a failed apprentice, now an accomplished drudge. His duty was simple enough, yet bizarre. Waddling to accommodate a clunky pail, he prowled along the inner perimeter of the mill with a long ladle in hand. The floor's cervices and corners bloomed with occasional patches of luminous fungal parasols. Those blanched stems and broad caps seemed to serve as anchorage to a swarming fleet of aquamarine spores. The mushrooms were beautiful, eerie, and—it seemed obvious to Iz—not native to the world. Upon these glowing sporadic lots, the drudge ladled molten lead, which devoured the mushrooms and orbiting motes with seething efficiency.

There was something in that terminal flash of color that stirred in Iz a sense of familiarity. She had seen those motes of light before, though at the moment she couldn't recall where. Such a failure of memory was out of character, though nosing a crozier full of lightning was not exactly conducive to clear thinking.

"What is he doing?" Isolde asked her scowling warden.

"Minding his business," Victor Cholmondeley said from the crack in the loading doors. The industrialist's socks were muddy, his pant cuffs crudely rolled. It was a dishevelment that seemed to extend to his expression: He looked harried, though he tried to hide it.

Isolde wished to take advantage of his discombobulation, to knock him further onto his heels, and so she announced the secret of his fortune. "Braid magic. You know, of all the veins of magic, I think the erosion and abandonment of braid magic is perhaps our greatest cultural loss. As I recall from my anthropological studies, scholars believe the very first commercial use of magic was a magic knot wound around a sheaf of wheat that made the berries a little plumper. This was, what, two millennia ago? Such a useful innovation that was unfortunately lost—or so we all thought."

The industrialist's aplomb was gone; his shoulders hunched nearer to his ears, gathered by stress. "That is a trade secret, Ms. Wilby. If you reveal it, I'll sue. I'll take your practice, your house, everything you have."

Iz shrugged. "I'm not interested in how you make your smog, Cholmondeley."

Warren stumbled through the gap in the loading gate, his shambling entrance apparently initiated by Silva, who steamed in after him. The head of her crozier radiated energy. Her face was similarly alight, but with outrage and embarrassment. Isolde could only imagine the moment when she had burst into the powder room only to find it empty and the window open.

Scouring the faces in the mill, Silva's gaze alighted on Isolde. Her iron crook flashed with gathering electricity as she bent one knee and dragged the other leg back, adopting the first figure in a mortar spell that had been quite popular during the Meridian War and was perfectly illegal now. Isolde stretched her neck in defiance.

"No." The industrialist pointed at Silva.

Begrudgingly, his alchemist drew in her legs and let the lightning in her iron staff disperse.

Cholmondeley turned back to face his wayward guest. "Why are you snooping? I invited you here, and yet you invade my privacy. I speak of the future, and you only seem obsessed with the past."

If the industrialist knew that she was hunting after the prince's ring, he was doing a very good job of concealing it. And still, he struck Isolde as hardly innocent. He was a presumptuous bully, a hedonistic misanthrope, a person who was accustomed to getting whatever he wanted. Which at the moment seemed to be an apology.

Too bad for him.

Sweeping the catchweed hairs from her coat sleeves, Isolde replied in her haughtiest tone, "It's not personal, Vicky. I told you I vet my partners, and thoroughly. To be frank, I had hoped that you were more clever—the sort of man who displays the least of his treasures for purposes of security. I hoped you were hiding the good stuff behind the curtain, as it were. Well, it turns out, you're just a man with crumbs in his beard pretending to have come from a feast." She stepped nearly upon his soaked toes, and clenched her teeth like a bulldog. "You have *nothing* to offer me. I'm insulted by the invitation and offended by your offer."

"Quite the threat, coming from a burglar."

She scoffed. "Call the police. The only thing I've robbed you of is your pretense."

Cholmondeley's gaze flattened. "Well, there's that famous tongue. Sharp as ever."

"I haven't even whetted it yet. Give me a drink."

"I think we've both had enough. I'll have a car brought around."

A COSMOS IN A COBWEB

Warren Wilby popped the top button on his trousers as if it were the cork of a bottle and fell back upon their bed with a prodigious sigh. As he reveled in the reclamation of his blood flow, he said, "You suppose that's what got the Umbrists in the end? A giant tongue?"

Seated at her vanity, Isolde snatched the pins from her hair with practiced efficiency. She had already divested herself of her evening wear in favor of a shabby silk robe; it bore a pattern of swimming koi whose bright waters were further colored with blotches of black tea and merlot. "If any of them got out alive, I doubt they'd ever dive back in again to test their luck a second time. Whatever they awoke down there with all their splashing about is still emphatically alive."

War wriggled from his trousers with all the grace of a spawning salmon flailing up a shallow stream, then paused to dig through the pockets. He extracted the small black ring that Isolde had asked him to carry on their ride home because she couldn't bear to have it on her person a second longer. "Can we file this away in the *Do Not Use Under Any Circumstances* drawer?"

"Absolutely." Isolde plucked out the last hair pin.

Warren dropped the Umbra Annulus into the coin dish at his bedside where it chimed upon the pennies. "It shall be done...first thing in the morning. And catchweed? Is that really what Cholmondeley built his fortune upon—sticky willy?"

"Yes, but exponentially enlarged, of course. Victor rediscovered a plait for turning a flowerbed into timberland. It's ingenious, really. Nearly all of the knowledge of braid magic has been lost, but it's the oldest of the orders—the original magic. Or nearly so." She scratched her scalp until the serpentine curls on her head regained some of their glory. "Our regretful host appears to have some genius for reinvigorating the lost arts. That, or he employs someone who does." At the top of Isolde's very short list of candidates in that regard was Silva, who had tipped her hand by adopting a stance that was the beginning of a mortar spell. Isolde only knew it because she had, while at university, pored over the battlefield photographs from the Meridian War, when the alchemists were primarily deployed as artillery. If Silva had finished the extraordinarily illegal casting, she would've immolated Iz and probably a quarter of the industrialist's mill. Iz wondered if that wasn't the only reason Vicky had told her to stand down. Regardless, it suggested that Silva had the ability to research thorny and obscure stuff. Perhaps braid magic was within her reach.

Warren peeled the socks from his broad calves. "So, those snips you nicked, they were enchanted? Are they what broke the spell when you cut the cord?" He watched his wife rise to pace and chew her thumb. He recognized in her demeanor an indifference to sleep—a state that presently called to him with such enticements.

She stomped to the window and back, shaking her head at the floor. "No, they were just common snips. That's the thing about braid magic, and the reason why it ultimately dwindled into obscurity: It's limited, fiddly, and vulnerable. Horribly vulnerable. The littlest snag, the slightest cut, breaks the spell. Works well enough on a static conveyor belt, but you can't wear it into battle. Come to think of it, it's strange that the atmospheric violence of the Entobarrus doesn't break the spell, though perhaps it just transforms the braids into thalanium along with the rest of the organic material. But you know what's really got me going—"

Warren sighed and collapsed back onto the bed. "Iz. I love you. I know you need to dwell on this, but I need to dwell upon my eyelids."

"I'll take it downstairs."

He reached out to her with the wide paw of one hand, and she came to squeeze it. "I know there was a lot of huffing and puffing at the end, but the impression Victor left me with was one of insecurity. Which isn't to say he mightn't be capable of terrible cruelty."

"But he didn't strike you as a mastermind?"

"Not particularly." War rolled nearer to kiss her fingertips. "Don't stay up all night."

"No, no. I'll be up in a bit."

In the urban dark of an unlit room amid the peeping light of streetlamps, a barefoot Iz picked her way over the battered carpet.

The rug would never be the same. The cinders ejected by the mandrake's collapse into the fireplace had left blackened divots everywhere. At first, Warren had attempted to shift the furniture to cover the worst of it, but the result was just an inhospitable jumble. They would simply have to learn to live with those scars, as they had with so many others, or buy a new rug.

Iz had come downstairs to conscript a little company, assuming Felivox was still awake. Under the ledge of the mantelpiece, Iz knelt to retrieve a long match from the kindling box. Striking it on the flagstone, she was about to rise to unlock the hidey-hole when her attention was arrested by the sight of a miniature meteor shower falling from the open flue onto the spotless hearth.

She leaned nearer to study the cascade of teal sparks. Cupping one hand, she reached out to catch some of the unusual particles, then reconsidered. Withdrawing her hand, she shook out the match and rocked back from the curious light show.

She retreated to the kitchen and returned with gas mask in tow and an electric torch weighing one pocket of her robe. She adjusted the straps on the boar-nosed apparatus—a relic from the war that Warren sometimes donned when he went to battle with that deathless foe: dust.

Through thick and wall-eyed lenses of bottle-green glass, Isolde lay on her back with her head pillowed upon the fire grate. She peered upward into the darkened throat of the chimney.

The spider had spun its web in a cavity in the crumbling clay liner. Iz wondered if it would be protected there from the brunt of a fire, or if it was simply an opportunist taking advantage of a cold flue and the insectile traffic that found its way down. While she pondered and watched, the bustling spider began embroidering its web once more. As the silk unspooled from the bobbin of its abdomen, atoms of pale azure drifted down toward her.

She slid out and sat up and spoke into the muffling mask: "Well, that's not good. No, I don't like the look of you at all."

Isolde's attic laboratory reflected the angle of the gambrel roof, resulting in a sort of polygonal womb of rough boards, joists, and ashlarings, all pressed upon by uneven shelves built of loose bricks and floor planks that bowed under books, scientific instruments, and apparatuses. The furnishings were modest: a long workbench; a sitting chair shrouded in quilts and her thinking coat, Splodge; and a foot pouf held together with drapery cords. The environment was as candid as a nest, and every bit as comforting.

A smattering of dirty dishes further contributed to the space's casual milieu. Once a month, Warren would impose upon his wife to return his crockery. Otherwise, he left her alone, believing as he did that an untouched, ungoverned refuge was essential to his wife's well-being. Betwixt her sanctuary and the kitchen there stood the seldom-used lifeline of an old butler's bell, which Warren could ring if there was a housefire. Otherwise, she was blissfully secluded from the interruptions of peddlers and postmen.

Still wearing her green-eyed gas mask, Isolde attempted to find room on her workbench for a crystalline bell jar, a procedure that was overseen by the tipped-over and propped-open carpetbag.

"A little to the left. You've got a teaspoon under you. My god, woman! Your desk is a disgrace," Felivox said. From the dim transom of the open portalmanteau, his amber eyes glowed like the dials of a dashboard.

"I asked for company not criticism," Isolde grunted.

"I'm afraid company is the white in which the yolk of criticism swims! Can't have one without the other!"

Isolde adjusted her tack and set the oak-footed terrarium down. She lurched back, shaking out her tired arms, and removed her cumbersome mask. Rubbing the red lines from her cheeks and chin, she said, "So, what do you know about the Entobarrus?" She clicked a fingernail against the glass where the spider she'd evicted from her chimney now huddled.

"Ah—well, dragons share an ancestor with one of those beasts: the Maoi Kabril, the Behemoth of Eist. I'm given to understand, he's a bit of a bighead. Prefers worship to small talk."

"I don't suppose you've ever heard of a leviathan that dwells beneath the shadows. Something large. Quite large. I only got a look at its tongue."

"Are you referring to the Gloaming God? I've read about him. No relation. Here's a little-known fact: He's mostly tongue. Well, it's not really a tongue—more of the corpus of a celestial bivalve. Oh, did I tell you Warren fed me oysters yesterday? Mmm-mmm, oysters! More of that, please."

"What about the flora over in the Entobarrus? What's it like?"

"I've not been there myself, of course. But from what I've managed to glean from your father's library—"

"Why don't you just bring me the book?"

"Can't, I'm afraid. It's on fire. Forever inflamed, but never consumed, conveniently. It's shelved with the Infernals. Even I get a bit warm when I peruse it. But really, Ms. Wilby, it's mostly tedious stuff. It's just family manuscripts. And it turns out, dragons aren't the best writers. There. I said it. Tell the world! We're terse when we should be descriptive, and effusive when we should be abrupt."

Isolde raked her face in frustration, then swallowed her impatience and resumed. "All right. What have you read about the Entobarrus's herbage?"

Felivox barked like a calving iceberg, a sound Isolde took for laughter. "Oh, it's uniformly horrible—its poisonous or carnivorous or full of acidic sap. So, in one sense, it's entirely alien, but in another sense, it's not so unlike your native plant life. It's naturally expansive, or *invasive* as your agricultural ministers prefer to call it, and their life cycles are reliant on predictable environmental stresses: sand floods, volcanic tides, electromagnetic inversions—"

"All perfectly normal," she drolled.

"Indeed. But why the sudden interest in the Entobarrus? Of the Eleven Realms, I'd classify it as the least interesting ... after your own, of course."

Isolde arranged the gooseneck of a magnifying glass to bring the cowering arachnid into clearer relief. "I saw some rather strange mushrooms growing in the alchemist's mill."

"Mushrooms! Ah! Did you know that fungi are much more closely related to animals than plants? Some philosophers have raised the question of whether eating mushrooms is even moral, proposing the possibility of a diffuse but shared consciousness between toadstools. Some even say it is tantamount to cannibalism! Seems a stretch to me, but as someone who has tasted the embryos of my would-be siblings, I don't find the prospect repellent. Surely, discovering that one's own self is delicious only increases your stock in the universe. I would prefer to believe that not only am I lithe, wise, and beautiful, but delectable as well! Who would want to walk around believing themselves to be a nasty nibble? I am delicious! Mushrooms are delicious! You are delicious!"

Isolde frowned at the merry eyes that watched her from her grandfather's satchel. "I'm getting the sense that you're hungry. Do I need to fetch you a snack?"

The dragon rumbled. "I'll wait for Mr. Wilby, thank you. He knows how I like my rashers cooked. Now, tell me more about these curious mushrooms."

"There were phosphorescent and shedding spores."

"Such things are not unheard of in your own world." Out of the mouth of the portalmanteau came the luffing sound of turning pages, heavy ones. "Let me see...here we are! You have the honey mushroom and the lilac bonnet and the—"

"I know we have our own bioluminescent varieties, but it was how the alchemists managed these little outgrowths that piqued my curiosity. They drenched the beds in molten lead."

"That does seem a bit dramatic. You think these toadstools hopped over from the Entobarrus? Is that allowed?"

"It's very much not allowed." Isolde went on to explain that when the alchemists first introduced thalanium and electrahol to the world, a number of questions regarding the associated dangers naturally arose. The answers the industrial alchemists initially supplied were not exactly comforting: There was a *slight* risk of dimensional collapse, demonic invasion, and environmental devastation. The outcry was predictably swift. There were protests, parliamentary debates, and increasingly shrill headlines—which for once were not without merit.

The difficulty was that even while everyone argued about whether panning the rivers of hell for gold was a safe and sensible thing to do, the applications of electrahol exploded in the national consciousness. Visions of racing jaunts and well-lit homes and wireless entertainment did more to alleviate the public's concerns than any reassurances the industry produced. It was the promise of convenience that settled the debate. It was electric kettles that swayed the world.

Isolde concluded, "In the end, the alchemists were allowed to propose their own protocols and safety standards. That's how we got the Haloist and the Flail on the thalanium extraction line. They represent the first of very few safeguards. There have been accidents, of course. Alchemists have died. Cover-ups abound. But no devils have ever been loosed upon the world. Or so I thought."

Isolde continued her examination of the truculent spider. She tormented it with a tuning fork, plied it with a small electric current, chilled it with one hex only to warm it with another. She even caught a live fly and introduced it to the environment, hoping to excite some response, some movement, some further release of those curious glowing atoms. The glassed-in arachnid remained unmoved and petulant.

"What are you doing?" Felivox asked.

"Trying to get it to produce those glowing spores again. Why did it start? Why did it stop?"

At her elbow, the third volume of the *Hexod Florilegium* lay open. The entries of the instructional index included detailed diagrams of how each hex should be drawn, depictions that were necessarily unfinished, the final step having been relegated to verbal instructions in the supporting text. An index of completed hexes would simply have been too arduous. The mere presence of such an ill-advised object would've sucked the life out of the reader, if not the room. The industrialist's Goat's Eye window had been exhausting to stand under, and it bore only sixty or seventy major hexes. The *Hexod* held more than two thousand.

Isolde's search for a hex to enliven the spider was a strain upon her already fatigued eyes. The print of the *Hexod* was vanishingly small, and the light of the brass chandelier overhead insufficient. She lit an oil lamp amid her piles of dishes and passel of books, and shifted her index to better receive the light.

The spider's response was immediate. Its legs snapped open like a silkless parasol, and it scuttled against the wall of the bell, though it was a hopeless offensive.

Isolde turned her attention from the index's tea-brown pages to the agitated crawler. On a hunch, she levered the crystal dome open. The spider shot out at once. Even as Iz recoiled, fearing it meant to attack her, it sprang upon the base of the oil lamp and ascended to the wick with magnetic swiftness.

Isolde laughed in surprise as the spider embraced the flame. The fuel of its small life made the fire leap.

Out from the arachnid's shrinking remains blue sparks rose. Those effervescing motes tumbled and drifted like fledglings experimenting with flight.

Isolde brought the crystal bell down over lamp and swarm, bottling both.

The flame dimmed as it consumed what little air was left to it. The ashen spider broke and collapsed as the last of the light turned to smoke. Within this polluted nimbus, the shining particles continued to swirl. The spores appeared perfectly indifferent to the absence of oxygen.

Having no molten lead on hand to tame them with, she thought to try a much simpler solution. She traced the diagram of a minor hex with her finger on the side of the stormy bell jar. The quatrefoil knot was neither particularly draining nor difficult.

The shimmering particles strobed and flickered, sinking lower in the lingering smoke as, one by one, they surrendered their light and drifted as dead ash to the tabletop. "Well, that's interesting."

"What did you do?" Felivox asked.

Isolde answered in a meditative singsong: "A clover string for a fairy ring, an itch without a bite."

The next morning, Isolde sat at the kitchen table clutching a teacup with both hands like a beggar bowl as her husband carefully refilled it. The jutting of her hair suggested a recent electrocution, though it was only the result of having spent the night sleeping in her attic chair under her thinking coat.

"So, you believe I have Cholmondeley to blame for a smashed basement door, your assault, all those holes in my carpet?" Warren seemed to excise his ire on the charred base of a roasting sheet. He scrubbed the floor of that pan as if he meant to erase it from existence, and the moment that chore was racked, he began to prune leaves from the potted basil in his windowsill with the tender snips of his thumbnail and forefinger.

Though she was still groggy, Iz's indignation was quite awake. She grumbled, "Yes, I think you probably do. At first, I was doubtful that an alchemist could open a portal into our basement through all of my hexes, but having met Cholmondeley's staff...I think he lassoed the mandrake with a braid to make it grow, and Silva hurled it into our cellar. But first, Vicky infected that poor woodland golem with the spores that drove it mad, hoping that even if it didn't kill us, it would infect our house, and consequently us. It was an assassination attempt, pure and simple. Cholmondeley found out the Crown had engaged us to investigate the prince's missing ring, and feared we would trace it back to him."

With a fresh towel, Warren gently patted dry a sheaf of green herbs. "But why invite us to his house if he believed we were being paid to poke about his past?"

"I think he probably would've preferred to rescind his old invites, but doing so would've stoked my suspicion. Besides, I think he might be vain enough to think he could get away with strangling our necks with one hand while patting our backs with the other. All that talk of pooling our resources, opening a museum. What a smarmy bugger!"

"But what now? Go to the police? Tell the king? Lodge a formal complaint?"

Isolde sighed and twisted her teacup as if it were the dial of a safe she hoped to crack. "With what evidence? Think of Mr. Horace Alman and that tin drum of *proof* that he so loves to bang! The crazed mandrake, the glowing spider, the mind-altering spores from the alchemist's mill—all incinerated. We still have no ring, no body, no witnesses. We have nothing!"

"We have breakfast." Warren settled a triangle of basil-sweetened quiche before his wife.

Feeling a little consoled by the sight of food, Isolde picked up her fork and attacked the savory pie. She spoke around a mouthful. "I'd like to interview one of the other children. It seems like all the adoptees got the boot as soon as they turned eighteen, all except Henry, of course, who only got to stay because he was buried in the family plot. I sincerely doubt Papa Cholmondeley told us the whole story there. Perhaps one of the other victims of his experiment would be more forthcoming."

"Well, it just so happens I might be able to help on that front." Warren blotted his damp hands upon his apron and retrieved from its pocket a folded square of paper.

Opening it, Isolde read aloud, "Emma Morris, Unit 119, Building J, 2488 South Hull Street. Morris, Emma Morris... Why is that name familiar? Where did you get this?"

Settling down before his own steaming breakfast, Warren cracked the pepper mill over his plate and allowed himself a moment to enjoy his wife's amazement. Then he regaled her with the chance meeting he'd had shortly before they were ejected from Victor's party.

After observing his wife skulk across the catwalk over the crowded lawn, Warren had excused himself from the industrialist's tobacco cloud to summon reinforcements. He had hoped to get out ahead of the impending disaster by contacting Detective Smud, whom Iz had once helped to resolve a personal matter. Though Smud had a reputation for gruffness and seemed an aspiring curmudgeon, he secreted a great affinity for animals of all kinds. The menagerie in his apartment had continued to swell despite the complaints of his neighbors because he was incapable of letting a stray animal pass unadopted.

It had been this inclination that was the ultimate source of the detective's trouble as he accidentally invited into his home a succubus who presented herself as a lovely long-haired silver cat. Within two weeks of opening his door to the imp, Smud was entirely under the creature's sway, an enthrallment that had inspired him to ask for the cat's paw in marriage. It was a desperate time for a man who was generally slow to accept the assistance of his fellow man. Isolde had intervened (against his protests), driving out the vampiric imp and saving the detective's life. Though there were not exactly an abundance of warm feelings between Smud and Isolde, there remained a sense of indebtedness that Warren expected would have to be called upon forthwith.

War would alert Smud of the incoming complaint about a burglar, who naturally would be his wife, and with any luck, the detective would arrive at Cholmondeley's gates the same instant the industrialist thought to summon the law.

Unfortunately for the Wilbies, the manor's only public voxbox was in high demand. Warren joined the queue awaiting a turn at the baroque cabinet mounted beneath an epiphanic yellow light bulb. At present, a young man wearing a grease-paint beard and a broken top hat was bullying the instrument. He shouted into the vox's mouthpiece: "The wedding's off! Off, I tell you! No—no...I didn't say I caught her *flirting*. I said I found her in flagrante delicto...on her hands and knees-o! My god, Mumsy, aren't you listening?"

Rocking from foot to foot and resisting the urge to stick his fingers in his ears, Warren soon became aware of some activity in the adjoining sitting room. Giving in to curiosity, he took a peek. Two leathered alchemists were roping in a third who they'd caught drinking from the ladle of an unattended punch bowl, though that offense did not seem to be the cause of the accosting. "We have an unaccounted-for guest. Come on. We're on the south wing." Then the three hurried out into the adjoining hall.

On tiptoe, Warren bounded after the retreating sentinels, certain they would lead him to his wife, who had always seemed to find her way to the center of a scandal. His thoughts were aroar with a litany of dire possibilities: She could be stuck, she could be hurt, she could be worse. He hoped she had not run afoul of the Umbra Annulus. Oh, how he hated that mystic trinket, which took his wife where he could not follow. *Shadow swimming—bah! More like skinny-dipping in an abyss!*

Despite his brisk clip, he soon lost the guards in the snarl of the mansion's central rooms, which was a plethora of redundant parlors, studies, and niches, all joined by a catacomb of fussy corridors. As the noise of the spreading alarm seemed to crash upon him from every side, War felt the sort of throaty panic that grips the visitors of a mirror maze. He was lost, alone, and seemed to find himself confronted, again and again, by looking glasses that placed his flushed and unhappy face in a golden frame.

Then he rounded a corner and had to dig in his heels to keep from barreling into a tall woman posted before an ornate frame on the wall. Her severe uniform identified her as the manor's housekeeper. Her perfect poise was unruffled by the bullish arrival of a red-faced man.

Feeling chastened by her calm, Warren collected himself. He took up rank beside her and clasped his hands at his back like a museum-goer, one who wished to reassure the other patrons that he was not out of breath because he had been running after (or from) the guards.

Mr. Wilby was so busy arranging himself into an attitude of innocent observance that it was a moment before he absorbed the subject of the painting before him. When he did, he gasped.

"The children!" he murmured. They were posed much as they had been in the newspaper clipping, leaving him to wonder whether one predated the other, or if the industrialist simply preferred this representation of his adopted family. They stood in two rows while the patriarch loomed behind them. Their faces were not as homogenous as they had seemed in the *Times*'s oversaturated photograph. Warren marked the variety of their races, their features, their hair. Yet their expressions were all of a single note: one of strained unease.

"The children?" the housekeeper said, turning her head at last to regard him.

Fearing he had unwittingly revealed something he should not have, War recovered with a cheerful sigh. "Oh, I was just thinking how rewarding it is to cook for children. They are sometimes a bit hard to please, of course. Yes, they can be picky, but they are so generous with their delight. No one has ever uttered a more sincere *yum* than a child!"

"Do you know who they are?" The housekeeper studied him with a disarming intensity.

Warren coughed to cover his surprise at her scrutiny and still seemed to choke upon the truth: "They're the adopted ten...the, em...the experiment."

The housekeeper turned to observe the ranked children once more. "*Experiment.*" The word flew out with the spontaneity of a curse.

Sensing her discomfort, Warren tried to soothe her with a confession. "I have an adopted sister myself. Well, I *did*."

The housekeeper squinted with concern. "What happened to her?"

"Well, Annie *was* my adopted sister, now she's just my sister. She's smarter than me, I hate to say, but I can still beat her at draughts...if she's tired and doesn't have her glasses on. Her flan is better than mine, but please don't tell her I said so. Since she's older than me by a few years, she would give me haircuts when I was little. I don't think anyone ever feels so vulnerable nor so doted upon as when they're getting a trim." Warren breathed in deeply to give himself a chance to swallow a few wistful tears that had arrived unexpectedly.

"Children aren't experiments. These children certainly weren't. They were my...my misses and masters. They were..." The housekeeper spoke as one strangled both by the expectations of her station and deference to her continued employment. She glanced about as if in anticipation of spies.

Seeing she was afraid and wishing to encourage her, Warren said, "I heard Master Henry is buried in Mr. Cholmondeley's own plot."

She shuddered as if curdled milk had passed her lips, then recovered and said, "Yes. Yes, Henry is. But they weren't all so . . ."

Warren watched as she deflated into the gulf of some private and still very immediate regret. He hurried to supply her with some escape. "Oh, madam, please, forgive my rudeness. I'm so sorry. My name is Warren, Warren Wilby. And you are?"

"Ms. Eynon." She tucked her chin, raising the bun on her head even as she lowered her voice. "I know who you are, Mr. Wilby." The sound of rushing feet and shushing leather skirts that had been fluttering in the distance seemed to drum like an approaching downpour. Ms. Eynon produced a pencil and scrap of paper from her pocket and wrote with the quick half-attended strokes of a professional. She squared the scrap and pressed it into his palm, leaning in close enough to cause Warren to resist the urge to recoil at the intimacy. Her gaze sparkled with unanticipated but fleeting emotion. "I hate to think Henry was the lucky one."

The alchemists stormed toward Warren from either end of the corridor, brandishing spiral-headed croziers and speaking in the strong terms of nervous drudges.

"You, there! You're coming with us!" the foremost said.

Tightening his necktie like a man preparing for court, Warren discreetly stuffed Ms. Eynon's note into his shirt. Then he raised his hands, presenting a man eager to surrender. In answer, a pair of Cholmondeley's guards roughly grasped his arms.

When Warren looked again to Ms. Eynon, she seemed as distant as a steeple.

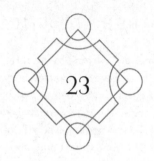

23

THE ✦OUROBOROS✦
SWALLOWS

The factory floors, wharfs, and sweatshops had sponged the life from the rookeries of Dove Town. Though it was noisy midday on the boulevard, it was solemn dusk in the valleys of the huddled apartment blocks. Crowded laundry lines formed a tangled canopy of bedsheets, footwraps, and diapers. Milky tusks of ice clogged detached rainspouts and barred the entrances of keyhole alleys that overflowed with rubbish and a stench that not even winter could temper.

Isolde walked ahead of her husband despite the fact that he was the one carrying the map. Having just reclaimed her favorite coat, Poppy, from the cleaners, she clasped its sweet-smelling lapels, fat as fox tails, tight to her throat. Warren held the portalmanteau pinned under one elbow as he animated the accordion of unwilling paper, turning the grid of needle-thin throughways this way and that, as if a new angle might reveal their present location or their ultimate destination.

"I'm sorry, dear. I think we're going round in circles. We seem to have doubled back on our double back," Warren said between muttering inspections of a pair of weather-beaten street signs, one that dangled by a single pin from a bar, another that lay facedown in the gutter and had to be inspected with the assistance of his boot. "What are you planning to ask when we finally locate Miss Emma Morris?"

Isolde opened a gate of iron bars that capped the backstreet, eliciting from its hinges a loathsome yowl. The secluded courtyard beyond served as a junction for three other identical alleys that cut through the clustered high-rises. Though to call it a "courtyard" seemed a touch grandiose. In truth, it was a pad of cracked cement, one spacious enough to entertain the most miserable playground Iz had ever seen. There was a seatless seesaw, a saddle-less swing set, a climbing frame that was as inviting as a hangman's scaffold, and a tilted merry-go-round whose edge had been honed by contact with the pavement. The only feature of the courtyard that was not aggressively grim was a hopscotch court—a lattice of imperfect squares and carefully chalked numbers. Otherwise, the quad seemed a punishment rather than an instance of architectural mercy. The playground equipment, Iz supposed, had been either tacked on by the builder as an afterthought or donated by a philan-thropic foundation who doubtlessly congratulated themselves for consider-ing the children. Gazing up that shaft of rusted fire escapes at a stingy ration of sky, it was difficult to believe that anyone at any point in the construction of this inhuman pen had spent much time thinking of the children.

Isolde pranced down the hopscotch board, pivoting on one foot when she reached the final square. "You're worried I'll be blunt."

Warren passed between the empty chains of an absent swing. "Clubs are blunt. You're direct. I suppose I'm not perfectly clear on the purpose of our visit. What are we hoping to learn?"

Isolde skipped back as she'd come, answering as she went. "I have two questions. First, I'd like to know if Vicky Cholmondeley, her unaffection-ate father, paid Henry Blessed any special attention. That might give us a better sense of whether and when Cholmondeley knew about the ring and Henry's tentative connection to the Crown."

Warren turned in a slow circle, scouring the four open gates for a street number or compass point, anything to direct them. "That seems a per-fectly reasonable line of inquiry."

Reaching the start of the board, Iz paused to catch her breath. "Second, I want to know if she saw her brother drown."

"Ah," Warren said, lowering his map to better see his wife.

Isolde advanced upon the skeletal seesaw, lowering and raising the bar with her foot. It moaned like a bent tuba. "I want to know if she saw his last breath foam upon the surface, whether she witnessed his body float downstream."

Warren made the face of one going to some trouble to swallow a belch. "Well," he said at last. "That certainly is a *direct* line of questioning."

Isolde dug her hands into her pockets, spreading the wings of her coat as she expounded upon her point. "I just want to be certain he's dead. Drowned in a river sounds suspicious to me. There's no body, most likely no investigation; not even Old Geb could root out those bones. It's too convenient. And I don't like the fact that there's an empty grave, especially one that an egotist of a father went to some pains to immortalize. It just doesn't sit right."

"I spoke to the housekeeper. I watched her expression. The Cholmondeleys were not a happy family. So, everything you're saying makes sense . . . but—" He pinched his fingers as if gingerly plucking a ripe berry from a bramble. "Maybe you could let me approach the subject a bit more . . . *in*directly."

"If you think it's best. Do you smell sulfur?"

"Honestly, I'm sorting through a lot of aromas at the mome—"

The tattoo of clanking metal rang in a circuit around the courtyard as the gates clapped shut, one after the other. A black cloud slid like a pot lid over the sky. The sole streetlamp that presided over the park flickered on, casting a lagoon of sallow light around the pitiful swing. A wind gusted in from each compass point, all at once, as at the courtyard's far end, a vortex of lightning began to bud, flowering like a rose, blazing like tinder. A strobing fistula between dimensions opened, and a fiend pressed through.

The centimane flowed into the courtyard upon the voluble carpet of a thousand tar-black tendrils. It was faceless, featureless except for its ubiquitous ever moiling mass of limbs and the roaring sinkhole in the universe at its center that swallowed everything in its path, including its own arms, though those were never in short supply as more constantly sprouted from its scalp. The centimane, one of the Entobarrus's most merciless predators, spilled over the sharpened disc of the merry-go-round, gulping whole those haggard plates, the shattering pavement, a nonplussed pigeon, a cyclone of rubbish, its own flails, and the Wilbies' screams.

Flinging open the portalmanteau, Warren unsheathed the Archsword of the Cloven God. The fuller that veined the claymore's length beamed forth with an emerald light, a display he'd never witnessed before. The blade seemed to quiver in the presence of the centimane, though War couldn't say whether it was out of terror or zeal. The beast was as large as a bull elephant, but fortunately less swift. Its advance was as deliberate as a saw through a trunk—and similarly portentous.

Dropping the portalmanteau, Warren widened his stance and raised the Archsword to give his wife cover while she worked. Iz marked on the back of his overcoat with her stick of chalk the tangled petals of a Hex of Aegis. The moment she closed the knot, the lines began to shine like wet lapis. An armor of livid blue light flowed around Warren's chest and flushed down his limbs, cladding him in a gauzy protective skin.

"I'll try the gates," Iz said, gathering up Grandad as she hurried back the way they'd come. As she ran, she cracked the magic satchel open and shouted into its recesses, "Any thoughts on how to defeat a centimane?"

Felivox's voice echoed back, "A *centimane*? Where are you? What have you—"

"No time to explain! Maybe something from the—" When Iz gripped the bar of the southern alley gate, it felt as if she had stuck her head into a cannon. The spell that sealed the exit repelled her with such violent intensity, it threw her into the air, and sent her tumbling over the hopscotch court.

She landed hard on her hip and ribs and tumbled to a stop, though her vision continued to spin. Through pain and clouded eyes she saw a second portal open. A figure, dressed in the common armor of an alchemist, stepped from the seething oval. Though her leather raiments were ordinary enough, their white coloration was not. Iz could only wonder at the rarity of the unpigmented beast who'd given its skin to defend this interloper. In addition to the cowl, she wore a mask over the bottom half of her face, which in combination with her hood rendered her identity inscrutable. And yet Isolde recognized her at once. It was Silva come to settle the score from the previous evening.

She strode with such purpose, Iz thought she'd kick her where she lay. She was momentarily relieved when the pallid alchemist merely stooped to collect the portalmanteau with a gloved hand. Then Silva turned on her bootheel and strode back to the fiery gate she'd come by with all the nonchalance of one collecting the morning milk from the front stoop.

Once again, Cholmondeley had sent his hounds to do his bidding. Since he could not burgle the portalmanteau, nor wheedle it from her directly, he meant to rip it from her hand.

Anger and indignation flooded Iz's veins, and she leapt up like the arm of a catapult.

Staring into the gyring maw of the beast, Warren was reminded of a spiny sea urchin—one birthed by devils in a pit.

He swiped at the monstrosity's squirming foundation. The Archsword passed through the grasping legs like a scythe through dry wheat. The centimane sucked in the amputated limbs, and no sooner were they consumed than new legs sprouted to replace them as the abomination plodded on. War repeated the harvest several times, and on each occasion the wounds, though terrible enough, were quickly lapped up, and the tentacles renewed. As brightly as the Archsword blazed, he felt like a man trying to beat back a wildfire with a wet towel. It didn't improve matters that this was a sentient catastrophe; the centimane appeared to sense his presence. War could scarcely guess how, given its blatant lack of sensory organs. Still, whichever way he leapt or feinted, the beast corrected its path to champ after him.

Seeing that he would not be able to cut the thing off at the knees, Warren sought higher ground out ahead of its deliberate advance. It was only then that he saw the white-clad alchemist, the flaming portal, and his wife vaulting back to her feet. He thought to rush to her side, but feared that doing so would only bring the centimane's attention to her. It was not the sort of notice he wished to share.

He surveyed his options, decided on the most defensible spot, and leapt upon the bottom rungs of the gymnastic apparatus. It received him with a shower of rust and a disconcerting groan. As he summited the climbing frame on all fours, he kept one eye on the centimane, simmering like a vat of pitch, sucking like a drain, and trampling ever nearer. The longsword occupying the grip of one hand clattered and bounced upon the rungs as he scrabbled upward.

Cresting the rusting triangle that capped that wretched dome, he would've liked to have chewed a little longer upon his morsel of a plan, but already the scaffolding beneath him shuddered with the touch of the centimane's whipping arms. In another second, his high ground would be swept away.

Warren split his fingers, two to a side, behind the guard of the Archsword and, drawing the pommel back behind his ear, heaved the awkward javelin down at the monster's crown.

The blade struck the center on the centimane's pate and sank deeply into the bed of thrashing tentacles. The green light of the sword beamed forth with the undulant radiance of the northern lights. The hole at the soul of the beast reverberated with a terrible screech as the wound shot out geysers of jade-clad fire.

Gaining his balance, Warren threw up a triumphant fist and cried, "Right on the beezer!"

The staving sword slid forward and down the slope of the monster's indiscernible brow. As the Archsword approached the engulfing inkpot at the heart of that heinous beast, it emitted such a light that Warren had to shut his eyes and turn away. A great warmth lashed the side of his face. The centimane's shriek pealed higher.

Then the Archsword's light stuttered, and War looked in time to see his sacred sword vanish into the bottomless orifice—carrying with it both light and hope.

The centimane, who'd momentarily piaffed in place, now pressed into the jungle gym, bucking Warren from his tenuous roost.

There was little in the world Isolde despised more than a surprise. Surprise guests, surprise parties, surprise revelations in the third acts of poorly written plays in which all previous clues were simultaneously overruled by the introduction of an unearned revelation. Warren had once jokingly rechristened a casserole "chicken obvious" in deference to Iz's famous aversion to surprise.

In Isolde's opinion, a clear mind was better than a crystal ball for predicting the future; the more astute and deliberate a thinker was, the surer their immunity to shock and upset would naturally be. Indeed, Isolde's knack for unraveling mystery was less the result of delighting in riddles, and more indicative of her deep-seated intolerance of uncertainty. At times, she even struggled not to interpret the capricious turns of existence—the sun showers and train delays—as implicit critiques of her intellectual prowess. It was, she knew, an absurdity that revealed more about her own insecurity than the nature of entropy, and yet she could not help but feel every surprise was a slight, one that inspired in her the same visceral response: *anger.*

She was furious to have let herself and Warren go capering into what she should've immediately identified as the perfect setting for an ambush: ungenerous exits, inaccessible reinforcements, relatively unpopulated buildings. Yet, she had been caught hopscotching and chattering like a monkey, and why? Because she believed that she was two strides ahead of everyone involved in the unraveling conspiracy against the king. But no, *not so.* It was she who had fallen behind once more.

Her retreating foe wore a long, flowing tippet around her neck. That gold-trimmed scarf featured two dozen alchemy blazons—defensive wards that would discourage the attention of certain cursed beasts and unhappy spirits, though Isolde didn't have time to study which ones exactly as she chased after the person who'd just robbed her of her most treasured possession. Iz drew a Hex of Disgorging in the air over the alchemist's back, hoping to interrupt Silva's march with the violent intrusion of her breakfast. The moment the hex was complete, its shimmering ring shattered—broken by the presence of some competing ward. Silva continued to storm toward the waiting portal that churned like a galactic pinwheel. Iz tried to get a glimpse of what lay through that flaming pore in space, but could only make out the murky shadows of a room. She quickly carved a second sign with her finger: a Hex of Somnolence, hoping to anesthetize the alchemist, or at least make her stumble with fatigue. The completed figure cracked and dissolved as swiftly as the first. Having drawn three hexes in fewer minutes, the only one who seemed to be winded was the caster herself. Isolde chugged like a marathoner.

Infuriated by these dispellings, Iz grasped the flapping tippet and pulled upon the alchemist's scarf as if it were the reins of a horse. The maneuver broke the thief's stride, if only briefly.

At first, Isolde had been relieved to see that Silva had come without her iron crozier, a rod imbued with great power in addition to its heft, which made it also an effective club. Iz supposed the alchemist had elected to travel light, intending to pop in and out, without confrontation, allowing her bidden fiend to do her dirty work for her. The ease with which she had defeated Isolde's hexes was astonishing since they were relatively trifling spells, and not the sort of thing one wasted space or energy preparing to rebuff.

The pallid alchemist swiveled around, and, in turning, animated the skirts of her leather cassock. The robe parted long enough for Isolde to glimpse the rows of hexes that crowded the scarlet lining.

Isolde said, "You aren't Silva, are you?"

Then the alchemist shook from the long leather sleeve of her armor what briefly seemed a humble stick. Then all at once Isolde understood who she was facing, or rather what. This woman demonstrated the expertise of an alchemist: She summoned portals and borrowed from the Entobarrus's unholy zoo. She could also bear the great psychic weight of a coat full of hexes, the sheer number of which would've been sufficient to flatten Isolde. And to these dazzling talents, the masked stranger now added a third.

Gripping the wand that had slipped from her sleeve, the white-clad woman raised the corkscrew of polished cypress and began to mutter a string of ancient words. Even as the wand's tip began to glow white with siphoned energy, Isolde understood that, unexpectedly, she had engaged herself in a duel with a plurician—a polymath of magic—alchemy, hexegy, and wizardry. She had stumbled upon an implausible savant. A once-in-a-generation confluence of genius and physiology.

Or as they were more commonly known, a *sorcerer*.

Oh, how Iz loathed surprises.

225

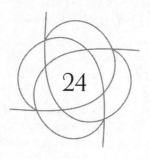

24

THE HOPEFUL SEEDS OF A
BITTER CROP

As a child of parents of modest means, Warren had grown up dreaming of swings. He could scarcely think of a more glamorous, urbane, genteel thing than a smooth plank lashed to the stout limb of an oak by a twist of jute. A swing was a carnival ride in your own back garden, a miraculous indulgence upon which you could animate yourself just by kicking wind. In the storybooks young Warren had read, children who had swings took tea on vast, weedless lawns, wore unstained pinafores, and had private tutors who taught them improbable instruments like the bassoon. Mounted upon ivied swings, those blessed youths laughed and shrieked and wheed at their tantalizing proximity to flight. How he had wanted a swing!

And yet, as Warren yanked the chain down from its rusted hanger and cracked it like a whip at the gobbling void, he couldn't help but feel some of the swing's romance had been lost. The climbing frame, which the centimane had slurped up like noodles from a bowl, had neither slowed its advance nor slaked its thirst. It all seemed rather hopeless.

Then, quite unexpectedly, the snapping of his chain appeared to divert the monster. It turned and began crawling upon a new track.

Warren's relief was short-lived as he realized its new target appeared to be his wife. Iz's attention was still absorbed by the white alchemist, who now brandished a . . . *was that a wand?*

While Isolde's hexed armor had preserved his bones from breaking on the rungs of the jungle gym as he fell to the ground, War had no doubt that her ephemeral chain mail would present little more than a candy coating to the centimane, should it get him in its throat. And yet, he was fully prepared to heave himself into that wretched gob in defense of his beloved.

No sooner was the thought considered than the tip of Warren's whipping chain strayed too near that insatiable gullet. He dug in his heels as the black hole at the heart of the centimane began to reel him in. Warren felt like the ambitious fisherman who had hooked an unwilling whale.

The centimane seemed to sense that War had been caught. The swarm of leeches quailed with delight. Warren wound the chain around the swing post to shore it up, not because he believed he could shackle the beast, but because he hoped to pull it off target, to deter it from plowing onward after Isolde. Incredibly, the centimane's progress slowed as the chain snapped taut as a bowstring.

It was then, while tugging the leash of a gorging abyss, that Warren was seized by a questionable epiphany. But what were his options? His holy sword had been gobbled up and the portalmanteau was in the clutches of a masked alchemist who continued to zestfully punish his wife. It was a desperate moment.

He rummaged through his vest pocket, sorting through the loose change and peppermints he'd absentmindedly scooped from his bedside bowl that morning. He hunted after that dreadful object that he had intended to file away after breakfast and somehow forgotten. Discovering the trinket, he checked it by the gloom of the mummified sun before pressing it into the slot of a link.

He released the chain, and the fiend devoured the line, baited at its end with the ancient passport of assassins, a key to the shadow realm. The centimane gulped the Umbra Annulus down, and Warren held his breath.

Across the courtyard, the overcast pavement began to ripple like a mirage. Then the shadows opened their secret reservoir, and the darkness swallowed the devil whole.

The chaos that had gripped the courtyard abated at a snap. The unearthly roar rumbled to extinction. The unnatural wind died. The squall of paper and rubbish drifted back to the earth. The remaining chains on the swing set chimed as sweetly as a cat bell. Mr. Wilby had banished the beast.

And yet, a nagging sense of menace lingered. Had Iz been at his elbow before he relegated the centimane to the shadow realm, she might've reminded him that the beasts of the Entobarrus sometimes presented themselves very differently on their native soil. Much like a fish reeled up from the ocean floor is unrecognizable when dropped upon the deck of a boat, the physiology of those diabolical animals was changed by the atmosphere of the living. On earth, the centimane resembled a ravenous sphere, but inside the Entobarrus, it was a gluttonous mat, a living quicksand, a hectare of death.

The dread Warren had felt a moment before did little to prepare him for the blooming that followed.

The shadows of the dismal park—the recessed windows, fire escapes, and eigenlicht alleyways—all began to writhe. Inky black worms rose everywhere at once as if drummed up by a cloudburst. Those tentacles stretched and fattened as they grasped flowerpots, ash buckets, straw whisks, and lines of laundry. They attacked the edifices, pulling out sills, drainpipes, bricks from the walls, dragging all of it down into the bubbling murk.

As the centimane's multiplying arms flailed up from the ground all about Warren's lamplit island, he murmured again, "Right on the beezer."

Wand spells, though most often offensive in nature, varied widely in their potency. While a novice wizard might cast a tongue of fire scarcely sufficient to warm a teapot, a white-haired master could summon a geyser of magma capable of consuming a company of soldiers en bloc. Regardless of the spell's efficacy, both novice and master typically needed a minute to compose themselves and regather their strength. The military application of wizards had always been limited by their stamina. Generals had complained for generations that you could fire and reload your artillery thrice in the time it took one knackered wizard to catch their breath.

Isolde was disappointed to discover that the plurician before her was not so easily sapped.

The pale sorcerer cast a sphere of purple static so near Iz's head it felt as if a buzzing cicada had flown into her ear. Even as she ducked, Isolde observed the markers of the scalding missile. It was a Bolt of Dissolution, a blast that would've transformed her into a puff of cinders if she hadn't dodged it. The missile cracked upon the foot of an apartment tower, vanishing a great bowl of foundational stone with a skull-rattling boom. Iz began to formulate a rejoinder of her own even as she charged. Like a boxer with a shorter reach, she knew distance was to her disadvantage. If a wizard's projectiles were akin to cannon fire, a hex was a bayonet. She needed to get in close. If worse came to worst, she could always poke the sorcerer in the eye.

She fashioned an aggressive ward: a Hex of Vacillation. She hoped the injunction would fill the sorcerer with crippling indecision, or at the very least cause her to second-guess herself. That was all Iz would need to snatch Grandad back—just a second of hesitation.

Before she could close the sigil, the sorcerer leveled her wand once again and loosed a missile at Isolde's very core.

The slug of mortal erasure would've consumed her like flash paper had she not been saved by the grip of a monster.

One of the centimane's myriad arms leapt from the gloom beneath her feet, wrapped about her calf, and hauled her down into the shadows. Plummeting into the roily depths, Isolde gasped to fill her lungs, even as the darkness closed about her throat.

Blindly, she reached up and seized the sorcerer's hem. Iz pulled her rival down with all the insistence of an anchor.

The stygian brine, though recently toured, struck her as perfectly strange. The warped plane of the surface, which deformed the fragile light and muddled the shapes of the world above, was now partly obscured by the reaching tendrils of the centimane. The fiend branched into a palpitating anemone, its black-violet limbs boiling out into the void.

Iz had no choice but to kick off one boot to free herself from the centimane's grasp, but the moment she slipped loose, she received a kick of her own. The sorcerer clipped her on the ear. Iz lost her grip and nearly her breath. Through one eye, clouded with pain, she saw white-clad legs scissors-kicking upward, coursing between the phalanxes of tentacles, reaching after the rippling ceiling.

Isolde was about to chase the sorcerer and the surface when something below caught her eye. Twisting about, she saw the familiar colorful patches of her father's satchel tumbling toward oblivion.

Without hesitation, she dove after the portalmanteau.

In all directions beyond his little refuge of street light, the arms of the centimane reached up from the shadows.

Warren wore the anguished expression of a man who had inadvertently set his own house on fire while trying to kill a spider, touching off a conflagration that could leap to the homes of his neighbors, consuming first the block, then the city, before turning its insatiable hunger toward the nation's borders. From the comfort of his ring of light, Warren could not help but wonder if he'd not just infested the bedrooms of Berbiton's children with an actual, ravenous monster.

Then his thoughts turned to Iz.

She was nowhere to be seen. She had been dragged under.

His first impulse was to throw himself into the grotesque fray, to dive down into the nest of headless wagging snakes in search of her. But how would he bring her back to the surface, back to his meager raft of the streetlamp, if he were himself drowned? Desperation made for a fine quartermaster but a terrible captain. He needed to think. His gaze lighted on the five remaining chains of the swing set, and he began to yank them down, popping them from their hangers with a grip shored up by his ephemeral armor.

He began to knot the chain ends together, an undertaking that proved more difficult than he had hoped. Even as his hands began to quake with the growing certainty that his wife had been consumed by a demon or drowned in a bottomless shadow, a sudden, violent commotion brought his head up.

The white-clad alchemist clawed her way up from the darkness onto the strand of cement that was lit up by her blazing portal. She seemed considerably less composed now, and Warren soon discerned the cause of her distress. Her breaching of the shadow realm was followed by the pursuit of a trio of probing tendrils. Though Warren felt certain she had called the centimane to the courtyard, the fiend was clearly not her lapdog.

From bent and splayed knees, she cast a red javelin of light that barked like a revolver. The missile exploded against the trident of reaching arms, blowing the alchemist flat on her back. The blast was strong enough to spatter Warren's turned cheek with the pulp of the centimane's flesh, even from half a courtyard away. When he looked back, she was on her feet, and seemed about to leap back through the portal behind her. Then she skidded to a halt on the sandy pavement, turned, and stared down into the frothing shadows. She leveled her wand and loosed a ball of violet static into the turbulent gloom.

Like a depth charge rolled into the path of a skulking submarine, the shadows swelled into a titanic bubble that burst and foamed upon the air.

Warren tied his dodgy knots a little more quickly.

Whisking her legs—one shod, the other bare—in pursuit of the sinking carpetbag, Isolde performed in her head an elaborate (if entirely speculative) equation of time, breath, and distance. Just the evening before, she had vowed she would never so much as dip her toe into the abyss again, yet here she was—diving straight down its throat. All the while, above her the sprawling flails of the centimane continued to colonize the surface, blotting out more and more of the dwindling light.

Her stretching fingers grazed Grandad's tumbling corner, its brass clasp, its stitched side. But the satchel seemed made of heavier stuff, a material more determined to sink than she could keep pace with.

She was still kicking and straining when she saw the field of gray stars rise from the void. The specks appeared in tidy rows that brightened as they emerged—though "bright" wasn't quite the word for it. The nodes pulsed with hues more vivid and strange than anything that colored the world above. She had known it was coming, and still she shuddered at the sight. The broad, humped tongue of the Gloaming God swelled toward her.

And yet she didn't turn back. She dove on—reaching, grasping, despairing.

With a final lunge, she hooked her father's satchel by the handle. Twisting about, she kicked toward salvation, but too late. The heavy buds of the god's unending tongue had caught her by the toe. She struggled against its grip, piercing as an ice bath, but found she had neither strength nor breath for such a fight. Clutching Grandad to her chest, she sketched within the closing gap a simple Hex of Radiance.

The disc of light ignited at her closing stroke. All at once, the blue medallion began to rise, eager as a bubble, carrying her along with it, towing her free of the god's bitter hold. Isolde balled herself about the portalmanteau as the darkness foamed around her rapid ascent. A flutter of hope tickled her heart. Perhaps she had gotten away with it; perhaps she would once again skirt the consequences of a choice rashly made and fanatically pursued! Then she beheld the tangle of tentacles that barred the way, and knew that she had escaped one terrible fate only to career into another.

The sorcerer's missile burst overhead, igniting the bramble of tentacles and touching off a shock wave that frothed the void. For a moment, everything was a pell-mell tousle of heat and severed limbs. Tossed about by the maelstrom, Iz lost all sense of up or out or self. Then she broke the surface and greeted the light with a gasp.

Isolde heard Warren shout her name, and turning on her floating hex that bobbed like flotsam in a storm, she saw him toeing the edge of his circlet of light, his armored trousers sparkling just outside the groping range of the centimane. He began to swing a knotted chain over his head like a lariat before she shouted, "It's coming! Get away from the shadows!"

Then the ground began to shriek.

As Iz's little boat of hexed light bounced upon the black-capped sea of murk, the centimane's widespread limbs all curled at once. The skins of the apartment buildings, now dressed in black fishhooks, seethed as the beast's arms first spasmed, then shriveled. Though Isolde could not see the exchange from the surface, she and the other castaways of the courtyard could feel the moment the Gloaming God lapped the centimane from the dish of their daylit world.

The quivering feelers vanished in waves that fled down the facades, and in from the alleyways, and over the plain of the derelict park, as the centimane's unappeasable hunger collided with the appetite of the abyss.

Then the stormy shadows fell still.

In the abrupt calm that followed, Iz looked for Warren. She found him, leaning upon the pylon of a swing set, a grateful, dreamy smile on his face. Though his expression quickly tightened as he saw something she did not.

From the threshold of her open portal, the sorcerer threw a Barb of Retrieval. The ray of pinkish light enveloped the portalmanteau where Isolde still held it pressed to her chest, and snatched it away. The sorcerer reeled the satchel to her hand.

Jaw clenched, Isolde raised a finger and scribbled a hex of such inconsequence few recalled it save those who had a spouse who, on occasion, put his undershirt on backward. Iz's Hex of Reversion struck the sorcerer squarely, swiveling her cloak about.

Blinded by her backward hood, the sorcerer staggered, her grip loosening on the portalmanteau as she fought to clear her obstructed view. Iz rushed forward and snatched away her father's satchel, an effort that the stumbling sorcerer could not see well enough to rebuff. Even as the empty-handed plurician scratched at her shrouded face, Warren arrived, shoulder down. He rammed her with a full head of steam, sending her tumbling gracelessly back through the portal. The moment the sorcerer collapsed into the obscured room beyond, the door in space clenched like a fist, and the fiery ring evanesced from ember to sparklet to ash.

Regaining his feet in the suddenly serene courtyard, Warren embraced his wife. They searched one another tenderly, first for injury, then to reassure themselves that they had survived. They shivered and murmured endearments until Isolde confessed she had to sit down and catch her breath.

Still panting, she nodded at the length of chain that encircled her husband's middle and dragged behind him like a tail. "What was the plan there?"

He raised his arms and chuckled at his handiwork. "It seemed a good first step, though I hadn't quite figured out the second."

"I'm sure it would've been spectacular." She hugged her knees to keep herself from splaying out flat.

"No doubt." Warren dislodged the poorly knotted chain from his waist with a shimmy of his hips. "That wasn't an alchemist, was it?"

"No. I'd hoped it was Silva. But I think that was someone else, someone new. We seem to have made a rather extraordinary enemy."

Warren assessed the devastated courtyard—the centimane's trajectory that furrowed the concrete, the miserable remnants of playground equipment, the bite the sorcerer's missile had taken from one tower. "What a mess. We should go home. Regroup."

"Absolutely not. The only good thing about an ambush is it tells you you're on the right track. If anything, I'm more determined than ever to speak with Ms. Morris."

Warren deflated with a sigh, then plumped his chest again with a laugh. "Aye, Captain. But perhaps we should start by finding you another shoe."

UNRAVELING A
BACKSTITCH

<hr>

The door bore so many layers of dappled and flaking paint that it resembled a topographical map. The stenciled number that centered it was eroded, but legible. Still, Warren checked and rechecked his crumpled note.

When Ms. Eynon had slipped Warren the address for Miss Emma Morris, he had assumed it was attached to an apartment, a rented room, perhaps a dormitory. Instead, their destination was quite clearly some sort of commercial enterprise, albeit a squalid one. The door lay at the bottom of a narrow stairwell that was pinched further on either side by rusted dress forms, broken sewing machines, and a multitude of warped boards from the hearts of spent bolts. These dreary artifacts were made all the more dismal by the thick layer of carp snow that cloaked them. The ichthyic stink of thalfall was so strong it brought tears to their eyes.

Warren knocked, first tentatively and then after a moment's silence with more authority. The door flew open, and they were confronted by a podgy man brandishing the leg of a dining room table. His shirt collar was cocked up, and his gray hair brushed back. He had the blown look of someone who'd been driving in a jaunt with the windscreen down—evidently amid a light rain. His cheeks, pitted and whiskered, coursed with sweat.

The trio scrutinized each other upon the cramped landing, all sharing a mutual sense of surprise and misgiving. Behind the dewy brute, sewing machines barked like a machine gun nest. The heat that fumed from the space beyond steamed against the winter air, carrying with it competing aromas of anxiety, motor oil, and lavender talc.

Raking Isolde up and down with his eyes, the windblown gentleman absorbed her rumpled coat and her missing shoe, replaced by a cast of newspaper and baling twine, and smiled. His stained and gapped teeth recollected nothing so well as a sewer grate. "You'll do. Pay is a quarter spar a seam. I dock half a spar for every missed stitch. If you can't run a sewing machine right, you're going to walk out of here owing me money! This isn't a charity." He glanced at Warren. "No men. No concerned husbands, brothers, managers, or pimps, either."

Isolde smirked at the gentleman's witlessness. "You are confused, sir. I'm not here to inquire after work. I'm here to interview a woman named Ms. Emma Morris. Is she under your employ?"

"Who, the Countess? My god! You must be joking! She's already got more sticks up her than a girdle. An interview? What are you, the press, the police? No, course not. Look at you! What is it, then? Does she owe you money? Get in line! She owes me money, too. She's been two weeks out on her wages for six months."

"No, we're not the police. Though I could come back with my friend Detective Smud. Let him have a look around, if you like. Perhaps he'd discover only a respectable little clothes mill—perhaps he'd find evidence of exploitation, maltreatment, fraud. What an exciting gamble! Either way, you'll lose production hours. Better to be reasonable, I imagine."

The man slapped the table leg on one fleshy palm. "Or I could just sort it out here."

"How much?" Warren asked, rooting around in his coat pocket.

"One hundred gallets," the sweatshop boss said.

Warren's heavy brow dropped like an axe. His voice was quavering and low when he said, "How about ten?"

The boss raised his chins. "How about two hundred?" A young girl in a flour sack dress scooted through the door past the boss and fled up the stairs with her head down. "And if you're late again tomorrow, Nan, just stay home! I binned your sister, and I'll bin you!"

Warren closed his wallet, his shoulders dropping. He shifted Grandad out from under his elbow and passed the satchel to his wife. "It's been a long morning."

The boss jeered. "Oh no! Should I call your mum? Perhaps you need a hot choccy and a kiss on the—" Warren snatched the boss's club from his grip and broke the heavy shaft over his knee.

Dropping the two ends of the shattered bat, Warren gripped the sweaty boss by his shirt front, jostling him backward through the door. The red-faced man crashed against the iron railing of a landing that jutted over the sunken sweatshop. Scores of whirring sewing machines thundered on the open floor below.

Revived by the presence of his employees, the gentleman was inspired to attack. He laid his doughy hands to Warren's throat. Mr. Wilby headbutted him twice on the nose. Blood flowed from both nostrils as if from a tap. As the supervisor gibbered profanely, Warren pressed him harder over the rail until the gory spring began to course up the slope of his face, into the wells of his sunken eyes. Warren said, "You know, I used to box at night in the bars and clubs. Such an effective way to excise the little furies that accrue over the course of a day. I'd thump prizefighters and professional bruisers until the moon set and I could sleep. Oh, how I slept! Like an infant! Like the unconscious men I left on the mat. Now, I bake. I beat eggs. I knead dough. I put things in the oven. I pull them out again. And I feel a little better. But, sometimes...oooh, sometimes I miss the evening pummel. I miss it!"

Through a mask of blood, the boss found Iz's gaze and mewed, "Help."

"I did try." She shrugged. Then after a second more of observing Warren bend the man like a cooper, she laid a hand on her husband's straining arm and said, "You know what, War, let's come back another time. I'm sorry. I've pushed too hard again. I've been selfish. You know how I get. Obsessed. You were right. We should regroup. Let's go home."

Still shivering with anger, Warren's grip softened as he focused upon his wife. Swallowing hard, he pulled the supervisor up and set him on his feet. As he smoothed the trembling man's bloody shirt, Warren said, "No, no. I'm sorry. That was unexpected. It sort of snuck up on me. I'm all right now."

"*You're* all right?" the man whimpered through the handkerchief he pressed to his nose.

"I'd shut up if I were you." Isolde patted him on the shoulder as he slunk down the stairs. The supervisor sequestered himself in a clapboard assemblage that clung to the corner of the sweatshop floor like a wart. The tar-papered door bore a crudely painted sign that read MANAGMENT.

Despite the season, the subbasement air was sweltering. Beyond the rows of machines, women loaded finished dresses into steam presses that barked and plumed like a bank of artillery. The women labored in cotton shifts, nightgowns, and thin housecoats while sitting on stools that were padded by their winter coats. They hunched over their machines like jockeys to their mounts. A few had observed the commotion above, but most seemed too absorbed by their work, too deafened by the ruckus, or too cowed by their manager to notice.

Isolde drew a Hex of Amplification in the air, conjuring a star that shone like a cut persimmon. Pressing her lips to the small, glowing ward, she said, "Excuse me! Hello! Can I have your attention, please!" Her enlarged voice outshouted the din. Gradually the noise abated as the sewing engines slowed to a stop. Into this pocket of quiet, Isolde Wilby said, "We'd like to speak to Ms. Emma Morris. Is she here?"

Amid the clogged rows, between racks of hanging blouses and dresses, a woman rose, straight as a needle. She lifted her hand.

Isolde smiled. "A mutual friend referred us. Could we have a moment of your time?"

Emma Morris's thick spectacles migrated from the bridge of her brow, down to the tip of her nose with inexorable determination. While the pace of their progress varied depending on which way she held her head, their goal never seemed in doubt. Her glasses were destined to slip from her face and fall disastrously to the ground. Yet what saved them—or rather, what perpetuated the drama—was the seemingly unconscious chop of her hand, which shot up, again and again, as if in salute, catching the specs on the left corner, forcing them back up her nose just in the nick of time.

Emma Morris struck Iz as an interesting soul. At odds with her suicidal spectacles was her formal posture. She wore her ratty housecoat like an evening gown and spoke in the clipped, quick style of the upper class. Even upon the filthy doorstep of a sweatshop, her poise betrayed the training of a youth spent under Victor Cholmondeley's roof. Though only in her midtwenties, silver already threaded her carefully styled curls.

After hearing the Wilbies' business involved her foster father, Emma Morris had seemed ready to turn the rumpled pair away. Then Warren explained that it was Ms. Eynon who'd given him her address. He showed Ms. Morris the slip of paper as evidence, and she recognized the house-keeper's pinched cursive instantly. She agreed to hear them out.

Iz allowed Warren to pursue the usual pleasantries, a back-and-forth that revealed Ms. Morris was unmarried, had no children, held few acquaintances, and fewer friends. She was self-sufficient and settled, at least as much as anyone in exile could be.

"Exile?" Isolde repeated the word. "So, you still consider that life, the Cholmondeley estate, as the place you most belong?"

Emma Morris chopped her spectacles back into place and smiled like someone who'd just gracefully withstood an insult. "If you beat manners into a child early and long enough, the resulting neurosis becomes indis-tinguishable from a personality. And even so, if I'd been allowed to stay, the browbeaten girl that I was would've been quite content. I would've been happy living as the dimmest, meanest candle in a blazing chandelier. But after years of studying how to please the gentry—learning the sort of wit that they like, the politics they prefer, their invisible hierarchies and enigmatic codes—my father chose to make that world suddenly and irre-deemably *inaccessible*. Such a dismissal leaves one feeling like a living faux pas. I am reminded every day by my taste, my etiquette, my enunciation what a wretched disgrace I am." Ms. Morris patted the carefully laid ring-lets of her hair. Isolde wondered how early she rose to style those locks, only to have them gradually wilt over the course of her workday. "Yes, I would say *exile* is the word for it, Ms. Wilby. Though I know some of my former siblings have described their departure from the old homestead as more of an escape."

"Cholmondeley was abusive, then?" Isolde asked.

Morris exhaled through her nose—a fossilized laugh. "He hardly ever spoke of anything but his displeasure with us. Though I don't believe he ever really wished to be pleased. It's not the egregious cruelties that stand out to me now. It's not the canings, nor the frozen nights in the attic, nor the endless mortifications that he passed off as curative exercises for overly effete children—unclogging chimneys, flushing gutters, clearing the stones from a field . . .

"No, what I remember most are the early breakfasts in the great hall, my brothers and sisters and I all sat in a row across from him at the big table. And at our back, through the gallery of windows, rolled his jade lawn and his prized bosk of firs and the sun rising over the cusp of the world. All alone on his side of that horizon, Papa would poke his yolks and eat his soldiers and gaze at the view behind us and declare, 'The nation's greatest painters could not compete with the exhibition of a Berbiton sunrise!' And we, made to watch the dawn by the gray mirror of his face, would gasp like witnesses of creation itself." Ms. Morris beat her glasses back up her nose. "The privations of a narcissistic parent are sometimes subtle but rarely unimaginative."

Isolde studied the woman intently. "Then you were aware that you were part of a social experiment."

From a baggy pocket in her overcoat, Emma Morris retrieved a small enameled tin, which she opened and delved. Lifting a pinch of snuff to one nostril, she gave a practiced snort, changed sides, and sniffed once more. "My earliest memory is of my father documenting a mistake." She sneezed several times in rapid succession, the dainty paradiddle sounding like a tabby with a snoot-full of catnip. Dabbing her nose with a tissue she continued: "I was five years old, and I had an accident in the night. While a nursemaid changed my sheets, my father stood in the doorway with his little black ledger, tut-tutting and detailing the failure of my bladder for his records. I keep calling him *Father*, but of course, he was not, and never allowed us to be confused on that point. He was Mr. Cholmondeley. We all kept the surnames we came to him with, and he called us by them or unflattering nicknames."

"What was yours?" Isolde asked.

"Piss-Pants." Emma Morris saluted her spectacles once more.

Warren sighed and rubbed his mouth. Through a break in his fingers, he said, "He likes to present a very different sort of persona at his parties. He's all ha-has and compliments."

"Oh, Father had a different face for every crowd, every evening, every hour."

Isolde extracted her notepad and began to scratch upon it, an activity that seemed to distress her interviewee. Warren gently laid a hand over hers to stop her scribbling. She looked to him and he smiled in a manner that communicated this was not the time. Isolde stowed her pad and composed a more cordial expression. "Do you remember a Henry Blessed?"

"Of course, I remember Henry. We all loved Henry. He was so good at sponging up our father's wrath, which spared the rest of us a bit of it. No one spent more time sleeping in the attic or breaking our father's canes with his back than little Blunder Britches. That's what Father called him. Which was tragic, because Henry was always so eager, so determined to please. It just seemed to make Father hate him more. Then it all changed."

"When he drowned?" Iz said.

"After the ceremony," Emma answered.

"Cholmondeley mentioned something about a crucible—a ritual incineration. It occurred, as I recall, on the occasion of your sixteenth birthday. He had you burn whatever possessions you'd come to him with originally. Is that right?"

Ms. Morris righted her spectacles and tilted her head back to better grip Isolde with her telescopic gaze. She appeared to undertake several calculations of her own. She evaluated the steaming hatch of her employer and scanned the clogged stairwell to the ghetto's bleak canyons. Isolde discerned in her stocktaking a mortal deliberation.

"You don't have to answer." Warren spoke with lowered chin. "You should know, we've been pursuing this inquiry for a relatively short time, and already some innocent parties have been hurt...killed. We have been assaulted on more than one occasion ourselves—very recently, in fact. Powerful interests lurk around the edges of these questions. It may not be safe for you to answer."

Iz's amiable smile tightened like a stitch. "I promise you that, though I have come in a hurry, the decision to seek you out was not made lightly. There's much at stake. Even so, whether or not you aid our investigation, our being here probably necessitates a change of address and employment. I have a friend, a captain of a gambling boat—a very fine one. He is presently in need of a cashier. The pay is reasonable, the work tolerable, and they have a number of cabins, berths really, available for employees. The accommodations would be snug, but the boat is well guarded."

Ms. Morris swept the slipping lenses from her face and rubbed her eyelids, purpled with fatigue. "A casino boat? I remember those. We went sometimes with Father. Or rather, we milled about on the wharf while he hobnobbed on those floating palaces. Such pageantry! I'm sure it's changed, but when I was a girl, everyone wore suits and gowns fit for a coronation." She snuffled dryly, a sound that seemed to fall somewhere between weeping and laughter. "Is it awful that I just wish to be near it again? It always seemed like a play, a performance, but it was a show that I had prepared for—trained for. I don't like this about myself, but I hate to think all of that... *cultivation* was wasted. Is that wrong? Is that shameful?"

Producing a peppermint from his pocket, Warren offered her the lozenge as he answered. "I don't see anything shameful about this life you've made for yourself. And I'd never insult you with any armchair moralizing. If you're looking for someone to judge you, you won't find a jury in us. We are the ones, after all, who barged in on your life."

Emma Morris unwrapped the mint and, holding it to her lips, said, "Not a life. Just an exile."

"We will do whatever you prefer," Iz said.

Her decision apparently made, Ms. Morris clacked the hard candy over her teeth before stowing it in her cheek. "Father called it the christening. If we had proved by the age of sixteen that we were cultured and deserving enough, he would bestow upon us his last name. That was the promise, at least. He called us up, one by one, to a firepit on the roof, and there, made us burn our infant blankets and swaddles and rag dolls—things we'd not seen since the day we arrived at the manor, things that he forced into our arms with a match and a scowl. I'd like to say that my bindle still smelled of my mother, but it only reeked of mold. Then, as each of us on our day watched our infancy burn, he informed us that we were unready, unrehabilitated, and beyond help. He, in his largess, gave some of us a year or two of probation—time we could use to redeem ourselves in his eyes. Though none of us ever did."

Isolde nodded in receipt of these tragic facts, but her next question leapt out eagerly enough: "But it wasn't the same for Mr. Blessed?"

"After the christening, Henry was strange; Father was different with him. They both made a grand show of announcing that Henry was on probation, having not had the family name bestowed upon him. But I remember, there was a flurry of late-night visits. I could hear Henry through the ceiling as he departed his more-or-less permanent confinement in the attic and squeaked down the stairs. I followed him once. I couldn't believe it at first when I saw him slinking into Father's study in the dead of night. At the time, I wondered if it didn't indicate some much worse form of punishment. Then, days later, he drowned. We all saw it happen. We were having a picnic on the riverbank between the bridges with Father, which was strange. Then Father began to bully Henry, as he so often did, about being a weakling. Which he was. Henry was small, always short of breath, always pasty. Father challenged him to swim across the river, and Henry, ever eager to please, stripped off his shoes and shirt and dove in. We observed him first by eye, then binocular, as he splashed deeper into the current. He was midway across the Zimme when he sank from view."

"But that wasn't the end of it," Isolde said.

"There was the funeral, of course. Father made us all stand around and listen to him as he elevated his most abused son to the status of sainthood. He went on and on about the myth of innocence, and the redemption of hubris. He said if Henry had made it across, he might have been king someday. The rest of us, he said, didn't have one-tenth of his courage. I think we all knew then and there, that was the end of it. None of my sisters or brothers were particularly surprised when Father told them their probation was over, and they would be dispatched to their new life on a dairy farm or tugboat or quarry.

"I was the youngest...the last to be shown the door. My probation went on much longer than it should've. I think Father liked the vestige of his little familial troop, liked sitting there across from his children over the levee of a table, eating his runny eggs and praising the beauty of a sun that seemed to rise just for him. I was such a meek little witness. So easy to overlook. I said all the right things, which most of the time was nothing at all.

"Then one day, Father had a visitor: a young man with an undeveloped mustache, exquisite grooming, and better clothes. It had been four years since he'd drowned, and still I recognized him straightaway, though I was smart enough to pretend not to, even after Father introduced him to me. He presented Henry as a dignitary's son, a recent university graduate, and his newly hired private clerk. Henry bowed and blinked and seemed as aloof as a camel. I'm sure it was a test, a test of how convincing his transformation was. I admit, it was startling: He was taller, fuller framed, not handsome exactly, but striking."

"And what was the name of this familiar stranger?" Iz asked.

Ms. Emma Morris hacked her spectacles up her nose once more. "Mr. Horace Alman."

26

THE APOSTATE

---◇---

He wore his hat on his knee. But of course...he had to," Isolde muttered to the nearly empty tram. Since hirable jaunts seldom ventured into Dove Town, they'd been compelled to take a clattering street trolley home. Warren had elected to squeeze himself into one of the unforgiving bench seats that telegraphed each junction in the track directly to his spine. Iz stood with one arm raised to grip the rail, the chill of which cut through her glove. She swayed in sympathy with their slaloming progress through the sloped blocks and gazed out the frost-tinted windows at the gray blur of the passing slums. The racket of their transit insulated their conversation from the few other riders, who sat rocking and slack-faced, caught in the commuter's trance.

"Hats? Knees? What? Wait a minute, wait." Warren ground upon his brow with the knuckles of one hand. "I'm trying to wrap my head around this: Horace Alman, the king's secretary, the man who hired us on behalf of the Crown, *is* Henry Blessed, the would-be royal bastard and orphaned experiment. Is that right?"

Standing on one foot like a crane, Iz absentmindedly itched the trussed paper of her pulpy boot with the edge of her remaining sole. "That letter, the threatening one the king received, always struck me as strange. Alman referred to it as blackmail, but blackmail comes with terms, doesn't it? It proposes a clear consequence, demands a specific reward, suggests a time-line, a means for avoiding the unwanted revelation...But that letter was more of an announcement, really. It didn't propose any particular action on the king's part because that wasn't its purpose."

As Warren listened to his wife, he strove to shut the cracked and whis-tling window by his ear, though the rusted frame resisted his tugging. Surrendering the effort, Warren shook out his sore fingers and said, "So what was the point of it?"

"Let's consider what we've learned so far..."

Jessamine Bysshe, after slaying the unhappy father of her unborn child, had gone on to bear a healthy boy who she named Henry. At the advice and direction of the prince, who had come to her aid on that faith-ful night in the midwife's alley, Jessamine had gone into hiding. While awaiting the prince's promised installation into the ranks of her would-be relations, the Larklands, Jessamine had succumbed to the pox, but not before reenacting one of the superstitions Cousin Valerie had taught her. On the occasion of her first day as a nurse, her cousin-mum had sewn into the hem of Jessamine's uniform a coin for good luck. Inspired by the tradition, if not the result, Jessamine Bysshe had sewn into her infant's swaddle Prince Sebastian's royal signet ring where it would remain hidden until years later when the industrialist's ritual burning of the orphan's rags revealed the stitched-up signet. As a collector of rarities and a man obsessed with the royalty, it had not taken Cholmondeley long to divine the ring's significance.

Perhaps Jessamine had hoped that the prince's ring would be a passport to a better life for her son, but as Horace Alman noted during his original interview with the Wilbies, possession of the ring of the king-to-be was not evidence of relation. A claimant would require surer proof. Undoubt-edly, Cholmondeley made every effort to connect Henry to the Crown, a search that had most likely begun at the orphanage and ended at a grave-stone carved with the pseudonym Jess Blessed.

Though Isolde's review of the case began on the banging tram, she continued her account as they disembarked at High Street, and covered the remaining blocks home on foot. After a brief abatement, the thalfall had returned with gusto. The carp snow had chased much of the citizenry back indoors, leaving the sidewalks clear for the ashes to more neatly fill. The Wilbies scuffed the opalescent fluff as they walked, heads pressed together to share the canopy of Warren's overcoat and to keep their voices from casting the king's secrets into the street.

And still, Isolde had yet to finish her appraisal of the facts when they arrived home. As Warren brushed the snow from their HEXOLOGISTS plaque, Isolde unlocked the front door. Marching inside, she turned to the burl-clad secretary, and there rummaged around for a pair of shears. Carrying the scissors to the couch, she set about the chore of snipping off her wet and dissolving boot.

"But why the change of persona?" Hanging up his coat, Warren frowned at the trail of pearly soot they'd tracked in. "Surely having Henry rename and remake himself would only further obscure his connection to the Crown."

"I'm sure Cholmondeley was careful to document the makeover. Should it ever come to light, he could say that he had only helped his adopted son reinvent himself to skirt the stigma of his past, perhaps even his association with the industrialist's spurned experiment. At least, that would be the excuse I'd make. The real reason for the change of name, I think, was that Victor knew his adopted heir would be unlikely to be given any position on the king's staff, and they needed access. Since the record of the prince's indiscretion could not be ferreted out via investigation or from the public archives, they felt they had no option but to scour the regent's private records for any indication, any hint of an association with Jessamine Bysshe. So they concocted an identity that was, no doubt, designed to be both innocuous as to not arouse suspicion but bearing a sufficient pedigree to give our Horace Alman the opportunity to insinuate himself into the king's home."

"Yes, I'm beginning to catch on." Warren slid Grandad back into its furtive alcove over the fireplace. "But then what? Let's see...I suppose after a few years of searching, poor Henry started to get a little desperate. Even with all of his access to the king's intimate records, he still hadn't found anything. So, maybe he thought he could scare a confession out of the king. The threat certainly seems to have taken a toll. But why bring us on? Why invite the scrutiny?"

"The letter provided him with the excuse he needed to hire us.

Remember what he said from the start: He needed *proof* that the black-mailer's claim was illegitimate. But what he hoped for was that we would discover the opposite: a chain of evidence that proved his privilege. He knew us well enough to know we would not suppress the truth to please the Crown. The evidence that we brought him—that he was in fact the son of Rudolph Atterton—came as a terrible disappointment."

Depositing her slit-open paper cast onto the fire grate, Isolde retrieved a blank card and envelope from her writing desk and began to scribble upon it as she continued: "Looking back to our debriefing in the tearoom, I see now that what I mistook for distress at the uncovering of the king's conspiracy to cover up a murder was in fact disappointment at his own lost cause. The question is, what will Alman and Cholmondeley do with the knowledge of the king's involvement in the death and cover-up of Rudolph Atterton now that we've spoiled their claim to the throne? Will they approach the Atterton family? Will they attempt to incite some sort of aristocratic revolt?" Sliding the card into a stiff envelope, she licked the flap, sealed it, then set about addressing it.

War retreated to the kitchen and continued to shout his thoughts as he opened and rummaged through the icebox. He called over his shoulder, "I almost feel bad for our Mr. Alman. I can't help but think of what Emma said about knowing it was all a farce, and still feeling no option but to play the part." He returned to the living room with a hastily buttered heel of bread capped with a rough slice of salami. He paused in the doorway to consider his snack, then murmured, "I need to feed Felivox. Poor boy. Always so patient." He bit into his crust, then dashed the crumbs from his mustache. "But what does any of this have to do with hats on knees? What were you ahaing about on the tram?"

Isolde slid her bare feet into the fraying slippers by the door and stepped out onto the age-scalloped stoop. Two fingers to her mouth, she piped a sharp whistle, then waved encouragingly when she attracted the attention of a courier, a capped boy in bracers. Slouching to his level, she offered him the envelope along with a five-gallet bill. "Deliver this, wait for a reply, and return it to me. There'll be twice as much waiting for you if you do. Quick as you can."

The slap of running feet accompanied Isolde's slamming of the door. She faced her puzzled husband with an expression that beamed with the dawn of manic delight. She pointed at the empty chair beside the cold hearth. "The royal secretary sat there with his hat on his knee throughout our interview. Students and stevedores sit with their hats on their knees. But a gentleman—certainly an emissary of the Crown—would keep his cap in his lap, or more customarily, he would relinquish it to the rack, which as I remember, you offered him more than once. But no. No, our Alman clung to his hat, and he sat there with it on his knee because he was covering up a stain: a wet spot from where he knelt in our soggy alley."

"What was he doing stooping in our alley?" Warren crammed the last of his snack into his cheek.

"He was depositing the mandrake into our basement through our old chained-up coal chute." Isolde pounded up the stairs, tugging loose the buttons of her blouse as she ascended.

"But the mandrake was seven feet tall!" Warren shouted as he chased after her.

"Only after its growth spurt!" She pulled her arms from the sooty sleeves of her shirt, and cast the balled-up garment toward the wicker hamper in the corner of their room. "Before you cut it in half, do you remember the odd cord belt around the golem's waist? I only recognized it recently for what it was: braid magic, of the very same sort that I saw in Cholmondeley's mill. The same knots the industrialist uses to enlarge his catchweed, Mr. Horace Alman employed to transform the mandrake from a spud into a tank."

"But the mandrake attacked him." Warren watched Iz dart about the bedroom, inspecting socks for runs, searching for a pair of pedal pushers among the strata of partially clean clothes that humped the seat of a high-backed chair that existed only to defer the ever-looming crisis of laundry.

Isolde answered, "But did it really attack him? You remember how Alman asked that we build a fire, chase off the chill, and how he positioned himself just beside the mantel, how he sweated through his clothes? He knew the mandrake would be drawn to the flames."

"How did he know that?" Sensing that a change of attire was in order, Warren sat on the bed to better free himself of his damp socks and playground-dusted trousers. Turned up, his cuffs drained an alarming amount of rubble onto the bedroom floor.

Isolde snatched up a tube of lipstick from her vanity, which she blithely applied as she ran into her closet. She answered from that dim depth: "Because

Alman had infested the mandrake with spores from the Entobarrus. Remember the spider I caught in our chimney, the one that shed blue embers and immolated itself on my candle? It was blighted with the same fungus that Cholmondeley's alchemist doused with molten lead! Those toadstools seem to rely upon fire to disseminate their zygotes, which makes perfect sense considering the flaming landscape they're native to. When you split the mandrake in half, his fibers were aswarm with those shining motes. They were enticing their host to its fiery end and their own beginning. Those mushrooms are deviously parasitic: They take the reins from the minds of their helpless host."

Warren rubbed his bare knees and squinted at the ceiling. "That's a grim fate."

"Yes, it is. And it was to be ours. I believe they hoped we would survive long enough to finish the investigation and then succumb to the urge to throw ourselves onto the pyre. I'm glad I put on your gas mask. But I think, both the braid and the spores mean that Mr. Alman was acting under Mr. Cholmondeley's influence, if not his explicit direction. Alman sat in front of the fire because he *knew* the mandrake would be drawn to it, making him appear to be the target."

"But why?" Warren stood and searched the chair of half-clean clothes.

Isolde hopped about as she worked her legs into a dun-colored pair of knickerbockers. "Perhaps to remove himself as a suspect, or maybe to conjure the specter of some other bad actor."

"Speaking of which, where does the murmuring flock and our pale alchemist—or rather, the sorcerer—where do they fit into all of this? Are they working for Cholmondeley?"

"I doubt it. The flock has tried to discourage our investigation from the start. Remember, it was an inquiry that both Horace and Vicky wanted."

"So, Alman isn't the only one who's been following our investigation. And may I ask, what are we dressing up for, dear?"

"I've just dispatched a request for a royal audience."

Warren dropped a frilly shirt he'd just been sniffing. "You what?"

Isolde slapped through a hanging rack of nearly identical white blouses. "I'm sorry. Couldn't be helped. Now, what does one wear to meet a mad king?"

A half hour later when the freshly dressed and recomposed Wilbies answered the knock at their door, they were somewhat surprised to see the six-wheeled gold-clad jaunt idling on their curb. The young courier who Iz had dispatched now stood on their stoop wearing the wide-eyed astonishment of a fish who'd lately been carried many miles through the air in the talons of an eagle. Shivering, either from a surplus of nerves or the lack of a scarf, he presented Ms. Wilby with an envelope that contained a card, thick as a shingle, which read, *Ms. & Mr. Wilby are hereby invited to attend the court of King Elbert III this very afternoon. Please carry this note, board the carriage, and leave all luggage at home.*

Paying the young courier his due and two gallets more, Iz and War nodded to the chauffeur as they piled into the voluminous back seat of the jewelry box of a jaunt. The Wilbies were accustomed to cab seats with squeaking, prodding springs and air that reeked of whatever the driver had had for supper. The royal jaunt resembled a rolling parlor, complete with rug, tasseled lampshades, and a plush sofa that embraced them as snugly as a slipper. Often, Iz passed the time during their transits auditing the troubling moles on the backs of her hired drivers' necks, but the royal chauffeur seemed as remote as a ship's figurehead. Still, his voice carried well enough when he informed them that he had been charged with driving them to the royal château with all due haste.

They were hardly underway before they became mired in traffic, which first slowed, then crawled, then stalled altogether. After idling for some minutes, the chauffeur got out to investigate the cause of the delay, and returned to report that a pedestrian bridge had collapsed. There were a number of injuries, but no fatalities, and the Department of Works was laboring to clear the debris. When Iz asked if the driver had heard what caused the collapse, he said the initial suspicion was that an excess of accumulated ash, which had been tamped down rather than cleared, had overburdened the girders and caused them to buckle. The bridge had been brought down by a permafrost of carp snow.

Watching the drifting flakes cascade past his foggy window, Warren mused, "Do you ever feel as if we're just straightening the picture frames on the walls of a burning house?"

Iz, who was flipping through her little memo pad and reviewing her notes, answered without looking up. "What do you mean?"

"Only that the longer we go on, the more I suspect we're attending the wrong crisis. I think Nurse Percy was right. Does it really matter who sits on the throne in a nation of ashes? Why even fight over such a distinction? Who wants to be the lord of soot? The world is burning. How long can we indulge our neutrality? How long until we have to choose a side?"

"One catastrophe at a time, dear," Isolde said, squeezing the top of his hand where it clenched the edge of their gold-piped seat. She asked the chauffeur if he wouldn't mind raising the opaque privacy screen.

Warren tugged at his black necktie. He'd chosen his funeral suit to visit the palace. The choice seemed to complement his uncharacteristically bleak mood. He said, "The person I feel most sorry for in this whole sordid affair is Jessamine. She only wanted to belong, to be loved. Yet, she died alone, in secret, and was buried under a false name in a pauper's plot. And her child . . . her poor child . . ."

As was often the case at the end of an investigation, Isolde observed in her husband the breaking of a dam that had been taken for granted, neglected, and stressed. The work affected him in ways she could not feel, and too often it was left to him to look after her while she flung herself headlong into obsession. It was not that she was insensible to the suffering they encountered. The misfortune they witnessed disturbed her, and profoundly, but she knew he felt it in a more visceral way. That quality was part of what made him such a wonderful partner. Still, a large heart is not light. Even the most cherished burdens must sometimes be laid down.

With hands cupped over his eyes, he wept with an empathic sorrow that could no longer be deferred. She held him and stroked his hair and whispered endearments in his ear. She lay, half draped over his chest, murmuring affections and encouragements until her lips slowly transitioned to a different sort of language, and she kissed along his jaw.

Warren pulled back, wearing a look of bemusement. The blush brought about by his tears now began to mix with a different sort of pink. "Really? Here? Now?"

Isolde rocked her head in deliberation as she stroked one of his earlobes. "I know: It's not the time. Would be outrageous. Absolutely scandalous. But then again, I doubt there'll be another occasion when we have a moment alone in the back of the king's car."

Warren chuffed with disbelieving laughter that turned into a little moan as she threw her leg over his and settled upon his lap. "If we're going to be scandalous, we should be quick about it."

She rocked forward and murmured, "Quick?"

"Well . . . within reason." War took her by the cheeks and pulled her mouth to his.

Following in the wake of a swift-footed doorman, who was dressed as starkly as a domino, Warren Wilby tried not to gape as they traversed the grand rooms of the palace, passing a host of ancestral busts, foreign gifts, and paintings so large he could only suppose the château had been built about them. The furniture that decorated those chambers appeared to have never suffered the indignity of a posterior. Warren would've sooner sat on the knee of a courthouse judge than have dented those cushions with his common rump.

Though Isolde trotted onward, her own thoughts were elsewhere. She was pondering those lingering loose threads of the case that pestered her like an overly starched collar. She might've remained in that distracted trance had she not discovered the doorman was leading them toward the most capacious mirror she'd ever seen. Though the towering pane gathered to its frame the great distance of the palace, the stranger effect was of seeing her own image grow from a far-off animate blot to a recognizable, striding figure. It was only then, in the blaring light of chandeliers, in that opulent circumstance, that she absorbed how disheveled and wild she looked. She had entered the royal carriage in a state of semi-composure, and had departed it appearing as rumpled as fish wrap. She suffered a rare flutter of self-consciousness, a flicker of doubt, though there seemed to be something in the mirror itself that magnified the feeling. It was almost as if she were looking not at her own honest reflection but at the eyes of an impostor peering back at her from the silvery depths.

It was a relief when the doorman veered away from the monumental looking glass before they drew any nearer.

All at once, they found they'd arrived at their destination. They blenched to hear the doorman, who had remained mute despite Warren's nervous attempts at small talk, now trumpet their full names and at full volume. Then their herald abandoned them, and they looked up to discover they had been left in the audience of someone who was decidedly not the king. And still they bowed deeply and with lowered eyes.

Their show of deference was somewhat tainted by the rushing transit of five children, who charged through the Wilbies as if they were a pair of turnstiles. The children, who ranged in age from six or seven to twice that, were engaged in some version of tag that involved great lengths of fat ribbon that snaked and snapped behind them. The eldest girl and boy embodied that awkward late-stage infantilism that so often accompanies privilege and coddling. They trotted and screeched like gangly toddlers, even as pimples brightened her cheeks and his voice cracked.

"Ah, the famous Hexologists!" Princess Constance of Yeardley said. She received them in the royal sitting room, which seemed half court and half parlor. The princess, dressed in a contemporary sleeveless green tea gown, sat in a high-backed chair whose crest was barbed with a dozen golden finials. Her skin was poreless and pale as pear flesh. Her bare neck was thick and erect. Her blond hair hung in a bob, its wingtips brightened by the silver of her age. Her face bore the prominent cheeks and full lips common to her family line, and yet, nothing about her appearance was half so pronounced as her presence. She exuded gravity. Her children seemed to orbit her like devoted moons.

Before broaching the occasion of their visit, the princess, as the nation's socialite in chief, engaged in some civilities. She chatted and smiled even as her children scrambled over and around her well-clad personage. These intrusions Princess Constance bore as placidly and nobly as a lioness endures the affectionate pestering of her cubs.

The princess inquired after the Wilbies' health, how they had spent the recent sunny day, and how they'd found their ride to the palace, asking which jaunt had been sent to retrieve them. Nodding and smiling at Warren's description of their carriage, the princess said, "Ah, yes! Queen Mother Yeardley's Golden Swan! How she loved that car. She would spend morning after morning touring the town, waving from the windows, and knitting socks for the nation's premature children. In the end, she neglected her health to work those knitting needles. There's still talk of christening her a saint and turning her chariot of goodwill into a shrine."

"It was a very pleasant ride," Warren said through a rictus grin.

The parlor's walls overflowed with a collection of formal portraits of several generations of beloved pets. In the shadow of these pink-bearded hounds, cross-eyed calicos, and a single white stoat, the princess's children played their evolving game that at present seemed to center upon stitching the pillars together. All through their boisterous romping, the wildlings were careful to steer clear of the minute tea table set just beside the princess's knee. The willowy coral stand looked as fragile as dried pasta, and held aloft a similarly delicate teapot.

As Warren waggled his fingers in greeting of the youngest boy, who was presently garroting a column with a length of blue trimming, Iz took a moment to compliment the princess. "Your Highness, in university, I was made aware of your effort to reinvigorate the national dedication to the study and application of hexes. Your campaign to bring attention to hexegy was instrumental to my own determination to pursue it professionally. I had the privilege of attending both of your lectures. I still have my notes."

Princess Constance smiled with the cold, sharp precision of a filleting knife as she leaned forward to pour a splash of tea for herself from the pot, the spout of which was so small it seemed incapable of ceding much more than a dribble. Isolde observed in the ritual a performance of domestic independence. By pouring her own tea, the princess wished to communicate her autonomy, but the small scale of the effort was intended to express her acknowledgment of the minor mortification. "You are too generous, Ms. Wilby—prodigy of the magic arts, prodigal of the law, and champion of the downtrodden. The city's constabulary still suffers from your retirement and boggles at the vacuum left by your early departure from service. The nation languishes in your absence."

"That's quite a flattering estimation of my brief tenure with the police. By all accounts, that grand institution appears to be pegging away as well as it ever did."

"Why did you quit the Office of Ensorcelled Investigations, exactly? One woman to another: Was it the culture that drove you out?"

"I just grew tired of investigating defamations, conspiracies, forgeries..." Isolde opted to air a diplomatic answer rather than the unvarnished truth, though even in this she could not keep from veering into unsolicitous territory, concluding: "The OEI was always dispatched in defense of the wealthy, but rarely the poor."

"Oh, we don't call them *the poor* anymore. It's such a hostile, dispiriting word."

"What do you call them now?"

The princess lifted her teacup as if to toast the genteelism she proceeded to rattle off. "The ascendant class, the social marrow, the nation's backbone."

"Inspiring titles. Do any of them come with better pay?"

The princess donned a patronizing expression. She looked like a mother patiently explaining where the sun went to sleep to a child at bedtime. "It's a question of *respect*, Ms. Wilby—the insistence that there is nothing shameful about their status."

"But there is something shameful about it, isn't there? I mean, the purpose of a euphemism is to shield the speaker from the difficulty of the subject. We say *passed away* instead of *died*, and *put out to pasture* instead of just admitting an elder was unceremoniously removed from gainful employment because a younger, cheaper hire applied for their job. You may pretend that these circumlocutions are for the benefit of the victim, but they're not. They are for the comfort of the speaker. We call them 'ascendant class' because it makes their suffering feel less shameful for those of us who refuse to address the role we play in perpetuating poverty to the enrichment of ourselves. I say, let's call them *the poor*, and help them."

Warren brushed his wife's elbow as he coughed into his fist.

Princess Constance hailed her children. Calling them each by name, she gathered their attention and then dispatched them. They departed in a file. The ribbons they'd lately woven about the pillars of the room drooped and slipped, gathering in colorful welts across the marble floor. When the last of her children's retreating footfalls were swallowed by the palace's recesses, the royal's gaze sharpened as she leaned forward on her tearoom throne. "Let's come to the point of your visit. Your note said you had information regarding the ongoing extortion of our king. I'm sure you can imagine my surprise—I had not known that you were probing my brother's difficulty."

"Our services were engaged by the king's secretary, Mr. Horace Alman. I take it he has not kept you apprised of our investigation?"

"He has not. I was very clear on that point, I believe. This was to be a private inquiry."

Isolde bowed and Warren followed suit. "We apologize for any intrusion upon King Elbert's privacy. We believed we were acting under royal direction. And if we have overstepped, then we beg forgiveness and ask your pardon, as we remove ourselves from your—"

"Oh, stop it." The princess rose and approached them. Rather than step over the tangle of ribbons that lay between them, she pinched the corner of her green skirt, baring her knees, and lifted it to better allow herself to kick the streamers aside. It seemed a small, cathartic release, and Iz perceived in it a woman of placid surface and fiercer undercurrent. "I know it's not your fault, Ms. Wilby. That Alman is always bowing and scraping and scampering off to do as he pleases. He's the worst sort of toady—the ambitious sort." She came to a halt within arm's reach of her visitors, and peered at them both in turn. "So, tell me, what have you discovered?"

"We had hoped to share our revelations with the king himself, Your Royal Highness."

She swatted the air dismissively. "That's impossible, I'm afraid. My brother is recuperating from the recent resurgence of an old illness."

"And his recovery isn't going particularly well, we're told."

"Alman gave it all up then, did he? I'll have to review the meaning of the word 'discretion' with him. But I assure you, the king is on the mend. I'm only receiving you now in his stead to allow him another day or two of rest."

Warren bowed again, an operation that appeared unpracticed but heartfelt. "We are relieved, Your Highness, to hear that His Majesty is on the road to recovery!"

Isolde smiled crookedly, as if she had something lodged in her teeth. "And if it's any consolation, Your Highness, we have labored in the knowledge that all information we have been made privy to is of an extremely sensitive nature. We do not gossip. However, it would be, I believe, to everyone's advantage if we were to communicate our discoveries to King Elbert directly. They do pluck something of a personal chord."

Princess Constance pretended not to have heard her. "I really should've sent Alman off months ago. But our trusty secretary is so accommodating. You hit him with a crop, and he offers you a club. Never met such a cowed creature in my life."

"Are you aware that the king has been poisoned?"

The princess seemed to cover her surprise with a laugh that was as rote and ready as a shop bell. "Is that what Alman told you?"

"No, Your Highness. The royal secretary merely described the king's malady: his obvious emotional distress, his marauding insomnia, his sudden interest in ovens. But I'm not surprised Mr. Alman didn't mention the possibility that the king had been poisoned, because I suspect he is the one who did it. And I believe I know the cure."

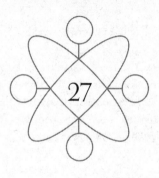

HARMLESS

Warren felt like an old stump in a sharecropper's field—an impediment, a thing in the way, but deftly avoided by the capable hands who seemed quite accustomed to inconvenience. Maids and nurses coursed about him, filling the king's sanctuary with activity and purpose. The Wilbies had interrupted the changing of the royal sheets, the sponging of the royal body, the salving of the royal bedsores, and the lashing of the royal limbs to the posts of a stately bed. The staff worked in their winter coats. The high chamber, filleted in gold and fluted with lapis, overlooked a central courtyard, onto which the tall windows stood open, permitting a bitter draft and eddies of ashen snow. The wind flowed over the inflamed coal that was King Elbert III, though he appeared insensible to his fever, his servants, and the strangers who had invaded his sanctum.

The king appeared half-starved, his noble features enlarged in contrast with the valleys of his cheeks and eyes. Warren stood by, wrenching his hat by its brim. He watched the monarch, whose politics he detested, contort like a beheaded snake, and felt his heart ache with pity.

His wife appeared considerably less affected by the moaning sovereign. Iz's attention was elsewise absorbed.

Upon being admitted into the king's sickroom, Isolde discerned several of the princess's untruths at a glance. Princess Constance had said that she was unconcerned by the king's disorder, and yet the high papered walls of the royal bedchamber were crowded with sophisticated hexes. Some were drawn in soot, others in paint; still others had been carved into the plaster at the point of a knife. The room was as tattooed as a sailor. Even the royal headboard was spotted with hexes—intricate, common, and obscure. Iz perceived in this collection the mania of desperation, and she felt in her bones the heavy presence of so many wards.

The second, more obvious of the princess's dishonesties was that the king's health was improving. He lay upon a stripped and yellowed mattress in a new nightshirt that was already beginning to cling with sweat. He struggled against his restraints with a determination that seemed almost automatic. He spasmed like the caught cog of a watch and moaned through his teeth. Rather than a man on the upswing of his health, he seemed like a corpse-in-waiting.

Though her arrival did not seem to change his distress, the presence of her brother had a marked effect on the princess's bearing. Her former detachment tightened into a hunched skulking. And Iz had the distinct impression that she was not so much concealing her brother's incapacitation as she was hiding her own frustration with her inability to heal him.

Before guiding them to the king's bedside, Princess Constance had summoned the head of the Royal Guard, and dispatched him on the urgent errand of arresting Mr. Horace Alman. She concluded her command in a daunting baritone, saying, "Bring him in unbruised. I don't want any accusations that a confession was coerced. Besides, the royal executioner prefers to work with an unmolested neck."

Standing at her brother's bedside, the princess bent to test the temperature of his forehead with the back of her hand. She sighed as she straightened. "Alman will pay for this."

"I don't believe he was acting alone," Isolde said.

"A conspiracy? Involving who?"

"Victor Cholmondeley."

The princess's chin recoiled as if indented by a hiccup. "Cholmondeley? I realize he's not exactly a patron of the race, but I've always considered him rather benign, if not a little silly. What makes you suspect him?"

Standing at the foot of the king's bed, observing him wrench his ankles against his leather cuffs with grim determination, Isolde smiled, though without pleasure. "Ma'am, it has been a strange and snaking road."

"Well, let's hear the notable turns."

Iz rehearsed the broad details of their investigation, quickly confirming her suspicion that Mr. Horace Alman had not apprised the royals of the Hexologists' recent tearoom debriefing that outed the king's blackmailer as the son of Sir Rudolph Atterton. When Isolde revealed that the prince, in defending Ms. Jessamine Bysshe's honor if not her person, had contributed to his batman's death and the subsequent cover-up, the princess appeared incredulous. What proof did they have of King Elbert's involvement in a murder?

"We had a witness," Isolde said.

"*Had?*" the princess echoed.

"Yes. The midwife, Charlotte De Lee. She died shortly after our interview, under what I would consider suspicious circumstances."

"Suspicious? How?"

"She appears to have been killed in her sleep by a neglected cigarette. But we know she didn't smoke."

"That is odd." The princess fished a rag from the white bowl at the king's bedside, wrung it out, and dabbed her brother's temples with the cool cloth. "And this Ms. De Lee—was she the only one who could've disproved Alman's claim?"

Isolde noted the staff who flooded the room seemed to be drooping, either under the pressure of the royal presence or the ambient radiation of so many hexes. It was a fog to which she and Warren were fortunately acclimated. As each finished their chore, they fled the room, with arms full of linens or dishes or pans full of carp snow. "We also have in our possession the midwife's intake form where Jessamine Bysshe lists the father of her unborn child as Sir Rudolph Atterton."

Princess Constance paused her mopping of her brother's brow. "*Atterton?* That's unfortunate. I mean, it's good in a way, I suppose. At least my brother was not—but...my god. Thank you. I'm sorry to hear life has been lost over this whole tawdry affair. But the king—you said you could heal him. How? Look around you. I've applied every healing, mitigating, invigorating hex I could think of. What have I missed?"

Isolde held up an inch of white chalk. "May I?" The princess nodded, and Isolde leaned over the king's rolling head. He stared mindlessly with dry, red eyes as she took the sleeve of her coat and cleared a spot on the headboard, erasing away the edges of a number of the princess's futile hexes. As Isolde began to draw, she explained, "His Majesty has been poisoned with the spores of a fungus from the Entobarrus. The same toadstools grow in Cholmondeley's thalanium mill, and I believe they were used by Mr. Alman to spur the mandrake he deposited in our basement into a self-destructive rage. The spores drive their infected host into open fires because that is the medium in which they propagate. Cholmondeley sterilizes the mushrooms by encasing them in molten lead, a treatment that obviously won't work for the king. Fortunately, there is a simpler, less invasive way to destroy the spores."

Princess Constance squinted over Isolde's shoulder as she drew. "A Hex of Antitinea? You're administering a treatment for ringworm?"

"Ringworm is a fungal infection, and we are fortunate that the mushrooms of the Entobarrus and our world evidently share a common ancestor." Iz closed the hex that resembled a clover-shaped knot. Standing back, she nodded in satisfaction as the sigil began to luster like fresh lacquer. The effect upon King Elbert was both instantaneous and marked. His fitful tossing slowed as his tensed limbs relaxed. His staring eyes blinked and then closed; his hoarse hyperventilation turned to deep and shuddering sighs. "There we are."

The princess gasped in amazement as she drew her hand down her brother's tear-strewn cheek. "Cholmondeley did this? Why?"

Isolde dashed the chalk dust, first from her sleeve, then from her hands. "To say the king was driven mad by guilt? To clear the way, perhaps? Personally, I suspect that Cholmondeley and Alman knew how to cure the king's ailment, and would've done so to reinforce Alman's claim. Horace Alman believed he would stand where I am, that he would be the one to save the nation by healing the king. That would put quite a bow on his petition for recognition, don't you think?"

"Speaking of our criminal secretary..." The princess returned to the chamber door, cracked it, and spoke to the guard standing in the hall. After a moment's back-and-forth, she closed the door and turned to announce: "Mr. Alman has departed the grounds without notice or permission. He is, it would seem, missing."

"It's only unfortunate that we were asked to leave our luggage at home. I might've employed some of our relics in the search."

The princess's expression puckered with displeasure. "What are you talking about?"

Isolde gave a small bow to apologize for knowing something the royal did not. "The reply to our request for an audience with His Majesty was very specific in that regard. We were welcome, but our portalmanteau was not."

The momentary vulnerability Princess Constance had displayed at her brother's bedside had now entirely fled. "And who do you think receives such requests, Ms. Wilby? Do you think the king opens his own mail?"

"Alman," Iz whispered.

"Why would he ask you to come without your satchel?" Princess Constance asked.

Bowing her way toward the door with her husband at her hip, Isolde said, "My apologies, ma'am, but I'm afraid we must beg your leave to return home and with all possible haste."

In the back of Grandmama Yeardley's rolling shrine, Isolde and Warren Wilby sat with hands gripping the leather handles of the doors as the crystal pendants of the chariot's sconces chimed in sympathy with its jolting progress through traffic. Isolde had adjured the chauffeur to hurry, citing as cause the fate of the kingdom itself. Based upon the urgency of their conveyance, it seemed a command that the driver had waited his whole life to receive.

With body pinned to the seat by the heedless speed of their car, Isolde looked not particularly alarmed as she mused to her whey-faced husband, "Ever since I deduced that Mr. Alman was responsible for planting the mandrake in our basement, I've been bothered by the whole theater of it. Why take such a risk? To heighten our anxiety? To make us believe in the existence of a shadowy conspiracy? To divert our suspicions away from him? It all just seemed so needlessly melodramatic."

Warren clenched his teeth at the sound of the jaunt's tires chirping around a corner. "But I thought the point was to infest our chimney with those mind-eating spores. You were nearly infected, weren't you?"

"But there are surer ways to kill me if that were his goal. No, I think he needed the violent scene."

"Why?" A fanfare of complaining horns accompanied a sharp jerk and acceleration of their jaunt.

Isolde reached for and found her husband's hand, which she squeezed. He was surprised to turn and find her staring at him. Tears stood in the corners of her eyes, though he could not say if they had swelled out of frustration, anger, or fear—though in truth, it seemed a touch of all three. "Alman did it to compel us to reveal where we keep Grandad hidden. He had to shock that out of us. I'm afraid we gave away the shop, War—from dust to deed—we gave it all up."

They arrived home to find their front door ajar. The strike plate and wooden frame bore the scars of a wrecking bar. Drawing a heavy black-thorn cane from the umbrella stand, Warren led their cautious advance through the vestibule.

Their parlor appeared to have been used to entertain a bull. The chairs and sofa that huddled about the hearth lay toppled; papers were strewn across the beleaguered carpet, which had gathered more and grimmer stains. Blood spattered the ground and climbed the walls in whips of red.

The royal secretary sat propped against the bearing wall beside the kitchen entrance beneath a crater in the plaster. The portalmanteau lay deflated and closed on its side between his splayed legs. His lacking chin was piled upon his starched and bloody collar. The right sleeve of his jacket was torn nearly to the yoke. The arm it had recently contained was now absent.

Dropping his club, Warren rushed to Alman's side, unbuckling his belt as he came. He hooped the leather strap about the stump of the secretary's arm, binding a wound that had already spilled so much life upon the rug. He cinched the belt tight, exciting a groan of protest from the half-conscious man. War shouted over his shoulder, "This is mortal, Iz. Keep the belt tight, and keep him awake if you can."

Surrendering his spot at Alman's side to his wife, Warren charged back to the street in search of a constable, emergency services, help.

Kneeling, Iz raised Alman's rolling head, pressing her face close to his. When she saw his eyes focus upon hers, she said, "There you are. Nice to see you. Don't be in such a hurry to go."

The royal secretary attempted to swallow, gagged, and coughed wetly, though he closed his mouth to spare Isolde the result. He swallowed again, painfully, and said, "There appears to be a dragon in your purse."

"I told you that there was back at the tearoom. What were you thinking?" Iz tugged a clean handkerchief from her sleeve and pressed it to the overwhelming and still draining wound.

Alman winced at the contact. "Desperation makes a man optimistic. I hoped you were joking."

"I never joke about dragons."

"So I've gathered." Alman rolled heavy eyes toward the front door, which stood open. "I don't think your husband needed to have bothered. I won't be long."

"Then perhaps I can help with the pain." Unpocketing her nubbin of chalk, Iz drew a quick hex in the plaster above his head. The king's treacherous secretary sighed with relief. "Tell me, Henry, how did you infect the king?"

"Henry? You know who I am, then?"

"I do. Tell me, did you put the spores in his food?"

"He always insisted on doing so much of the official correspondence himself—answering cousins, sending congratulations, the usual back-and-forth with other heads of state. He has a terrible habit of second-guessing his drafts. He tears them up, writes them again, over and over. Always unhappy with his efforts. I used to think that was a sign he really was my father." Alman smiled, though his lips soon twisted into a tortured sneer as some barrage of pain occupied his entire sentience for a moment.

"You didn't answer my question." Iz flicked Alman's ear.

The secretary groaned and blinked like a deep sleeper resisting his alarm call. "Are you interrogating me just to keep me awake or because you want answers before I die?"

"Well, you'll just have to stick around to find out. How did you poison him?"

Alman chuffed a laugh that quickly turned dire. He pawed at her with his remaining hand. Thinking he sought only comfort in his final moments, she was surprised when his grasping delivered to her palm a hard nut. She opened her bloodied hand to find he had passed to her the prince's golden signet ring. She expected he would address the gift, but he appeared to have another point to make. "The king licks his nibs. Bad habit from his school days, I suppose. A few spores in his inkpot were enough."

"You went to such lengths to find yourself in his service: You labored, and jockeyed, and kowtowed, and none of it was sincere. Seems such a waste of a promising career."

"Then it was a chore I was born for. I always knew I was a waste. There was a time, a wonderful time, Papa Cholmondeley really believed I was a prince . . . believed I would one day sit on the throne, and he upon my shoulders, of course. He loved me then, I think. He spoke to me like a person. But then . . . my god, how he laughed when he heard I was nothing but the bastard of a dead baron—a father who despised my existence so completely he gave up his post and his life just to be rid of me."

"That's not what happened," Iz said, though Horace seemed hardly to hear her. She regarded the papers strewn about the floor, and recognized the tawny dossier they'd spilled from. "What were you trying to accomplish here? Destroy the record of your birth?"

"I read about your Demiurge's Brush in the papers, how you used it to trick that forger. If it fooled him, I thought it might fool a court. I wanted to change my father's name to Yeardley. I would've been a prince. Mr. Cholmondeley would've had to forgive me, then." Alman's eyes quivered and fell as lightly as the page of a book.

Iz raked his sweat-matted hair from his forehead with her fingernails and pinched his drained cheeks. He snored a breath and opened his foggy eyes in search of hers. She smiled in welcome of his return. "I'm sorry to tell you, Mr. Alman, the Demiurge's Brush only amends oil paint, not ink. But if you stick around, I'll show you how it works."

Alman raised a whisper of a smile. "It doesn't seem fair that a man should live long enough to disappoint two fathers."

"Your mother loved you very much," she said quickly as his head fell against her cheek.

His last breath fled over her pulsing throat as she hearkened to the approaching roar of belated sirens.

A TWO-FACED HEADSTONE

The Wilbies found themselves in the unusual position of being the only ones concerned with the final repose of the man who'd tried to rob them and then bled to death in their parlor. The Crown had not yet decided how much of their recent private debacle they wished to have on the public record, and Victor Cholmondeley was steadfast in his insistence that Alman had long ago and only briefly passed through his care as a favor to a foreign client whose village and lineage had subsequently (and quite conveniently) been obliterated by a typhoon, and was most certainly not Henry Blessed in disguise. The police held the body long enough to complete a rather perfunctory autopsy, and then having finished with the corpus and finding no ready family to receive it, had placed a notice in the *Times* that if the remains of Mr. Horace Alman were not claimed within twenty-four hours, he would be added to the weekly grave: an ever-expanding pit outside of town where deceased prisoners and the recently executed were anointed with lye and interred by steam shovel.

The Wilbies, knowing well enough that they could abhor a man's choices and still cherish his humanity, volunteered to be responsible for his body. Normally, the discovery of a one-armed corpse in a private residence would've prompted a long and likely public inquest. Such gory events, when parceled with a victim from the king's own inner circle, would've proved irresistible to the scandalmongering gazettes. The Crown, wishing to resolve the matter of their treacherous secretary as swiftly and discreetly as possible, brought their considerable influence to bear. The cause of Mr. Horace Alman's untimely death in the city's coroner's report was listed as "General mayhem and misfortune," which struck Isolde as both tragic and apt.

Isolde called upon Arnold Hollins, groundskeeper of Honewort Cemetery, asking a favor that, once explained, was readily agreed to. While there was not enough room at the proposed site to bury the gentleman plank-straight, Mr. Hollins said that if the deceased was willing to be laid to rest upon his side and slightly curled, then he believed he could slip the boy in at his mother's hip.

While a coatless Warren and Len dug the crooked grave with all the care of archaeologists, Isolde and Arnold—observing from above—conferred on the details of the headstone.

Iz inquired after the possibility of revising Jess's marker to read JESSAMINE BYSSHE, but the groundskeeper quickly dismissed the idea. "I can't go around changing names higgledy-piggledy, Ms. Wilby. I'd be arrested for fraud. I've had names misspelled on forms before, and those misspellings have been consecrated by chisel because paper is more stubborn than stone. Changing an official log requires an attorney, a dozen forms, and a court order signed by a willing magistrate. And let me tell you, those aren't easy to come by. There is no graft here; no voters, either."

Isolde gritted her teeth, suffering the familiar bristle of old frustrations. "And I suppose you can't bury a body under a different name than you received it?"

"Do you think I have the power to rechristen the dead just because I don't like their names? Why, just last week we interred a man named Iffy Gibbets. Do you think I want an Iffy Gibbets in my yard? Do you know what sort of attention an Iffy Gibbets attracts? There is an entire subspecies of human who goes around collecting rubbings of gravestones with humorous names. They trample my grass and leave crayon shavings everywhere." The old groundskeeper checked the top form on his board, the clip of which bit upon a sheaf of pink pages, all crinkled and soiled. "But let's see who we have here . . . one Mr. Horace Alman. That's not so bad!"

Peering over his shoulder, Iz said, "But entirely fabricated."

"So is his mother's name, according to you." Mr. Hollins pressed his papers to his chest as if he were shielding the secrets of a nation.

Iz made no reply. And for a time the conversation was taken up by the pair of shovels that rasped against the sandy clay. Raising a spade-full of earth, Warren looked up at his wife, a smile brightening his dirty face. She had worried a return to the cemetery would be traumatic for him given their last visit, but War had insisted it would be therapeutic. He said that if he was going to start being skittish around boneyards, he'd have to look for a new line of work.

If at that moment Iz had been pressed to explain why she was so stuck on the question of Henry's epitaph, she would've struggled to supply a convincing answer. Perhaps it was a manifestation of her latent aversion for misclassification. Like her mother, she hated to see a thing improperly shelved. Or perhaps this was an expression of her frustration with a case that had spiraled out of control. She was only quibbling over this detail to pacify her injured pride. Or perhaps she perceived in the ill-fated mother and son a shared heartbreak, an echoed tragedy, a congenital desire that had underwritten so many of their sympathetic but inadvisable choices. And she hadn't her father's body to bury; it was a lack she could only address via substitute.

Iz drew a breath through her teeth to keep the drifting dirty snow from her throat. "Both Jess and Henry spent their lives striving to find their place, their people, their family. Neither ever did. The closest they seemed to have come was when they were together as mother and child. The surname *Blessed* might've begun as a gibe and been assumed in a moment of irony, but it is still theirs and theirs alone. It belongs to them, and they to each other."

The groundskeeper watched the backs of the pair toiling in the hole beneath him. "I read in the paper yesterday that astronomers believe there are planets out there that don't ride on a rail around a star like our rock does. They call them *nomads*. These nomads are up there wandering around without a sun to warm them, an orbit to guide them, other worlds to keep them company. They just float around in the dark—aimless, forgotten. These scientists think the galaxy might be full of them. All we ever see are the stars, but the night sky is a crowded graveyard."

Isolde snuggled her chin down into the fat lapels of her coat. "I didn't know you were a poet, Mr. Hollins."

The groundskeeper puffed at the compliment and returned to his clipboard, whose pages he shuffled more as a prop than for a purpose. Finally, he turned to her, searching her face for some kinship or agreement. He appeared to find what he was looking for in Isolde's inscrutable expression. "I could put in an order for a two-sided stone—carve his legal name on the back and his mother's name on the front."

Isolde signaled her gratitude with a curt nod. "That seems fitting and generous."

"Fitting, maybe. But as for the generosity..." Mr. Hollins rubbed his fingers together. "I'm afraid I'll need a little help with that."

In the days following the royal secretary's subdued funeral, the Wilbies received three callers, only the first of whom was expected—and yet somehow still not without surprise.

The parlor's violet rug and its slowly eroding gold-threaded maze had been abused beyond revival. No scooting of furniture or tactful placement of throw rugs could redeem it. A removal company was summoned, and arrived midmorning in a troop. They shunted the furniture about as freely as chess pieces as they prized and cut and pulled the voluminous rug from the parlor floor. Warren observed the massacre from the kitchen door with glassy stare and fist to chin. He grimaced when they slashed the three-hundred-year-old rug into strips, rolled them up, and shouldered them out the door. He cringed again at the whump those dusty scrolls made as they filled the back of the workmen's lorry.

When an insensible Warren did not respond to the workmen's shuffling and coughing and idle remarks that they'd best be off to their next job, Isolde intervened, dispatching the men with a check and a recommendation that they attend to the front wheel of their truck, which she suspected was ripe for explosion.

When she turned to find Warren now sitting, knees splayed and head hung, on the settee huddled in one corner with the rest of their furniture, she approached him with puzzled laughter.

"I never knew you liked the rug *that* much."

Warren straightened a little but with a wretched sigh. "Why would you say that?"

"Well, you always said nothing matched it—it was fraying and rotting and impossible to keep clean."

He rubbed his knees as if to warm them. "It wasn't how it looked. It was how it felt."

"Scratchy, you mean?"

"You don't remember?"

"Remember what?"

"It was before your mother took her apartment, when she was still living here, sleeping upstairs. We'd just met, and you invited me home to show me your collection of... what was it? Something unlikely, something absolutely unbelievable..."

"Cobwebs." She sat down beside him and took up his hanging hand.

He chortled. "That's right. You wanted to show me your collection of cobwebs. But as soon as we were in the door, we were all over each other. The upstairs with your sleeping mother seemed too daring and the couch seemed too small, and so I threw you down—"

"Oh, *you* threw me down?"

"All right, we threw each down on that funny old carpet and you made me feel, I think for the first time in my life, truly beautiful. And now..." Warren gestured at the barren floorboards, mottled with long-concealed stains and freckled with the black heads of iron tacks. The wood was paler for its preservation, and yet somehow more homely than the darker periphery of lumber that had endured years of traffic, sunlight, and wax.

"You thought I was making love to the rug?"

"No, of course not, it's just that—"

"War, I loved you right through that rug, past the floorboards, into the basement, under the foundation, straight down to the center of the earth. And I hope to see all of those things wear away as we grow old and our love stays young. Now, come on, let's warm up the floor before the new carpet arrives..."

The second visitor came in the dead of night.

While Warren lay snoring like a mountain pass, Isolde stared at the ceiling of their bedroom and worried.

A soft rapping brought her head up from the pillow. Unsure if it had been the tapping of a receding dream, she observed the streetlight flicker through the break in the curtains. Reassuring herself with a peek at her slumbering spouse, she rose, snatched her nightrobe from the radiator, and approached the drapes.

She parted the velvet and the tulle, then cracked the window on the swirling snow, stained orange by the city lights. The coated road was empty but for the trenches of taxi wheels. Glancing about, she began to believe she had imagined the noise, then she looked down at the corner of the sill and found the perched starling, its shoulders capped in snow. She opened the window a little more and presented her face.

The bird looked at her and croaked a single word: "Roof."

Isolde traversed the halls and curling stair first by the hint of external lamps, then by the light of her memory. She dallied just long enough in her attic laboratory to collect Splodge from her nesting chair. Feeding her arms into her thinking coat, she surmounted the bare spiral stair. Cracking the rooftop hatch, she squinted in the uptown midnight that shone just like the dawn. She scrambled out onto the picketed widow's walk, tightening her lapels against the tumbling, frozen ash.

As she lifted a hand to shield her eyes, it took only a moment's appraisal to discern she was surrounded. Her neighbors' shingles, gutters, and spouts all bore the weight of a vast flock. The plum-, blue-, and black-headed starlings sat in stony observance of the Wilbies' frail turret.

Facing the sheet of inky birds, Iz said, "To what do I owe the honor, Princess Constance?"

The flock roiled, flapping in a spasm of surprise. "You know us?" The words emerged with the sharp staccato of a typewriter as each member of the flock contributed the only note their throats could hold, the only word each brain could contain.

"You're a *patron of the race*, are you not?" Iz tested the planks of the beleaguered observation deck as she advanced to the railing. Everything underfoot seemed soft and unready.

"A slip of the tongue," said the flock.

Iz smiled to herself. Part of her wished to pounce upon the princess's momentary uncertainty, to goad her with more revelations and accusations and see what the royal would confess when pressed upon her heels. But it seemed unwise to play all her cards at once, and so Isolde chose a more diplomatic approach. "How fares the king?"

The delay in answer was marked by a meditative muttering among the birds that emerged as a sort of organic static—the hum of an untuned hyaline. The birds, as they waited and muttered, shifted about restlessly, pattering this way and that. After a beat, the flock fell still and answered, "He is mend-ing. He will be well soon. Thank-s to you."

"That's good to hear, but I'm sure it's not the incentive for your visit, ma'am. Do you come with a new request, or perhaps you only hoped to disturb my sleep much as you disrupted my investigation?"

"An un-fortune-ate re-quire-ment."

"So, you weren't sure that there wasn't a legitimate claim to the Crown? You suspected your brother might have, in fact, sired an heir with Miss Bysshe."

"It was a con-cern," answered the flock.

"What sort of hex are you using here? How did you trap these birds? Perhaps an adapted Hex of Ambuscade? I admit, it's quite impressive."

"I have a flock. You have a dragon."

"Yes. Well. I must ask again, ma'am: What do you want?"

The starlings fluttered as one, their crepitation sounding like a deeply drawn breath. "We ask for dis-cre-tion. The king is still frail. This is not the time to en-live-en old mis-takes."

"I will release all of my evidence to your representatives in the morn-ing, and I will promise my discretion in exchange for a single guarantee."

"Which would be?"

"You will not call on me again." Isolde leaned upon the insecure railing to better loom over the rooftop horde. "I do not work for the Crown. I will not be party to your machinations, ambitions, or scandals. I am a private citizen. I serve the public."

Isolde could not tell whether it was a breeze or vexation that riffled the birds' wings, but still she was relieved when their answer came: "We are agree-able to this."

Toes stinging from the cold, Isolde was about to return to the warmth of her bed, when one of the worries that had been keeping her awake occurred to her once more. She swung about. "I am sorry to think that Cholmondeley won't be held accountable for the evil he has done."

"Leave the al-che-mist to the courts, Miss Will-be. They have a way of get-ing it right in the end."

"I'd be careful around Mr. Cholmondeley if I were you. He may have a sorcerer on his payroll. And there could be a military connection. I can't say for sure."

The flock's reply seemed tense with surprise. "A sore-sir-er? Are you sure? The last was kill-ed in the war years a-go."

"I thought so, too, but apparently not." Hands in her pockets, Isolde flapped the snow from her coat, seeming for a moment to be attempting to join the flock as it began to take wing.

"This is die-er news, in-deed. I will look in-to it, Miss Will-be. The na-tion is grate-ful for your help."

Isolde gave a brisk bow. "And the help thanks the nation to leave her alone."

29

POST SCRIPTS

The third and final visitor proved to be the most surprising of all, though their arrival was inauspicious enough.

When the doorbell rang with pronounced and determined tones the next morning at nine, Iz expected to find a royal messenger come to collect all the evidence of their case. Instead, she was greeted by a sleepy-eyed courier in a uniform two sizes too large who seemed to have fallen asleep while pressing her bell. The delivery girl, roused by the abrupt unlatching of the door, straightened, saluted enthusiastically but form-lessly, and presented Isolde with a package that looked to have recently been employed as a pillow.

Exchanging the parcel for a tip, Isolde inspected the paper bundle as she retreated to the kitchen, where Warren stood shaking his head over the sink as he peeled potatoes and lent his ear to the open satchel on the counter, from which Felivox orated in apologetic tones: "I'm ruined, my dear boy. Absolutely ruined! Having dined at some of the nation's finest restaurants, and sampled the piquant fare of street carts, and filled my belly with the fruits of your stove top, the taste of an uncooked, sleeved human arm was nothing short of profane!" The bagged dragon broke off here to voice three barks of self-pity. "When that unfamiliar arm appeared

274

and swatted me on the nose, I snapped it off by instinct. Oh, but what a wretched impulse!"

"He didn't fare so well, either," Warren said wryly.

"And I've apologized! But I would also remind you of my pact with your wife. She made it clear that not only was there an allowance that I feast upon whatever trespassers impinged upon the sanctity of my home, but it was practically a duty! I am, after all, the guardian of the professor's treasures, am I not?"

"No one is blaming you for Mr. Alman's death," Isolde said as she set the parcel on the table and retrieved a steak knife from the drawer beside the sink to assist her unwrapping.

"Thank you, Isolde! And I do not mean to present myself as the only victim here. I am merely saying that my palate was a little traumatized. I had to eat the Infinite Goat again just to get the taste of man out of my mouth, and I think the goat resented it! He'd gotten accustomed to not being devoured every day. Oh, the look of betrayal!"

As Felivox continued to natter, Warren quit his peeling and dried his hands on his apron as he joined his wife at the kitchen table, where she now stood reading an uncovered note attached to a ribboned bundle of brittle papers. "It's from Lady Lily Atterton," Iz murmured as she read. "She says she has not given up hope that the full story of her brother's disappearance might one day be known. She's emptied out Rudy's old desk drawer and sent us the contents..."

Even as she spoke, Warren began to spread out the bale of papers. The sheer number of sheets and the minute nature of their script soon convinced him it would not be a quick survey. "This is going to take a little sifting," War said.

Seated at the kitchen table, Iz and War leafed through Rudolph Atterton's papers, many of which proved to be the anodyne scraps of an academic youth. There were records of his time in the military's officer training academy, including his grade cards in Skill at Arms, Tactics, Field Craft, Casualty Drills, Communication and Signals, and Intelligence. He proved to be a poor student, scoring better in Intelligence than anything, but distinguishing himself in nothing at all. It seemed a quality that reflected Duke Atterton's characterization of him as a lackadaisical playboy.

Among the jetsam of receipts, playbills, and lines of adolescent dog-gerel, War discovered an unsealed envelope that was addressed simply to "Cousin Mary," a name that the Wilbies suspected at once might be shared with Mary Soames, Atterton's cousin who would go on to marry Prince Sebastian, be crowned queen, and then tragically perish long before her time.

Disappointingly, the envelope proved to be empty.

"Perhaps Lady Atterton removed the letter. That, or ol' Rudy never got around to writing it," Warren suggested.

"If Lady Atterton was trying to preserve this corner of her brother's privacy, why leave behind the empty envelope? And who addresses an envelope before they write the letter? No, that doesn't sit well. May I see it, please?" Taking the envelope, Isolde peered into corners. Doing so brought a wrinkle to her nose. "Here, what's that smell like to you?"

Warren leaned over and sniffed the fine linen paper. "Old cheese?"

"Or sour milk." Isolde scooted back from the table and carried the envelope to the stove top, which she lit and then held the paper to the gas burner's blue flower. "Let's see if Rudolph remembered anything from his courses in Military Intelligence." As the paper warmed, brown letters began to appear. "Ah, there we are. Milk makes a reasonably good invis-ible ink because the lactose darkens more readily than the paper. It seems the duke was right: The royal cousins were passing notes, and secret ones, at that."

Isolde returned to the table to show her husband the envelope and the message that crowded its front and back. With fist on her hip, she read it aloud:

Dear Mary,

It was more fun pretending to be spies with you when I had nothing secret to report, and we could fritter our cream on barbs about Flo-rian and Quinn and all our wretched relations.

But now I fear I must spoil the game with unhappy news. I'm cer-tain now that my suspicions were correct, and our mutual friend is more than grateful to his nurse. I can't help but feel I'm to blame for exposing her to him. I was the one who kept asking for her because she was a familiar face. I think you may have met Jess at a croquet match. That's where I knew her from. She was a real cracker with a mallet. George Larkland and his wife adopted her some years back, but the rest of their clan never accepted her. She was a black sheep. Like me. And you know how black sheep like to flock!

If you are to marry him, as everyone says you must, you should at least know what you are in for.

If my fondness for you cannot make me brave enough to confront him, I will be proven a hopeless coward. But I do hate him. I can't help it. He was given the greatest treasure—the emeralds of your attention, the sapphires of your company, the diamonds of your love—and he shrugged and frittered it like spare change. It is an insult I cannot forgive.

Now and Always, Your Loving Cousin,
Rudy

Warren's chair creaked as he leaned back, cupping his jaw even as it fell open. "I don't understand. Rudy was the one who dallied with Jessamine, wasn't he? He's Henry's father."

"Clear a spot on the table, will you?" Isolde fled to the front room and attacked the crate that sat between the spindly legs of the writing desk. She returned to the kitchen with the midwife's intake form flying overhead like a flag. She passed the blood-flecked sheet to Warren, then drew out her stick of chalk and began to draw an intricate hex on the kitchen table.

Isolde finished the final jot, closing the Hex of Palimpsests. The involute medallion began to shimmer, and as the grain of the wood ignited with the waxed-over scratches and knicks of generations of use, Isolde took the midwife's form from Warren and laid it upon the glittering altar.

The lines, letters, and blood spatters that graced the sheet rose up from that brittle cradle and began to float upon time's languid currents. The Wilbies observed as the name R. Atterton riffled up from the record, revealing the eminent name it concealed, a name that had been carefully bleached from the document, either by charm or chemical, the name of Sebastian, Prince of Yeardley.

Warren rocked back in his seat, hand over his eyes. He murmured to the ceiling. "We got the wrong man."

His revelatory moment was quickly spoiled by the rapid tattoo of a professional knock upon their home's front door. The Wilbies looked at one another, sharing an expression of dreadful comprehension. That would be the Crown come to collect all the evidence of the case, and just when it had gotten interesting again.

Isolde darted into the parlor and returned with her coat. Stuffing Prince Sebastian's signet ring into her pocket, she spoke to Warren in a harried whisper. "I need you to buy me a little time. I'm not ready to give this up quite yet."

"What are going to do?"

"Darling, you know I can't *not* know. I need to be certain, and I'm tired of being deceived. I have to know what happened in the midwife's alley. Not the tatters of ghosts or the memory of a traumatized, guilt-ridden, and distant witness. I need to know the whole truth." Capping her hair with a hard tug of her cloche, Isolde bounded for the back door before stopping and returning to the drawer of miscellany beside the oven. Rummaging through its jangling contents, she muttered, "Where are they, where are they? Ah! There." She snatched out something small.

"Where are you going?" Warren asked with arms spread in question.

"Where I'm not welcome. I shan't be long." She nearly stood on his toes when she came to kiss him on the chin. "Keep the king's men busy, will you? I'll explain everything when I get back."

Warren watched the back door shut behind her, then observed the top of her head bob across the horizon of the garden window, and she was gone.

Putting his fists on his hips, Warren said to the empty room, "I don't think she had breakfast."

A firm pounding from the parlor made him hop in startlement, though he quickly composed himself. Before hurrying to the front door, Warren snatched up the portalmanteau and spoke from the corner of his mouth into its recesses, "Play along, will you, Felivox? We'll need to make a spectacle of ourselves, I'm afraid."

Clutching the portalmanteau to his chest, Warren encountered on his doorstep a new royal secretary of pleasant poise and forgettable features who introduced himself as Mr. Louis Neesland. Secretary Neesland stood with three soldiers and an idling royal jaunt at his back. "We've come to collect—" the secretary began to say.

Jerking the satchel this way and that, Warren shouted, "No more flames, Felivox! No more!"

And in answer, a geyser of fire broke from the satchel, scattering over the head of the secretary and the now-ducking guard.

Contriving to wrestle with Grandad's clasp, Warren pinched off the spurting fire, and quickly apologized to the king's terrorized retinue. "I'm so sorry: You caught us at feeding time. If we don't feed our dragon regularly, he gets a little—" War cracked the case and a sheet of orange fire nearly blasted the nose from his face. Clamping it shut again, he said, "Could you possibly come back in a few hours? I just started carving the boar."

From the alleyway beside their home, Isolde could hear her husband's front stoop theatrics. She smiled as she knelt before the rain barrel, which still lay where she had left it, tipped over and empty. She opened her hand around the mismatched yellowed dice, murmuring, "This better work."

She cast the martyr's bones into the barrel. They tumbled along the slimed staves and bounced upon the base that still bore the scorched ward of a neatly knotted squid. She watched expectantly. After a moment, when it became clear nothing would happen, she retrieved the dice and repeated the cast, and then a third time and a fourth. Each time, the unlucky result of the throw was the same: a one and a two. "Come on, now. I know you'd like a snack."

She was just beginning to doubt the intuition that had inspired her to crawl into a rank keg to play craps with herself when the sigil in the wood before her began to shimmer. She had just taken up the dice to hurl them again when the bottom of the drum began to ripple and shine like a stirred bowl of mulled wine. Isolde smiled, "Ah, there you ar—"

The tentacle that coiled from that lightless depth grasped her about the neck and snatched her into the dark.

Isolde broke the lilied surface of the wizard's reflection pool with all the poise of a dunked cat. She thrashed to the tiled edge, eyes widened by shock. Throwing her arm onto the shore of the wizard's palace, she was greeted by a tuxedoed Obelos. He stood nearly upon the tips of her trembling fingers, sipping from a cocktail glass. His untied bow tie hung loose over his neck. He seemed a man coming in from a long night rather than one greeting the new day.

Isolde reached up for his hand, but he did not hasten to help her. Instead, he sipped and watched her haul herself and the deadweight of her sodden coat out of the water.

"You stole my dice," he said.

She lay panting on her back for a moment, swiping the hair from her eyes and blowing the water from her nose. "An honest mistake."

"What do you want, Wilby?"

Isolde wrung out the wings of her coat as she again marveled at the galleries of the wizard's home. "I need your help."

"No."

Gaining her feet at last, Isolde found she had to clench her muscles against the cold to keep from trembling. Obelos seemed to stare through her as if she were but a reflection on a train window, an impendent clouding a grander view. Or perhaps he was just drunk.

Undeterred, she bullied on. "If there's one person I think you dislike more than me, it's probably the king. Well, here's your chance to embarrass him. Elbert seems to have sired a bastard. I think he may have killed his orderly to cover it up, but I can't be sure. He's swept up his tracks rather well. I need your help uncovering the truth."

"You're right. I don't like you." He dashed off the last of his drink and shook the glass by its frail stem. The glass refilled from the bottom up like a hole dug in the sand by the sea. "And jolly old Sebastian isn't the one who keeps tripping over my doormat."

"What do you want? Everything's on the table."

The wizard parted his fingers before his mouth. An olive appeared in the gap. He sucked the red pimento from its center, then threw the remainder at his pool. It vanished among the verdant pads with a satisfying *bloop*. "A favor."

"Name it."

"No, not now. Later. Soon, perhaps. But you can't say no when I ask for it."

"All right." She stuck out her arm.

The wizard smiled as he took her hand. "You really are the most reckless person."

"Said the man with a monster in his pond." Isolde dredged Prince Sebastian's signet ring from her pocket. Holding it up, she said, "Now, to your end of the bargain."

Iz relayed the details of the case to Obelos across a nacre-topped café table overlooking a sea of undulating clouds.

It had not really occurred to Isolde to ponder the true location of the wizard's sanctuary until he opened the glass doors onto the loggia, and she was greeted by an unearthly landscape. No mountains peaked in the distance; no coastlines broke the uniformity of the view. In every direction, pacific clouds lapped upon a flat horizon. Above them, an unfamiliar galaxy ribbed the starry firmament.

His demeanor softened considerably after the promise of a future favor, which Isolde chose not to linger over at the moment. He poured her tea from a pot that was presumably self-heating because steam never stopped sliding up from its porcelain spout. He took off his tuxedo jacket and rolled up his cuffs, giving the impression of a gentleman settling into some evening work. He no longer seemed to be gazing through her, but pulled his attention from loftier vistas to consider her. In these small acts, she glimpsed the friend from her youth, though she was not deceived. This was a performance she had purchased, and perhaps at a dearer price than she would care to admit.

She omitted nothing when she communicated the details of her investigation, which she did as succinctly and dryly as possible. He quickly understood her obsession with the events of that evening in the midwife's alley, and quizzed her more thoroughly on the details of the environment. When she, in passing, mentioned the presence of a gargoyle, he pounced, saying, "That's our way in, those are our eyes. You want to see what really happened that night, we just have to ask Muir Be'wyn."

The name was familiar, but only distantly, like something she had learned one evening in school while cramming for an exam. Oh, how many hours she'd wasted preparing to forget! "I know the name," Isolde lied.

"I hope you're still feeling as charitable with your favors when you meet her. She does not part with her secrets lightly." Obelos rose and, pinching up one leg of his trousers, stepped onto the top of the low balustrade that fenced the ranging clouds.

Isolde refused to flatter him with a gasp, and even still, she felt the tendons in her neck tighten when he offered her his hand.

She accepted the unusual gesture with a determined frown.

The moment her toes were upon the edge, he released her and spread his arms, forming brackets in the air. He began a guttural chant.

At first it seemed as if he were only muttering to himself, but soon his invocation rose in volume. What had at first seemed insensible grew distinct, if not more intelligible. He spoke in the language of the Eidolon, a dead tongue all but lost to the world. Each word was like a dormant seed that now, watered by the wizard's throat, began to bloom. The air about them changed. She felt electricity enliven the wires of her veins. The oceanic clouds darkened and ruffled, unsettled by a coming storm. Eels of light began to swim in the void between the wizard's cupped hands, their number growing as they snarled and knotted into an orb of spermatic energy.

Thunder pealed in the distance. Obelos released his grip upon the serpentine sphere. The ball of lightning plummeted and was swallowed by the agitated mists.

"Ready?" Obelos watched her from the corner of his eye.

"Ready for what?"

He slipped his wand from his sleeve, and holding that crooked length of hazel before them, conjured a little light to its point. "Muir Be'wyn lies straight ahead. You just have to start walking."

She wavered, searching the turbid atmosphere before her for any hint of a portal, a foothold, a bridge.

The wizard said, "It's not too late to turn around. You can climb down, go home. I'll forget the favor."

"Anything to see the back of me, eh?"

Obelos appeared to swallow a yawn.

When she strode out upon the air, Iz anticipated the sickening reel of free fall. Instead, her heel cracked upon hard stone, and in the same instant, the squally heavens, the railing, and the wizard's palace all vanished, and she found herself standing in a cave, dark except for the thin yellow light that emanated from the wand.

At her side, Obelos maintained his stolid mien. His calm made her realize that she was panting for breath. "Thought I'd let you fall?" he said.

"You'd not let me off that easy."

"You're right about that, Wilby." He led the way, his footsteps echoing out ahead into the murk.

The cavern was covered, above and below, with the fangs of mineral drippings. Multihued stalagmites and stalactites rose to her shoulder and descended nearly to the top of her head. The path, such as it was, through these winnowed spires was narrow and winding. The candle of Obelos's wand beaded the wet rock with light and threw stalking shadows upon the wall. As they went, Isolde resisted the urge to quiz her guide, to ask where they were, and whether this place was among the realms of the living. Had Warren been present, he would've likely had a different sort of inquisition in mind, one comprising different iterations of a single question: *What on earth are you doing, Iz?*

Then the cave opened upon a craggy chamber. Isolde noted the absence of other exits and any hope of escape, though where would she go without her guide? The space held an oppressive air that reeked of old water and older magic. And all at once, she remembered what she had long ago committed to memory and subsequently forgotten. Muir Be'wyn was a stone spirit, an ancient power, an uncomfortable remnant of the uncertain past. She was called the Goddess of Grotesques, the Mother of Spies.

Clogging the end of the chamber was the strangest statue Isolde had ever seen. Three times the height of a man, the figure was a pastiche of many anatomies. It bore the mane of a lion, the face and arms of a woman, the chest of a wolf mounded with eight teats, the grand haunches of a bear, the taloned claws of an eagle, and the tail of an oar fish, which curled around in front of it, forming a pool that plashed with the stream that drooled from the goddess's mouth and spouted from the point of her chin. Rather than having been carved from a granite block by hammer and chisel, the figure bore the rough edges of a natural feature—one shaped by glaciers, calderas, and shifting continents.

Even as Isolde realized the depth of the pit she had walked into, Muir Be'wyn smiled. From her throat rumbled a voice like a gnashing millstone. "Isolde Ann Always Wilby, what do you wish to see?"

A COVENANT, MOST GROTESQUE

The dribbling fountain played the water's surface like a celesta. The
quiet that accompanied the melodic splashing seemed immense, as
if they were not only buried under earth but beneath an age as well.
Isolde had the impression that Obelos had brought her here expecting
her to cower in the presence of such ancient magic, to reconsider her silly
errand, to run home with her coat thrown over her head.

As she once had.

And as she would not again.

The stony goddess did not move, and still she seemed to loom over the
small mortals who had imposed themselves upon her. Her petrified mane
seemed to writhe and her frozen claws scratch upon her perch when she
said, "I have many sons, many daughters, many others. I guide the hands
of your sculptors. Always so eager, they are, to welcome my children to
the world. But those beautiful stones are but shells until a soul possesses
them. Which is where our bargain begins."

Gathering herself up, Isolde contrived a cordial smile. "What do you
mean, ma'am?"

Obelos answered for the goddess. "Muir Be'wyn only accepts one form
of payment for her favors, and that's the currency of time. After you die,

your essence, your consciousness, will be poured into a gargoyle or grotesque on some facade of her choosing. And you will serve as her unblinking eyes and untiring ears to that little corner of the world."

"For how long?"

Obelos rolled back his head, dramatizing what appeared to be a grueling calculation. "Oh! Well, it depends upon the question—its difficulty, how many follow-ups you have, and how often you ask."

Isolde marveled. "*How often?* Have you done this before? Have you taken this deal yourself?"

Obelos bowed toward the goddess of quilted parts, and with a mirthful scoff asked her, "Mother, how deep am I in the hole?"

"Eighty-six years," the goddess rasped.

Isolde startled at the fact that the wizard had just called this fearsome deity "mother" and also the realization that followed. "So, when you die, you have to live in the head of a gargoyle for eighty-six years?"

Obelos shrugged, though it seemed to Iz an affectation covering over some deeper dread. "So what? Life is short and lively, and death is long and deathly boring. If I have to spend eighty-six years staring at the rumps of a few pigeons to get the answers I want, it seems a reasonable trade."

Scowling both at the cynicism of her former friend and at the terrible bargain she was herself considering, she said, "Muir Be'wyn, Your Holiness? I . . . don't know how to address you—"

"Call me *Mother*," the goddess hissed.

Isolde cocked her head to one side. "Mmm. Let's come back to that. How long would I have to serve to see what happened in one particular alley on one particular night?"

The water that poured from the goddess's mouth bubbled and seemed to run faster like the slaver of an excited predator. "One year."

Isolde squinted reprovingly at Obelos, who dug his hands into his trouser pockets and scuffed the grit at his feet with the petulance of a lad. "Oh, don't give me that look, Wilby. I've had a lot of questions."

Isolde thought of Warren, thought of what he would say if he knew she was here and considering this morbid contract. A year apart. But then again, if she died first, it would hardly matter. He'd just be reading the Sunday paper while she was off staring over a roofline. She wondered if that would really be so bad, to spend a year in quiet contemplation . . .

Even as she rationalized, she realized her mind was already made up.

"One nosy woman to another, is it satisfying—knowing all the secrets of the world? Is it enough? Are you content, or does the ever-swelling bubble of reality make fulfillment impossible? After all, every soul on the planet is out there right now, studiously making a mystery of their life. They're lying, faking, pretending... Is it better to admit your limitations, to not only allow for, but to insist upon the necessity of the unknown? Is ignorance the basis of sanity? Do we need mysteries to survive?"

"Choose your fate, Isolde Ann Always Wilby."

"Oh, very well. I choose madness. I accept your terms, Muir Be'wyn."

The flow of foul water that spewed from Muir Be'wyn's mouth first slackened, then stopped. The mother of chimeras said, "Close your eyes and picture the night you wish to see, then bathe one hand in my waters, and I shall reveal what has been hidden from you."

Isolde approached the pool in the grip of the goddess's tail. The closer she drew, the larger the statue before her seemed to grow until it was a vertiginous monument. She had to roll her body over the round hump of the pool's edge to reach the water, and even as she stretched after it, she felt her more temperate half shriek: *Stop! Don't! Think, Iz, think!* This was too much, even for her. She could still quit. She could turn around and go home and learn to live with the uncertainty.

Her hand trembled over the black and motionless surface.

She bit back her caution and pushed her hand into the inky pool.

On contact, the surface of the cistern stiffened as if seized by a sudden frost. The water shone like a skating rink under the noonday light. As she peered down into the brightening past, the familiar alleyway emerged, as glimpsed not by the midwife from her elevated window but from the vantage point of a goat-headed grotesque.

From above, it seemed as if the two men in the urban trough were engaged in a curious dance. One would move away, only to be hooked by the arm and brought back around by the other. The one who did the reeling-in sported a well-tailored suit. The man who was attempting to escape wore the formal parade dress of his military station. A ceremonial saber wagged in its sheath at his hip. It was only after the gentleman managed to drag the soldier a little nearer the alley entrance that the lamplight revealed it was Rudolph Atterton, in uniform, attempting to distance himself from the nation's future king.

Finally disengaging from the bellicose two-step, Atterton spoke at a perceptible volume when he said, "You'll do the right thing, Sebastian, and that's the end of it!"

The prince lurched in a circle, snatching at the air as if he would choke it. "But why ruin three lives when you can save two? An unwanted child is to no one's advantage, least of all its own!"

Backlit by the spotlight of the street, Jessamine Bysshe put a hand to her mouth. The passing shouts of revelers seemed to echo her surprise.

The prince wrenched at his shirtfront as if he would wring out his own heart. "You know I care for you, Jess, that I will *take* care of you when the hour is right. But this is not the time! This would be the end of all our aspirations—all of your dreams. Your child would have to console you for my lost station and your bankrupt future, and that is an awful lot to lay at the feet of a bantling who was groped into existence inside a hospital closet."

"You're being cruel," Rudy said.

"Better now than later!" The prince paced toward Jessamine but found his way blocked by his former orderly's raised arm. The royal pled his case over that bar. "Can you imagine, toeing your own death for weeks and weeks and then waking up and seeing your face—your beautiful face— and feeling again the rush of blood through your veins. You are my angel of salvation! I adore you." Prince Sebastian tapped at his chest as if he would pound a nail into it. "I am a decent man. My conscience is clean, and I take care of those who are loyal to me." The tempo of his speech quickened: "I know a discreet physician. There are pills for these things, and—"

With a stricken expression, Jessamine said, "It's not a thing! It's our child. I didn't ask for this; I didn't ask you for anything. And I don't want any—"

The prince crowed his *aha* like a sun-swatted rooster. "Oh, you say that! You say that now! But once I've been crowned, you'll have a change of heart. They always do. And there we'll be—at each other's throats on the front page of the *Times*—another randy royal and his silly strumpet."

Atterton wheeled about and cuffed the prince across the jaw.

Sebastian faltered under the blow but quickly gathered himself and leapt upon his friend.

The two grappled, their legs tangling as they attempted to throw the other from his feet. The prince's eloquence turned to grunts as Atterton punched him twice in the ribs. The prince broke from their embrace, which seemed to the lance corporal's advantage, and stumbled toward the wood pile. He grasped a billet from the stack and swung. The log crashed into the side of Atterton's head, just above the ear. The corporal fell flat and spasmed upon the cobblestones as blood poured from the wound.

A drowning silence claimed the alley.

The prince staggered toward Jessamine, cradling his ribs as if to emphasize how much he had been abused by the brief scuffle. It seemed to Isolde a transparent performance, and yet, his once nurse stood as if caught in a spider's web at the mouth of the alley, shivering while a dying Rudolph convulsed himself cold.

Charlotte De Lee had been right about one thing: The fight had been brief. Isolde wondered whether, if they had wrestled for another minute or two, their passions would've cooled.

The prince gripped Jessamine by her dangling elbows. "Oh my god. My god. Please, please. We need to be careful here. We're in dire straits, Jess. We need to think. We need help. We need—"

Abruptly, as if stirred by premonition, Prince Sebastian looked up from the alley floor. His gaze fell upon the light of a parted curtain and the shocked visage of Charlotte De Lee.

"I'll call the authorities." Not waiting for an answer, the prince fled toward the street.

"Nothing very interesting happens for a little while," the goddess of gargoyles announced, and the scene before Isolde's submerged hand blurred with the passage of time. "So, on and on we watch the world and on and on and then..."

The mouth of the alleyway was now clogged by the rectangular back of a military transport. And yet, despite its presence, no enlisted men trooped about under the eye of attentive officers. The alley was all but empty. Jessamine and Charlotte De Lee sat upon empty veg crates, pressed up against one wall. The body of Rudolph Atterton lay sprawled on his back in a swollen puddle of blood. The prince stood over his dead friend, tugging his own ear as if he would remove it, as if he might begin to suck his thumb.

And there was a new figure, too. She was dressed in white and she moved among them with the authority of a commander. At first, her long white uniform made Isolde mistake her for a nurse—just as Charlotte De Lee had. The mysterious figure's mouth was covered by what seemed a surgical mask. But as she moved between the two dazed women and the fidgeting prince, Iz saw that she wasn't wearing a paper bonnet, but a leather cowl, and what covered her face was not a surgical mask, but an all-too-familiar cover.

The sorcerer who'd tried to kill her and Warren upon the rusted playground knelt before Jessamine and her midwife, holding one hand up, fingers pinched together as if to show them a needle. She lowered her voice, but the hearing of the wide-eared gargoyle was keener. She said, "It was dark. It happened quickly. Rudolph Atterton fell upon his own sword, which you were holding, Jessamine. You drew it by accident, just on impulse. You didn't mean to kill him. Or perhaps you did. Perhaps he stumbled; perhaps you lunged. It all happened so very fast. But before he died, Atterton was absolutely enraged, upset that your child would reveal his indiscretion. He rejected you. But he was no patron of the race; he was a cad. You do not feel much guilt."

As was so often the case, the discovery felt less like an epiphany and more like a repudiation of Isolde's supposed genius. She should've put the pieces together much sooner. Princess Constance was not just a champion of hex-casting, a paragon of domesticity. She was also a master of alchemy and wizardry, perhaps more. She was the sorcerer, and she had been using her powers to protect her brother for a very long time. That she had been unable to cure the king's malady had surely been a source of great frustration, and the fact that Iz had succeeded in that regard was probably the only thing keeping Warren and herself alive. But there would be limits to the sorcerer's gratitude, no doubt.

Even as Isolde grappled with her revelation, the prince's sister continued enchanting the memories of the midwife and the nurse who sat in wooden observance. "This was all an unfortunate accident, but you will recover. You will move on with your lives. And you will never speak of these things again."

Isolde recognized in that dreamy cadence the same automatic rhythm Charlotte De Lee had later used over her smoky kitchen table. The sorcerer... *Princess Constance* had hypnotized both women, inventing a reality. Though obviously, the spell had been imperfect. De Lee's horror at seeing the prince slay a man had colored her recollection—the prince had not been so utterly absolved in her retelling.

The leather-clad sorcerer straightened and approached the prince, who continued to tug upon his ear, swaying near the foot of the man he'd recently slain. "And you—pull yourself together! What are you doing? Idiot! I can't leave you alone for a— Stop that! Put your hands down. Listen to me. This did not happen. And if it ever comes out that it did, it won't be your fault." As Princess Constance spoke, she hipped him aside. Circling the body in a stooped position, she sprinkled the ground with salt from a sachet taken from her belt.

"What are you doing?" The prince paced after her. The sorcerer was not shy about shoving him out of her way as she set at the five points of the dead man's body a drop of her own blood, pricked from her thumb. "He was my friend, Connie. I didn't mean to hurt him."

"Shut up. I'm working," Princess Constance snapped as she stooped over Rudolph Atterton's wan face. She began to sing, the notes long and low and sliding together in an unfamiliar tongue. The halo of salt leapt and bounced like frozen rain, and where the sorcerer had squeezed out her blood, the ground began to glow with a sanguine throbbing light. She pulled the dead man's chin down, and bent with parted lips as if she meant to kiss Rudolph Atterton with open mouth.

The prince cupped his ears and seemed as if he might scream.

Then the sorcerer stood back and the bouncing salt fell still and the light of her blood faded.

"Get up," she said.

Rudolph Atterton sat up. He straightened his neck, raising a terrible crack.

The pale sorcerer beckoned him with a flick of her finger, and he labored to his feet. She pointed to the back of the boxy transport that blocked the end of the alley, and the noble lance corporal began to shuffle toward it.

Leading him, Princess Constance opened the back gate. "Rudy was supposed to ship off in the morning. And he still will. I'll go with him. He'll cross the sea, stay in his cabin, keep to himself, march to the front, and die in the trenches. That was to be his fate anyway. You'll stay here, and keep your mouth shut."

The sorcerer waited until the reanimated batman had lowered himself onto the empty bench, then shut and locked the doors. She pointed to Jessamine, who still sat on her crate, placid as a porcelain figurine. "Go back to your room. Pack only what you need. Tell no one where you are going. You are a fugitive and must live as one." The sorcerer swung her finger to Charlotte De Lee. "And you, I want to see your records for this woman. We have some corrections to make."

"What should I do?" Prince Sebastian asked as he watched the sleepwalking women rise in answer to the commands they'd been given.

"Go home. Go to bed. And—look at me. Look at me!" Princess Constance pointed her finger as if she were preparing to poke him in the eye. "You will never see this woman again."

The surface of the black reflection pool broke with the return of the water that sprang from the ancient's mouth, dispelling the vision. Isolde snatched back her hand in surprise. Drying her fingers on her coat, still heavy from her recent dip in the wizard's pool, she turned to regard Obelos, who seemed, for the first time, unnerved. The brassy hue of his complexion had turned sallow; his expressive mouth stood clenched in a line.

She said, "But Atterton never made it to the trenches. It was in the paper for weeks and weeks. It was a whole scandal—a noble son running from his duty. He sent some old man in his uniform to die in his place."

"That's the thing about reanimating the dead, Wilby. It's easy to make their bones walk around, much harder to stop their flesh from rotting. I'm sure it was Rudolph Atterton's corpse that fell in battle, but it would've been weeks after he died. He probably didn't look much like his old self by then. Of course, that's just a guess."

Muir Be'wyn's voice rumbled from her throat like an approaching army. The longer Isolde stood in her presence, the more she felt cowed by her power. The goddess said, "I can show you what happened next. I have eyes on every corner of every block of every city of every nation throughout all time. I can show you everything, Isolde Ann Always Wilby. Another view for another year of service. You could be sure. You could be certain."

Isolde shivered, already regretting the bargain and dreading the thought of telling Warren. She felt a pang of shame that she had allowed her obsession to carry her so far from her senses. "No. No, I don't want to know. I just want to leave. Please."

Muir Be'wyn tut-tutted, the sound like two stones knocking together. "The world is a curious place, Isolde Ann Always Wilby. So many hidden wonders. So many buried answers. There's no shame in wanting to know, to understand, to see."

"Yes, Mother," Isolde said, and flinched at a word she had not intended to say, and yet, on reflection, she realized she had no power to resist it, either. She felt the closing of a cage about her heart.

"I look forward to our next visit," said the Goddess of Grotesques.

The chamber went dark. A roar filled her ears, trumpeting the death-like silence that followed.

Isolde blinked her eyes and found herself sitting again on the wizard's patio on the shore of a nimbus sea.

Obelos sat across from her, rubbing his finger meditatively, his brow puckered by worry.

"You know her, too—the sorcerer?"

"She is why I live under a bridge, why I keep a monster in my koi pond, and why I wish you would've left me alone. Sorcerers don't like wizards, or rather I should say, they seem to rather enjoy killing us." He reached for the half-empty teacup before him. His fingers trembled at the prospect; reconsidering, he made a fist and set it upon the cloth.

Isolde drew a shuddering breath. "This is why I don't work for the Crown. I told her as much last night. I'm done with all of this."

"You still think you have a choice? Oh, what a naïf! What a dear! What a sap." Obelos leaned forward in his chair as if preparing to pass a secret. His expression seemed to reclaim some of its former nonchalance. "She is a mongoose, Wilby. She eats little snakes like us and thinks nothing of it. You are alive because she has chosen to let you live. Perhaps she has a plan for you; perhaps she just wants to play with you before you're a corpse."

Isolde stood, knocking the table edge with her knees and making the cups and saucers clatter. "I have to get home."

"I'll call you a cab."

"I was hoping for something a bit more direct."

*   *   *

Warren was doing his best to occupy himself to avoid worrying about his wife. At present, his occupation was *percussionist*. He banged his pots upon the range and clapped the oven door open and shut, open and shut. He ran the tap and splashed the flow and shook the drawers full of knives and forks. The charade was for the benefit of the royal envoy who had ensconced himself in the Wilbies' parlor to await the end of the dragon's morning tea.

Felivox accompanied the performance, though his focus was waning. His roars and flames had turned to grumbles and oaths, that had evolved into smoke and protests, that veered suddenly into soliloquy. From the depth of the portalmanteau, which lay open on the kitchen table, he said: "I have to admire humans in two regards. First, they are delicious, and second they are very adept at making their atrocities so snaking and circuitous, it's hard to know what's happened, how it happened, and who's to blame. Man is quite a devious snack! Take your knights, for instance. They slaughtered my ancestors by the score! But not wantonly. No, they slew us because they were told we'd stolen their king's gold and snatched away their most desirable virgins...Though it has never been adequately explained to me what on earth a dragon would want with either."

Warren dashed his butcher's knife up and down his honing steel, and shouted for the benefit of his guests. "Open wide! Here comes the ham."

But Felivox seemed to have entirely forgotten the purpose of the ruse as he became more enamored with the point he wished to make. "And when it turned out my ancestors had neither gold nor virgins, the knights bogged off, leaving the peasantry with the almighty rotting corpse of a dragon to dispose of."

"I said, here comes the ham!" Warren called and then more pointedly spoke toward the bag. "Don't forget to chew."

Felivox seemed not to hear him. "And somewhere along the way, one of you lot decided that our fire bladders cured impotency and our scales reversed hair loss. Within a generation, your merchant class hunted us nearly to extinction just so you could grind us up and sell us at market. And when it turned out that our guts gave you cancer and our hide carried leprosy, the cities sent their armies to eradicate our dwindling population for being harbingers of disease! Apparently, my kind has always been hell-bent upon inconveniencing yours with our meek and distant existence! Personally, I blame your storytellers and their overfondness for—"

The back door swung open, and Warren, who'd been improvising a drum routine on the copper kettles with a pair of wooden spoons, fell still at the sight of his wife. She was drenched and shivering; her bare neck was scarfed with dozens of circular bruises; and her eyes shone with manic intent.

"My god, are you all right?" he said.

Isolde hurried to the table and gathered up the sprawled contents of Rudolph Atterton's desk drawer. She pitched the disorderly sheaf into the open mouth of the portalmanteau. "Felivox, file this away somewhere—somewhere deep, please. I hope to never see it again, but don't lose track of it."

"What happened? Where have you been?" Warren asked with all the calm he could gather. He did not wish to interrogate her, to inflame her uncertain state with his own concern.

Iz began raking up the documents of their investigation. "The damage is done. We have to think of ourselves."

A tap at the kitchen door made her leap.

Coming up behind her, and settling his heavy hands lightly upon her shoulders, Warren whispered, "That's the royal secretary—well, the new one, anyway. Do you want me to invite him to leave?"

Isolde came around to face him. He stiffened when he recognized it was fear, primal and entire, that assailed her. "No, no. We give them exactly what they came for and pray they don't ask for more."

"You'll tell me what happened?"

"Yes, of course, but not now."

"Have you done anything unwise?"

She gripped the straps of his apron, and steadied herself. "Yes, I have."

He stroked her hair. "All right. I love you."

The royal secretary cracked the kitchen door, and imposed his uncooked custard of a face upon the domestic havoc. The sink was about to overflow, the drawers and cupboards stood open, the gas range sissed, the Wilbies stood in an intimate embrace before the open and still smoking portalmanteau.

"Excuse me, sir, madam, but if the dragon is fed, we really must be on our way."

Isolde snatched up the disorderly folio of documents and notes and urged them roughly into a paper sack. She presented the untidy mass to the royal secretary with her best impression of a gracious smile. "There you are! There's everything and with our compliments. Thank you for your patience, good sir. Here, let me get the door."

31

A BROKEN BRIDLE

Victor Cholmondeley felt uncertain.

It was a shameful state that he would never admit to publicly and could hardly confess to in the protectorate of his own heart.

Indecision went against the very nature of his character. In the rapids of life, there was no morality—sin was a turmoil invented to invigorate the shallows, shoals, and oxbows of mediocrity, a thing made to entertain minnows. Yet, the error of ambiguity was quite real and likely to get you killed. He knew all too well that bold mistakes were better than methodical aspirations. He had never been the smartest, the most talented, nor the most fortunate of his peers, some of whom had bungled their way to greatness, but the main of whom had been dragged under by the capricious currents of fate, a flow that seemed capable of forgiving almost anything but *uncertainty*—that perennial and tireless enemy.

He lay sprawled upon the mattress of his four-poster bed, naked as a newt though not so vulnerable. A strategically deployed sheet barred his loins, arranged not in the name of modesty but in anticipation of a grand reveal. He needed this. He deserved it. It had been a disappointing week. He had lost one of his best-placed assets. Little Blunder Britches had died going after the Wilbies' bag—something he was explicitly told not to do, not yet, not while her guard was up. Of course, all might've been forgiven if he'd succeeded. But he hadn't. Now, instead of an heir to the throne or a bag of magical treasures, all that remained was an enormous mess. The boy had lived up to his name even to the end.

Cholmondeley lounged under the watchful gaze of what the local rabble liked to call the Goat's Eye—as if it were but a harbinger of dread, rather than what it really was: a guardian and a bulwark. The indurated room was toughened against all magic. In the presence of that charmed dial, not even the world's most powerful practitioners could conjure so much as a fanciful fart.

He was safe. He was certain . . . or nearly so.

Before arranging himself upon the bed, he had uncovered the mirror on the wall in anticipation of her arrival, halving and setting aside the tapestry of a knight mounted upon a unicorn. And still he startled when he saw that argentine surface warp and pile and break about the appearance of her foot, grim and beautiful as a shark's fin.

The rest of her followed, her figure robed in a diaphanous fabric that did little to disguise the beauty of her form. Her nightgown was as thin as an eyelid shut against the sun.

"You've been busy," Princess Constance said as she padded barefoot across the floor. She approached the ice bucket in its stand beside the bed and lifted the chilling bottle to read its label. She spared an admiring frown before dropping the vessel back into its bath. Shaking the sleet from her hand, she said, "You made quite a mess."

Victor shimmied languidly, plumping the carefully maintained muscles of his shoulders and chest. "If you wanted someone who lacked ambition, you had better options at your disposal, my love."

"And here I believed I was enough to sate your appetites." The princess smiled without warmth as she crossed to his desk, opened the colorful box, and selected a cigar. She trimmed the tip, placed the roll to her lips, and lit it with the cut crystal table lighter. Puffing to establish the coal, she returned and settled upon the edge of the bed. He reached for her with his foot, and she blessed the tips of each toe with the tap of one finger. He laughed. She did not, though she offered him the cigar, which he took as consolation. "I gave you the braids; I showed you how to use them. I brought your little mill back from the brink, saved you from bankruptcy, but it wasn't enough, was it? No, no, you had to go and install a spy in my home."

Victor puffed and chuckled around his cigar as if a private joke had been shared. He felt a little perplexed that she did not reflect his merriment. She was in a mood. He caressed her veiled thigh with the sole of his foot. "I'm grateful for all the gifts you've given me, my love, but I only know how to chase what I want."

She rolled her head back, her mouth stretching with incredulity. The noise she made seemed a mockery of laughter. "A title! Yes, of course. Nobility. I was never confused about what you wanted, and I explained why you could not have it. You couldn't be my proxy in the industry if our association was suspected," the princess said, alluding to the moratorium on the Crown owning stakes in certain markets. "It was your distance that made you useful, Victor."

"And I hope that hasn't changed. I'm always happy to be of use." Cholmondeley dragged the sheet from the stage of his hips and smiled as he puffed his cigar.

The princess looked down, her lips curling like a dinner guest observing a fly bob to the surface of her soup. The expression made Victor think to cross his legs, then she said, "You tried to kill my brother and put your little runt on his throne."

His surprise made him cough. "No!"

"No?" She smiled with the perfunctory indulgence of a shop clerk.

He coughed again, trying to clear the tickle in his throat. "We both know who's next in line to rule, and it would not be a half-noble unknown prince. It would be you. Don't you see?" He reached for her arm, bared by the split sleeve of her robe. She shrugged away, leaving him to fondle his own fingertips. He laughed at her coyness. "I only wished to give you the little push you needed, my love. I tried to help clear the way for the ascent of the *empress* that our nation so badly needs." His phlegmy throat compelled him to cough again. His eyes watered as he continued, "Yes, I admit, I hoped Henry would have a place in your court and—"

"And his adoptive father, too." She stood and presented him with her back. The chiffon of her peignoir shone like the flow of an ornamental waterfall.

"I don't understand why we have to hide what we are." He reached for his coupe of wine, took several swallows, though it only inflamed his throat more. "What is the point of power if you have to skulk around, to lurk in the shadows, to hide from the daylight?"

The princess regarded him over the august banc of her shoulder. "Daylight is not the point of power. My dear Victor, attention is the dissolution of control, of influence, of freedom. Enduring power is furtive. It is not boastful. It is not vain. Perhaps that is why men such as yourself are so desperately feckless when given even a modicum of authority. Do you truly believe that if I wanted the throne I could not take it for myself? Do you not know me at all?"

"I just thought—" He broke off to hack into his fist.

"Ah, but you didn't have to. No, all you had to do was *listen* and *do*. Now...well, now I can neither trust you nor use you." She dashed a hand over his recumbent figure. "And frankly, all of this has begun to bore."

The curve of Victor's smile finally straightened for good as he absorbed that this was not the usual pillow talk. She was in earnest. "You wish to end our partnership?"

"Something like that." She took up the sheet he had lately been using as a fig leaf and began to twist it into a rope. He wondered if she meant to garrote him with it. Without her magic, she was no match for him, and he found the prospect of her trying to strangle him almost arousing.

He said, "You forget, you have no power here, my love."

"Oh yes, yes—your window. It is quite something, I have to admit. It took me a little while, but I eventually hunted down every glazier and carpenter who worked on your Goat's Eye. Even the little boy who boiled the lead." She wound the twisted sheet about the neck of the chilling wine bottle and knotted it in place. "I killed them all. I can't have another one of these in the world. One was too many."

Feeling abruptly vulnerable in his exposed state, Victor sat up at last. The change in position reinvigorated his cough, which had turned the cigar smoke sharp as acid in his lungs. The princess turned the mouth of the leashed bottle to her own lips and drank as she observed him from the corner of her eye. When she pulled the bottle neck away and sighed, she seemed to exhale a little cloud of orange sparks. To his further surprise, those fiery scintillas did not sink or dissipate. Instead, they converged again upon her lips and crowded into her mouth.

He examined the chewed end of his cigar. A small swarm of ember-bright mites scrambled about the rolled and moistened leaves. Even as he recoiled, the little brutes leapt into the air and floated after the princess. Terror tightened his confused expression as another spasm gripped his lungs, and he began to cough anew.

Victor gaped at his retreating visitor. The bottle of sparkling wine fizzed and spilled upon his floor as she dragged it by the leash of his bedsheet like an unwilling dog back toward the mirror she had come by. She spoke loudly to be heard over his breathless wheezing. "Do you know, I was recently acquainted with one of your adopted daughters, Emma Morris. Wonderful woman. Self-possessed. Well mannered. I think, with a little help and a few timely revisions, she'll be able to mount a credible claim to your estate. What a pleasant, unexpected homecoming that would be! She will have lost a father, but gained a home. Goodbye, Victor."

The princess stepped into the liquid mirror. Her disappearance raised a chop on that silvery surface. The tethered bottle bounded along behind her, even as the face of the mirror began to calm. The looking glass hardened just in time to receive the trailing wine bottle. The glass shattered at the impact, spangling shards falling about the unbroken magnum as it spun and spilled its bright contents upon the floor.

Though Cholmondeley had dropped the cigar, smoke continued to pour from his mouth and nose. He tried to rise, to make for the door, the hall, and help, but he collapsed after the second step. He tried to speak, but hadn't breath enough to cough, to gasp, to scream. Floundering onto his back, he felt the fire come, swift as rapture, and just as ruthless.

As the bombs of his lungs burst into flames, melting the cartilage of his throat, blackening the flesh between his ribs, underneath the agony that convulsed him, there flowered in his combusting heart the familiar coolness of surety. He felt no doubt, concealed no questions.

In the end, there was only certainty.

Warren Wilby sat on the cusp of the sofa, hunched over a typewriter that stood, crooked and sunken, upon the crown of a pouf. He pecked at the keys with his head tilted back to accommodate the reading glasses perched on the end of his nose. His halting progress was further interrupted by the new carpet, which enticed his eye to its unfamiliar garden maze—its flowers and vines, tangled and overgrown, and possessed of many colors, though predominantly green. Despite being novel to them, the rug was a hundred years old, which only seemed fitting given its new environment.

"I don't know. Maybe we should've gone for the red one," he murmured.

"It's fine. You're just going through your regret stage, which of course we both do after a major purchase." Isolde stood on a stepladder by the mantel, drawing a hex in salt water high on the exposed stone of the chimney. Once dried, it would be nearly invisible, but no less effective. "You remember how sad the new mattress made you?"

Warren broke off his typing. "What are you talking about? I liked that mattress from the very first night! As I recall, you enjoyed it, too."

"You said it was like sleeping on the devil's knuckles." Finishing the sigil, she craned back to check her work, winking one eye as she did. "Well, we won't have to worry about any more cursed spores floating down our chimney."

"May we all sleep a little better for it! If only you could chalk us up some sorcerer repellent."

"Still something of a tender button."

"Sorry, darling. You know me—always trying to make light of heavier things. Princess Constance certainly had me fooled. I hope you're not thrashing yourself for overlooking some invisible and probably imaginary clue."

"I'm not," she said.

But of course she was. She found her own inability to see through Princess Constance's charade absolutely galling. The princess had looked her in the eye and feigned perfect ignorance about the Wilbies' investigation even as she dispatched her flocking mouthpiece to discourage them from the pursuit. And Iz had accepted the lie without a whiff of suspicion. Why? Because the princess was a hex-caster who publicly supported the continuation of the tradition. Iz had let herself be duped because the source of the lie had been a kindred spirit. What a broad and nearly fatal flaw! Though wasn't that, Isolde reflected, just one of provincialism's many flaws? The errant belief that it was the outsider, the alien, the *other* who was the real danger ignored the fact that most violent crimes were intimate in their origins. A clique was quite content to devour its own. She should've known better.

Warren yanked the page from the typewriter with a flourish. "And that's the invoice done. I decided to charge the Crown for the carpet. Why not? Let them dicker. I'll take them to court."

Iz descended the steps, skipping the last two, and set about collapsing the onerous scaffold. She wrenched and wrestled the stepladder's hinges, and it appeared to parry her attacks. "Do you really want to start a back-and-forth with the royal lawyers? I say let's be done with them and move on. Call it an expensive lesson. We keep to the private sector."

Warren reconsidered his recent work, barked a note of angst, and crumpled the page into a ball. "You still haven't told me what happened that made you so eager to turn over our files. Or why your neck was wreathed with bruises."

"I told you, a large squid carried me home."

"It wouldn't be the first time I was jealous of a cephalopod. Did I ever tell you about Oppie, the ship's mascot? He was an octopus who could fit his entire self into a bottle. Quite a feat. Never tried to kiss him, though." Warren's attempt to feed a new page into the typewriter was interrupted by a knock at their door. He gave his wife a speculative look, and she waved him off as she released the stubborn ladder and let it clatter violently to the floor, announcing, "I'll get it."

Answering the summons, Isolde was a little surprised to find a breathless Detective Aloysius Smud on her stoop. The stocky gentleman stood gripping his knees as he labored to catch his breath. His dark suit, flocked with a variety of animal hair, was muddied at the joints. "What's happened?" she asked.

He straightened and through gasps said, "Sorry to barge in on you, Ms. Wilby. But there's a horse loose on High Street." Smud's square face bore the rings and lines of one who had recently suffered a sleepless night only to be greeted by a disappointing morning; Iz recognized the expression as his everyday wear.

"That's not exactly our subject of expertise, Al."

Detective Smud hauled his hat from his head and smoothed his sweat-thinned hair. "The mare is as big as a house, and shooting flames out her nose. If that's not your business, I don't know whose it is."

Isolde's ears pricked to the distant crack of gunfire and the whinny of a beast that clamored like a landslide.

Patting the detective on his damp shoulder, she said, "Let me get my bag."

THE ADVENTURE CONTINUES!

The story continues in . . .

Book Two of The Hexologists

GLOSSARY

Belloc Islands, the — A collection of desirable islands in the Garrean Sea over which the Meridian War was fought. The islands produce timber, mace, nutmeg, guano, and gold.

Berbiton — The capital and commercial hub of Luthland.

Berbiton Times, **the** — Luthland's primary newspaper of record and Lorcan Magnussen's employer.

Caffery Room, the — A private study room in the Cardinal Library.

Cardinal Library, the — The nation's largest library that purports to conserve all printed materials; also the employer of Dr. Luella Timmons-Wilby.

Coats, Isolde's — Isolde's once-identical coats are composed of felted gray wool and deep pockets. The six coats have accrued stains and scars that now distinguish them, inspiring the names: Tabby, Splodge, Notch, Fussock, Reef, and Poppy.

Conch of Enoch, the — A charmed conch shell that amplifies imperceptible echoes.

Court of Commons, the — A governmental body of elected commoners that shares legislative duties with the House of Peers.

De Lee & Gwatkin, the Offices of — A clinic of midwives and monthly nurses that Jessamine Bysshe visits.

Dove Town — An old, poor neighborhood near the waterfront district in Berbiton known for its violence and high crime.

Eidolon — A (presumed) extinct supernatural race of stone giants whose language is still sometimes employed for incantations.

Glossary

Entobarrus, the — A fiery realm adjacent to our own from which thalanium is extracted by industrial alchemists.

Felpurian Empire — A historical age, some two thousand years in the past.

Gloaming God — The only permanent inhabitant of the shadow realm that is sometimes described as a celestial bivalve.

Hammerstone of Knorrl — A tool used to flake the arrowheads that helped fell the Wraith Army of Bosaken.

House of Peers, the — A governmental body of nobles that shares legislative duties with the Court of Commons.

Hyaline — A wireless receiver of audio broadcasts.

Garrean Sea, the — The major body of water between the nations of Luthland and Intarsia.

Gallets — The national currency of Luthland. A tenth of a gallet is called a spar.

Gray Plains of the Unmade, the — A transitional plane between the living and the dead.

Hazel of Want — A transient magical tree from which wands may be inadvisably pruned.

High Street — The main thoroughfare of commerce in Berbiton.

Honewort Cemetery — A cemetery near the heart of Berbiton funded by a trust and generally reserved for the impoverished.

Hymn of Hems — A clothier in downtown Berbiton.

Intarsia — A nation that has antagonized Luthland in the past.

Lithoverse — A theoretical biome beneath the earth's crust that may or may not be populated.

Luthland — A venerable nation and home to the Wilbies.

Glossary

Maoi Kabril, the Behemoth of Eist — A demigod of the Entobarrus who is fabled to be related to the world's population of dragons.

Meridian War, the — Waged from 4012 to 4033 between Luthland and Intarsia over control of the Belloc Islands and associated shipping routes, the Meridian War ended in an armistice that sharply curtailed the use of magic on the battlefield.

Marcus and Evanne — Ill-fated lovers from the Felpurian Age whose use of magic resulted in their being stoned to death. Their hip bones were used to make a pair of cursed dice.

Nethercroft, the — A spectral realm in which the dead can create memorial scenes of important events from their life.

Office of Ensorcelled Investigations, the (OEI) — Berbiton's short-lived law enforcement agency that responded to supernatural incidents under the leadership of Isolde Wilby.

Saffoi Towers, the — Luxurious apartment buildings in Berbiton.

***Sangfroid Hand of Heaven,* the** — A lavish and famous casino boat anchored at Luthland upon the River Zimme where Obelos is a frequent gambler. Captained by Emin Dursun.

Second Kingdom's First Victim, The — A history by Sir Dudley Foster.

Spillway Public House — The drinkery that is haunted by Old Geb.

Stare of Ancients — A relic that resembles a domino mask made of jade, the Stare of Ancients allows the user to glimpse fixtures from the past.

Umbra Annulus — A small onyx ring that, when enclosed inside the mouth, allows the bearer to dive into the Unlit Realm.

Umbrists — A vanished clan of assassins who employed the lost art of shadow swimming to attack their targets.

Vaward Bridge — One of the three bridges that span the Zimme from Berbiton's shores.

Glossary

Voxbox (Veebee) — An increasingly common device used for telecommunication.

Winterbourne Military Hospital — The hospital where Prince Yeardley was once a patient, now a ruin.

Wynn University of the Thaumatic Arts (WUTA) — The academy that Isolde and Obelos attended in pursuit of an education in magic's history and practice.

Zimme, the River — The broad river upon which Berbiton is built.

Excerpts from

THE HEXOD FLORILEGIUM

(An Index of Hexes)

Nota Bene: The range, efficacy, and longevity of a hex depends upon a number of factors that include, but are not limited to, the focus and craft of the wielder, the receptiveness of the intended object, the ambient atmosphere and environment, and the materials used in the creation of a hex. Much like the application of an herbal medicament, the effect of a hex is sometimes tangential, counterintuitive, or even surprising. As much as some would like to present the drawing of hexes as a science, it is still inarguably an art.

Acuity
An enlarging and clarifying hex that brings minute and faded texts and images into sharper relief.

Aegis
A common defensive ward that supplies broad (if limited) protection to those who employ it.

Ambuscade
Sometimes referred to as the "bloodless mousetrap," the Hex of Ambuscade is useful for catching small animals.

Amplification
An advanced hex that, ideally, captures and magnifies the sound of receded echoes, but often produces a cacophonous roar.

Excerpts from the Hexod Florilegium

Antitinea
A common antifungal hex often employed by nurses to ameliorate cases of athlete's foot, ringworm, and thrush.

Conviviality
While this hex may loosen the tongues of those who are already predisposed to gossip, it is generally ineffective at compelling the unwilling to share their secrets. Comparable to a stiff drink.

Declaration
An elementary hex that reveals the presence of hexes in the immediate vicinity. Still, the hex is an imperfect candle, incapable of illuminating the work of the most advanced practitioners.

Deplaquing
Often used and reliable, this hex is a staple of dentists and considered essential in teeth cleanings.

Disgorging
Most often abused as a prank by new students of the form, the hex's practical purpose is as an expectorate of phlegm or to clear the contents of a stomach as necessitated by poisoning.

Empathy
Sometimes used with unconscious patients or livestock, this hex allows the wielder to glimpse the emotional state of the intended subject. It is widely considered to be a hex of some consequence upon the wielder; practitioners are cautioned against overuse.

Fecundity
Elementary in nature, this relatively minor hex is often deployed to revitalize and fertilize house plants and small plots and to encourage the ripening of green fruit.

Palimpsests
An advanced hex, this form is useful to uncover erased, overwritten, and expunged texts, glyphs, and images. The Hex of Palimpsests allows the wielder to peer into the past, though the result is occasionally similar to divining the secret message of a bowl of alphabet soup.

Excerpts from the Hexod Florilegium

Radiance
The most basic of illuminating hexes, this sigil is simple enough to be constructed in the air with a finger. The resulting light, while often insignificant, can be considerably magnified with sufficient preparation and expertise.

Reversion
A common nurses' hex, this figure is often used to assist in the dressing of wounds, the turning of bedridden patients, and the reorientation of backward garments.

Somnolence
Most often employed as a rudimentary anesthesia for dental procedures, this hex hastens the onset of a deep, if brief, slumber. The efficacy of the hex is improved by the participation of the subject, though it can elicit some drowsiness even in the unwilling.

Tranquility
Intended to diminish the anxiety of a subject, the Hex of Tranquility is a staple among the staff of sanatoriums. While some believe it has been exploited to incapacitate unwell persons, the ward is still considered a useful tool in the treatment and management of disturbed individuals.

Vacillation
Originally used to interrupt bouts of mania, this hex is most often used to inject hesitancy or uncertainty in a subject's engagement of a purpose.

Vigilance
A defensive ward of some renown, though its efficacy remains in question. Often regarded as more of a decorative ward, the Hex of Vigilance remains a popular banner of good luck and home defense.

ACKNOWLEDGMENTS

Novels require a willing suspension of disbelief, not only from readers who may be asked to accept, for example, the existence of a gourmand dragon or the convenient availability of taxis, but also from their authors, who must believe in the project enough to undertake the daunting task. Scrawling that hubristic phrase "Chapter One" is itself a profession of faith.

But the truth is—legal contracts and public promises notwithstanding—each time I have sat down to pen a new book, I have been privately convinced that I would never manage to finish it. The end of the novel is as illusory as a will-o'-the-wisp, a flitting light that haunts a swamp, baiting incautious travelers to brave the quicksand seas and the alligators who sail upon them.

So it was with fatalistic doom that I began to write this book.

Fortunately, it was not left to me alone to believe in this effort. Indeed, I sometimes felt as if I were being crowd-surfed toward the finish line, borne aloft by the many hands of my family and friends, my confreres and collaborators. I owe the completion of this work to them.

I wish to thank my parents, Barbara and Josiah Bancroft, for being a regular geyser of pride and enthusiasm. I'm also deeply grateful to Carol and Robert Bricker for their sustained encouragement and support. I must thank my sister, Jesse Batstone, for being a superior listener and advisor, and salute Kim Bricker and Josh Urso, whose own considerable creative endeavors have informed the growth of my own. And many thanks to Will Viss for his commiserate camaraderie, adventuresome spirit, and invaluable insights on an early draft.

I am indebted to Ian Drury and Lucy Fawcett of Shiel Land Associates Ltd., whose expert representation has yielded many new opportunities. I wish to thank Hachette Book Group, the entire publishing team at Orbit Books, and my editor, Bradley Englert, who saw the potential of this work even before it was finished. Additionally, I must express my gratitude to everyone at Subterranean Press and particularly to Bill Schafer, whose generosity and vision have been a boon to me both personally and professionally. I would also like to thank my munificent Patreon supporters. Their excitement, good cheer, and financial backing have helped keep this whole unlikely enterprise rattling along. All of my readers benefit from the charity of these discerning, determined fans.

The dazzling art and decorative flourishes that distinguish this volume were created by Ian Leino. Much as his incredible talents embroider the finished face of this book, his kindness and sagacity shaped its composition. I am the writer that I am because of his friendship. I also wish to thank my daughter, Maddie, for being full of wonder and wonderful. My life has been marked by privilege, but none greater than being a father to her.

This book is dedicated to my wife, Sharon, without whose love and support I would never have finished a single novel, much less five. It was Sharon's patience, humor, and wisdom that inspired me to conceive of the Wilbies' marriage, a union defined not by dysfunction, doubt, or resentment but by the shared desire to bolster, dote on, and revel in the inimitable gift of a loving partner.

meet the author

Kim Bricker

JOSIAH BANCROFT is the author of five novels, a collection of short fiction, and numerous poems. His books have been translated into eight languages. Before settling down to write fantasy full-time, he was a college instructor, rock musician, and aspiring comic book artist. When he's not writing, he enjoys strumming a variety of stringed instruments, drawing with a growing cache of imperfect pens, and cooking without a recipe. He lives in Philadelphia with his wife, Sharon; their daughter, Maddie; and their two rabbits, Mabel and Chaplin.

Find out more about Josiah Bancroft and other Orbit authors by registering for the free monthly newsletter at orbitbooks.net.

orbit

Follow us:

 /orbitbooksUS

/orbitbooks

/orbitbooks

Join our mailing list
to receive alerts on our
latest releases and deals.

orbitbooks.net

Enter our monthly
giveaway for the chance
to win some epic prizes.

orbitloot.com